REALM LEAPER

Realm Leaper

Book 1 of the Realm Leaper Series

P.E. CRAVEN

Little River Raven

To my husband, my own personal Fated-Mate:
Thank you for always jumping on board for all my crazy
ideas, hyping me up whenever I doubt myself, and being
the very best supporter I could ask for.

I couldn't have dreamed of a better partner if I tried.

Chapter 1

✧✦✧

She was falling.

Faster. Faster. Blinding.

She could hardly think as that one singular word kept pounding through her head: falling.

She hurtled through space; through darkness and time; falling for eternity; she was sure of it. A weight pressed in on her like a fist squeezing the air from her lungs. Her hair fluttered against her face, scratching at her eyes and nose as air whipped by her like bramble vines.

She breached the impenetrable darkness, squinting against the streaks of white painting the sky. The darkness was still a void she plummeted through, but now she fell amongst patches of stars and bursts of debris. A gasp was torn from her gut as she gulped for air, trying to relieve the lurching of her stomach.

And still, she fell.

Below, a massive shape loomed as she tumbled through the air, flipping end over end. She tried to control her limbs, pulling them tight into herself, but it only made her plummet faster. The sensation of spinning pulled at her insides, threatening to rip her very soul out through her throat and mouth.

Suddenly, a blinding light flashed. She crested through clouds, hurtling towards the ground. She would not, could not, survive this.

"Help..."

"Help me," she whispered.

She was picking up speed; falling faster. A bright shield of fire formed around her, creating a solid ball of flame as she plunged toward death.

"Help," she growled, baring her teeth at the flames licking at the air around her.

She should be burning, could not remember whether she could burn, or if this was how fire was supposed to behave.

Water came into view below her as she surpassed the clouds. Water and lands unfamiliar and strange, unwelcoming, as she tumbled towards the end.

She thought of the water and whether there was any possible way her body could survive smacking the surface. Whether she would hit the surface and be knocked unconscious and drown. Or maybe the gods would have pity on her, allowing the sweet end of instant death from the punishment of hitting the rolling ocean below. The idea of letting go teased her sweetly as panic surged through her. She inhaled deeply, the hot air singing her throat and chest as she readied herself.

Only, she wasn't heading towards the ocean anymore; a city was coming into view. She didn't want to hit the city. Her impact would not be small. How she knew; fuck...how did she know anything?! She just couldn't fall there, she knew it.

"I. Said. Fucking help me," she grunted between clenched teeth. She shoved her hands against one side of the fireball, briefly amazed that she could touch it and not be burned alive, even as the skin of her palms blistered and cracked. She pushed hard, until her arms quivered with the effort, sweat beading on her forehead. She stifled a cry of pain. A force rolled her away from the city.

Faster. Faster. Gods...this was going to hurt. Not the ocean. Now she was heading for a small peninsula; an outcropping of stone and trees rising up from the water. The wind howled in her ears, against her body. The force of falling squeezed her from all sides as tears streaked from her eyes.

No, no, no, no, no, no. She didn't want to die.

She'd accepted that fate before, but she was scared now.

She did not want to give up. Not here.

Not in a place she didn't know.

Not when she had so much to do. What, she couldn't remember just now. But it was important.

"NO. Help me!" she cried out to gods she could only vaguely remember. The ground was so close, reaching up to swallow her now.

"NO!" she demanded again, reaching her hands up and gasping loudly as she tried to stop her ball of flame from hitting the ground. She slowed, the ocean surging forward up the coast to meet her, and she hit the ground with an explosion of water, steam, rock, and debris.

That. Hurt.

The water flowed away back to the sea, leaving her lying broken, bruised, and exhausted in a crater of red dirt, grass peeking over the ridges. Something warm ran down her face, warmer than the rest of the water soaking her body.

The sun beat down on her over the trees. She closed her eyes; it hurt. It all hurt.

She opened her eyes, straining against the sun hanging overhead before slipping back into a brief darkness.

When she managed to peel open her eyes once more, three winged figures stood on one side of the small crater, staring down at her.

Angels. They'd come to take her spirit away. She blinked, silently thanking Cerridos for sending angels to this unknown world to carry her spirit to the beyond. Light flooded her as she opened her eyes, and...

They weren't angels. They were warriors; menacing and terrifying, with crude, antique weapons in their hands and strapped to their bodies.

She tried scrambling up the slope of the crater. Making to stand, push to her feet, to scream, to get away. Dirt scraped away from the crater, embedding below her nails and sticking to her bloody elbows as she felt her legs give way.

She tumbled back into the pit. Nausea clawed itself into her mouth as she felt bone protrude from her leg.

"Help," she pleaded softly. "Please."

A feeble rumble of earth from the crater was the only response as she fell once again into darkness.

Gavin stood on the balcony of the Obelisk towering over the city, Veritasailles. He let himself admire the wind whip through his hair and tousling the wild curls of his commander, Meliza.

She stood, leaning against the archway of the balcony that led back into the tower which housed the private training center and accommodation for some of the chosen members of the King and Queen's Court. Gavin avoided making eye contact with his Commander, a fierce leader who had proven her merit in combat in addition to being the sister of the King.

Not only was Meliza a fierce leader, she was a hell of a fighter. Gavin had a wound wrapped in bandages on his arm to prove it. Could he have avoided Meliza's downward thrust? Probably. But Zeke, the army's General, had made a distracting comment about Gavin's form. That moment of distraction had cost Gavin. He wasn't mad, though. If he was honest, being stationed in the Obelisk and serving in the city had been some of the best fun he could remember having.

The country of Felysia had spent the last one hundred years under the control of a genocidal psychopath. King Rankor murdered the leaders of every sovereign state on the continent, using forbidden blood magic to serve his purpose. The conquered people had been thrown into work camps where they'd been abused for a century.

Gavin rolled his shoulders, willing the uneasiness of memories better left forgotten to trickle out of his muscles and into any other place but himself. He might still be burning for vengeance deep down inside, but he was content to ignore that need as long as the Tri-Goddess would allow him to.

Just then, Meliza tensed. She pushed off from the archway and strode towards the edge of the balcony, peering into the sky.

"What is it?" Gavin asked.

Meliza ignored the young fae, keeping her eyes shielded to the sun just cresting towards the other side of the sky. Gavin tensed as she remained still.

A boom erupted in the sky, and a small fireball broke through the cover of fluffy white clouds smattering the horizon. It didn't appear to be anything malicious; a falling star perhaps?

A watery voice echoed from behind Gavin and Meliza. "Meliza- do you know what that is?" Gavin and Meliza turned to meet the gaze of King Symon. He stood in his transparent form, a projection of his true form which likely stood in his study.

"I do not," Meliza replied firmly, twisting to look again at the strange star falling to the land. Which now seemed to be heading directly towards the Obelisk.

"Shit," the three of them muttered in unison.

Gavin stilled, scrambling to come up with some way to be useful against the meteor plummeting towards the city and destroying everything in its path. He could use his wind powers, but would that be enough? Glancing at Meliza, he could see similar calculations running through her mind. Her power over earth and stone, while impressive, would likely make the situation worse. A mighty wind roared across the beach and appeared to *push* the falling object towards a distant peninsula, avoiding the city itself.

"Was that you?" Symon asked Gavin, a small smile in his voice.

"No," Gavin replied, shaking his head.

"Get Zeke. I want to know what it is as soon as it hits the ground," Symon ordered. "Go."

Gavin could sense Zeke sprinting up the stairs, clearly having sensed the danger already. As soon as Zeke hit the landing, the three fae warriors leapt from the balcony and plummeted towards the ground. Simultaneously, they shifted into their feather-winged form, spearing towards the clearing.

The wind sang in Gavin's ears as they soared towards the outcropping of rocks that bordered the city and sea. He whispered a quiet plea to the Goddess herself as they prepared to shield the city from whatever might come next.

But their trajectory was too closely aligned to that of the blazing fireball. Without warning, Meliza pulled up towards the sky, steering the trio upwards so that they could observe the damage from a safe distance. Gavin hovered slightly behind Meliza, Zeke a short distance to his side.

Gavin allowed himself to focus on the mission at hand, letting the beating of Zeke's wings lull him into a trance-like state of hyperfocus. It was close now; any second the fireball would crash into the dirt, no doubt annihilating whatever trees and brush grew on the grassy point. He braced himself, remaining steady in the air, prepared to dodge any debris. But just before the fireball hit the ground, time seemed to slow. No, not time. IT slowed down. And as the fireball slowed the sea rushed towards the peninsula, swallowing it whole. The impact, although not as destructive as it could have been, was brutal. The clearing smoke and dust revealed a steaming crater scarring the earth.

"What, the-" muttered Gavin. Zeke whistled between his teeth. The trio beat their wings in the air for just a moment before they quickly swooped for the crater as one.

Gavin dove to the crater, but stopped short before reaching it. In the center of the crater was a petite girl with short, cinnamon hair, battered and crushed, lying completely inert. He gasped, "It's a girl."

"Very perceptive," Zeke hissed.

"Funny. I just meant, what is a girl doing inside a fireball?" asked Gavin through his teeth.

All three hit the ground a few yards from the crater and ran towards it. The girl seemed unconscious, battered, but breathing. Her cinnamon hair reflected the glow from the sun.

Gavin, Meliza, and Zeke stood together at the rim of the crater, peering at the strange girl who'd fallen from the sky. Slowly, the girl's head moved, and her eyes fluttered open. Fear masked her face. She tried to scramble up to the top of the crater, as if to get away but stumbled.

Meliza stood her ground, waiting. Gavin watched as Meliza assessed the girl's state, waiting for her to lose consciousness. Gavin had seen soldiers with lesser wounds succumb to the relief of unconsciousness on the battlefield. He could sense her pain and panic, and something urged him forwards. Gavin stepped forward to approach the girl, but Meliza grabbed his arm to stop him.

The girl, still scrambling up the crater and trying to stand, hit the ground and rolled back down. A slight tremor murmured through the clearing, and the girl passed out. Gavin jumped in, scooping her into his arms, careful to avoid hurting her clearly broken leg.

"We've got to get her back to the Obelisk. Raphael can help," said Gavin.

Zeke barked, "You and Meliza go to the Obelisk, get the girl to Raph. I will get Symon. He can help." Zeke moved without pausing, scooping up a brown lump sitting, steaming, on the edge of the crater before bolting back into the sky. From Gavin's perspective, it looked like a satchel of some sort, but he couldn't be sure. If it were a bag, maybe it could provide some answers. After all, there was no telling how long it might take for the girl to heal enough for them to question her.

Not wasting a second more, Gavin shot into the sky, followed by Meliza. They raced toward the Obelisk.

Above the wind roaring in his ears, he heard Meliza mutter curses beneath her breath. Gavin couldn't help but agree to some extent. What was this? Was it an omen? Was the girl a weapon in disguise? They would find out soon enough. Meliza would surely wield her Truth Teller powers on the girl once she had healed enough to think coherently.

How fast Gavin flew. He couldn't remember a time he'd flown so fast. His heart thumped in his chest with a primal instinct to protect the girl in his arms. Thoughts raced through his mind as fast as he flew, and he had no idea where the urgency to protect and save her came from. He looked down at her limp body, hair whipping across her face.

This girl, this small girl. She was strong. How else could she have survived? He wasn't sure he would have survived an impact like that; shit, he wasn't even sure Zeke could. That huge wave, summoned mysteriously from the sea, had likely softened the blow. But she was hurt- brutalized from the fall.

Blisters covered part of her face, her palms, along the back of her arms. Her leg was broken, the bone sticking through her pant leg. Blood soaked both sides of her face, and trickled from her ears. She was breathing, and he could hear her heart beating, but barely. Thank the Goddess Raphael was there. And with luck, Symon and Zeke would arrive at nearly the same time.

She squirmed in his arms."No. Don't," she croaked.

"It's fine. We're going to help you. Just hang on. Keep breathing," Gavin said over the wind roaring past. His wings beat harder as he speared to the Obelisk. So close. They were so close.

His feet hit the balcony floor at a run, closely followed by Meliza, and together they bounded up the stairs towards Raphael's medical ward. Gavin tried to stabilize her head as he tackled the stairs two at a time, trying desperately to avoid worsening her injuries. His jaw worked as he ran, conscious of her ragged breaths, simultaneously trying to block out memories of cradling warrior friends injured in bloody battle.

"Just hang on. Almost there," Gavin said again as he burst through Raphael's open door.

"Gavin, that better not be you again," drawled Raphael, not bothering to look up from the text he was scanning.

"Raph. Hurry," demanded Meliza as Gavin placed the girl on a medical table in the center of Raphael's room.

Raphael turned and took in the damaged female on his table, face changing from a look of annoyance to dignified purpose.

"Meliza, roll that cart over here. Gavin, be ready in case she wakes up. I need to assess her. Keep her calm. Yes, Meliza, that one. Quickly. NOW."

Symon may be King of Veritasailles, but Raphael was lord of this domain. Raphael spoke with a soft, lilting voice. His long dark hair, dark brown eyes, and long eyelashes often had people curious about his gender. But when he was in the midst of healing, his soft voice carried no questions, only commands.

"Symon," directed Raphael in his cool manner, not looking up from his work on the girl as Symon and Zeke entered.

"I need you on pain management. Use her mind to numb the extremities. She's in shock, and we need to sustain her vitals." Symon stalked to her head, and placed his hands on either of her temples.

The moment his fingertips brushed her skin, she bucked.

She. Bucked. Back arching off the table, her arms reaching up as if she would pry Symon's fingers from her scalp. Symon inhaled sharply, but remained focused on her mind while she continued to thrash upon the table.

No one should be able to resist Symon like that; Gavin hadn't witnessed anyone resist Symon's mind control in the slightest before.

Gavin stared at the girl, pulling her hands away from Symon as she glared at him, pleading, "Please don't. Don't let him take me," she sobbed.

Symon grit his teeth, and Gavin could tell he was reaching further into his power.

"No, please," the girl screamed as she flailed her broken body. The blisters on her arms left bloody streaks along the table, staining the sheets a sheer crimson. Gavin trembled as he tried to keep her arms on the table without hurting her.

"It's ok. Look. Look at me. I won't let them hurt you. Trust me," promised Gavin. "I won't let them hurt you."

He wasn't sure why, but he meant it. She looked up at him, still trying to reach for Symon's hands, and held his stare. They looked at each other as Gavin whispered again, "I won't let them hurt you."

She nodded, exhaled loudly, and let Symon into her mind as she closed her eyes. Gavin could feel her body lose its rigidness, but he could also feel that little heart of hers slow down.

"Raph," warned Gavin.

"I know, I know," barked Raphael. "Just hold her. Meliza, come hold this leg while I set it. I need to get the bone back in to help slow the bleeding. Symon, be ready. She might fight this."

Raphael and Meliza headed toward the end of the table. Gavin glanced back at the pair before turning his attention back to the girl. She was so small. He couldn't imagine what could have caused something like this. How she could have survived. He stared at her face, this impossible creature, waiting for her to surge back off the table as Raphael shoved her bone back into her leg before using his powers to help heal the tissues and sinew, stopping the bleeding. He knew Raphael could fix this; had seen him fix worse injuries with fewer advantages in the final battle with King Rankor. Gavin had only been fifteen then. A babe in the eyes of the fae.

Gavin glared at the girl. Willing her heart to beat strong, for breath to fill her lungs.

"Gavin," muttered Zeke, as a breeze fluttered the wrappings on Raphael's medical cart.

"Sorry," replied Gavin.

Gavin had always struggled to manage his wind power in stressful situations. Gavin prided himself in being in total control, however, his connection with the wind was less controlled. The wind was his brother, had sung to him during the darkest nights as a boy. The wind had led him into battle, shielded him. But now was not the time for a raucous wind to bellow through the tower.

"Symon, ease up a little. I fear the numbing may be dimming her will," Raphael said.

Her eyes began fluttering, but not with consciousness. Raphael rushed towards her head, pushing Symon and

Gavin out of the way, while Meliza continued wrapping the injured ankle, the skin already beginning to heal.

Raphael placed his hands on the girl's chest, light glowing beneath his palms.

"There is some internal bleeding. Gavin, keep air moving through her lungs. Symon, manage her pain. I will try to locate the damage and repair what I can," Raphael glanced at her face and shook his head, clearly confused as to what could have brought her to him.

Gavin noticed it then. The stark differences between her and them. As fae, everyone in the room exhibited extreme physiques. Muscular, well-built bodies, honed for predatory lethalness. Each warrior, and healer, had the tell-tale fae tipped ears. And then there was her. She looked every bit the mortal of lands across the sea. Panchaia, the continent they were on now, was home to the fae, while Meropoli was home to the mortals, humans. Those without access to natural powers.

Gavin focused his energy on her breathing. Trying not to force air too quickly into her while Raphael worked to repair the damage inside. It seemed eternity stretched in front of Gavin while Raphael worked.

At last, Sage's heartbeat steadied, her breathing stabilized on its own. Her face relaxed slightly and Gavin felt a moment of relief as Raphael turned and said, "That should do it. She is out of immediate danger. Meliza, Gavin, you can go. Zeke, Symon, a word. And then I will see to these burns."

Gavin released his grip on her arms, preparing to leave.

"My dear, what have you done," whispered Raphael into the strange girl's ears, checking her burns and lacerations. Gavin had to physically force energy into his legs as he headed for the open door of Raphael's ward. All of Gavin's training was poured into not looking back to that strange girl lying on the table as he left her to Raphael.

He couldn't wrap his mind around why she was here, or how she'd gotten inside a fireball. Her clothes didn't look like those from Meropoli. Instead of a tunic and breeches or a chiton, she wore coarse blue pants and a striped yellow shirt, cut tight to her body.

And her pack. Not made of homespun, or leather. Something different. Something pliant and... different. Canvas maybe? With straps and extra pockets designed for long and efficient purposes. Completely different from the simple, homemade packs typical of the people of Meropoli. Who was this girl, and where had she come from?

Gavin reached the door, and despite his best efforts, he lingered, looking back at the girl. At her apposing stubborn will and diminutive fragility as she slept under Symon's influence.

Meliza cleared her throat, standing just behind him in the door frame. She gently placed her hand on his shoulder, steering him away from the medical ward. There was nothing left for them to do. Gavin headed up to his room to try and gather himself, and pray to the Goddess for answers.

Chapter 2

✧◆✧

She awoke.

Her mouth felt like it was full of gauze. Hot. And dry. She tried to swallow and grimaced at the thickness of the saliva pooled near the back of her throat.

She pushed herself up onto pillows, arms trembling.

Pillows? She was in a bed. She couldn't remember the last time she was in a bed. She couldn't remember...anything.

"Did you sleep well?" a quiet, husky voice asked.

Her head snapped to the direction of the voice, too fast, and bright stars popped before her eyes. She blinked rapidly, trying to adjust her sight as the room she lay in came into focus. Soft blue walls surrounded her, accompanied by full-length windows bright with sunlight on the far wall. The room was pleasantly furnished but felt foreign and strange. Like wearing the skin of someone else.

Goosebumps prickled her arms as she noticed the two figures sitting near her bed.

Two fierce-looking women sat in wingback chairs, mere feet from her. One woman wore coral red, the color of hot steel, and the other wore cold steel gray. Two opposites of the same coin. One radiant with warmth and fire, the other cold with biting resilience.

Something about the clothing seemed off. The shape and texture of the draping material made her wonder if the women were in costume. The gray woman, with skin like cream and hair like a moonless, cloudy night, wore a chiton, swept up to her shoulders and pinned with dark metallic brooches. Meanwhile, the red woman, with bright blonde hair and dark olive skin, wore a similar gown. Except it wasn't a gown, but a one-piece that ended with pants cuffed at the ankles. The fabric pooled around her relaxed legs along the seat, and she could make out the strength hidden beneath the soft swaths of fabric.

"She said: did you sleep. Well?" replied the gray woman, ice coating each word.

"I don't know," was all she could reply. "Where am I? Who are you?" she muttered as she sat up further on her pillows.

Her body ached. Welts and bruises twinged as she pushed herself into a sitting position. Her left leg throbbed, and she wondered what accident she'd been in to cause the spinning sensation behind her eyes. She squeezed her eyes closed before opening them and focusing once more on the women.

"My name is Meliza. This is Petra," answered the red woman. "You are in Veritasailles. You are not in danger, but we do have some questions for you. What is your name, and where are *you* from?"

"I don't know," she replied.

"Where are you from?" snapped the woman named Petra.

"I don't know," she answered again, more urgently. Her hands gripped her sheets. Sweat began collecting along her palms as she took deep breaths. The realization that she could not remember who she was or where she came from clanged loudly through her mind.

Meliza glanced at her body, scanning for something before whispering to Petra, "She's telling the truth," then shifted forward in her chair, "Do you remember how you got here?"

She paused, and tried to remember. The panic was rising in her veins and she took several calming breaths, trying to remember something.

Falling. She was falling. She clenched her eyes shut as tears burned behind her lids. Her heart threatened to beat right out of her throat.

"I remember falling. I remember hitting the ground. I remember him holding me down, not letting them take me away," she replied through pants. A tear slid down her cheek and she clenched her teeth to keep her chin from wobbling. Gods, she felt like a fool. "I don't remember anything else."

"Here," said Petra, shoving something towards her clenched hands. "We found this in your pack."

It was a small note on a piece of paper torn from something, and Petra laid it beside her on the bed. The paper was bright white, but wrinkled with stains as if it had traveled at the bottom of a pocket for a long time. A spidery script scrawled, *"Sage- Hope this helps. G'luck."*

"Sage. My name is Sage?" she asked.

"Looks like it. Does it feel familiar?" inquired Meliza.

She contemplated the question, rolling the question around in her body, around her mind and soul.

Sage.

Sage.

It did feel familiar. Like a sweater she'd had for years and years, or a blanket atop her bed every night.

Sage.

That was who she was.

Sage nodded. "Yes. I think that's my name. But I can't remember anything else. How'd I get here?"

The tears she tried so hard to hold in began a slow trickle down her cheeks. She tried, tried and failed, to meet their eyes with steel, but there was tangible fear cascading through her body. She could taste the fear mixed with panic as nausea began to claw its way towards her throat. They could do anything with her. Still, she lifted her chin, refusing to show just how terrified she felt.

Petra's eyes slid to Meliza, and Meliza nodded confirmation. Sage supposed she had somehow convinced the women she told the truth, despite having no reasons to be untruthful.

Meliza began to stand and announced, "I know this is very difficult for you, but we have the best healer in the city here. He will visit you later and see to your injuries as they continue to heal. Perhaps he can help with your memory loss."

Leaning back against the pillows, Sage opened her mouth to ask where she was, but Meliza held up her hand to quiet Sage. "I will see that your pack is delivered to you soon. You should rest. If you need assistance, rest assured you are welcome to stay here until you have an idea of where you need to go."

"If you remember anything, you should tell my sister," quipped Petra who stood as well, glaring at Sage.

Apparently, Sage was not to be trusted, even with Meliza's approval. Sage took the brunt of Petra's stare and willed herself to return the sentiment.

With a soft click of the door, the two women exited the room and Sage sank into her bed again, letting herself succumb to bone-deep weariness and despair.

Minutes, perhaps hours, passed before the tears dried up. Slowly, Sage peeled herself from the bed to make her way to the large windows flanking the side of her room. She was halfway there, limping on her sore leg, before realizing her bladder was full. Gods, she hoped one of those doors on the opposite wall was a bathing room.

Sure enough, two of the doors held closets, and the third opened to a modest bathroom complete with a tub, toilet, and sink. All you could hope for, she supposed as she went about her business. She tended to her needs, swished her mouth with a tonic supplied in the bathing room, and gulped down several glasses of water before finishing her trek to the windows.

Finally making it to the windows, she admired the floor-to-ceiling panes glinting in the sunlight. She peered out over the city below. The view had her stomach dropping completely from where it belonged. She had to be at least fifty floors off the ground. So high up. If she leaned against the window, it almost felt like she'd fall again.

She teetered, her legs quaking beneath her as she made to step away from the window as a gasp escaped her lips.

The door burst open behind her, just as Sage's knees lost the battle to keep her upright. A dark figure ran towards her at astonishing speed and scooped her up before she hit the floor.

He gently set her in one of the wing-backed chairs. As he moved away from her, she took deep breaths, willing herself to calm down.

"Are you Zeke?" Sage asked, as she gathered her senses, reminding herself she wasn't actually falling.

He almost blushed as he replied, "Me? No. I'm Gavin. Zeke sent me with your pack. Let me get it for you." He hurried to the door where he had dropped the bag.

It was made of stiff, olive-green canvas. The bag was covered in pockets and zippers. It was marked in dark patches from their fall but was otherwise unharmed.

She jolted. She had clutched it to her in the final moments before she hit the ground. Praying to someone that they'd send help.

"Here you go. Meliza told me your name is Sage?" Gavin set the bag next to her as he moved to a chair next to hers.

Sage stared at Gavin, slowly taking in the male sitting in the chair next to her. He was well built. Clearly meant for something athletic. He wore his thick, dark hair cropped just long enough for him to brush his fingers through. His skin was olive-toned and kissed by the sun, and Sage could just make out warm hazel eyes rimmed in a brown that reminded her of dark tea.

His body was honed from training, but still showed the signs of youth. Not young like adolescence, but young in a way the two females before were not. Males and females. Sage began to notice the striking differences in Gavin she hadn't noticed before. Tipped ears, a stillness to his posture more like a wolf or a jungle cat than man, and an alertness she hadn't quite experienced before.

He just sat there while she examined him, and he examined her back.

"I'm sorry. What is with everyone here? What are you wearing? Is this some sort of play-acting place? Are you guys, like, antiquity actors? Gods, that clothing belongs to several centuries ago." Sage demanded with a huff, standing up and walking towards the fireplace. What was with this place? And who put a godsdamned nightgown on her?

"I'm fae," Gavin answered slowly. "We're in Veritasailles. In the Kingdom of Felysia. Under King Symon?" Gavin delivered each answer as if it were obvious. A slow smile spread across his face as if he were trying to hold his laughter. He leaned towards her and whispered "Do they make plays about us in Meropoli? Put on costumes and pretend to wield our power?"

"Meropoli? Where's that?" Sage replied, shaking her head as she sat back in her chair.

"So, you truly can't remember? You have no idea where your home might be?" whispered Gavin, almost to himself, as if he were assessing her and what awaited them.

Home. Pain lanced through Sage's head, and she crumpled over herself, laying her head in her hands. Flashes of streets bustling with machines, covered in steam and mist flooded her sight. A familiar hand passing her a book with a note; a whisper of "Be safe," rang in her ears as Sage gripped tight to herself, folding into a ball.

"Hey, hey, hey...what do you need? Should I call Raph?" Gavin was in front of her in an instant, offering a glass of water from the side table that hadn't been there a second before. His hand rested gently on her knee.

"How'd you do that?" demanded Sage after taking several hasty sips of cool water, nodding to the glass she placed on the table.

"Probably Raph. He's likely eavesdropping, trying to be sure I don't disturb you too much before you're fully healed. You were quite a mess when we got to you."

"I'll try harder to make myself presentable next time I fall from the sky," muttered Sage.

Sage looked down, her cheeks warming as she suddenly remembered she was in a nightgown and glanced at Gavin who was staring back at her as if he, too, had just realized. They stayed there for a long moment, eyes locked, with Gavin in front of her on the floor, his hand resting on her knee. Gavin jerked his hand away, clearing his throat while tucking his hand behind him as if it had embarrassed itself.

"Would you like some food? And if you'd like, there's clothing in the closets. Pick whatever suits you, and I'll be back with some food."

"That'd be great actually. Thank you."

Gavin jumped up from his spot and practically marched to the door, before turning back, lingering by the door.

"I'll be back in twenty minutes. If you need help dressing, just yell for Raph. He can help you dress; he got you into that nightgown. Don't worry about modesty with him. He's a healer and immune to naked bodies." Gavin winked as he opened the door and strode out.

Like hell was she going to ask a stranger, a *fae* stranger, whatever the hell that meant, to dress her. She could do this.

Sage strode to the closets and opened them again, scanning for familiar clothing. Hanging from the racks were various chitons, some in dress form, some in jumpsuit form ending in banded pants legs. She chose a dress of pale sea green, and carefully removed her nightgown.

There was a vanity with a large mirror across the room, and Sage took a moment to assess her body. There were marks along one side of her face, and what looked like welts that had almost fully healed down the backs of her arms. Bruises littered her torso, arms, legs, and under her chin. Her leg all the way to her ankle was wrapped in stiff dressings that made it hard to move freely.

How long had she been asleep to be healed over so much? She remembered, suddenly, her leg had been badly broken. Bone stuck through her sock when the three warriors found her. She knelt to feel her leg. It was still the slightest bit tender, but didn't feel broken at all. A break like that would take surgery and six weeks to heal back home.

Home. The word drummed through her head again as she slipped the dress over her head. The straps didn't attach, and she selected two copper-looking pins to fasten the straps atop her shoulders to her liking.

Home. She couldn't remember it at all, beyond those flashes earlier when Gavin said the word.

But she knew it was much different from this place. For one thing, these clothes. No one dressed like this where she was from. And machines. Machines had been everywhere. Large vehicles on the ground, and planes in the air. Clanging and beeping devices dominated the surroundings and large bright signs on nearly every surface.

This is what she knew as *home*.

Sage slowly hobbled to the large windows again and peered out on the city below her now. If she steadied her breathing, she could hear the sea. Not a machine to be heard.

Instead, the streets were populated with people on foot, or horseback. Horses pulled wagons loaded with people and goods.

The white stone buildings, pieced together with red clay mortar, dazzled in the bright sunlight. Many of the buildings sported colorful domed roofs. Those closer to the sea were crowned with cyan blue domes, while those in the center of the city displayed patinated copper domes. Further still, the buildings on the border of where Sage assumed the city ended were capped with ruby red domes.

And in the center of the city stood a massive, sprawling estate. Clearly the prized jewel of the city. Dotted with gardens, tiny outbuildings, and one large mansion- no, not mansion- a castle. Atop the castle stood a peaked, golden crown of a roof, ending with one long needle of a spire reaching towards the heavens above.

Sage had never seen anything like it before. Well, she assumed she hadn't. She rubbed her hands over her face as she began to pace in front of the fireplace in the center of her room.

Not remembering who she was, where she came from, or *why* she was here was going to suck. Suck, so bad. A growl of frustration escaped her chest.

She could feel warmth building in the center of her body. Hot ore slithered through her veins, bubbling up from her diaphragm and spilling into her limbs. The molten heat squirmed its way along, building and trying to escape. Sage sank to her knees in front of the fireplace, not sure if she was going to vomit or pass out, but sure she wouldn't make it to the bathing room again before it happened.

On instinct, Sage lifted her hands towards the fireplace, stacked with logs and awaiting a spark, before she flexed her palms and fingers open. A blinding flash escaped her palms, and fire erupted on the logs in front of her.

She sank onto her backside, panting from the relief of release.

"So, you're a fire wielder?" Gavin interrupted her brief respite. "I thought humans couldn't access our powers? How'd you do that?" Gavin stood in the doorway, tray in hand and lips pressed tight.

Sage blinked. "I don't know. Water? Please?" she answered, still gasping for breath.

Gavin placed the tray on the table beside the two wing-backed chairs and hurried to help her up. He then turned and waved his other hand, floating one of the chairs to where they stood with his wind power.

Gavin made to summon the other chair when Sage halted him. "Wait. Let me."

Sage took a deep breath, easing herself from Gavin's gentle hold, and opened her palms by her side. With a flourish of her hand and wrist, a breeze scooted the chair along the floor next to Gavin's chair.

"Fire and wind. Well, shit."

"I think...I think water, too. But not now. I need to sit now. And drink. And eat." Sage's stomach growled in response, loudly enough to coax a smile to her lips. Food, water, and rest. Then she could figure out more about herself. Maybe that could wait until tomorrow. She was tired. But, she realized, not tired enough to want to be alone.

"Sit with me?" she asked Gavin sheepishly.

"Of course," he smiled back.

They sat together, digging into the refreshments he had ransacked from the kitchen earlier. The tray bore fruits, nuts, hard cheeses, boiled eggs, olives, and rolls of several varieties.

"I wasn't sure what you liked, so I just grabbed whatever was lying around," Gavin chuckled.

"It's perfect. Thank you," Sage replied. She tried to contain her excitement over the cherries. She remembered cherries and knew she liked them. Knew, somehow, they were a seasonal treat back home. So maybe she could remember some things? Just no people or places. Nothing important. Like memories of her home.

That word again. Sage sighed as she ate her cherries. "So, Gavin. I can't remember my home. Maybe you would care to share a bit of your home?"

"I don't have one. Not yet anyways," Gavin answered, and continued when she didn't ask any further questions. "I was born in a work camp. Our country was conquered and ruled for a hundred years by a tyrant. Symon- our king- his father was murdered when he wouldn't give in to a madman. As a result, all our people were captured and enslaved. Many others were killed. It's only been ten years since we defeated him and began reconstructing our lands. So, as a result, I'm kind of...in between places for now, I guess." Gavin lowered his eyes from hers and stared into the fire. She had the sense that he was filtering through memories, choosing what to share and what to keep close.

Gavin shook his head a little, and grinned apologetically. "I'm sorry. I'm not sure you were asking for our tragic backstory when you asked about my home."

"It's not like we can change our stories, Gavin. Trust me, I would if I could."

"It's not all bad, I still have family. They live in Mystaira, which will eventually become my home, I guess"

"You don't sound especially excited about that."

"It's a long story. I've probably overshared already," Gavin said. He rolled his shoulders, something Sage noticed was a habit of his when he felt uncomfortable.

"I saw a flash of my home. A small piece of a memory, I suppose," offered Sage. "It wasn't at all like this. It was noisier. The air didn't seem quite so clean. Where are all the machines kept in your lands? I noticed there wasn't even a single automobile driving around the streets below. Is there a ban from driving here?"

"Automobile? I'm not sure I understand," Gavin asked as he refilled her water.

"You know. Cars, buses. Trolleys. Big giant trucks that bring deliveries," Sage explained.

Gavin hummed to himself a little before answering, "We have wagons, and horse-drawn caravans for that. But I'm not sure I would recognize a...bus."

"So there truly aren't any machines here?" asked Sage.

That would explain the clean and quiet air. To be honest, she wasn't sure she'd miss the noise and pollution from what she gathered in her snippet of a memory. "So how do you have running water?" Sage questioned.

"That was an improvement sought out by King Credeus, early in his reign," began Gavin. "His Queen disliked the smell of the city. She had come from Nysa, a much less populated land. The stench drove her mad, especially in her first pregnancy. So, the King demanded someone find a solution. It was actually Raph's parents who figured it out. They had already been looking for ways to combat diseases that came from contaminated waterways, and won special favor from the King and Queen when they proposed the solution. Veritasailles is one of the few cities in Felysia to boast such an achievement."

"We were conquered just a few years after the city completed the project." Gavin gazed mournfully toward the window.

"How old are you?" Sage asked.

"Twenty-five," answered Gavin. "A babe if you ask Meliza, which she gets a kick out calling me. I don't particularly like it," he scowled.

"And how old is Meliza?"

"Meliza is 150; Symon and Zeke are 175 years each; Petra, their sister, is 140. She was the last child born from their parents."

"175 years old?! How is that even possible?" Sage sat forward, astounded

Gavin grinned, "Fae. Remember? That's not even all that old for us. Many fae, when there is not war or famine, have lived more than 300 years before succumbing to death. At that point, it seems we can choose to just...lie down and be done if we want." Gavin shrugged off the statement.

"But that's without war."

"And famine."

"So...you were born in the war camp?" Sage asked.

Gavin exhaled slowly, rubbing the faint stubble on his chin. Finally, he replied, "Yeah. I have an older sister and a younger brother, too. We were some of the few children born there. I've never understood why my parents chose to have children, but I suppose I should be grateful we only spent a couple decades in the camp."

Gavin grew pensive again, and Sage couldn't help but feel an ache for all this male had gone through. A similar feeling seemed to weigh on her, and she felt the presence of a memory hover in the back of her mind. Like a gentle caress, a feeling of remembrance tried to push its way forward. The ache in her chest grew stronger, and she chewed the inside of her lip to try and keep the ache inside, lest they turn to tears once again.

With a tremble in her voice, Sage set down the napkin she'd been nervously wrapping around her hand and said, "I don't know why I'm here, but I know I was escaping—something. Something horrible. An awful fate. I left behind everything. And I know it's important for me to remember, but I think part of me wants to keep forgetting. Part of me is afraid of remembering." Sage closed her eyes, trying to focus on her breathing as the caress of memory in her mind continued to try and gain her attention. The faintest outline of a woman's face began to filter into her thoughts when the relative peace of the room was shattered.

"Enjoying ourselves, are we, Gavin?" came a familiar clipped voice. Sage started as she met Petra's icy glare. She fought to keep her eye roll to herself, but Petra's intensifying stare informed her that she'd failed to remain stoic.

"Meliza sent me to check on you," Petra said as she approached Gavin, who was rising to stand.

"Petra. Be nice to her, will you?" Gavin said.

"You were supposed to be on sentry duty five minutes ago. I would be more concerned about how Meliza will react to you being late, if I were you."

Gavin once again rolled his shoulders, then turned to Sage. "Don't let her bully you. She's not in charge around here, regardless of how she might act." Gavin boldly looked towards Petra, then started off towards wherever his duties took him.

Sage had risen from her chair, making towards the bed. Petra stepped in her way before she could make any sort of progress. "I heard what you told Gavin. You *do* remember something. Interesting that you hadn't told any of us yet."

"I only just had the memory, like, just before you got here. It's not like I've had time to find you all. Besides, I wouldn't even know *where* to find you. Now, I'd really like to get some rest."

Sage made to push past Petra once more, but the female grabbed her arm with a cold, strong hand. "I'm not done. You remember more don't you. Don't think that you can fool us, girl. We will get our answers from you."

Just then, inky shadows began to swirl around Petra's feet. Sage yanked her arm free and stepped back. "What are you doing?" Sage asked.

Petra advanced again, "Tell us what you are hiding." Shadows, thick as coffee, snaked their way around Petra, some of them seeming to take shapes that resembled haunted faces.

The molten ore that had bubbled in Sage's chest before began making a reappearance. The fire in the grate seemed to reach out towards Sage, licking upwards like hands grabbing at prey. Sage stepped back again, "Like I told you before," she said through clenched teeth, "I just remembered a little about my home. I haven't even had a second to try and find you."

Sage's back was now pressed against the window. She was trapped. The floor began to vibrate below her, the stone walls trembling slightly. Petra's head snapped to the wall, taking in the fire flickering in and out of its grate. "Are you doing that?" she asked Sage.

A soft voice danced through Sage's mind, *"My darling, you will need to hide these talents,"* Sage shook her head, trying to dislodge the voice while still keeping Petra in her line of sight. *"They will come for you if they find out. I won't be able to hide you, my love."*

The water in the pitcher began to splash, and the vibration in the floor intensified, making Sage's head ache. "You are dangerous. They never should have kept you here," Petra snapped at Sage, and made to grab her by the arm again. Sage thrust her hands outward, and the stone floor buckled slightly beneath Petra.

Petra stumbled backward but caught herself quickly. Shadows like hounds rippled out from Petra, growls adding to the rumble that was now constant in the small room. "Stay away from me," Sage gasped.

"You will not destroy us," Petra threw towards Sage. "I will take you to the dungeons, where you belong." Petra's hounds leapt towards Sage. Sage reacted, pulling the water from the pitcher. With a slice of her hand, the water formed a ball that smacked Petra in the face. Her hounds faltered. Sage pushed out again, and a wind surged forward, pushing Petra against the far wall. "Stay away from me!"

Petra hit the wall. The wind died and she slumped to the floor before jumping up again. The walls rattled so hard now, her bed seemed to hop merrily across the floor. A chair tipped over, and the water glasses tumbled to the ground, smashing into a hundred tiny pieces.

A giant male burst through the door, holding himself upright against the trembling building. Sage kept one hand stretched outright towards Petra, and used the other to stabilize herself against the window.

"Zeke," Petra gasped, pointing at Sage. "You have to get her out of here."

"Stay back," Sage warned.

"Now, just calm down. I'm not here to hurt you," Zeke replied with a rumbling voice. The fire jumped from its gate in warning as Zeke took a step toward Sage. The carpet singed, and the room filled with the smell of burnt hair.

"Stay back!" Sage warned again.

Just then, a beautiful male with dark, curling locks appeared from thin air. "Petra, what have you done?" he asked, exasperation thick in his voice.

"She's dangerous, Raphael. She doesn't belong here! She'll kill us all!" Petra screamed. She pushed herself forward like she would launch herself at Sage, her shadows coiling and expanding through the rumbling room.

"Get her out of here," Raphael said pointedly to Zeke before turning his attention back to Sage. Zeke grabbed Petra around the waist, and with a nod towards Raphael, he disappeared into nothingness from the room.

"My dear. Please calm down. We can't help you if you bring the building down on top of us, now can we?" Raphael smiled slightly and took the smallest step toward her.

"I told you. Stay back."

"I know. But I can't do that, now can I? Not when you are so worked up. Please, let me help you." His voice was soft, and he walked towards her with both palms exposed, trying to placate her. "Just take a nice, deep breath for me, dear, and we can't fix all of this."

Sage shook her head. This was it. They were going to capture her; this is what she was running from, what that woman's voice had warned her of. Sage looked back, glancing out of the window. She'd fallen from the sky and survived once. Maybe she could break the window and do it again? Her breath shook as she exhaled.

"Don't do that, Sage. It will be very difficult for me to heal you again. That's assuming you aren't splattered from the fall, this time."

"Just stay back!" Sage exclaimed. Spider veins of cracks began to slither down the windows.

Just then, Raphael jumped forward, wrapping one arm around her waist, and forcefully pushing his index finger to her head.

"Sleep," he whispered before she could react. Sage pushed to fight back but felt her mind fade quickly, a curtain of black falling over her consciousness. She gripped Raphael's shirt tightly just before she felt herself fall into oblivion.

Chapter 3

Raphael sat at his desk making notes on his newest patient. The fact that she was a mortal and bore elemental powers strong enough to shake a building was worrisome. The fact that she seemed to possess all four elemental powers made her downright terrifying until they learned more about her. Nevertheless, he wasn't afraid of her, necessarily. But he couldn't blame his King for being wary of the girl.

"Speak of the demon himself," Raphael muttered as Symon and Gavin walked into his ward. Raphael knew Symon to be a benevolent and fair king, but the male was built for war. He was a creature of contradictions, even in the clothes he wore: a tunic made of charcoal fabric and embroidered with reds, blacks, and gray. His mid-length golden hair and brown skin contrasted with his eyes, the color of the deepest ocean, a color so cold Raphael often wondered if they'd frozen solid during his years of confinement.

Sunlight from Raphael's floor-to-ceiling windows danced across Gavin's face and training armor. The younger male was often in good spirits, his spirit seemingly untainted by his early years being shaped by the brutality of servitude.

But today Raphael noticed his smile failing to reach his eyes as he strode to greet the healer.

"Morning, Raph," Gavin said with false cheer.

"And to what do I owe the pleasure?" Raphael replied, acknowledging the young warrior and King with a quick nod.

"We're here to talk about the girl." Symon spoke in a melodious voice, rich and warm, but brimming with a quiet, steady power.

"Of course. Although, I'm surprised you waited until the morning. And that you brought Gavin."

"The boy, here, seems to be one of the few people who can make sense of her. She's unafraid of him."

"I just fed her," Gavin responded defensively, clearly affected by being referred to as "boy."

"And she opened up to you," Symon replied. Turning his attention back to Raphael, he continued, "I think you could also get through to her."

Raphael considered what his King said, chewing over the best questions to ask. "I take it you are after a particular thread of information? Maybe, wondering what she has to do with the disappearances along the Nysan borders?"

Symon had walked towards the large windows to gaze out at the city while Raphael sat quietly. At his questions, Symon's head whipped back to stare at Raphael. "How'd you hear about that?"

Raphael shrugged. "Symon, you know very well that I sit on your Queen's council, in addition to the duties I hold as court healer. Besides, young Gavin here *also* sits on Aryael's council. Though he does a good job of shirking his responsibilities to it."

Again, Gavin exhaled sharply. Clearly, the boy thought his little rouse was working. He wasn't fooling anyone. In fact, Raphael would bet that Symon had brought Gavin here to spur the boy on to acting like the Lord he ought to be by now.

"Well, since you brought it up, I suppose I should fill Gavin in." The King began while walking back towards Raphael's desk. He lithely dropped into the elegant wingback and laid his cheek on his palm. "The Dark Born Twins are on the move. They've assembled a stronghold on their side of the Speridesse Pass. There have been reports of several companies of soldiers going missing, as well as some Nysan civilians. Our diplomats have sent word that Speridisia is likely to blame for the disappearances." Symon waited, letting the news settle over the room.

Gavin dragged a spare wooden chair next to Symon and sat. He leaned forward, elbows on his knees, hands clasped below. With his head dropped, eyes on the floor, Gavin asked, "You think Sage might be one of them?"

Symon passed a hand over his tight, curly hair, and grimaced slightly. "I don't know. And that's what worries me. She could have been abducted from the human lands, though we have no word that their defenses have dropped. As far as we know, any fae trespassing in Meropoli without permission is still a fatal mistake. Plus, we found something in her bag yesterday that suggests something else." Symon paused, visually carefully choosing what information he shared. "There was a book in her bag. It mentioned Cerridos. And Allyra."

That caught Raphael's attention. "Cerridos? The realm leaper?"

"Aryael thinks the girl might be one of them. A realm leaper. They used to come to us when we were in danger."

"So that means she isn't a threat to us?" Gavin asked, quickly sitting taller, becoming even more invested in the conversation.

"That means we will have to wait to see. In the meantime, Raphael, you will train her. Even if she was sent here as a gift, she will destroy the city if she can't manage her powers."

"Hmm...agreed. And should we return the book to her?" Raphael asked.

"No. We will hold on to it a while longer. I would like for Aryael and I to compare notes on it. See what else we can learn in the meantime."

Raphael nodded in confirmation, although he didn't quite agree with the King. Keeping the girl's belongings from her didn't feel right.

"And you," Symon finished, turning to Gavin. "You will get close to the girl. Get to know her, observe her. And when she opens up, when she shares her memories as they return, you will report them to me. Do you understand?"

"You want me to spy? I'm not a spy Symon. What does Aryael think of this plan?"

"Boy, you may be my Queen's little pet, but I am still your King. You have pledged your fealty to me just as much as you have to her. You will report what you discover to me, or to Raphael. Raph, you can forward anything to me in the usual fashion."

"Very well," Raphael replied.

"Her training starts today," Symon ordered, making his way toward the door.

"If she's feeling better," Raphael replied. Symon turned, ready to demand obedience. "It will do no good if we push her before her body is ready, Symon, and you know that.

Let me do my job. Now, if I could make a request, maybe you could visit your sister, and remind her that Sage is still a guest under our protection. Hmm?"

"Of course. Gavin, I expect an update before supper tomorrow." Symon disappeared into thin air before Gavin replied.

Gavin glared at Raphael. Rather than saying anything, the young male strode to the door and slammed it closed on his way out. The frame rattled in his wake, and Raphael let out an exasperated sigh.

"No need to be dramatic," he called out, knowing the boy could hear him as he hurried towards the training ring, no doubt eager to work off his frustration. He would be back later this afternoon, most likely covered in wounds from fighting Zeke. The boy would forget his training, probably lose his head with the acknowledgment that they had caught on to his little game. Or maybe he was upset at having to spy on the girl.

Raphael pondered the interesting turn of events as he climbed the flight of stairs that led to Sage's floor. He would fetch the girl, inspect her wounds, and take her to breakfast. The best way to spy on someone, after all, is to make them feel safe and cared for. This wouldn't be the first time he'd been used by the royals to keep an eye on people. He'd been spying on Petra for years now.

Raphael reached Sage's door, and smartly rapped on the cream-painted wood.

Sage was sitting against the window, shoulder pushed up against the glass. Miraculously, the windows had been repaired while she'd been...asleep? Sedated? She remembered

vividly the scene that had played out before; Petra screaming at her, shadows lurching with menace and hate, and
the arrival of the most beautiful man- no, a fae male. Tall,
elegant, lithe, and commanding. His kind eyes beseeching
her to let him help. He had laid one hand on her and she'd
succumbed to sleep.

Suddenly, that same male voice followed the staccato
knock at her door. "Sage, may I come in and check your
wounds?"

"If I say no, will you go away?" Sage replied hopefully.

The door opened slowly, and Raphael stuck his head
around it. "I'm sorry, my dear, but no. I really must insist on
checking your wounds." He stepped in and closed the door
behind him. "Healers orders."

Sage pushed herself to stand. They stood still, quietly
observing each other. He didn't seem menacing. He didn't
seem like he meant her any harm; in fact, he seemed quite
genuine.

"I'm just here to check on you, maybe make sure you get
some breakfast?"

Raphael gestured to the side table, and a teapot, mugs,
and a tray covered in cookies and pastries materialized.

"How'd you do that?" Sage asked.

"My power allows me to provide what my patients need.
Sometimes that means water, and sometimes that means
cookies. Help yourself," Raphael inclined his chin to Sage
as he leaned forward to pour the tea.

Carefully, Sage approached the chairs, and accepted a
mug of tea. The warm liquid slipped down her throat like
nectar from heaven. She couldn't stop a groan of pleasure
from escaping. "I guess I like tea," she sighed. She barely
stopped herself from mimicking the sound as she bit into

the cookie. The cookie, dusted with spice and filled with dried fruits, flooded her senses. Spicy cinnamon, vanilla, and tangy fruits forced her body to relax despite her best efforts to stay on her guard.

"Thank you," Sage whispered. "I suppose you are here to ask more questions?" Sage studied Raphael as he glanced at her over his tea cup. He gracefully placed the cup back on his saucer.

"I will ask you questions, when you feel up to it. In the meantime, I'm content to ensure you make a full recovery."

"I don't remember anything new, if you're wondering. I'm sure Gavin filled you all in yesterday after I...well, you know."

"He did. So did Petra. He told me that you think you might be suppressing your memories?" Sage responded with a nod. Saying it out loud was a more painful admission today, it seemed. Raphael remained quiet for a few moments, staring into the embers of the fireplace, which had once again quieted to a low crackle. "Sometimes, forgetting seems like the easy way out. But everything has a price."

Raphael stirred, turning his body more towards Sage. "Would you like to know what *I* know about you so far? Would that be helpful?"

"I'm not sure what you mean. How do you know anything about me?"

"Well, when healing you, I was able to discover a few things. For starters, you are not fae. But you are not human, either. At least, not kin to the humans I'm used to encountering. Your body responded to some of my healing powers naturally, but also rejected others. In contrast, your body also didn't entirely respond to mortal techniques of healing. This leads me to believe that you are not from here."

Sage froze. She stared at him for a beat, then burst into a fit of laughter. "You think...I'm from somewhere else? Geeze. Get this guy a badge. He's a regular detective!" Sage gestured towards Raphael as she rocked back in her chair, laughing in hysterics. "Of course I'm from somewhere else!" Flames crackled to life in the fireplace. "I fell—to the ground—in a fucking fireball. How many fae, how many 'mortals', do that?!"

Raphael waved her off. "Yes, yes, my dear. You are *quite* hilarious." He sipped daintily from his tea. "If you are done with your little show, I can proceed with what else I know about you. And your powers."

That shut her up. In mid-breath, Sage jerked to a halt. "What powers?"

"Oh, you know. Fire," Raphael gestured at the fireplace. "Earth, powers," again, Raphael waved his hand towards the windows. "And, if I'm not mistaken—and I rarely am— water and wind as well. Quite powerful, even by fae standards."

Raphael continued sipping his tea, giving Sage time to absorb the information. Picking up a flaky pastry, he continued, "I also determined you are likely twenty-two, maybe twenty-three years of age. And quite underfed. I imagine you've been on the run for a while." Raphael took a small bite out of a croissant. "It's been two days since you fell to us. I'd like to take a look at your leg before taking you to breakfast for more substantial food."

"Two days ago? How'd you heal a broken leg in two days?" Sage asked in disbelief. "Magic?"

"I'm no sorcerer. I'm a healer, that is where my power lies," said Raphael with a flourish of his hand. "I have the ability to...encourage healing in the body. Most of the time, it is a simple matter with the fae. You deary, were a different matter. But I like a good challenge, which means we will be good friends. I've already decided."

"If you say so." But Sage got the feeling he was correct. He was not unkind, and his sense of humor seemed very similar to her own.

Raphael sat in front of Sage and unwrapped her ankle to reveal a deep pink scar that ran a length of six inches, at least. The wound felt tender to the touch, but was healthy enough to walk on.

"That's incredible. How....how did you do that?" remarked Sage.

"Powers," winked Raphael, as if that was all the explanation needed. Raphael grabbed a pair of sandals from one of the closets and strapped them to Sage's feet before standing and offering her his elbow. "Shall we?"

"That depends. Will there be more tea at breakfast? I can't promise I will be good company without a nice, big pot of strong tea," whispered Sage, suddenly feeling like she'd really, really like to crawl back into bed. The sun was just peeking over the ocean and greeting the town behind her. Apparently, she wasn't a morning person.

"I promise, there will be tea," grinned Raphael, and he tugged her out of the room and into the waiting hallway.

Chapter 4

Raphael escorted Sage to the dining room of the tower, passing Meliza, Zeke, Petra, and Gavin before they arrived at a small table set for two alongside an open window facing the sea. As promised, a steaming pot of tea sat on the table next to plates of eggs, toast, and fresh fruit. Her stomach clenched with hunger, but Sage forced herself to sit politely and wait as Raphael poured them each a mug of tea.

"Eat. You need the sustenance," was all Raphael said, indicating the food in front of them, as if he could sense the hunger beckoning inside her.

Sage helped herself to eggs and buttered toast, and nibbled on the fruit with enthusiasm.

"I was able to determine that you are quite malnourished while I worked on your burns. It would seem you've gone a very long time without a proper diet, or rest for that matter. Does that information seem surprising to you?" asked Raphael.

It didn't. Sage had noticed how visible her ribs were when she'd dressed yesterday, but hadn't thought much about what it might say about her or the events in her past.

Sage shrugged as she chewed on her toast and stared out at the sea.

"I would say our first point of business is seeing that we build up your strength and get your body strong and recovered before doing anything too drastic with your memories. They may come back on their own. We will start with a healthy diet." The statement was rhetorical; Raphael was not consulting Sage on a plan for medical treatment. No, this was Raphael telling her what was going to happen.

Sage bristled. "I appreciate your concern, but I'd really like to know what the heck I'm doing here."

"And I have no doubt we will figure that out," said Raphael. "If you've finished your breakfast, we can go ahead and take a look at those injuries. Perhaps I can smooth out any lasting damage before the scarring becomes permanent."

Raphael stood and offered his arm to Sage again, leading her out of the dining room and away from the fae who had been eating their own breakfasts at a separate table. They had been awfully quiet. In fact, Sage hadn't heard a single word spoken between the four of them; she hadn't even heard the scrape of a fork.

"They were listening to us the whole time, weren't they?" whispered Sage once they had cleared the doorway.

"Very perceptive. Of course they were. You are the shiny new thing, full of mystery. A problem to be solved. I imagine you will be the most popular creature in the tower, well, next to me of course," and Raphael winked at her as they entered his medical ward.

Three tables lined one wall, dressed with white linens awaiting patients. Sage wondered how many patients the fae healer could have in a tower where she had only seen five other creatures. She was sure the King resided in the castle at the center of the city, so that meant Raphael lived here with the others. Surely, they couldn't need medical help that often.

"Go ahead and undress, Sage. There are linens on the bed there you can use to cover any areas you are uncomfortable with me viewing. Although, I may need to tend to some sensitive areas. Your burns were extensive," Raphael waved a hand to the tables as he hung a sign on his door, informing others he was with a patient and mustn't be disturbed.

As Raphael walked across the room to appraise his medical carts and the trappings laid atop it, Sage did as she was told, laying a wide strip of linen across her breasts and another strip over her hips, and waited for the healer to approach.

Raphael inspected the marks on the side of Sage's head and face, gently prodding the tissue to determine tenderness and the status of her healing before repeating the process along her body. Raphael stooped, prodded, felt, and even sniffed each mark and bruise on her body before arriving at her ankle.

He took care to examine the facility of her ankle joint, pausing to inspect the deep pink scar that had formed higher above where the bone had once jutted through her skin. He rubbed his thumb across the line and a faint glow emitted beneath the pad of his digit. He passed over the scar again, and Sage snatched her leg away, choking on a giggle.

Grinning, and biting her teeth together, Sage cried out, "Sorry! That was just...that tickled." She grinned sheepishly at the healer.

"Not to worry. I forgot the sensation would be new to you. The others are here often enough, I don't even have to tell them how to sit or to prepare themselves. May I?" asked Raphael, gesturing back to the leg Sage still held curled up near her torso.

"Sure. I'm ready. I'll be still."

"Good," smiled Raphael. "It may help to talk while we do this. To keep your mind occupied. This is simple enough work, I should be able to keep up while I see to this mark."

They sat in silence for just a moment, Sage trying hard not to yank her leg out of the healer's hand as the soft glow seemed to erase the scar from her skin. "Most of you guys are super old. How come no one looks ancient?"

"Well, I suppose it's just the way we age. Humans age faster because they live faster. We age slower because we live slower. How old do you think the others look?" asked Raphael.

"Well, if I didn't already know better, I would have guessed King Symon, Meliza, and Zeke to be somewhere in their forties. Petra doesn't look older than thirty-five, you too. But I know they are all over one-hundred. Except you, how old are you?" Sage asked.

Raphael finished working on her ankle and turned to his cart, preparing a tonic of some sort. "Would you believe me if I told you I was older than all of them?" Raphael teased.

Sage gaped. "But you definitely look younger than Symon, and Meliza for that fact. How?!"

Raphael hummed to himself, smiling a bit, clearly enjoying this conversation. "Well, lifestyle likely has something to do with it. I'm no warrior and have no intention to learn how to bang a sword around or smash rocks apart. And, my healing powers might have some other, self-serving purposes. Why bother with these powers if I can't at least maintain this gorgeous complexion of mine," Raphael was positively beaming at Sage now, and she grinned widely back.

Sage giggled, "You have an excellent point. I think I'd rather like a power that could make me an everlasting radiant beauty."

The two continued joking about Raphael's so-called "vanity routine" for the next several minutes while he finished the tonic he was preparing before he commanded she "Drink up." It was bitter, but filled her with warmth and ease. She could feel knots of tension held in various parts of her body relax as she finished the glass.

Sage began dressing as Raphael wheeled his cart back to where it had been when they arrived. "Can you tell me more about the others? More than just...how old they are?" she asked. "I get the feeling they aren't necessarily thrilled I'm here."

"You worry the others feel the same as Petra?" Raphael asked with his lilting voice. Sage nodded her response.

"Yes, well, it has not been that long since they were all separated and fighting desperately to get back to one another. You had us all quite scared when you arrived; I don't know that the others aren't fully convinced you haven't come to attack us."

"But you don't think that?" asked Sage.

Raphael paused, staring at her, "No. No, I do not. I think you tried very hard to get away from something—or someone—and ended up here by accident."

Raphael gestured to a pair of chairs facing a desk on the opposite side of the room. The ward was large enough to house the three medical beds, a large desk, and three chairs, plus an entire wall of shelves stocked with the various accoutrements of his vocation.

"Symon, Meliza, and Petra are siblings, all fifteen years apart. Zeke was the son of their father's hand, and their best friend. When we were conquered, our enemies were clever enough to split them apart, send them to different parts of the continent-"

"That's awful!" Sage was genuinely moved by the story. No wonder everyone seemed so uptight.

"Yes, well, eventually, all four found each other again," Raphael continued the story, picking at lint on his pants, "and they were able to covertly form an alliance with other conquered kingdoms and overthrow our repressor. Petra and Zeke are paired, and King Symon is of course married to Queen Aryael, whom you haven't met yet. And then there is Meliza who leads the City Guard as General. They've faced, and lost, so much this last century, and they are finally beginning to see the fruits of their sacrifices. Give them time," Raphael promised, patting Sage's knee.

Sage contemplated this information for a bit. "You said Petra and Zeke were paired, but King Symon married? I don't really understand the difference," Sage chewed on her cheek, contemplating the details Raphael had offered her.

"Fae relationships work differently than those on Meropoli, with humans. Marriage is a symbol of formality, and not all Fae choose to go through with it. Fae often become pairs, lovers, and partners, but do not marry. Many choose to become hand-fasted over the institutionalized practice of marriage. And then there is the bond, a powerful connection between paired fae. The bond is something that surpasses marriage, hand-fasting, and whatever other nonsense we might think up when pursuing love. The bond links a paired couple in a primal way, similar to birds of prey. We are lucky to have a King and Queen who have bonded, as it increases the control and abilities of their power; and I suspect Petra and Zeke have the bond, but they have not declared it if they have."

"What happens if one of the bonded fae dies, but not the other?" asked Sage.

"It is very difficult for a fae when their bonded partner moves on. Many choose to die alongside their loves, but others continue on. Some even find other partners, and may even find a bond again," explained Raphael.

"So you can be bonded more than once?" retorted Sage.

"I suppose that was a gift from the Goddess, blessing us with more than one opportunity for love to go alongside our long lives." Raphael shrugged off the conversation, and Sage could tell he grew weary of the topic.

"Gavin told me your family is responsible for the running water in Veritasailles. Did they make it out?" asked Sage.

Raphael loosed a long, tight breath. "They did not. My parents were proud, innovative healers. 'Champions of the people,' is what they called themselves. When we were invaded, after the murder of King Credeus and his Queen Cissa, my parents were very outspoken against our new rulers. They were executed in the Castle Gardens. Along with Zeke's father. His mother was so distraught she found a memory-walker in the work camp she was sent to and had them erase all the memories of her husband. In the end, the memory-walker had been so thorough she can't even recognize her own son any longer."

"Gods...that's awful."

They sat in silence for a while, as if to make space for the memories to find their way back to where they belong, to honor the lives lost.

"You speak of gods. Can you recall your gods?" asked Raphael with a tilt of his head, once she'd made herself comfortable.

Sage started to roll her eyes at him, because of course, she couldn't remember. But she stopped suddenly, grasping her stomach in shock. "I do. I remember their names, actually." Raphael sat up in his seat, extending one palm in a gesture for her to elaborate. "We, where I'm from, have four gods. Therisyd, god over earth; Cerridos, god of wind and air; Allyra, goddess of water; and Brighid, goddess of fire. Except, it's not really fire. It's more like... energy. Like the vibration between all living things that makes fire come to life." Sage gaped at the wall beyond her. She remembered. She didn't have anything else to go on, besides some flashes of ancient-looking statues and drawings, likely portraying the gods, but she knew they were real. They were hers.

Raphael smiled slightly, "That's good. I overheard you tell Gavin you saw a bit of your home, in your mind?"

"You really are a gossip, aren't you?" Sage replied, side-eying the fae.

"It comes with the trade," Raphael replied with a shrug. "What you described does not relate to anything in this world. Symon spent the evening, after that spectacle in your room," the fae smiled teasingly, "perusing his library for any mention of machines like the ones you described. I think....Well, I think you came from a different world somehow."

A different world. Honestly, that really wasn't all that shocking of an idea once you had hurtled to the earth in a fireball. She tried to remember what happened when she fell from the sky, but it was like her brain was a toddler, stomping its feet and declaring, "NO!"

"I just wish I could remember what I was doing before coming here. In my memory, I saw a book. An old thing; and hands passing the book to me. I had hoped the book would be in my pack, but all that was in there were blankets, socks, and gauze."

Raphael squirmed slightly in his chair, sinking a bit into the seat. "Do you remember what the book looks like?"

"Old, like I said before. The binding was stiff leather, with some adornment around the edges. But it wasn't elaborate. Just a little black border. But I couldn't see the title. I could just tell it was important to whatever I was doing." Sage stood and walked to the windows on the back side of the room. She supposed, being in a tower, every room had windows. She felt so very tired all of a sudden.

"Right, well. That should do it for today. I will walk you back to your room. Once you've begun to gain a little weight, and I'm satisfied with your recovery, we will begin training with your powers." Raphael was already heading for the door when Sage stopped him.

"Training? For what?"

"It is Symon's belief that you should be practiced with your abilities. You know, so you don't bring the Obelisk down upon our heads."

Cold snaked through Sage's insides as they walked towards the stairs leading to her room. "And what if I don't want to?"

"Come now, dear. You wouldn't truly wish to be at fault for...tearing down a building, or lighting an innocent person on fire because you lost control, would you?"

They stopped at the door to her room, Sage considering Raphael's suggestion.

"No. I don't."

"I will see you tomorrow," Raphael bid Sage goodbye at her door, turned on his heel, and sauntered down the hall, humming to himself.

Sage just stared at him, trying to keep her shock from rising to the surface. She opened her door slowly, reeling from the idea that one false move, one moment of uncontrolled emotion, could result in her unintentionally hurting someone - or worse.

Her spirits lifted when she saw a tray of food on the side table; a small note lay next to a bowl of cherries. *"I noticed you preferred the cherries yesterday. I decided you could use more today with your lunch. -Gavin."*

Sage smiled softly to herself. She really did like cherries. She ate her modest lunch of cherries, cold meats, and cheese, sipping on sparkling water that had been left next to the tray before deciding she would explore the tower. Raphael had mentioned books yesterday; there had to be a library somewhere nearby, and he hadn't said she *had* to stay in her room.

Raphael left Sage at her room, and walked back to his ward. She remembered the book, which was alarming. That she remembered it in such detail suggested the book was more important than they had guessed. He had hoped that detail would refuse to surface for a while longer so they could analyze the item a bit longer, but he supposed they wouldn't have that luxury after all.

Raphael sat down behind his desk, and pulled out a yellow leather-bound notebook, with a winged lion embroidered in reds, grays, and black floral embellishments. He flipped to a random page and began writing.

She knows about the book. I don't believe she suspects we have it, but we should hurry with our examination.

The writing faded off the page as if it had never existed. Several moments passed, and Raphael contemplated setting the book down and coming back later. The King was likely busy with some other business at present, and would write back at his leisure. Raphael leaned back in his chair, pondering the girl. Her powers were unpredictable. He couldn't tell if she had a complete lack of control over them, or if her mastery of them were intuitive. It was possible that her response to Petra had been a simple survival response.

She was a curious creature; he felt sure she hadn't been sent here in an act of malice, but he hadn't decided if she meant to come here at all. There were old stories of gods passing through portals of time and space, coming to walk alongside fae and humans to give omens or blessings. Could she be one of the gods who'd passed through the wrong portal?

A tight, neat script flowed across the open page of his journal.

Perhaps she isn't as helpless as she'd like us all to believe.

The book will be returned to her when we've determined where she is from, and what she plans to do here.

I want to know about her powers, and how she got them. If humans are now coming equipped with powers, there's no telling how Rankor's sons might use them in their retaliation.

Raphael had feared a response like that from his King.

He didn't enjoy being deceitful, especially when the girl seemed to trust him so willingly. King Credeus had once held a family captive in one of the castle's wings for several years, suspecting them of allying with King Rankor and plotting to overthrow him. It had been that determination to squash out dissent which led the family to do just as they were accused of. In hindsight, had King Credeus been more willing to listen and believe his subjects, Felysia may never have been conquered at all.

Raphael stood, shaking his head, and walked to his shelves of medical supplies. That was all a thought and a problem for another day.

It was time to head to the market where Gavin and Meliza had already set up a booth. He would spend the rest of the day seeing to the ailments of the Veritasailles people, helping them to the best of his ability. Most of it would be simple tonics and salves, already prepared and waiting for the day, but he was sure there would be a few surprises waiting for him when he arrived.

He finished filling his portable medical chest, and cast himself into the market, shimmering into nothing and re-appearing out of thin air. He landed gracefully in the chair Gavin had placed at a table for the healer.

"I will never understand how you do that. How do you know exactly where I'm going to put the chair?" Gavin said.

"Because I'm wise and all-knowing," winked Raphael, before standing to greet the first patient of the day.

Chapter 5

Gavin matched Meliza step for step. The normally stealthy warrior practically stomped down the expansive marble halls, a clear indicator she wished her presence known.

If Meliza had been blessed with powers over fire, Gavin imagined flames would ripple from her spine down her back. In fact, he was surprised that stalagmites weren't erupting from the castle floor with the anger that emanated from her. He carefully remained adjacent to her, never daring to take the lead. He tugged at his tunic, rolling his shoulders to ease the tension, and readied himself for the sibling squabble.

Reaching the gold-embellished double doors of Symon's study, Meliza unceremoniously slammed through them.

"You should get a dog whistle. It'd probably take less energy than using your spectre to hunt me down."

"I'll keep that in mind," Symon replied, glancing up from a black, leather-bound book he was bent over.

"What was so important you interrupted my line-up?" Meliza asked, balling her hands into fists at her side. "I expected to find the castle under siege based on your message."

Gavin looked around the room, noting the piles of scattered books and wondering if maybe an intrusion hadn't happened in the King's usually tidy study.

"I want to know what you've discovered about the girl." Symon looked at Meliza, then turned his steely gaze toward Gavin.

"I told you the same thing Raphael told you. The memories will likely come back on their own," Meliza replied, stepping in front of Gavin. "She isn't lying about what she knows, or doesn't know. Surely even you could have sensed that."

Symon glared at Meliza. Gavin knew Symon usually heeded Meliza's advice. That he wasn't able to accept her word implied something else was going on. "What's going on? What do you know that I don't?" Meliza demanded, clearly thinking along the same lines as Gavin.

"Did Gavin inform you of her flashback? Of the powerful machines she saw?" Symon set the book down, stepping toward them. "Did Raphael, or Zeke tell you about her lapse of control over her powers?" He backed away, a gleam in his eyes that seemed unfamiliar to Gavin. Symon walked toward the windows facing the palatial gardens.

Symon turned to face them again, "Not just fire, or water, or wind, or stone. All four. *How* does a human attain all four powers, and wield them? Is that the plan of Abbadon and Apyllon?"

Abbadon and Apyllon. The Dark Born Twins: quite possibly more blood-thirsty, more crazed than their father. The twins hadn't attacked in the past ten years. Their decimated armies and resources were the most likely reason, but could they have something more menacing in mind?

"You know, as well do I, that no son of Rankor would stoop to work alongside humans. They detest them. Abbadon and Apyllon would sooner conquer Meropoli and enslave the continent before they would align with them. But they can't do that, so long as we and our allies are here to prevent them," Meliza calmly replied, clasping her hands behind her, in Commander mode once again.

Symon scrubbed his hands down his face before advancing once more. "Unless they've already begun the process. What if she is the first weapon they intend to send us? She could have been sent here with powers she can't control, what mortal could? Sent here to self-destruct, and take us down with her." Symon hung his head and turned to face his sister. "I can't let us fall to ruin again. I can't be separated from all of you again."

Meliza approached her brother- brother now, not King- and slipped her arm around his waist, hugging him softly. She was strong, and tall for a female, but he was stronger and taller. In that moment, Gavin could imagine them when they were younger, their close bond, the way their minds worked in tune with each other. "We won't fall, brother, not while we're still here."

"For what it's worth, I don't get the sense the girl is here with malicious intent," Gavin interjected. "Nor do I think she was sent here by someone else. I get the idea that very few creatures would be able to make her do anything she didn't want to do. I sense a very strong will within her; I think she sent herself, and something just...went wrong along the way."

Meliza pulled away from Symon and considered his words. "Gavin is on to something there. I will meet with Acantha and Epyllo this evening after dinner. I'm sending them to the Nysan borders to spy on the brothers to try and get a grasp of what they are planning. I won't send them into enemy territory just yet, but at least we should be able to get an idea if they are up to something. In the meantime, brother, let's give Gavin a chance to do what you've ordered him to do. I will try and listen in when I can, but I will be busy the next month." Meliza had begun to walk to the door before she turned and took in her brother's confused look.

"Oh, Goddess. You didn't? You forgot!" Meliza grinned, trying to hold back her laughter. Gavin choked on his own laughter. Aryael would have Symon's balls in a vice if he had forgotten her birthday. Gavin wanted to say that Symon would lose his head if it weren't for Meliza, but he wisely held his tongue. The King was nonplussed enough as it was.

"If either of you breathes a word to her, I'll demote both of you to stableboy. She's already accusing me of ignoring her counsel," Symon grumbled. "I just, I have to know what that girl means to Felysia."

"You should listen to your wife!" Meliza tossed over her shoulder as she left, chuckling to herself as she headed out of the study.

"Gavin, wait," the King called before Gavin could follow.

"Yes?"

"You will get to know the girl, but keep this information to yourself. We need to keep her unaware of our suspicions in case the knowledge triggers some unfortunate reaction."

Gavin stiffened but nodded his understanding. Symon kept his gaze for a moment, and Gavin fought the urge to squirm under the intensity of the King's attention. Finally, Symon dipped his chin, a signal that Gavin was dismissed.

Gavin left the palace, trailing after Meliza, but she'd already gone so he headed back to the Obelisk. Gavin was starving. He'd missed lunch, punishment for being late to his sentry duty the other day. He shifted into his hawk form and flew to the tower. Gavin landed and proceeded towards his room, stealthily trying to avoid Petra. He was already on her bad side after pestering her over Sage's lunch. The cherries were his idea, and the note had been an afterthought. He hoped the note hadn't been too forward, but in his experience, a friendly gesture went a long way to disarming people.

He had overheard Zeke and Petra whispering after breakfast as they headed to the small training gymnasium in the tower. According to them, Sage possessed all four primary powers. There were stories of fae wielding power like that, but that was millennia ago when the realm leapers still visited. He wished she could tell them how she, a human, came into power like that. Maybe they could practice wind wielding together.

Gavin used the hour before dinner to wash up and try to develop a game plan for getting close to Sage. The training idea had real appeal, but he would have to play it right. Sure, the others apparently knew he had been suppressing his powers, but maybe they would let him keep up the ruse a while longer. Gavin quickly dressed and headed to the dining room.

He'd just got himself seated when Sage entered with Raphael, chatting about something she'd read while in the library. He should have thought to show her that. Of course, she would get bored here with no training or responsibilities and no way to venture into the city. Raphael steered Sage towards Gavin's side of the table, where she chose a seat next to him.

After taking her seat she leaned over and whispered, "Thanks for the cherries. You were right. They are my favorite," she smiled.

"Then we will have to make sure you have them every day," said Gavin.

"You know too much sweetness is bad for the humors," said Petra.

Zeke smiled at his partner from the corner of his eye before saying, "Isn't she the best," toward Gavin.

Petra swatted at Zeke as they both took their seats. Briefly, Gavin watched Petra's mask slip as Zeke sat and a knowing smile passed between the pair. When Petra turned her attention back to the table, the mask of detachment slid firmly back into place.

"How are we feeling today, Petra?" Raphael asked while pouring water into Sage's glass.

"She's fine," Zeke replied, his tone indicating that the subject would be dropped.

Petra straightened, lifting her chin in answer as Zeke mirrored Raphael in pouring wine for her. Symon was a King in his birthright, but Petra could have been an Empress, thought Gavin. The female held herself together like she was a fortress built of iron. Rarely did she lose control; all the more reason they had been surprised and concerned by her outburst in Sage's room. Clearly, Symon had spoken to her about it because she treated Sage with polite aloofness for the moment.

Gavin interrupted the brief silence that had settled on the room. "Are we waiting for Meliza?"

"She won't join us tonight. In fact, she won't be here much for a while, what with the Queen's birthday."

"There's much to prepare. Ah, lovely," Raphael said as a heavenly array of food appeared in the dining room, courtesy of enchantments Symon had ordered when the Obelisk was rebuilt.

Gavin served himself a generous portion of roasted chicken and root vegetables and grabbed several pieces of buttered flatbread before glancing at Sage. He was glad to see she was well enough to eat, and he could see the lines and bruises were fading from her skin. Already, her skin had a healthier flush to it, though dark circles still lingered below her eyes. She was wearing the sea green dress from yesterday, and it emphasized her bright green eyes. He also found himself noticing how the copper pins holding the straps of her chiton accentuated bits of copper in her hair. More than once, he found himself caught by Sage as he stared at her.

Gavin smiled and asked, "I overheard you talking about the library; did you find anything interesting?"

"I'd say it's all pretty interesting when you're in a strange land with no recollection of your past," she replied lightly, "but I did find a book of fae children's stories that seemed curious."

"And don't forget the romances," jabbed Raphael, a smile on his lips.

"You wretch!" Sage rolled her eyes, but Gavin noticed her smile. He got the sense that Sage and Raphael had become friendly. For some reason, that pleased Gavin, despite his knowledge of why Raphael was getting close to Sage. Still, the idea of Sage having a friend here made him glad. "So, you like romances?" Gavin asked, unable to resist teasing her.

"Well, I don't *dislike* them, but I'm not opposed to reading other materials." Sage nudged Raphael once more, a reprimand for spilling her secret.

"How do you know what your interests are if you can't remember who you are?" Petra inserted coolly into the conversation.

Sage cleared her throat, looking down at her plate before answering, "It's just a feeling, for now I suppose. Who knows, by the end of this perhaps I'll be a completely different person."

Gavin suspected that was the wrong answer as Zeke, Petra, and Raphael all shifted in their seats. Perhaps she would be a different person. There was no telling what they would learn once her memories came back.

Gavin coughed, breaking the silence, "Hyacinth outdid herself tonight. The chicken is really good. You'll have to give her my thanks Petra."

"Who's Hyacinth?" asked Sage, looking at Gavin.

"She is our cook, and you are not to bother her," growled Petra.

Sage placed her fork on her plate and, looking at her plate and speaking through gritted teeth, said, "I am not here to hurt anyone. But of course, I will do as you ask."

Petra glared at Sage in quiet challenge as if she really thought she could take the female on in a battle of strength. Gavin had only seen Petra's powers released once, and the way the female carried herself— the way even Zeke would stand down at her command— made Gavin balk at the idea of a face-off between the two.

Zeke interjected, "Hyacinth is our cook. She was handled very badly during our time under King Rankor. She only speaks to Petra and does not feel comfortable around others. We ask that you do not bother her."

Sage's fork fell from her hand and all the color Gavin admired before leached from her face. "What did you say?"

"...when we were under King Rankor's rule-"

The name King Rankor was a battering ram to her conscience.

Sage could see him. The madman behind the pulpit, beseeching the country to follow him into glory. She could see the man with the wild, hungry eyes, reading her power like a book. She could hear his laugh, feel his gloved hand grip her face. He was going to kill her. He was going to kill her, everyone she loved, everyone that loved her, and anyone who had ever helped her. She couldn't do this.

Without warning, wind rattled everywhere. The walls began trembling.

"Sage. Dear, calm down," Raphael said softly. His chair fell back as he stood too quickly.

Sage stood, willing the wind to let her pass, and backed away from the table. The tremor in the walls became a dischorded song. A moan echoed through the halls. Raphael tried to come closer and she pleaded with a look for him to stay back.

"Sage. It's okay," Gavin called out against the rising wind.

She had to keep them there, so she could run. So she could escape. They didn't know; they might be spared if she left now. But she didn't know the way out. The wind was increasing its pressure on the fae at the table, and she could sense Gavin struggling against it.

A haughty voice crept through her senses. *"Ahhh...there you are, Sage."* Sage stiffened, throwing out her hands. Water began trickling along the walls.

"She's burst the pipes," Zeke muttered.

"Hyacinth," Petra exclaimed. She and Zeke shared a look, and with a nod, they disappeared into nothing.

"Sage. I need you to let me near you. We need you to calm down before you lose control." Raphael's voice remained calm, but there was a look of panic he was unable to hide.

"Raph!" Gavin yelled above the trembling of stone. "Let me. Stay back!" Gavin stepped forward again, trying to approach Sage.

"Sage..." That voice skittered across her mind once again. *"You can't hide from me now. Your powers will always call to me. I will find you, one way or another."*

She pushed harder, trying to keep the two fae away from her, but the pressure eased. A soft breeze fluttered across her neck, cooling the heat that had begun building in her center. She looked at Gavin, who was looking at her with a silent request to let go. So she did.

Raphael rushed to her side. Pushing his palm against her forehead, he commanded her into unconsciousness again. Her knees went soft under her, and she felt the floor meet her body softly as she crumpled, assisted by Raph. Darkness slipped around her as the hissing of pipes sang through the halls.

The disembodied voice's laughter rode her body as she felt Gavin lift her from the floor, and she slipped fully into the darkness of oblivion.

Sage woke later; not sure how much later, Sage glanced at the windows. Dark. Still the same night?

A lumpy figure filled a chair that had been moved near her bed. Gavin sat in the chair facing her, asleep against one of the high shoulders of the chair. His head lolled slightly on his chest, and Sage allowed herself time to contemplate the male. In sleep, there was a childish quality that shone through which was overshadowed by his physical prowess by day.

Eventually feeling awkward for staring, Sage chose to stare out the windows from her bed for countless moments before deciding she needed to use the bathroom. She was still in her dress from dinner and grabbed the nightgown she had left on the floor that morning before heading into the bathing room. When Sage reappeared in her room, she swore she noticed Gavin's body relax. But he continued sleeping, curled into himself on the chair. She felt bad for him, sleeping there, but also didn't want to wake him. She slipped a blanket off her bed and laid it across the sleeping fae before returning to her bed.

Gavin sensed Sage wake, but had remained still to allow her time to adjust to her current situation. A lifetime in work camps had taught him how to feign sleep.

He knew what it felt like to want to run away; to run and hide to protect those you cared about. Gavin knew what it was like to be hunted in the name of evil. His powers had marked him as a target in the work camp, and his family had always tried to shield him from their captors' eyes. But he had shown everyone just what he had kept hidden the first time he walked into battle.

Sage had gotten up from the bed and padded into her bathroom. Gavin was tempted to sneak out and head to his own rooms, or perhaps take a flight around the city to ease some of the tension brought on by painful memories. He was angry with Raph for intervening. He could have helped Sage without the healer knocking her out. But watching Sage command the wind, hearing her panic at the thought of being caught and sacrificed triggered a protective side of him. He couldn't leave her just yet, not when he could sense the uneasiness in her still. He wasn't entirely sure why he felt the need to protect her, or at least help her feel protected. Perhaps it was the promise he made as she was fighting Symon's control, that he wouldn't let them, or anyone, hurt her.

Gavin's eyes were open now, his focus on the sliver of moonlight that peeked through the windows. Shadows of clouds passed in front of the beam, and Gavin thought he saw the shadow of something, someone else pass by it. Most likely it was Meliza or Zeke, making one last patrol before turning in for the night. Gavin sighed quietly to himself, contemplating everything that waited for him, his impending fate.

He had been honored, more than that really, when King Symon and Queen Aryael had offered him Lordship of Mystaira. It would mean a home and safety for himself and his family, something he had never actually experienced before. But Gavin also knew that the moment he was inducted into his Lordship, he would be confined to the burdens of the position for the rest of his life. He was only twenty-five, for Goddess's sake. He'd like to see the world a bit before settling into one place. He had been imprisoned once before, and even though being the Lord of a fertile land was more luxury than he could fathom, Gavin couldn't help the feeling he was walking into a second imprisonment once the title was officially bestowed on him.

Sage walked into the room again, finished with the bathroom. Gavin quickly resumed his sleeping facade as she walked past him toward her bed. She reached the bed, and Gavin heard her pause before padding back to him. He tensed, expecting her to ask him to leave, readying his reply of respectful embarrassment at falling asleep. And then she draped something across him, a blanket, before patting his knee and climbing into her own bed. He counted her breaths and was relieved when he could tell she was asleep only a few moments after she laid down. Gavin blinked, surprised at tears rimming his eyes, and he had to look away from her. It had been a very long time since anyone had done something like that for him. Not since the last time he saw his family, a short visit five years ago to help them get settled in Mystaira, where they would wait for him to become Lord.

Gavin sat in his chair, blanket draped across him, until he could sense the dark make way for sunrise. With the first snippets of birdsong, Gavin stealthily escaped from her room and headed for the balcony above. As he reached the balcony landing, Gavin shifted into his white hawk-eagle form and launched into the sky, spearing for Mystaira. He would peek in on his family before returning. Meliza and Zeke would understand, and he didn't particularly care if they didn't.

Chapter 6

Warm sunlight flooded her room. Sage sat in her bed, holding tightly to both the thick blankets on her bed and the emotions which rode her like a storm. Gavin was gone. Raphael hadn't been in to check on her. And while she was thankful for the quiet, she was left feeling hollowed out and cold.

Memories from the previous night replayed themselves on repeat. The creeping voice that had wormed itself into her mind was a violation she couldn't shake. While she had expected some side effects to recovering her memories, what happened last night didn't seem like a memory. Rather, she was beginning to wonder if Petra had been right about her all along. Was she ready to learn the truth about who she had been in another life?

Sage raked her hand through her hair in frustration, then straightened. Throwing off the blankets, she slid from the bed and made herself face reality. She resolved *not* to cause a scene every time a new memory developed. Her situation was too urgent to lose control of herself like that. And the alternative, never learning who she was or why she was here, was not an option.

That meant the only way forward was the uncomfortable way. She had a feeling that had been a way of life for her for a while now.

Sage took her time getting dressed, choosing a dress of jade with dark blue, wooden painted pins adorning the straps. She ran a comb through her hair, and rummaged through the vanity in her room for any hair pins she could use to secure her chin-length hair out of her eyes.

Once she had comfortably situated herself, Sage left her room in search of breakfast. She was aware that everyone else in the building had most likely eaten, but hoped a pastry or some fruit might be left in the dining room. She hadn't finished her dinner last night, and hunger kept poking at her.

Sage entered the dining room and groaned to find it completely empty save the tables and chairs. She walked to the window where she and Raphael had eaten the day before and peered down at the city below.

She would have liked to go out alone, had she any idea how to get out of the tower. Yet, the thought of climbing down hundreds of stairs was unappealing. The idea of using her influence over air occurred to her, but she wasn't ready to announce herself that prominently to the public. Then there was the voice. *You can't hide your powers from me.* The memory of the voice lingered like a bad taste.

Nope. She was not ready for that test just yet. She would just have to find her way to the kitchens then.

Sage turned on her heel and exited the dining room, determined to find the kitchen on her own. She walked down the hallway, passing the stairwell, and began peeking into the doorways. She passed a couple of storage rooms, holding robes and linens, before finding a pantry- that led into a beautiful stone kitchen.

The kitchen was expansive in a way Sage could not believe. She turned on her spot trying to take in the sight. A large, wood-burning oven dominated one wall, as well as a fireplace holding a cauldron and several racks clearly meant for other cooking purposes. A wall of shelves and racks housed cooking utensils, bags of goods, fruits, vegetables, and even a jar of what looked like candied ginger beamed proudly across from the oven.

Sage remembered Petra's warning not to bother the cook, Hyacinth, and began to look around frantically for a tray, bowl, or plate she could use to quickly pile a few pieces of fruit onto as she heard a dish clatter in a room just beyond the kitchen.

"What are you doing here?"

Sage's insides rolled over as she slowly turned around, and raised her palms, "I'm sorry, I was trying to be quick. I didn't want to disturb anyone."

Petra glowered with cold rage as she stepped toward Sage. "What are you doing here? I don't mean in this kitchen, girl, I can clearly see you pillaging your way through our wares. I mean, what are you doing here, in Felysia?"

Sage was taken aback. Surely, Petra must remember the fact that s*he. did. not. know.* "I don't know why I'm here. I suppose *that* is why I'm *here*, in this gods-forsaken tower."

Sage hadn't meant to raise her voice, but she was finished with Petra's insolent attitude toward her. Irritation pricked at her skin, and she could feel the burning tension rising in her center. Sage took a deep breath, forcing herself to calm down. It wouldn't help if her powers got out of hand again.

Glittering ice sparkled in the depths of Petra's dark gray eyes as she stepped closer to Sage, "I spent a hundred years separated from my family. I watched as my people were slaughtered and burned. You, girl, will not be the ruin of us. So help me, I will summon the wrath of the Tri-Goddess if you so much as step on one of my people's toes."

Sage and Petra glared into each other's eyes, neither one willing to back down.

A gasp interrupted the stand-off as a young female with hair the color of burnished bronze entered the kitchen. Her body had gone rigid with shock, and she raised one hand to her open mouth.

"You need to go," whispered Petra, taking another step towards Sage, fists clenched.

But the female with bronze hair walked closer with out-stretched arms. "Celia, is that you? How?"

Sage looked behind herself, perplexed at the situation.

"Hyacinth, this is Sage. She is Raphael's newest patient," Petra explained with a softness Sage had not witnessed in the female.

"Goddess, I'm sorry. You just...look so much like her." Hyacinth said with tears in her eyes; she had reached the two females and grabbed Sage's hands. "Yes, I can see now, you aren't Celia. But you look so much like her. I just thought...I don't know what I thought,"

Hyacinth gave Sage's hands a quick squeeze as if reluctant to let go, and quickly left the room.

"You need to go, *now*," Petra commanded.

Sage glared at Petra for one more moment before grabbing her bowl of food, and stomping towards the library. She climbed the stairs, fiercely pushing the urge to erupt into flame down. Her back was coated in a fine sheen of sweat by the time she reached the landing, but her irritation was still coiling itself around her spine.

Sage reached the library, and thumped her bowl down on a table. She paced the room a few times before muttering, "What's her fucking problem? It's not like I asked to be sent to this gods-forsaken place. It's not like I *tried* to erase my memories."

She was just starting her fourth lap around the room when she heard a chuckle echo behind her. Sage whipped around, glowering at whoever dared interrupt her tantrum.

Gavin leaned against the door jamb, staring intently at Sage, the picture of poised male grace.

Sage quipped, "Enjoying the show?"

"Actually, yes," Gavin replied. "You might be the first one to actually voice their opinion about Petra out loud. I wouldn't recommend it, though," Gavin said, walking towards Sage.

"And why not? What's her deal?"

"Well...I don't know, actually. All I know is that Symon and Aryael have given her commands *not* to use her powers except as a last resort. And that's always been reason enough for me to stay out of her way."

Sage blanched; so everyone was terrified of Petra? What kind of power could she possess to make a fae king command her to keep them in check? A memory of shadows forming solid shapes resurfaced and Sage tucked her arms behind her back to hide the goosebumps that prickled her skin.

"Well, maybe she should stay out of my way, and I'll stay out of hers," Sage said softly, mustering all the false bravado she could manage.

"You should have asked me to go get the food. I'm happy to help, you just have to ask," said Gavin.

"I am a full-grown woman. I do not need anyone running errands for me. Don't forget, *I* was the one who survived falling from the sky."

"With our help," chuckled Gavin.

Rolling her eyes, Sage walked away from Gavin, picking up the bowl of food she had forgotten about, and with one hand, offered to share with him.

He grabbed a few nuts before asking, "Looking for anything in particular today? More...children's books...to hide your romances inside?" Gavin was grinning far too wide for Sage's liking.

"And what do you read? Tutorials on waging war? Self-help books?"

Gavin laughed again, "Yeah, a little. I typically stick to histories, accounts of famous battles and generals and the like. I find they offer me insight into what I might face in the future. Enlightenment, if you will."

"Enlightenment? For what? Aren't you just a soldier like Zeke and Meliza?"

"First off, they are not *just* soldiers. Zeke is the High General, commander of all armed forces in Felysia, and quite possibly the best warrior Felysia has ever seen. He answers to Symon alone; well and Petra of course," Gavin added with a wink. "Meliza, who is Symon's sister, is General of the City Guard. She controls the city. I, by formality alone, I assure you, am a Colonel, under Zeke. But more than that...someday..." Gavin paused as if unsure he wanted to share what came next, "I'll be Lord of Mystaira, an honor bestowed by the Queen herself." Sage watched as he rolled his shoulders, his hands tugging quickly at his tunic.

"So, you're a Lord?" asked Sage. "I'll have to start referring to you as... 'Lord Gavin'," Sage added, raising an eyebrow and putting special emphasis by switching to a mockingly dignified tone at the title.

Gavin grinned, "Indubitably," with an equally obnoxious tone, sounding like a horrible old aristocrat.

They laughed at their joke. "So, when do you receive this illustrious honor, Lord Gavin?"

"Ah, well...I've got to prove I've got the right disposition, show off my powers. I managed to gain some recognition in the final battle before we won back the Kingdom. I had always hidden them away before then. But rage got the better of me; I'd only fought with my powers once before then, in the battle to break out of the work camp I grew up in. But since then..."Gavin trailed off. "Can I tell you a secret?" Gavin offered. Sage nodded. Gavin leaned in, "I've been hiding my powers ever since the Queen bestowed the honor. I don't think I'm ready to be a Lord. So I've just been biding my time, training and learning. Hoping to get a chance to see a bit of the world before I'm tied down," he finished in a whisper. "My family is already there, setting up a life for themselves. I know I should just get it over with, secure their safety with my title, but...I just haven't been able to bring myself to do it."

Sage wasn't quite sure how to reply, other than, "Your secret's safe with me."

"Good."

He was still leaning toward her when she said, "You weren't there when I woke up."

"I had some business early this morning." Gavin stepped away, seeming to realize just how close they were. Sage forced herself to exhale, stepping back a little, and Gavin asked, "How would you like to visit the city tomorrow? I won't be training much for the time being, what with the Queen's birthday so close. Meliza and Zeke will be tied up securing the city; I'll have a bit of time on my hands, and I'd hate to be in Petra or Raph's way."

"I'd like that," nodded Sage.

"Then I bid you ado," replied Gavin, with his stuffy, nasally old-man voice, as he flourished his hand and bowed.

Sage couldn't help but giggle as she replied, "It will be a promenade," and curtsied.

Sage could feel his grin as he exited the library, and she turned to finally eat her breakfast and peruse the library. She was still smiling to herself as she thought of Gavin becoming a Lord. She couldn't imagine him attending court; his short, wavy dark hair slicked back, and him wearing tightly buttoned vests and coats, or whatever high society wore here. Gavin had such a youthful wildness about him, a playful aloofness that just made the idea seem far fetched. The thought occurred that she actually enjoyed his company, and was looking forward to touring the city by his side.

She drifted into a daydream, delicately placing food in her mouth with one hand, a random book held in the other.

"Reading up on the *History of Fae Healing*, are we?"

Sage dropped the book and whirled to find herself staring at Raphael, framed in the doorway. "Don't do that. You scared the wits out of me," She choked out around a piece of half-chewed grape.

Raphael grinned, "Sorry, you were so lost in thought, it was too easy. Come. We will work on those memories a bit today."

Raphael again offered Sage his elbow. She hesitated. Before, the gesture had been sweet, but after he had once again knocked her out without her consent, she was having second thoughts about the male.

"We need to talk."

"About what, my dear?" Raphael said, dropping his arm to his side.

"We need to set some boundaries, you and I. No more putting me under whenever you want." Sage crossed her arms, ready to dig in her heels when the fae argued with her.

Raphael sighed. "You're right. I'm sorry, my dear. But if you really want me to stop, you're going to have to get a hold of your emotions, and your powers. You burst our pipes last night and nearly tore down our balcony. We are used to dealing with our young with elemental powers, but they are rarely strong enough to tear down whole buildings in the throes of a tantrum."

Sage let his counterpoint hang in the air, considering that he made a pretty good point. If she lost control of her power and caused the Obelisk to fall, she would most likely be squashed under the rubble alongside her captors.

"Okay. I'll work on controlling my powers. And you'll train me, too?"

Raphael nodded. "Now, shall we start with memories?" Sage looped her arm through Raphael's elbow in answer and they began their descent toward the ward.

"Gavin offered to show me the city tomorrow. Would you like to come?" Sage asked.

"Oh, I wouldn't want to impose. Besides, I believe I will be busy with other matters tomorrow. That's why I wanted to squeeze in some time with you today. After you," Raphael gestured to one of the chairs near his desk as he closed the door behind him.

Raphael walked to his desk and glanced at a few pieces of parchment before looking up at Sage again. "The place to begin is for you to recount everything you know about yourself. Then, we will try a few things and see if anything pops up on its own."

Sage took a deep breath. "Ok. Well, I know I'm in my twenties, apparently twenty-two. I know my home was much different than here, full of machines. It was dirty and shadowed, and there were dark towering buildings everywhere. I know I was being hunted. I know that I was in danger, I was running from something—or someone—, and that's what brought me here." Sage chewed on her bottom lip, trying to dig deeper for any sliver of memory that she hadn't already uncovered.

"Good. That's very good. Now, I've been looking through some older manuscripts. I think there is a chance that meditation might spark some memories, or awaken a part of you that is resting or suppressed for now."

The mention of suppressed memories made Sage squirm. Was it possible she was subconsciously suppressing her own thoughts?

"Ok. Sure. I'm game to try, if you think it will help."

Raphael walked around the desk, and leaned the back of his legs against it. "We will start slowly. To begin, let's focus on stilling your mind. Come over here, to the windows." Raphael extended an arm towards the windows where Sage saw a blanket and pillow laid out. "Go ahead and lie down, get comfortable."

Raphael walked to a window that housed a hand crank, and began using it to open the windows slightly. The smell and sound of the sea filtered in, accompanied by the occasional sound of gulls.

Sage lay on the blanket, arranging her dress so that nothing bunched underneath her.

"Close your eyes, and try to relax your body. Focus on letting go of any tension."

Sage lay still, focusing on her muscles. She hadn't realized how sore her shoulders were. Taking a deep breath she tried to force the muscles in her shoulders to release, and when they didn't the space between her eyebrows scrunched together.

"Don't get frustrated. Let your body get acclimated. Let's transition our focus to our breath. Take a deep breath through your nose, and out through your mouth. Count the space between each inhale and exhale."

Sage wriggled slightly on the blanket and exhaled; as she inhaled, she counted to four and repeated the act. She continued breathing and counting, letting the sound of gulls and sea, the smell of the ocean, and the warmth of the sun coming in through the window wash over her.

She could feel individual muscles begin to loosen, to relax and succumb to the rhythm of her breath.

Raphael allowed Sage to continue this pattern for several minutes before prompting, "Now, as you continue your focus on breathing, I want you to also move your focus through your body. Take inventory. Begin with your toes; notice how each body part feels, acknowledge any aches and pains, take note of any asymmetry, but continue on through the body."

Sage imagined her soul lifting out of her body and began scanning each tiny part. Her feet felt strong; she felt a playful breeze skim over her toes, and noticed the lingering tenderness in the ankle below the leg that had been broken.

She moved into her legs, and acknowledged the tiredness in her calves, as if she had been running and standing for long periods of time. She noticed how her left leg felt slightly longer than the other, and her right leg turned out further as she lay on her back. Her hamstrings and lower back muscles tensed at each sound she heard, as if they were conditioned to responding.

The hollowness in her stomach yawned, even after breakfast, the skin stretched tightly across her ribs.

She checked over each part of her body, took note of what had felt unfamiliar before, and greeted it as her own. Even a scar behind her ear she hadn't noticed before, hidden among a bunch of tightened muscles connecting to her jaw.

"Now, take a moment, and thank your body for bringing you this far."

Sage did; she thanked her body for not giving up, for continuing on, even when everything seemed so impossible. Sage released a tight breath.

Raphael responded, "Ok, gently, ease your way back to center. When you're ready, roll to your side and push up to a seated position. Open your eyes whenever you feel comfortable."

Sage spent a couple more breaths acknowledging her body, coming to terms with what it had been through.

When Sage had gathered herself, she rolled to her side and pushed up to a seated position, legs crossed below her.

Raphael offered her a hand, and she allowed him to help her back to her feet. "That's all we will do today."

"What? That's it? But I thought we were going to try and learn about my past, who I was?" Sage exclaimed.

"We will. But we will take it slow. Today was an exercise to try and connect your body and brain. To reintroduce yourself."

Raphael gestured back to the desk, and they both took a seat in the chairs in front of it. "I heard you had a run-in with Petra."

Sage scowled. "More like Petra thinks she can railroad me into submission, to cowering before her."

Raphael barked a laugh, "It's about time someone had the nerve to stand up to her. And who better than the living fireball herself."

Sage couldn't help but grin, "Is that my nickname, The Living Fireball?"

"It's got to be better than being called That Girl. What a drab title. At least Fireball has some style to it," Raphael said with a side-eye.

Sage couldn't agree more. She hated being called "girl." She was a real, actual woman. A full grown-up where she was from. She thought.

"I met Hyacinth. That's what set Petra off. She called me Celia." Sage said, picking pieces of lint from the blanket off her dress.

"Celia? Are you sure?" asked Raphael. Sage nodded. "Celia was Hyacinth's sister. She was tortured and killed in the work camp they were kept in," Raphael explained. "Hyacinth doesn't speak to many of us; Petra is the only one, likely because she rescued her when they escaped the camp together."

"Petra was in a work camp?" Sage asked.

Raphael nodded, "They all were. Me as well. King Rankor was tactical, intelligent and calculated. He separated families, friends, and neighbors to minimize the threat of rebellion. His soldiers were ordered to treat us with a severe brutality I hope we never see again. Watching her sister die broke a part of Hyacinth that even I cannot mend. I think it broke a part of Petra, too." Raphael looked away from Sage, a faraway look in his eyes again, the same look he always got when sharing those painful memories.

Sage leaned forward to grab Raphael's hand, "I'm really sorry you had to go through that. I know me falling from the sky is probably not what you all had planned to do with your time; thank you for helping me." She squeezed his hand once for good measure, and he patted it with his other hand in recognition.

"I've had your dinner sent to your room. The rest of us have been summoned to meet with King Symon and Queen Aryael this evening. It appears even I cannot escape the excitement of birthday celebration planning," Raphael stood, rolling his eyes slightly.

"Thank you, again," said Sage as she stood, and she walked out of his ward to her rooms.

When she arrived, a tray of food sat on the side table that had become the focal point of her room. A covered bowl, holding some sort of fragrant seafood concoction, a plate of pickled vegetables, and a pastry made of cornmeal sat on the tray, along with a note that read, *"Sage- it was so nice to meet you. I'm sorry if I alarmed you. Please, any time you'd like, you are welcome to visit me in my kitchen. I would love to talk with you sometime. -Hyacinth."*

Chapter 7

❋❋❋

She was running through a pasture, a field where horses or goats might usually roam.

A smaller girl ran behind her; they were both laughing with the joyful abandonment of children, blowing dandelion seeds anytime they stopped.

"Sage, do the trick!" squealed the other girl.

Sage dropped her dandelion on the ground, and let her arms fall by her sides. She took a deep breath, and began moving her arms and hands in a pattern, as if she were pulling a rope straight up from the earth, her hands traveling up towards her face. A ball of water plopped from the ground and began floating, stopping when it reached chest height to Sage.

Sage moved her hands around the orb, and it spun, reacting to her magic. She pinched her fingers and moved them away from the orb, and the shape transformed. Sage rotated the water blob and flexed her fingers. The water resembled a crown, and Sage gently pushed it until it hovered over the other girl's head.

The girl looked up in wonder. Then— Sage let it burst all over the girl, and she darted off, back in the direction of a large white house in the distance.

"Hey! That's not fair!" screamed the other girl, chasing her Sage back to the house. "Why do you got to be a mean big sister? Not fair!"

But Sage was laughing and running and feeling the wind push her forward. They reached the house, and the other girl pulled a polished stick from her pocket. With a flourish, she sent a torrent of water spurting from the end of the stick, walloping Sage, and soaking her clothes through.

A man walked onto the porch, "Oh, good. That means we can skip baths tonight."

They all burst into laughter, and the girls climbed onto the porch, where the man made the girls hug before coming inside.

A light, singsong voice called, "Dinner!" and the girls raced each other to the door, slamming it shut behind them.

Sage sat bolt upright in her bed, soaked in sweat. Feeling thirsty, she reached for the glass of water next to her bedside table only to realize she wasn't soaked with sweat. She must have controlled the water through her dream. Or was it a dream? It had felt so familiar. Dawning realization settled over her as she realized it was a memory.

The idea that good memories were lurking somewhere in that brain of hers had Sage up and out of bed in a hurry. The sun hadn't risen, not yet illuminating the town below, and Sage rushed to get ready for the day.

She rummaged through the closets and got dressed. She brushed her hair, opting to leave it hanging down today, the better to cover her rounded ears. With a final look in the mirror, Sage gave herself a final mental pep talk to boost her confidence. She was nervous about leaving the tower, but the nerves rode atop a wave of excitement and curiosity.

Sage rushed through the hallways, quietly tiptoeing down the stairwell. She hoped she wouldn't regret this.

Hyacinth was busy, stirring what looked like ground meat in a pan over the fire, and occasionally checking flatbreads in the oven. Her bronze hair was tied up in a bun on her head, and her cheeks were flushed from the activity.

Sage cleared her throat, "Can I be of any help?"

Hyacinth paused in her tracks, turning to stare at Sage. After a moment, the pop of the meat in the pan brought them both back into focus.

"Yes. Thank you. I assume you can keep bread from burning? Just keep an eye on those breads, and slice those oranges. If you don't mind."

Sage got to work slicing several bright, fragrant oranges while keeping a close watch on the breads.

She quietly observed Hyacinth who was clearly in her element preparing the meat and putting the finishing touches on an egg pie that had been cooling on the counter.

A strange air of familiarity hung around Hyacinth, so much so that Sage forgot to watch the breads. Hyacinth yelped as one caught fire in the stone oven. Before Sage could react, Hyacinth summoned a ball of water and expertly smothered the bread encased in flames, leaving the coals on the bottom of the oven unscathed before sweeping in and scooping the remaining breads into the safety of her basket.

"Well, I suppose we should have stuck with one task at first," Hyacinth said to Sage with a side-eye.

"Sorry. I'm out of practice, I guess," Sage replied.

"Not to worry. Get those oranges in that bowl over there. Petra will be here any second to take all of this upstairs. Will you wait in that back room until she's gone?" Hyacinth pointed to the room Sage had seen her come from the day before. Sage nodded as she passed the bowl of oranges to Hyacinth, and headed for the back room. She was surprised to walk into a makeshift, slightly rustic bedroom, complete with a bed, a small table for dining or writing, and a vanity holding a wash table. The space felt unfinished, but somehow inviting, cozy even.

Moments later, Sage heard Petra enter, and Hyacinth directed which dishes were to go upstairs to the others.

"She's gone. You can come back in now," Hyacinth called out a few moments later.

Sage stepped back into the kitchen, where Hyacinth was fixing two plates of food. A second egg pie had been held back, and Hyacinth plated a slice of it for each of them, along with a few slices of fresh sweet peppers, oranges, and unburned bread. Sage's mouth watered, realizing how hungry she felt as she took in the spread. She couldn't help a wary feeling from climbing up her spine. "Are you sure Petra won't be back down here?"

"She won't make her way back here for a while. But I wouldn't worry about her if I were you." Hyacinth patted a stool, gesturing for Sage to have a seat.

"Why does she bother coming down here for the food anyway? Can't you all use magic to move the food like dinner the other night?"

Hyacinth exhaled loudly, "Well, I suppose it's just an excuse for Petra to come check on me, without seeming like she's actually checking on me. Now, sit. Let's eat while we have the time."

As Sage sat on the stool at the kitchen island, Hyacinth placed a teapot and two mugs down before taking a seat next to her. The two females sat in silence, staring at each other for several long moments. Hyacinth cleared her throat and poured tea into the two mugs, before gesturing toward Sage's plate of food.

Sage smiled, "Why did you want to see me? Petra seemed to believe you'd want nothing to do with me, or any of the others."

Hyacinth paused, her eyes sliding away from Sage like she was considering how to answer the question. Sage got the impression she was trying to decide how much to tell her.

Still not meeting her gaze, Hyacinth whispered, "You look just like her. I thought at first you might be her, somehow, but when I got close...your scent was all wrong, and your ears."

Sage felt her cheeks redden. She wasn't sure she had ever felt embarrassed about her ears before. A quick look at Hyacinth, grinning sweetly, took the sting away from the comment. Still, Sage untucked her hair from her ears, letting her locks drape over her rounded ears.

"You are so much like Celia, my sister. You have a similar sense of humor, too. You know, we were in the work camp with Petra. The three of us, we were close. We looked out for each other. Petra hadn't seen her family in decades when my sister, Celia, and I arrived at the work camp. We shared sleeping quarters, and we became each other's family."

"What happened to her?"

A long moment stretched between the question and Hyacinth's answer, "I was a willful prisoner, I routinely challenged our guards. I would make trouble whenever and wherever I thought I could get away with it. Petra did, too, and we often worked together to cause dissent among the other prisoners. Petty things, usually. I would over-salt the guards' food when I had kitchen duty, or would purposefully use food that had expired. Petra would leave burn marks on uniforms when she was sent to manage the laundry. Celia would egg us on, but wouldn't often join in. She was smart enough to fear the guards and their thinning patience.

"One day, Petra and I decided if enough of us prisoners joined together, we could overthrow the guards. They were in the middle of shifting units, so the full force of Rankor's men weren't there. We all had bands of iron soldered onto our wrists to keep us from using our powers, but many of us still had some access. Petra's powers were the strongest of all of us. So we laid plans to break out and make our way to the allies who were beginning to join up arms against Rankor."

Sage had been carefully taking bites of the egg pie, which was delicious, and set her fork down, "So you guys broke free?"

Hyacinth shook her head. "One of the prisoners had befriended some of the guards. I guess she got special treatment. I hadn't actually ever met her before, but she heard of the plans from someone else, and she informed the guards. They were waiting for us as we set our plans into motion. They put us down before we even got started. As punishment..." Hyacinth took a deep breath and stared at Sage. "Instead of punishing me and Petra, they stripped my sister and dragged her to the center of the work camp. They beat her. They held me and Petra down and forced us to watch. And then...then they executed her." Hyacinth looked away again. "They wouldn't even let me bury her. They tied me to the wall, and forced me to watch for days as the birds picked her body clean. Petra, too."

Sage pushed her plate away, the horror she saw in Hyacinth's eyes taking away her hunger. "Gods, Hyacinth. That is the most...I'm so sorry."

She wanted to cover her face, her body. Gods, why would she land here? Where she would force these people to relive such awful memories.

Sage didn't know what else she could say, and instead reached for Hyacinth's hand. "I'm so sorry. I wish I knew why I was here."

Hyacinth smiled, "You know, Petra is not so thrilled with you here. I reckon she will never forgive herself for what happened to Celia, for not being able to save her. But...just the other day, it struck me...I was beginning to forget her. Her face...I had a hard time remembering details about Celia. I couldn't remember her smile. And then there you were.

"The Goddess blessed me. I know you aren't my sister, but just seeing your face...it brings a little bit of peace to me."

Tears lined Hyacinth's eyes, and Sage wiped at her own, realizing she was crying, too. "I think I had a sister, too. I think you could have looked very much like her," Sage whispered, searching Hyacinth's face, her heart squeezing at the little details that reminded her of the girl from her dream.

They smiled at each other, and Sage surprised herself by reaching forward and hugging Hyacinth. They laughed at their mutual surprise, and as they parted their smiles lingered as they finished their tea and breakfast.

"Did the rest of your family survive Rankor? What about your parents?" asked Sage.

"My parents survived. They had actually been visiting some extended family in the Maracadian Islands, my mother's family is from there. The islands are enchanted. Rankor was never able to breach their defenses. They tried early on to find a way to free us when we were captured, but it was impossible. They settled there, but I haven't been able to force myself to go to them. Not yet. I write to them, though. I get to tell them about serving the Royal Family. I tell them all about Veritasailles, even if I don't venture out into it. I haven't figured out how to go back into the world after everything."

"Gavin is taking me into the city today. Would you like me to bring you anything?" Sage offered.

Hyacinth beamed, "I know I could ask Petra for this, but she does so much already... They've started selling art for the Queen's birthday. I would love a commemorative banner. I won't go to the celebration, but I will see it from the window in my room."

Sage grinned. She didn't have any money, but she would figure out some way to make that happen. She hugged Hyacinth again, "You've got a deal," then hopped off her stool before grabbing the plates and bringing them to the sink in the corner.

Sage was washing their dishes when Petra returned, carrying the dirty dishes from upstairs.

"I thought I told you—" Petra began.

"She's my guest, Petra. I invited her," Hyacinth cut in.

Petra glared at Sage as she dropped the dishes on the island, then exited with a swoosh of her skirts.

Hyacinth rolled her eyes, "It will take some time for her to get used to this."

Sage shrugged. She didn't really care if Petra ever came around. It wouldn't change her situation.

Sage had just finished washing the last plate, preparing to start on the pie dishes left on the counter when Gavin walked in.

"I heard you'd been put to work down here," he said, grabbing an apple off the shelf.

Hyacinth's face went white and she scurried into her room.

"Aren't you supposed to stay out of here?" Sage glowered.

"Sorry, Hyacinth," Gavin called in the direction of her room. "Should I stay and help?"

"Just go back upstairs. I'll be up there in a minute," Sage said, sharply, shooing him towards the door.

She was looking forward to her tour of the city, but felt protective over Hyacinth's space after hearing her story. Well, maybe she and Petra had some common ground after all.

"Sorry," Gavin replied, palms outstretched, as he backed out of the room. "Meet me on the balcony."

"He's gone," called Sage once she was sure Gavin was out of earshot. "He shouldn't have barged in here on you."

"It's ok. He means well. The first month he was here he tried every week to come help down here. Zeke had to threaten him with night sentry duty for a month to get him to stop. He means well, but... he just doesn't seem to understand," Hyacinth shrugged.

Sage finished with the pie pans, and drying her hands on the towel hanging by the sink asked, "Should I come back tomorrow morning?"

"If you'd like. I'd like that very much. Maybe I can teach you how to bake bread without burning it," Hyacinth teased with a smirk.

"Look out ladies and gents, she's got cooking skills and a sense of humor," Sage drawled before exiting the kitchen. "See you tomorrow."

Sage headed up to her room to tidy up before she went to find Gavin. She was just exiting her room when a whispered "There you are," had her almost jump out of her skin.

Sage whirled around to find Gavin grinning, like sunshine incarnate, his hand outstretched in invitation.

"Ready?" Gavin extended his hand to her. Sage laid her hand in his, and he guided her up the stairs towards the open balcony in the center of the Obelisk. "I was waiting on the balcony when I realized you probably didn't have a clue where it was."

"Thanks," she replied softly.

She was wearing one of the pants one-pieces popular in Veritasailles. The dark cream color complimented her sun-kissed skin, and Gavin couldn't help but appreciate the way that the pants emphasized her lean legs.

He cleared his throat when she caught him staring and asked, "How much do you trust me?"

Sage replied with a grin, "You? Hardly at all."

"Well, this is going to be a test for us both then," said Gavin.

Before her eyes, Gavin shifted, flexing his shoulder muscles and extending his white feathered wings, tipped in black, on either side of him. Sage opened her mouth as if to say something, blinked, and shut her mouth again, taking a step backward.

"What is that for?" she said, pointing at his wings.

"*This* is how we get down there," said Gavin, pointing to the city below. "Here," he pulled Sage towards him, "hold on here. I promise not to drop you." Gavin put her arms around his neck, and after gathering her legs into his arms, ran and leapt off the balcony.

Sage buried her face into his neck, "No, no no no no....Gods, oh my..." she whispered to herself. Her breath hit his neck in quick pants, and he squeezed her a bit tighter to his body.

Gavin couldn't help but laugh, "You mean fireball girl can't brave a short flight, with someone who knows what they're doing, mind you?"

Sage just gripped his neck tighter in response.

"Sage, trust me. Look," said Gavin. Slowly, she peeked her head out from his neck and gazed out at Veritasailles as they flew over the city.

The city glittered before them; dome-topped buildings glittering in the sun like jewels washed ashore from the sea. People below, dressed in chitons, tunics, and robes, went about their business, unbothered by one of their fellows flying above them. In fact, several other fae sported similar winged physiques, some of them calling out in greeting to Gavin as they passed by. Gavin noticed Sage smiling softly as she gazed at the city flying below them.

Gavin found an empty courtyard, and landed softly, gently placing Sage squarely on her feet and encircling her waist with his arms. She stood there, gripping his neck for a moment before taking a deep breath and taking in their surroundings, then stepping away from him and tucking a strand of hair behind her ear.

"I guess I prefer flying to falling, but I can't say I don't prefer solid ground," Sage said.

They had landed in a courtyard centered around a fountain. Floral vines grew around the walls of the courtyard. Several gated, open archways offered glimpses to the city beyond.

"Where are we?" Sage asked.

"This is one of the gardens on the outside of the palace. We're close to one of the markets; I thought you'd like to start there," Gavin explained and led Sage through one of the archways.

Sound and sunlight flooded his senses as they stepped through the opening and Gavin led Sage down the cobbled streets flanked by stables, trades booths, and sentries walking their routes.

Gavin waved politely to a few sentries and gently nudged Sage through the increasing crowds as they approached an intersection of roads. The outlines of the market were becoming visible, and the sounds and smells of bustling commerce increasing.

Even after nearly a year of living here, the abruptness of the street turning into a marketplace surprised and delighted Gavin. He smiled at the look of awe on Sage's face, mirroring his own feelings. The market was vast; what felt like an infinity of covered booths and stalls, selling handmade housewares, foods, spices, jewelry, clothing, upholstery, art, books, and anything else a fae could imagine or want stretching before them.

Gavin grinned; this was his favorite market in the city. It wasn't the busiest, definitely a plus, and it featured his favorite tavern, which offered a rooftop patio and musicians at most hours, day or night. The plan for the day included a stop there. He hoped she would appreciate the atmosphere.

They began their trek through the market by stopping by one of the abundant clothiers, where Sage ran her hand along the fine clothes, and admired the myriad of colors. A quick stop at a booth selling handmade jewelry then led the pair into a housewares shop, where Sage remarked at the artisan clay pots, hand-carved spoons, and glass jars used for preserving spreads.

"Gods, everything here is so beautiful. The small bits I remember of home can't compare to this," Sage remarked while admiring a set of copper mugs.

"What kinds of things do you remember, " asked Gavin.

"I remember things being made for efficiency, not beauty; where I come from, things are...colder."

They exited the housewares shop, and walked down the street again, occasionally pointing at something that caught their interest. As they walked, Gavin noticed the way their hands bumped against each other; he could have sworn he caught a touch of blush on Sage's cheeks when he noticed her staring at him in one of the market stalls.

They made it to the tavern, and Gavin gestured to it, "Would you like to stop? We could grab something to eat if you'd like." He could already hear the musicians on the rooftop and hoped he hadn't overstepped with this suggestion.

Sage nodded, "That'd be great...oh, but I don't have any money. We should probably just head back."

Gavin laid a hand on her back, "Nonsense. Allow me, please. My treat," and led her into the tavern and up the stairs that led to the rooftop patio. The barkeep greeted Gavin from behind the bar as they made their way to the stairs. They found a seat on the outer edge of the patio, a bit removed from the musician, to allow for conversation. A tavern maid met the pair at their table, and Gavin ordered some ales, bread, and asked for a small spread to be shared between them.

As they sat, enjoying their ales and bread, Sage stared out on the city streets below them. She grinned at the sights, and when a soft breeze began to pass by, she lifted her chin with closed eyes towards the sun in appreciation.

He wished he'd caused that breeze and made a note to remember that for the future.

"So, what do you think of our city so far?" Gavin asked.

"It's wonderful. Thank you for this. I think this is the most normal I've felt since coming here."

Their food, hummus, cheese, and smoked meats, arrived at that time.

"Your family doesn't live here; how come?" she asked while pausing to sip her ale.

"My parents never really appreciated the city. I think living in cramped living quarters ruined it for them. Mystaira is far less crowded; it suits them."

"Does it suit you?" asked Sage.

"At times. Sometimes when I need more space to fly— feel the wind— Mystaira seems like the only place in the world I'd want to be. It's surrounded by beautiful mountains and lakes; it's wide open. But it's also very isolated. I spent a long time feeling isolated; I like the variety in the city," explained Gavin as he finished his ale.

"I think I'd like to see that sometime. I had a dream about my home, my family. I'm pretty sure I have a sister, and I think I came from a wide-open place, but ended up somewhere else more cramped. Honestly, from the first memory I had, I'm not sure I'd want to go back to that," Sage said, leaning back and gazing out at the market below. After a while, Sage slapped her hands on the table, "Oh! I forgot....but I couldn't impose. Shoot!"

"What? What's going on?!" Gavin demanded.

Sage rubbed her hands across her face, "I promised Hyacinth I'd bring her something from the city. But I don't have any money, and I don't even know where to look."

She looked defeated at the thought of letting down Hyacinth.

"Don't worry about it. Just tell me what it is. I'd be happy to buy it. Think of it as me making up for my intrusion this morning."

Sage gave Gavin a side eye, "You really should know better, you know. Ok. I'll take that deal. She wants some banner, or art, or something for the Queen's birthday. Do you know what I'm talking about?" Gavin knew just where to look.

Within ten minutes of leaving the tavern, they were in a part of the market that popped up within the last week. Temporary stalls and booths were splayed out across a road that was blocked off to horse and wagon traffic, dedicated solely to pedestrian shoppers. Several booths boasted arrays of historical books and artifact replicas, while others displayed clothing decorated especially for the celebration to take place in a month's time.

As they walked, Gavin noticed a translucent figure walking alongside them. "Hello Symon," Gavin said softly.

Not one for wasting time on pleasantries, Symon replied, "There will be a formal reception in honor of the Queen for her birthday in three weeks. You will be there, to pledge fealty in honor of Mystaira. The girl comes, too. We can't afford to leave her to her own devices. She will need to be prepared, and in charge of her powers. You will see to it she, and you both are ready," Symon commanded.

"And if she doesn't want to?" Gavin asked.

Sage had stopped walking and was looking around her wildly, before giving Gavin a questioning look. He held up a finger, signaling her to wait just a moment.

"Just be a good Lord, and do as you're told," grinned Symon, knowing exactly which threads he was pulling with those words.

"Of course, Your Majesty," Gavin said, maybe a little sarcastically.

"Don't spend too much of my money out here," Symon replied, as he shimmered out of Gavin's view.

"What...who are you talking to?" Sage asked, peering around Gavin.

"That was Symon. He has powers specific to mind and mental control. He can spectre...cast his likeness into just about anyone's mind. It's one of the ways he sends messages to us cronies," Gavin explained.

"Mental control? Does that mean-" Sage's voice dropping to a whisper "-that he can control other minds?"

"Yes. It was one of the only reasons we defeated Rankor and his men. That and Aryael's fire."

"So he can just...control other soldiers?" asked Sage.

"For short periods of time." Sage looked at Gavin, stunned by the information.

"Has he ever mind-controlled you?" she asked.

"No. Or at least I don't know if he had. I don't even know if I would remember if he had, actually. I've never really thought about it," Gavin said.

Ready to shake the thought that he might actually have been controlled and not know it, Gavin led Sage towards a booth at random and began looking through the wares.

Sage followed, and admired the commemorative clothing made for the celebration; she lingered by a display of scarves embroidered with flames, a symbol of Aryael herself. She passed from the scarves and stopped by a display of Felysian flags. The flags were halved, one side a block of deep blue with a male lion and two female lions of red, all with wings, in a straight line; the other half of the flag was white, with a bold red flame in the center of its block. "That flag was made when King Symon and Queen Aryael were crowned; this half represents the lion-borne siblings, Symon, Meliza, and Petra. This other half represents Aryael. Their union, their combining of powers was the turning point in our revolution."

"Lion-borne; why are they called that?" Sage asked.

"Probably because that's how they shift. And their father was called The Lion when he was on the battlefield. Felysians love giving everyone dramatic titles," Gavin explained with chagrin. They finished perusing the stall, and headed towards another booth featuring paintings and storybooks of famous fae from various lands. Sage picked up a picture book featuring two fae holding hands and holding up rods with serpents. "That's the story of Amara and Eron. They founded the healing temples in Mystaira; they were bonded and devoted their lives to teaching fae how to heal and preserve life. They accepted those like Raphael, gifted with healing powers, and others who just desired to learn the healing arts. The temples were destroyed, but we've been rebuilding them over the past several years." Sage ran her hand over the book, and set it down. There was so much to learn about this new place she was in; Gavin hoped he wouldn't overwhelm her with information. He passed a coin to the female working in the stall and swiped up the book.

They wandered for a while longer before reaching the end of the temporary market space, and Sage peered through the stalls as they worked to produce the art pieces Hyacinth had mentioned. They sat, watching a fae female paint a rectangle block of various colors, then stamp the design on a piece of parchment. The end result was a mosaic that featured a nondescript likeness of Queen Aryael on the battlefield. It didn't show her striking features, but the telltale flaming sword, rich dark skin, and long amber-colored braids made it clear who the portrait depicted. In a booth across from them, Gavin pulled Sage towards a portrait painted of the scene they watched stamped.

It was Queen Aryael, dressed in battle armor. Her dark skin glistened with sweat and blood; her sword was lifted to the sky, flames engulfing the blade, and her long, amber braids whipped in the wind. Behind her, a lion roared, and the artist had taken pains to include many of the fae who had fought in the battles of the revolution, roaring alongside their King and Queen in victory as they defeated their oppressors. Gavin and Sage gazed at the portrait for a long time, before Gavin cleared his throat, "I think Hyacinth might like this one. What do you think?"

Sage gazed at it for a long moment, "I couldn't. This painting...it must cost a fortune. It's mesmerizing."

"It's perfect," Gavin replied and summoned the stooped male in the corner. "How much?" he asked, pointing at the portrait.

"Five krons," the male replied. Five krons was steep, even for a portrait of this detail. He had six on him, thankfully, but had never expected to spend it all. He grinned with tight lips and slapped the coins onto the table. The male nodded his head and took the painting to the back of his stall to wrap it in soft cloth to protect it on its journey home. "Thank you," Sage whispered, staring at Gavin. He just nodded, watching the male prepare their package.

A soft breeze brushed the back of his neck, and he stiffened. Something about the breeze seemed foreign, misplaced. A thread of malice tainted the air and refused to respond to his control. Simultaneously, the stooped male seemed to straighten and made his way back to the front with their prepared package. His instincts kicking in, Gavin edged closer to Sage.

The male's eyes were rimmed in red, as if he'd been crying, and he handed the package to Gavin before approaching Sage.

"You are her, aren't you? The girl from the sky."

Sage looked to Gavin before replying, "I don't know what you mean." The stooped fae male across from her suddenly seemed less frail, less friendly. His eyes glowed like embers in a flame. The intensity of his gaze burned.

She squared her feet and leaned away from the stall slightly. She felt like a doe getting ready to run from a wolf.

"You are her. He's looking for you. Do you remember? How he looks for you?" the stallholder asked, reaching across the table to grasp at her hand. The moment the stallholder's hand connected with Sage's arm, her knees buckled, a hand flying to her forehead, eyes shut tight in pain. Thousands of needles pierced her skin and her breath stole away from her. The stallholder's skin was clammy and slipped against her skin. But he squeezed tighter with a grip that belied his apparent age.

Gavin lunged forward to get her away as a scream was wrenched from her throat. She flung out an arm, and pillars of rock surrounded him. Even as the pain ricocheted through her body, glimpses of her past filtered through her mind. Amidst the pain answers awaited her, if she survived the onslaught.

A stark white room with incessant, rhythmic beepings. People carrying syringes, confused questions stuttering from people she couldn't see. A woman with a mechanical eye, an automobile smoldering. A van of dead or dying victims.

The stallholder continued whispering in her ear, dripping poison into her mind. "He's coming. Wait for him."

Tears lined her eyes, but Sage pushed Gavin away with a tremor sent through the earth so that he couldn't separate her from her tormentor. She could feel Gavin using the wind to try and pry her from the male holding her, but she clung back at him, determined to siphon any memory she could.

"My little prize. Stay where you are. I'll be there to get you soon." A burst of light flashed before her eyes, and she felt the male's grip slacken.

Just as suddenly as it began, the wind stopped. The stallholder straightened, released her arm, and then with eyes leaking blood instead of tears, he fell backward.

Sage fell, sagging to her hands, gasping for breath, and Gavin rushed to her. Booths and stalls, the entire marketplace was in chaos. She had created a minor earthquake that had upended displays, scattering banners and books everywhere.

Gavin helped haul her back to her feet before checking on the male stallholder behind the table. Blood rushed from the man's eyes and ears. Gavin could detect no heartbeat, his breath silenced forever. Something had taken control of this stranger and killed him in the process.

"He knew me. He knew. Gavin...he showed me," Sage whispered.

Gavin spoke quickly to the sentries who had rushed to the scene, giving them orders to get Meliza and Zeke to the booth, and shifted to his winged form. He had to get Sage out of there before her presence became too noticeable. He grabbed their package and scooped her up under her knees before shooting into the sky.

The feeling of her trembling in his arms was an all too familiar feeling at this point, and the fear of danger coming back to his home was an unwelcome companion on his flight to safety.

He flew her to the Obelisk and walked her straight to Raphael's ward.

Raphael turned from his shelf of tonics, took one look at Sage, and with a grim face, told Gavin to lay her down and leave. Gavin did as he was told, not saying a word to her as he left the ward to head back to the market.

His heart hammered a staccato rhythm as he flew, furiously, back to the market. Instincts to find the threat, and protect his own nearly sent him out of control.

Meliza turned as Gavin landed in the marketplace center. "Well, she knows how to make a day exciting," Meliza greeted. Gavin didn't bother to feign amusement. "Was it the dark borne?" he asked.

"It's likely," answered Zeke. "How'd they know about her?" Zeke questioned. The three of them stared at the dead fae male in his booth, pondering how he'd succumbed to such a fate and what it meant for their city and country.

"He told Sage someone was looking for her. She doesn't seem to remember who it is, but she is afraid of them," Gavin explained.

"Then we will keep them from her," Meliza answered.

Gavin nodded his agreement. Like hell was he going to let some defenseless human into the claws of one of the dark borne; and if they were involved with whoever was hunting her, Sage was in big trouble. Besides, Gavin knew Meliza had been itching for a reason to kill the dark-borne brothers, and he wouldn't mind putting a sword through their necks either. They were Rankor's sons and would be coming for revenge someday. Better to get it over with than to wait idly, in his opinion.

Meliza met Zeke's stare, and they nodded. "It's time to go talk to Symon"

Gavin waited two wingbeats before meeting his commanders in the sky. If only he could start the day over. Maybe they all could have remained hidden just a little while longer.

Chapter 8

You, darling, are very special. Special to me, and to your country. You and I are going to do amazing things. The cold voice echoed through her mind and cloyed her senses.

Sage had woken feeling exhausted again, just after she had begun feeling a little bit whole.

The events in the market had hammered her mind throughout the night, unlocking dark and twisted images that bore little context or truth about her past. An urgency to discover her past was erupting within her. The fact that her hunter followed, and found her, in Felysia and managed to possess the stallholder made her feel unsafe—watched. Unclean.

She sat by her window, watching the sun peek above the tower, the domes sparking to life as sunbeams slipped over them.

Her body was tense, bunched together, and on high alert. Her room was quiet, so quiet that it made her feel like a predator was stalking her, ready to pounce. She lay on the floor to practice the meditation technique Raphael had taught her. Willing her shoulders to soften, she exhaled through the tension trapped between her eyebrows and felt herself let go of the worries plaguing her mind.

She was just pushing back to a seated position, intent on seeing if Hyacinth needed any help in the kitchen when a soft knock on the door preceded Raphael gently entering her room.

"How are we feeling today?"

"Honestly, pretty shitty. But that meditation you showed me helped. I'm feeling a little better."

"Good!" Raphael beamed at her response. Meeting in the middle, Sage and Raphael took a seat near the fireplace.

"I just can't help but feel that me being here is playing into someone's trap."

"About that. I think we'd better start your training. I had hoped to increase your strength, but from what you told me last night about what happened in the market, I'd say you are strong enough."

Sage snorted. "Why do I get the impression you heard a different version of events from Gavin? I think he might have had his feelings hurt that I could contain him."

Raphael laughed in response. "Perhaps, but that wouldn't be the first time he's been restrained by someone else's powers. That's not so abnormal here, after all."

"So, are we training here, or do we get to go somewhere else?" Sage asked.

"We will have to stay in the building, for now," Raphael added quickly in response to Sage's put-out expression. "We feel that it might be best to keep you here until we have a better idea of what is after you. The Obelisk is enchanted, warded against anyone with malintent."

"Fine. Well, lead the way."

Raphael led Sage through the smooth, tan hallways and stairwells into a large, open room. One side of the room boasted large, open windows that allowed wind from the sea to trickle in. On the wall hung various swords, mace, daggers, and shields, none of which Sage knew the first thing about. "So...am I playing with those things?" she asked, pointing to a long row of swords.

"Now, what makes you think *I* could teach you anything about those? I'm a sophisticated male, remember?" Raphael continued through the room, coming to a stop by a large metal bowl.

"This is where we will train today. We will start with fire since this room is warded against the element. That way, we don't end up with burst pipes or a crumbling foundation." Sage rolled her eyes at the connotation. "No sass while training," snapped Raphael, smacking her lightly on the shoulder before walking to the other side of the bowl.

Inside, lay a damp rag. "So, I'm going to light a wet rag on fire?" Sage couldn't contain her skepticism as she looked inside the dark, hammered bowl.

"A rag soaked in accelerant, yes." Raphael replied smartly. "Now, usually, your powers appear when you've been triggered by a memory or experience strong emotions. The key to preventing *that* is by being able to use them when you are calm." Raphael stepped back from the bowl slightly and gestured with a hand. "Go ahead."

Sage looked from Raphael to the bowl. Ok, she thought, just light it on fire. No problem. Except, how does one start creating fire from nothing?

She concentrated on the rag, pummeling the limp linen with her stare, trying to conjure up the bubbling lava she'd felt before when Petra had pushed her too far. She stared and stared, willing heat to rise up from her center.

Nothing.

Nothing except a throbbing vessel on one side of her head. "Goddess, girl, you'll need to take a breath at some point," Raphael warned.

Gasping, Sage replied, "Well, how am I supposed to do this? What I'm doing now obviously isn't doing it."

"Start by breathing. Focus on your senses, be aware of your body."

Exhaling loudly, Sage rolled her head. Closing her eyes, she focused on her breath. She felt the air ripple through her nasal cavity and push down into her chest. She envisioned the air swirling around her lungs before galloping back out. Repeating the process several times, she began to notice subtle changes in the room. She could feel streams of wind brush over her arms, lifting wisps of her hair from her face. She heard the murmur of waves below, daggers clinking softly as the breeze shifted their position ever so slightly. She could feel the beams of sunlight caressing her feet, warming her toes and the floor.

Focusing on the warmth, Sage breathed in the sensation of heat. Focusing on the tingling response of her skin as the sun danced along the arches of her feet, Sage pushed her mind to concentrate on the warmth down to the very smallest pieces of herself.

There. She could feel it there, right on the top of one foot. It was like the faintest buzzing of a bee in another room, but it was there. Pulling the sensation of vibrating upwards, Sage felt creeks of warmth beginning to wind themselves through her body. Slowly, Sage was able to collect enough warmth in her abdomen that she felt confident she could shape the energy to her will.

Opening her eyes, but never letting go of the soft buzzing now growing inside, she stared at the rag. Breathing deep, Sage lifted both hands, palms facing the bowl. Pushing the energy up, pulling the warmth forward, she let the sensation collect in her palms. When she didn't think she could stand it anymore, Sage let go, releasing everything she could toward the rag.

Poof.

"What?!" Sage blurted as the smallest puff of smoke fluffed from her palms. Not a single spark reached the rag.

A booming laugh erupted from behind Sage. Whirling, Sage took in the hulking fae belly laughing from the entrance of the training room.

Zeke, shirtless, slapped his leg, bending over in a fit of laughter. Grinding her teeth, Sage slowly turned back to the bowl, only to find Raphael losing his battle against laughing at her failure.

"Why is that so funny?" she asked.

"You just...you were so..." taking a deep, gulping breath of air, Zeke finished, "You were just trying so hard. And then...Poof!" He doubled over again.

Not waiting for permission, Sage left Raph and Zeke behind to laugh about her puny "poof," aiming for the cooling breezes of the balcony above.

Feeling hot all over, not sure if it was from trying to light the fire or from embarrassment, Sage was still surprised by the cooling effect of the breeze once she reached the doorway. She hadn't realized she was sweating until the wind began gently sweeping over her, drying the moisture that had collected along her skin.

She leaned against the archway, staring over the city. Her body was sore; her abdominal muscles and legs felt like she'd been pushing a boulder up a mountain. There was a slight shake in her legs, and yet she felt a pleasant response to the exertion. Actually trying to use her powers on her own terms had been thrilling. Granted, she failed spectacularly. Nevertheless, it had been nice to feel in control for a moment.

She slid to the ground to rest her legs, letting the sun warm her skin while appreciating the cooling breeze. She looked up, noticing a white hawk-eagle flying over the city towards the tower, and smiled. She hadn't seen Gavin since the market. Maybe he had some time to spare for a quick fly over the city.

Gavin had worked sentry duty since the early hours of the morning. He'd been in a foul mood all morning. First, the events from the previous day weighed heavily on him; second, Symon had sent his spectre into Gavin's room berating him for taking the girl into the city as if he hadn't known what Gavin was up to. He supposed it had been risky, but how else was he supposed to get to know the girl if she was trapped in the tower? Plus, he knew she'd loved the time out in the city while it lasted. He couldn't find it in himself to regret taking the chance. Even with the lingering aftertaste of her being attacked.

Meliza landed heavily next to him as he turned a corner, heading towards the barracks to change shifts. Matching his stride, her wings disappeared as she shifted. Gavin found himself standing straighter around the Commander. Where her sister had learned to wield an icy mask on her waif-like body to fend off outsiders, Meliza had earned the respect of her comrades through battles and training. She was of a stockier build than her sister, whether that was from training or genetics, it didn't matter, her reputation and physique rarely lured anyone to forget who they were dealing with.

"We found out more about that fae in the market," Meliza said.

Gavin asked, "So we've heard from Epyllo?"

"No," replied Meliza. "We've not heard from the spies, which is concerning in itself. I did some investigating of my own. Some of the fae in the marketplace had gleaned that he was a foreigner while they set up their booths. It didn't take too much digging to find out where he came from. It does, however, offer some speculation. Do you find it strange that a fae from Nysa, which borders Speridisia, was the fae to be possessed?" Meliza turned to face Gavin. "What do you know of dark-born blood magic?"

Gavin paused, reluctant to answer in a public place, "I've seen them use it. Once, in the camps."

They'd reached the barracks. Meliza gestured with a lift of her chin, "Go get changed and meet me in my office. Symon will want to hear about this."

Taking his time, willing his mind to go into the cold place he'd created for reliving these memories, Gavin changed into his tunic and breeches. He rolled his shoulders as he reached Meliza's door.

Both Symon and Meliza were in the office, already in quiet discussion when Gavin walked in. They rarely talked about those times. Meliza, it seemed, was a fae who handled things internally just fine, and maybe Symon was as well. Gavin had only spoken to one person about it, other than what had been said between his family. His best friend,

Micah, had made it out with him; as soon as they were freed, Micah left for Maracadia, to find work as a merchant sailor.

Gavin cleared his throat, realizing they were both waiting for him to speak. "It's good to see you, Symon."

"Don't lie, boy. I know you're still pissy about this morning."

Meliza responded to Symon with a glare, apparently not approving of her brother's tone. "Gavin, it would help us if you explained what you know about the Dark Born and their use of blood magic."

Gavin rolled his shoulders again, pulling on his tunic to try and settle his body. These memories were ones that had been carefully locked away, then buried under all the others. It took him several breaths to steady himself before he began. "Once, Apyllon and Abbadon came to our camp. They were looking for those with enhanced powers. It had happened once before, so most of us knew to lay low. They found a child, he had some developed flame abilities. They took him to a guard's building and ordered everyone out."

"Go on," Meliza insisted.

Gavin swallowed, and looked away from Meliza, towards Symon who nodded, encouraging him to continue. While the King may have been frustrated before, a look of under-standing had overcome him.

"I was curious. Goddess, I was stupid is what I was. I was barely ten years old when this happened," Gavin took a deep breath and rubbed his hands over his face, speaking quickly so as not to lose his nerve. "I was able to sneak to the guard's building they took the boy to. They...they siphoned the child's blood right from his body. And Apyl-lon drank it. The boy was alive, right up until they drained the last drop, they did it so quickly. He made these awful sounds, like he was suffocating, and then he just..."

There were a lot of memories Gavin didn't let himself think about. This was at the top of his list. "When Apyllon drank the blood, he was able to wield fire, but briefly. What's more disturbing, I think, was that Apyllon knew everything about the boy. His parents had been secretly hoarding food, planning on trying to escape. The brothers set a trap, and captured the family a few months later, slaughtered the whole lot of them, and anyone associated with them. Only the father came back, and he was oddly loyal to the guards despite what had happened to his family."

Meliza and Symon stood silently exchanging a look, giving Gavin a few moments to collect himself.

"I think it's likely someone practiced blood magic on the stallholder, sometime before arriving in Felysia, possibly without his knowledge," Meliza said finally.

"But what happened here, that sounds more elegant...more...refined and practiced than what Gavin just described. Apyllon has never been one to wield his powers with much subtlety," Symon pondered.

"Abbadon didn't drink any of the blood. I saw him collect some of it in vials. But I left as soon as the boy was dead. I nearly got caught. I ran out of there so fast, I crashed right into some of the guards making their rounds before curfew."

"We need more time to think through this information. Not everyone in Speridisia practices sorcery, but there are enough of them there that we shouldn't put it past someone using blood magic to possess others," Meliza suggested. "What bothers me is whether they could do it from such a distance. Unfortunately, Gavin, your story doesn't answer the biggest questions that we have."

"Such as, what do they want with the girl," Symon said, advancing towards Gavin "Gavin, I'm going to need you to take over security of the Obelisk. The Queen's birthday ceremonies begin within the month. Zeke and Meliza will be increasing sentry rounds and patrols; I need you to take over the tower until the celebrations are over. Zeke and Meliza will move to the barracks for the time being."

Gavin nodded, his face grave.

The ceremonies of the next few weeks would be a tempting opportunity to strike Veritasailles, a time when their city would be flooded with lords and ladies coming from the countryside regions of Felysia. They wouldn't take it for granted that Abbadon or Apyllon already had infidels stationed within her city.

Symon broke through Gavin's thoughts. "Meliza, we are late for a meeting with Aryael. She'll send her regards, Gavin." Without so much as a nod of thanks, Symon looked towards his sister and they both casted out of the office leaving Gavin alone.

He left the office battling his feelings of defiance at the King's tone, opting to gather the few personal items he kept in the barracks before taking up his permanent station in the Obelisk. He didn't always stay there, but he kept a room just in case he was required to work late, and to keep up the facade of his station.

Gavin wondered if Zeke had already informed Petra, and was curious if she would stay in the tower or go to the palace in his absence. That would make one thing slightly more bearable; he and Petra had never really been friendly. Honestly, he wasn't sure if anyone besides Hyacinth could claim Petra as a friend. She wasn't even all that friendly with Zeke, if Gavin thought about it.

Gavin reached the balcony and shifted into his white hawk-eagle form, clutching the small bag of belongings in his talons. He would begin his watch now, a little on edge after the conversation with Meliza and Symon. He was sure, whatever they said, that his appointment as commander of the Obelisk was a test of some sort.

He assumed it would have happened at some point or another. That didn't mean he had to be pleased with it. He'd spent his whole life under someone else's command; unable to choose how he would spend each day; or where he would live. In all honesty, he felt like he'd escaped one prison to be trapped in a different sort of prison.

The guilt that accompanied his thoughts triggered a gust of wind to lift up below him. Gavin banked hard, and dove towards the beach, enjoying the thrill of falling and the wind singing in his ears. He soared along the water before catching an updraft back into the sky. Gavin circled the Obelisk, gazing across the sea, the forests around the city, and the city itself for hours before plummeting back onto the balcony, shifting just as his feet hit the ground.

Sage was on the balcony, on the opposite side, looking out on the city when he landed. He didn't acknowledge her, didn't particularly feel like chatting or elaborating on his current mood, and strode towards the stairwell.

"I thought that was you out there," Sage grinned.

Gavin merely nodded and kept walking.

"Um...did I do something?"

He turned and couldn't help but notice how her cinnamon-colored hair caught the sun, illuminating it like candlelight. "I won't be able to take you around the city this week, or next. You will need Raphael or someone to take you down and help you pick out the proper attire for the Queen's reception and her birthday celebrations. You're supposed to attend as a special guest of Her Majesty," Gavin replied flatly.

"Fine, but you didn't answer my question. Did I do something to you?" Sage said, folding her arms and glaring at Gavin.

"Honestly, yes, you did," he responded, unable to stop himself from stepping toward her. "I don't know if you noticed, but things have been a lot more complicated around here since you showed up," Gavin said, still in a flat tone, but he could tell that Sage felt the edge anyways.

"And *I* don't know if *you* noticed, but I don't particularly want to be here, either. I would be perfectly fine going off on my own. You lot haven't seen it fit to give me the option. Why don't you just go tell your little—fae majesties— that they can dump me on a ship, and I'll find my own way to Meropoli," Sage advanced towards Gavin with a glare, pointing her finger towards his chest.

Gavin blew a long breath through his nose. "I'm sorry...that our help is so difficult for you to bear," and he turned and walked away, not waiting for a reply from her.

As he began to walk down the stairwell, an unfamiliar wind barreled down upon him, knocking him into the wall. He turned and saw Sage standing on the landing, hands and teeth clenched before she turned and stalked back to the balcony.

✦ ✦ ✦

An ass. He was a fae ass.

Sage stood on the balcony, leaning against the wall and glaring at the stairwell for an uncountable amount of time. The sun was almost fully below the mountains beyond the city, the moon rising above the sea when she decided to go to her room. She stomped to her rooms loud enough that she hoped every fae shithead in the place could hear her and know that she was not in the mood tonight. She wrenched open her door and slammed it shut behind her hard enough that the stone walls seemed to rattle.

There was a hot energy building in her center, fighting to find its way out of her. She felt like she would combust; worst, she felt like a prisoner. In no way had she been offered autonomy on her stay here. No one asked whether she wanted to remain. No one asked her what she wanted at all! She had thought Gavin might be different. Even Raphael, who she had to admit she enjoyed, was under the King's thumb and determined to wring memories from her addled mind. The molten lava had reached an unbearable level inside her, and she flung her hands out toward the fireplace. It was too hot in there for a fire, but she figured it was better to have fire in the hearth than on her bed.

Sage paced in front of the windows for a few minutes, like a tiger trapped in a circus wagon. Finally, realizing she was wasting her energy, Sage stopped and decided to give Raphael's breathing techniques a try. She was on her fifth breath when someone knocked at her door.

She growled to herself and heard, "I can hear that. Just...please open the door."

Sage stomped to the door and wrenched it open, still glaring through her lashes. Gavin stood there, one hand extended upward, palm exposed, the other holding a wrapped package.

"I'm sorry. Here. I was...frustrated about something else, and...you were just there, and I'm sorry. Here," Gavin repeated, handing over the package.

Sage accepted the package, still not letting Gavin into her room, and opened it. A box of chocolates greeted her under the wrappings, and Sage felt one side of her mouth turn upwards.

"Fine," Sage sighed, "I suppose you want to come in?"

"Only if you want me to," Gavin answered.

"Sure."

Sage left him at the open door, plopping herself down onto one of the comfortable chairs by the fireplace.

"A little warm for a fire, don't you think?" Gavin stated.

"Well, it was the fireplace or I burn something else, so I think my choice was just fine," Sage said with a smirk, looking at the chocolates to determine which she would try first. It was a box of dried and fresh fruits, each dipped in a variety of wonderful smelling chocolates. She chose a strawberry first, and bit into the treat, trying and failing to hold back her hum of approval.

Gavin grinned, either in satisfaction or amusement, she wasn't sure.

"Where did you get these?" Sage asked with a sideward stare.

"I felt bad after we talked. I had wanted to take you to that shop at some point, but I figured maybe now was a good time to get you something from there. I flew down after I heard you go to your room."

"Must be nice, to just fly down to the city any time you want." She looked back at the box, trying to decide if she felt like sharing, and ultimately extended the box to him in offering. "Thank you for apologizing," Sage said.

Gavin nodded, selecting a chocolate. They sat together for a few moments.

"So what exactly do I get to do, as the Queen's special guest? Do I ride in on a unicorn, a symbol of mysterious and strange blessings? Or will I be chaperoned by Her Majesty's guards the whole time?" Sage asked.

Gavin snorted, "I hate to say it, but I think you and Her Majesty might find some common ground with each other."

"What's that supposed to mean?" Sage retorted.

"It means, she doesn't have the tendency to hold her tongue or her opinions to herself either. And she's gracious enough not to hold it against those who share that trait. Now, King Symon on the other hand...I'd recommend a bit more diplomacy."

"Tell me about the reception," Sage demanded, then popped another chocolate into her mouth.

"It's formal. You'll need dress robes for it. Lords and Ladies from all over Felysia will be there, to pledge fealty to the Queen, and the King by proxy. Each of us will be called down to the throne and will bow and make our pledges in front of the audience of those in attendance. I'll be escorting you," Gavin explained.

"And am I expected to pledge my fealty? What about you?" Sage asked, again more of a demand than a request.

"You will not. I...will be making my formal pledge. We will move to the palace at the end of the month." Gavin didn't seem particularly thrilled with the ceremony.

"Is that what made you upset? Earlier." Sage asked, leaning toward him slightly.

Gavin nodded. "I suppose it will happen sooner or later. I just hoped to see a bit more of the world before settling,"

Gavin shrugged, "Anyway, Meliza and Zeke are gone from the Obelisk. They'll be staying in the city and palace, getting ready for the ceremony." Gavin stood, "I'll be in charge of securing the tower, so, you will just have to rely on Raphael for your entertainment, I suppose."

Gavin walked to the door, and turned, "I'm really sorry you have to go through all this. I'll see you around," and he left.

Chapter 9

Sage stood on the balcony of the Obelisk, waiting in anticipation for Raphael to finish gathering his supplies. Her nerves jittered beneath her skin. The idea of leaving the Obelisk for training was both exciting and unnerving.

She'd spent the last week working with Raphael in the training room. It took her three days to light the rag on fire, and another four days to wield the fire in any manner that resembled control.

Today, they'd be going somewhere off campus, away from the Obelisk. What Raphael had in store she had no idea. She hadn't seen or heard from Gavin since he apologized for lashing out. She got the feeling he was avoiding her. Maybe he hadn't been sorry for what he said after all.

Soft steps echoed up the stairwell behind her, and she tensed, expecting Raphael to arrive to take her to wherever it was they were heading. "You really took your time getting ready," she said jokingly.

"Raph is still getting ready."

Sage turned, surprised to find Gavin standing near the stairwell entrance, arms tucked behind his back. His face was stoic, reserved, a quality she hadn't really attributed to him before.

"Are you heading out for duty?"

"My duties are to guard you and Raph for the day, so...yes."

A tightness clutched at her stomach at his tone. She'd assumed they had made up for their squabble, but it appeared he was still uncomfortable with her being here. That was fine. She could be reserved and stoic, too.

"I see. Thanks." Sage turned back towards the opening, facing out to the sea.

"Ah...everyone's ready to go, I gather?" Raphael's singsong voice rang out from the stairwell as he made his entrance.

"Shall we?" Raph asked, offering her his arm. Sage walked to his side and hooked her arm through his elbow.

"Can you fly?" she asked the healer.

A mischievous grin lit his face, and a soft pop rang through her head. Suddenly, she was flitting through velvet space, being squeezed from one reality into another.

Her feet struck soft ground, carpeted in grass. "Wha- How'd we do that?!" panted Sage when they landed. Her head spun, and she felt like she'd been quickly forced through molasses. A dichotomy of sensations battered her periphery as she regained her balance.

"We casted. Not all fae can do it. But those of us with extreme mastery of our power can will ourselves to anywhere we desire. Anywhere we've been before, at least. Within reason. I couldn't cross the ocean to Meropoli, that's too long a distance," answered Raphael.

"You've been to Meropoli?" questioned Sage.

"I have. I spent a decade there in my youth. Learned traditional healing techniques from human healers. While my powers encourage healing, it does not work on all ailments. I have a hard time combating infections. Viruses and bacteria work against my powers' affinity for keeping things alive. Meaning...my power shies away from killing, even when those things are lethal. So, I rely on medicine discovered and perfected by humans. They really do not get the credit they deserve, to be so resilient and so weak at the same time."

Heavy feet struck the earth behind Sage, and she whirled to find an unhappy Gavin striding towards them, wings shifting back into nothing as he walked. "Raph, a little warning next time? Or even, just tell me where we are going before you cast and leave me behind?"

Raph chuckled. "Oops. I just assumed you'd cast alongside me. You know, since you can."

Gavin rolled his eyes, walking to a large boulder and took a seat rather than taking Raphael's bait. Sage cast Raph a knowing glance.

They were in the field Sage had landed. The crater was slowly beginning to fill with grass and wildflowers, a shallow puddle forming at the very bottom. A slight film of sweat began to collect along Sage's palms.

"Why'd we come here?" she asked, looking at Raphael.

Raphael walked around the perimeter of Sage's crater, shaking his head to himself while he took in the scene, then said, "Not just because of what happened to you here." Raphael nodded toward the trees, to a slender trail barely visible. "There's a temple, an old abandoned thing, just down the trail over here. I figured it would be as good a place as any to continue your practice," Raphael gestured toward the trail and they began walking.

The abandoned temple sat in a quiet wooded peninsula. The stillness was absolute, like the absence of singing birds and rustling creatures after a heavy fall of snow. The animals of the forest were wary.

A nervousness grew in the pit of Sage's stomach, a kind of thrumming, nameless anxiety. But they arrived at the temple after a brief twenty-minute walk and Sage pushed the feelings aside. She tried ignoring the further lessening of anxiety when Gavin brushed past her to once again perch on a rock. Rather than looking at him, trying to engage him in any way, she focused on the crumbling ruins ahead.

"There, we should be far away now that we won't disturb anyone too much," announced Raphael.

Sage peered at the temple; it was not large, rather it was quite small to be considered a temple. The structure was no bigger than a small, single-person cabin, built out of stone and covered in lichen. The back end of the temple was built into a small hill, and the sides were open to the air. In the center of the structure, an insignia was carved into the floor, and a small stone statue stood at the far end of the temple.

Sage started: she recognized the insignia on the floor. Encircled three times, the insignia consisted of four spiraling lines moving out from the center where a small circle was engraved. Above the lines, four alternating triangles were carved, indicating the four elemental powers.

"This is the insignia of Cerridos, our wind god. What is this doing here?" Sage bent to touch the insignia, as she felt Raphael step in close to her.

"This temple has been here so long, most of us have forgotten about it," whispered Raphael.

"But what is it doing *here*?" asked Sage again. Raphael responded with a shrug. She looked up at the statue. The head had been knocked off, or perhaps it had just turned to dust from age. But the body showed a strong, muscled male body, holding large, impressive spears in each hand. The figure seemed to be in a mid-sprinting stride, poised and ready to launch its spears toward its opponents. Sage and Raphael had walked close to the statue and stared at it before turning in a circle and looking closer at their surroundings.

"Before we begin training, let's work on meditation. I'd like to try something we call Dream Walking. It takes a bit of trust between a healer and a patient. And I'll admit, I've only ever tried with other fae. But, seeing as I am so talented, I don't doubt we can find some success." The healer walked out of the temple. Sage followed, quick on his heels, not wanting to be left alone inside the ruins.

"Okay," Sage agreed reluctantly. "But we'll try training after?"

"Of course." Raphael gestured towards a blanket that materialized from thin air. Not needing the instructions, Sage laid herself down on the blanket. "I'm going to go through your memories alongside you." Gently, Raphael sat on the blanket and lifted her head so it was cradled in the basket of his criss-crossed legs. "You need to will my energy to mingle with yours, to signal that you are consenting to me accompanying you on this journey."

Sage, eyes still open, furrowed her brows. "Mmkay...and I do that, how?"

Exasperated, Raphael retorted, "Close your eyes and relax. Start with the breathing exercises and listen to my voice."

"Fine," Sage said. She closed her eyes and began the process of unwinding.

"Go back in your memories, and find someone from your family," Raphael directed.

Sage sifted through the dreams and memories she had recently recovered. Faces swam behind her closed eyelids. A girl with burnished bronze hair wildly escaping its ponytail, her face flush from running, a tooth missing in her wide grin. A woman appeared, with long, flowing blonde hair and pale blue eyes. Suntanned arms wrapped around Sage and her sister in a loving embrace.

"Good," Raphael's voice flitted between her memories, "Now, we are both going to dive a bit deeper."

Sage willed her mind to let Raphael join her; she envisioned a steel and brick wall, then commanded it to crumble. When it was dust, Raphael stood on the other side, and she realized she could see parts of her own body.

"This is the Dream World. We are going to use this space to try and recover more of yourself. Ready?" Raphael explained, before stepping over the remains of the wall and leading the way into darkness.

A short distance into the darkness led them to a schoolyard. Children ran and shrieked, pretending to fly while swinging, or playing chase. A small, lanky girl with chin-length hair sat on a bench by herself, looking at the ground.

"That's me," whispered Sage.

Raphael nodded, looking solemnly at Sage. She realized he was asking whether she wanted to approach. "They can't see us. We are less real here than they are," he explained.

"Okay. Sure, let's go."

Walking carefully toward the Sage sitting on the bench, they watched as a pretty woman in a floral dress came to the bench.

"Sage? I know it can be frustrating to get spells wrong in class, but you can't cast spells in anger. What you did today could have been very dangerous. Fire spells are not allowed for students below grade six. Do you understand?"

Tiny Sage wiped at her face, sniffling loudly. Her face scrunched as streams of tears ran down her face, and it was plain the child still harbored angry feelings. Nevertheless, the child nodded sharply.

"I still have to call home. Your parents will have to help pay for the burned cabinet. Is there anything you'd like me to explain to them when I call?"

The child only responded with a quick, sharp shake of the head. Her fingers gripped the bench so hard her knuckles had turned white.

"Well, okay," the floral-dress woman replied. "When you've pulled yourself together, you can join the other children on the playground."

Quickly, the scene disappeared, melting away like watercolors in a rain shower. In its place was a softly lit bedroom, pink walls surrounded Sage and Raphael, and a beautiful woman with long blonde hair lay on the bed with a freshly bathed Sage.

"Mama..." the young Sage said.

Sage gripped Raphael's arm, a sharp pang of longing gripping her so tightly she lost her breath.

"Sweetpea...I need to tell you a story," the woman began.

"A bedtime story? I thought I was too old for bedtime stories," tiny-Sage replied, wrinkling her nose at her mom.

"You may have started reading chapter books all by yourself, but you'll *never* be too old for a bedtime story from your Mommy." Her mom punctuated her claim by tickling Sage under her armpits, sending the girl into a fit of squeals and giggles.

"A long time ago," her mother began softly, once Sage had quieted and snuggled into her mother once more, "this world was filled with magic wielders powerful enough to raise nations from the sea floor, powerful enough to light every fire in every hearth across entire villages, and powerful enough to pull cyclones down from the heavens and flatten kingdoms at their will.

"While magic has always survived unchecked in this world, those with power over the elements were heralded as supreme to those of us with practical magical abilities. The gods saw that power, and demanded retribution. The elementals were hunted, and used as sacrifices to our gods, to show our gratitude for the blessings they've bestowed on us." Her mother paused, looking away from Sage towards the window overlooking a pasture.

"But over time, those powers have begun to wane. The elementals who used to roam our world are hardly seen at all now, mostly because we have destroyed them in our pursuit to keep the gods happy." Her mother stopped speaking for a moment, but stroked Sage's hair.

Sage looked up at her mother, "Am I an elemental? Is that why I'm no good at school?"

"Baby, you are just fine at school. You might have to try a little bit harder, but I know you can do anything those teachers ask you to do. But you do need to be careful; if someone sees your special magic...baby, you must keep it a secret. Mommy and Daddy will do everything we can to keep you safe, but you can't show any of your new friends your special magic. Okay?"

Tears lined the corners of her mother's eyes, and Sage, both present and past, felt like she would explode from the sight. She would do anything to keep tears from those eyes, so Sage watched as the child nodded enthusiastically and hugged her mother's neck.

Just as quickly as the scene had begun, Raphael and Sage were ripped away. Inhaling deeply, gasping as she opened her eyes, Sage's hands involuntarily rushed to her chest, clutching at her heart. "My mom..." she whispered.

Raphael carefully disentangled himself from Sage, gingerly laying her head on the blanket before pushing himself to stand and walking towards the temple. Slowly, Sage pulled herself back together and joined him.

"So sorcery is a normal part of your world?" he asked.

"Magic." The word danced in the air and delivered a thrill to her spine. In the distance, she could sense Gavin stilling, obviously eavesdropping. "It's part of everything there," Sage said in awe.

"Here, sorcery is not always well received," Raphael warned.

"It's not sorcery," Sage explained, "It's magic! I remember bits and pieces...there's alchemy, spell building, healing arts —kind of like you!" The memory wrapped itself around her. She could remember being a very studious child, but the magic had proved to be difficult for her to wield. "I don't think I was very good at it," she finally admitted to Raphael.

"Well, never mind that!" Raphael announced with a clap of his hands. "We will train what you *are* good at. Let's start with wind."

"Okay, we start with wind. How?" asked Sage.

"Let's start with breathing," he replied.

Sage rolled her eyes, "Oy, with the breathing. It's like you think I don't know how to breathe on my own. You know I do it every single day, for hours and hours without you around, right?"

Raphael chuckled. "Of course, but you could always do it better."

Sage made an ungracious gesture towards him, and while it might have been foreign to him, she was sure he got the meaning. "Fine. Breathing. Lead on, breath master," Sage said in retort.

Raphael had Sage sit on the grass, commanding her to find a calm, relaxed posture. Once she was ready, Raphael talked her through the routine they had practiced over and over again: beginning with slow, deep breaths, then focusing the energy of those breaths into various parts of her body. When they reached her stomach, Sage felt as though she could feel the energy begin to stir, searching for a way out of her.

"Now, open your eyes. Keep thinking of that breath, and I want you to take this feather," Raphael laid a white feather on the ground a few feet from her, "and move it into the temple. Extra points if you can get it to land on the insignia inside. I just made that last part up, but what a fun challenge it will be!" Raphael simply beamed at the last statement. Sage groaned to herself, not amused by the extra layer of difficulty Raphael added. He seemed to have a lot more faith in her than she did.

Sage centered herself again. Focusing on breathing, she visualized the air swirling around her lungs. Pushing the energy that had gathered in her center into the farthest part of her body, Sage lifted one hand. A small breeze passed over her palm, lifting pieces of her hair from her face so that they fluttered about her ears. Sage inhaled again and raised her second hand; with an exhale, Sage flipped her hands from horizontal to vertical, and pushed outward. A breeze pushed across the field, and the feather fluttered several feet— away from the temple.

Gavin laughed, and she glared at him. Quickly, he looked away, but she could still see his shoulders shaking.

Sage dropped her hands and glared at Raphael.

He chuckled, "Again. Try again."

Sage tried again. And again. And again, and again, and again. Each time she failed to move the feather further than mere inches, Raphael would patiently talk her through resetting her focus. His unwavering patience flustered her, and at one point she became so irate with him, she sent a blast of wind so forceful the feather flew off into the woods. Raphael simply procured a new feather and had her try again. Each time she missed, Gavin grew more and more boisterous with his laughter.

"WHAT is so funny?" she finally demanded.

He only shrugged, shifted into his bird form, and took flight, circling Sage and Raphael in the sky.

They stayed until moments before dark when Sage finally got the feather to float to the temple's edge.

"That will do for tonight. Time to go home," said Raphael, "Well done."

Sage, who had begun to stand, froze. "Home. That's the first time someone has said that, and it hasn't physically hurt to hear the word. What does that mean?"

"Only time will tell, my dear," answered Raphael softly.

He offered Sage his elbow and he cast them back into his medical ward.

Surprisingly, a moment later, Gavin arrived in the ward. "Dinner?" he asked in Sage's direction.

"So now you're going to be nice to me again?" she asked.

"I was never not nice to you today," Gavin replied.

They argued about who was and was not nice all the way up the stairs and well into dinner. Still, Sage enjoyed Gavin's company, even if he couldn't make up his mind about how he felt about her.

Raphael opened the journal that connected him to the King, and scrawled, *"Training with the girl showed promise today. I brought her to the temple of Cerridos. I think you have something there with your theory about the realm leapers. Would it perhaps be time to introduce her to the book?"*

He had grown to enjoy Sage's company— had actually grown quite fond of her. She was intelligent, perceptive, and she didn't seem to be bashful with sharing her opinions, especially when it came to training. It would be nice to have someone around that didn't take themselves quite so seriously, although he supposed Gavin fit that bill as well. Keeping the book from her had become a growing point of contention between himself and the King; it seemed important that the girl and the book be united. For what purpose, Raphael couldn't say other than his practically perfect intuition, and who would argue with that? Raphael waited for a reply.

"The book stays here for now. We've just received word from Acantha and Epyllo; a village in Nysa was raided. Several males have gone missing. The spies should be back by the formal reception to give us the full report. Be sure the girl is ready for the reception; I expect her to be in control at

the event. After that, we will see whether she's ready for the book. Trust me, Raphael. We will figure this out."

Raphael trusted Symon with his life. They had known each other since they were boys; Raphael had been a quiet, serious child whereas Symon and Zeke tended to keep the palace staff exasperated with their constant activity. But Symon had always been kind to Raphael, making sure Raphael was included, or at least invited, to palace events held for the children; Symon was also responsible for Raphael's life being spared when his parents were captured and executed. Helping Raphael to hide was likely what sent Symon to the work camps, along with his siblings.

He *did* trust Symon, he just hoped the king wasn't making the kind of mistake his father would have made, trying to hold on too tightly to control in order to avoid disaster. Trust was a shared pathway, after all.

Raphael closed the book, and looked over his notes from the sessions he had spent with Sage. So far, she exhibited rather good control over her wind and fire power. He turned to a book about wind wielders and ran through a few key points he might bring up at their next practice session.

It was minutes later he realized he'd been staring at the same line without actually reading it, lost in the thought that Sage might be a realm leaper, sent here to help defeat their enemies. He doubted she was dark-born. She didn't have any warring motivations other than finding her memories, Meliza had been sure to discover that.

Raphael shook his head, set the book down on his desk, and rose to head off to his rooms for the evening. Answers to his questions would have to wait for another day.

Chapter 10

Raphael helped Sage settle into place. They'd spent several days attempting to dream walk, but no memories had resurfaced. Nevertheless, both Sage and Raphael remained optimistic.

"I'm feeling good about this one, Raph," said Sage as he positioned her head in his lap.

"Good. Now, hush, let's get started."

Carefully, Sage let herself slip into her mind, drifting somewhere between wakefulness and sleep. Floating through worlds and thoughts, she let herself float along the boundaries of consciousness until something began to take shape.

Sage and Raphael landed in what appeared to be a stadium, hovering somewhere above the crowd. It took a moment for Sage to recollect the setting, her stomach dropping and her heart beating fast when she realized where they'd ended up. Memory-Sage was standing among a vast crowd of young people, ranging in age from very young right up to late teens. They were all peering at a stage where a man stood lecturing the crowd.

"As Principal of Tiernan Academy of Arts and Alchemy, I will preface today's presentation by reminding you all about the high standards we demand of our students."

A few boos echoed from one corner of the field, and several older master-level boys were swarmed by nearby faculty members.

"What's going on here?" Raphael asked Sage.

"This is my old school. I think this is where everything went wrong," Sage replied. She watched as the faculty members berated the boys into compliance. Memory-Sage waved across the crowd, and another student with brass-colored hair waved back. "There's my sister," Sage pointed out to Raphael.

The principal continued, "I expect all of our students to prove to our esteemed guest why Tiernan is the premiere academy of the Metro-Techeduin area. Now, if you will all please stand and salute as we welcome, our very own, President Ranquer."

The students and faculty let out a collective gasp and stood to salute. The Thuledain national anthem played over loudspeakers as President Ranquer and his assembly of advisors poured onto the stage. Ranquer was dressed in a silver-gray pinstriped suit, his thin cropped hair parted down the center, and his pencil-thin mustache visible on projector screens which slid into place on either side of the stage.

A gasp escaped Raphael, and Sage grabbed his hand. Seeing the President caused goosebumps to pimple her skin, even in the dream world. She was sure something similar occurred to Raphael.

President Ranquer stepped up to the microphone, "Yes, yes, yes. Thank you, students of Tiernan Academy. It is my honor and pleasure to be addressing you today, our future leaders and citizens of Thuledain. Please be seated." He paused, waiting for the students and faculty to settle themselves into their seats, all the while scanning the crowd with his politician's smile. "It is my honor to lead Thuledain as your President; over the past eight years of my Presidency, we have seen prosperous gains for our country; achievements that have been made in honor of you, our upcoming generation. Your parents, my cabinet members, your representatives, and your country have devoted themselves to building a wondrous nation for you to one day inherit. But we must never stop pursuing enlightenment. We must never stop striving for perfection."

The president grabbed the microphone and walked away from the podium. "As I gaze out on this audience, I recognize that I am staring into the face of progress. You, students, are the promise of a better world. We have been fortunate to live in many years of peace, of fortuitous blessings; but our enemies still lurk out there, in the places we cannot see. We must never lose our desire to learn, to discover every single mystery this world offers to us. It is up to YOU—" he jabbed his finger at the audience, "to pick up the torch, and carry us to victory!

"I urge each and every student to throw themselves into their studies. Become the greatest sorcerers that Thuledain has laid eyes on. Become the most recognized alchemists history will ever tell of. The most creative, diverse spellcasters our world will ever be blessed with!" He had reached the podium again, and began banging his fist on the podium. "YOU will be the salvation of our world!" He paused for a long moment.

"I know many of you are too young to have any idea of just how special you can be to our great nation." He scanned the audience again. "But I have faith that there are those among you who are most gifted, and will bless our nation with their gifts. In order to do this, I and my cabinet have established a special House of Youth Representatives to guide our nation into glory. In order to join this elite establishment, we will be testing each and every student at Tiernan Academy. Those of you who exemplify the standards required will be invited to join us immediately for the swearing-in ceremonies. Your parents have all been informed already, and we will begin the testing ceremonies immediately."

President Ranquer paused for a moment, then lifted his palms forward and shouted, "For the glory of the world!" The school repeated the phrase back in unison with fervor, everyone rising to their feet in applause.

As President Ranquer and his entourage exited the stage, the students burst into conversation, exclaiming over the prospects of becoming one of the first Youth Representatives.

Memory-Sage engaged in conversation with the girls who sat near her, and the scene began to shift. Shapes and figures blurred as Sage and Raphael were poured into another memory. Trying to grab onto Raphael, Sage gasped as she landed inside the body of herself.

"Raph? Where are you?"

Her voice echoed inside her head, and she winced.

She was in a testing area housed within a temporary, tented facility, with cool conditioned air. Bright fluorescent lights hummed along the lengths of the tent, and attendants dressed in black and white suits strutted along the lengths, checking clipboards, calling names, and directing faculty and students like puppeteers. Raphael was nowhere to be seen, and she recognized the youthful version of her own hands, a Tiernan Academy uniform cloaking her body.

Students, eager for their turn in the interview room, surrounded her, while it was all Sage could do to staunch the growing anxiety in her chest. Her palms felt slick against the schoolbook she clutched, *A History of the Gods and Thuledain*. She nervously ran her thumb along the spine of the book, trying to displace the fear that crept across her spine. A severe-looking woman called her name, and Sage flinched, bumping into the girl next to her.

"Shit...oh...sorry," embarrassed, she waved an apology to her teacher, who gave her a look that promised consequences for another slip-up. "Sorry, everyone," she muttered again, and tentatively followed the woman to the next tent.

What she had thought was simply a second tent was actually a long hallway, extending farther than she thought was physically possible. "What kind of charms did you use for this?" Sage asked, recognizing the tell-tale sign of magic-manipulated space.

"That's confidential," the woman answered, not even looking back at her.

In her head, she sought Raphael's voice again. "Raph? What's happening?"

"This is unusual, my dear. But don't worry, I'm here," Raph's voice echoed softly in her mind. His voice brought an immediate sense of comfort, and she squared her shoulders to follow the attendant down a long white hallway.

They arrived at an entrance, blocked by curtains, and the woman pulled back one of the curtains and gestured inside for Sage to go through. Sage continued through the opening and found several alchemists in lab coats, and more attendants in their sharp black and white suits.

Sage recognized one of the President's advisors from the assembly and moved toward a chair in the center of the room. The advisor gestured and she took her seat, trying to appear confident. The advisor wore a crisp brown jacket over a tightly buttoned shirt. His skin glistened with the effects of beauty-magic, and his smile stretched across his face. His eyes shone eagerly, and something nudged Sage to go, get out.

"You are Sage Brennan?" the advisor asked, not sitting like Sage, but standing to the side and staring at a clipboard in his hand. Sage nodded. "We need a small DNA sample from you, to confirm your identity. Don't worry, it won't take much, just a small prick of the finger," he chirped, now circling her chair. "I see here, you seem to be an excellent student, Ms. Brennan."

An alchemist in a white coat reached for and grabbed her finger; he swabbed something over it, then took a small device and pricked her finger. She flinched. This memory might not be real, but the sensation was. He collected several small beads of blood into a vial. She hissed as he squeezed her finger, working to try and catch a few more drops of blood.

"Honestly, I know my grades could be better. But I'm working on it," Sage said between her teeth, and the alchemist stopped with her finger as another alchemist walked forward and wrapped her finger in a bandage.

One of the alchemists signaled to the advisor, and he turned to Sage, asking, "Would you say you had any hidden talents?"

Sage pondered the question, trying to find an answer that might make her seem more desirable to the panel. "I have an excellent eye for research; I always get top marks on my research papers. And I'm a hard worker," she was floundering, grasping for anything that might make her stand out. Inwardly, she tried to take control of the conversation, but felt herself half-shout, "I'm a good dancer!", then instantly regretted it. She squeezed her eyes shut. Idiot, she thought to herself.

The alchemists muttered to themselves. Peering at the alchemists, the advisor stepped closer to Sage.

"It's a full match," she heard an alchemist say, and the advisor clapped his hands together, and rubbed them happily.

He stepped closer to her. "I have excellent news for you, Ms. Brennan. You have been chosen as one of the Youth Representatives. Now, Ms. Dullahan here will escort you to the holding room while we finish up. We will inform your parents of the honor, and the ceremony to swear you in will begin shortly!"

Before Sage could process what had happened, Ms. Dullahan—the sharp, severe attendant from before—scooped her up under the elbows, and half-dragged her through a separate, curtained opening. Within twenty steps, Sage found herself in a room with six other students. The youngest student couldn't have been older than eleven.

Is it just me, or do these students look awfully young? Raph's voice drifted through her awareness.

"I don't think you're wrong. And I'm afraid it gets worse," she said out loud, though no one seemed to notice.

Looking around, Sage realized she recognized at least one other student, a quiet girl in her sister's year. She couldn't remember her name but could remember her sister complaining about being paired with her the year before. It sounded as if she also struggled with spellcasting.

And that other boy sitting two seats down; that was Jamie, a boy who regularly caused trouble in the school, usually with outbursts of temper or mischief. In fact, there wasn't a single Exceptional student in the tent as far as she could tell.

A piece of pizza dangled from her grasp. She hadn't noticed when it appeared, but it felt unappetizing as her wariness grew. Something curled in the pit of her stomach, unraveling itself as realization lurked beneath her conscience. There was something off about this.

Time seemed to creep to a stop. The people around her seemed clueless to the unnatural circumstances. These were not students who should be representing the country. She took deep steadying breaths, and noticed a subtle breeze tickle her ankles. "No no no no...not now," Memory-Sage was panicking. Even now, experiencing the moment a second time, Sage felt the tremor and willed her memory self to control her emotions. Another deep breath calmed the wind, but she could feel warmth collecting in her center, sweat gathering on her palms.

Before she could entirely get herself together, the advisor from before walked in. "Welcome, Youth Representatives! We are so excited to welcome you; we have finished setting up for the next part of the ceremony, if you will each follow an attendant," and he waved for the attendants to gather the students.

She stood to follow and was whipped from the scene. Like mist rising from a hot road after a summer storm, her surroundings came into focus. She was in a stiff, white medical chair. Cuffs popped out and snapped tight over their hands and wrists. The cuffs pinched at her wrists as Sage squirmed, trying to slip free.

Panic began to set in, not just in Sage. Fear floated through the room like a heavy fog. Sage's insides turned into a roiling sea, sweat gathering on her skin.

Other students muttered, trying to ask each other questions, attempting to get the attention of the attendants hovering by the chairs. Their pleas were met with indifference, and the realization that they were in danger dawned on the children.

"Raph- get me out of here. I don't want to do this anymore." Sage tried speaking the words out loud, but her voice remained silent. She looked around, but the tilt of the chair kept her vision slight. She couldn't sense Raphael in the room, in her mind, anywhere. She was on her own.

President Ranquer stepped in then, strutting into the room and examining his collection of students, his expression unreadable.

"Ah, welcome to my new...representatives," His smile stretched across his face, genuine. Something like a shadow rippled in his eyes before he continued, "You should be proud to know that your service to your nation will become legend; not only will you represent the glory and victory we will achieve, but you, my dear children, will be the leaders of the most glorious era Thuledain has ever seen. Let's begin, shall we?" and he waved a hand, palm up, across the line.

The attendants, Ms. Dullahan included, stepped behind the students. Dullahan's cold fingers pressed into either side of Sage's head, and a tingling sensation skittered over her face, into her mind. She fought to retain her wits, trying to use her water magic to protect her senses, but lost hope as the edges of her vision faded to black.

She was lying flat on her back. She had been stripped and dressed in a white, flimsy gown. Air pumped into the room swept across her body sending goosebumps racing along her arms. Foggy memories of being restrained blinked in and out as she struggled to remember where she was. Trying to wrench her body upwards, following the intuition which told her to run, her forehead slammed against some sort of restraint holding her head down. The cold bite of steel at her wrists and ankles sending her body into a fresh panic.

"Raph?" Sage tried reaching for her friend. She couldn't speak his name out loud, but she whispered it in her mind.

Nothing. She asked again.

Again.

Again....nothing. She couldn't find him.

In the distance, muttering voices discussed a disappointment in levels. "Sir, it doesn't look like his levels will be sufficient enough to provide us the energy required for transfer."

"Hmm...that's too bad," Ranquer's voice snaked down the line of restrained children, curling around Sage's ears. "Well, we can still use him. Cian, please wake him, you know I prefer them awake."

"Of course," a soft voice replied. Sage tempered her breathing, straining to hear what happened next. Softly, the moans of a boy began to stir within the room.

"Where am I?" The question was interrupted by a *thunk*, and abrupt thrashing as the boy came to. "Let me go! Let me out of here!" His voice was too sharp, too high. Cracks emitted from his shrieks as a soft growl began to tremble through the room.

Sage felt a menacing heat begin to invade her space, a dark red glow seeped into the room. The boy screamed, thrashing against his restraints. Gurgles began to choke out his pleading. She couldn't move her head to watch the horror unfold, but she swore she saw the shadows of horns fill the wall before her.

The boy quieted. The glowing ceased, and bile rose in her throat as she heard the attendants peel the boy from the plastic covered chair. Unable to hold it back, a soft sob escaped her chest.

Sage– grab my hand. Grab my hand now!

Raph's voice in her head was urgent now. She looked around for Raph, ready to be yanked out of this nightmare. All she found was Ms. Dullahan's cold stare. Sawing sharp pants rose from her chest as the woman approached and observed Sage.

"Mr. President—I seem to have a live one here," Ms. Dullahan announced, peering down at Sage.

Sage tried to call out, to protest, but her mouth wouldn't —couldn't— move. President Ranquer stepped close to her, peering at her, his eyes seeming wild and untamed. A strange smell like burning brimstone permeated the air around him.

"Look at you, darling. You are very special, indeed," his cold voice crooned, punctuating each word as if he were stabbing a fat holiday roast. Looking at Ms. Dullahan he quipped, "May I see her levels." A clipboard appeared in his hands as he hovered by her bed. Flipping through the pages, a greedy light seemed to flicker in his eyes. "Very good. She will do nicely." He passed the clipboard back to Dullahan, and began to step away. "Put her back down," he called out.

Those cold fingers once again probed at her head, but she fought with all her might, not ready to slip back into the darkness.

"She's fighting the sleep," Ms. Dullahan murmured.

"No matter," the cold voice replied, coming near her once more, "just get the chip in and put her with the others. She won't be able to do anything once we get her to the plant."

An alchemist appeared, and Sage tried to shake her head, to plead, beg with her eyes. The cold swab of disinfectant on her neck came before a long needle pressed into her neck, just behind her ear. She tried to scream as the pain barreled into her, but she couldn't make a sound. When the needle was removed, she could feel something linger under her skin. Tears pricked her eyes.

Finally, President Ranquer placed his hand to her abdomen, and commanded, "Sleep. Now."

Lightning filled her body; everything writhed, spittle frothed in her mouth, and a thousand shards of glass filled her body. Inky blackness coiled around her, choking any hope from her. The pain lasted an eternity until finally, relief swarmed as she blacked out.

They were in a van.

It was dark.

She was slumped over someone else, and they were chained.

Sage peeled her eyes apart and tried to get a bearing on her whereabouts. Her head jostled against the knee of an unconscious body. A sticky wet substance slithered across her upper lip. The coppery taste of blood indicated her nose had begun bleeding at some point. Her neck was tender, and an ache behind her eyes made her want to close them and never open them again.

Forcing herself to stay aware, she tried to figure out where they were heading. They were in a transport van. The captors were all slumped on the floor. In the corner of the cargo hold, she could sense an alert presence, someone menacing who would hurt her if she caused trouble. The other students were all still unconscious. She tried to quiet her breathing, but terror was clanging inside her body like the bells of St. Agrona.

Shit.....shit, shit, shit. The stories her mother told her as a young girl started flooding back into her memory. How'd they find out? She'd been careful, hadn't used her magic in ages. She wouldn't even let her sister coax her into making water shapes like they did as kids.

Her blood.

Her stomach sank at the realization of what that would mean. If her real abilities were discovered.

A creeping awareness stole over her as she became aware of the lack of wind. The cold, hollowness that filled her stomach. The way she couldn't reach for the earth or sense the waters that ran below them. The magic she'd suppressed for so long, but had still been a constant companion, were now barely echoes of memory. Try as she might, the elements had gone silent.

Careful to not move her head, Sage glanced at her wrists, at the chains around them emanating an almost imperceptible green glow. Gods-damned her. They'd used radioactive isotope chains; she supposed it didn't matter if they were poisoned by the radioactive chains. They were going to be sacrificed after all.

Somewhere deep in her mind, a familiar voice tried to call out for her. She couldn't place the voice, tried to reach out for it. She thought she heard her name, like a whisper, run through her mind, but it disappeared as quickly as she noticed it. Her sense of reality felt watery. This couldn't be happening. This couldn't be real.

But it was. It was real. She was going to die.

Shit! Sage clawed through her mind, pleading for her magic to make an appearance. Nothing. She put all her will into seeking the tiniest hint that her magical powers were intact, lurking undetected by those who'd captured her. Still nothing. She took a slow breath to stem the rise of bile that threatened to choke her.

Sputtering memories sifted through her rattled brain. She wished she was back at school, back at home. Wished she was doing homework, safe in her room. An image of her schoolbooks drifted through her mind, and she almost laughed as she remembered the stacks of Religious History homework that would remain untouched, forever incomplete.

The Gods. She'd never been religious. Her family only visited temples on high holidays, and she wasn't even sure she believed they hung around anymore. But she was desperate.

She bent all her will praying to them. First to Therisyd, then to Brighid, then Cerridos. She had nearly given up when she got to Allyra.

"Allyra...Goddess...please, just let me live."

"Fall," a sweet, whispering voice brushed against Sage's mind.

A sob escaped her mouth, and she stiffened, hoping the guard hadn't heard, but it was mercifully covered by a particularly heavy bump. She knocked her head against a student's knee, and had to bite her tongue to keep from calling out in pain. She nearly shook her head from the shock, but then she heard it again.- *"Fall...fall through the chains."*

She prayed to the goddess once more, "Allyra...help me. Please. Just help me get out of here."

"FALL," the voice repeated, a command this time.

"If this is you Allyra, I don't know what you mean. Fall?" Sage responded in her mind.

"Fall. Like water from the ledge of a table. Like water falls between cracks and crevices. Fall through your chains."

Sage took a deep, quiet breath and tried to focus on the directions the goddess had just given her. Fall. She could hear water nearby, rushing. They must be coming to the Tiernan bridge; the river was swollen at this time of year.

Sage breathed, and focused on the sound of the river, so much quieter than the sound of the van.

She breathed, and thought about the river passing over rocks and boulders, sliding over weed and grass.

She breathed. She thought about the way the river wound and twisted through Thuledain.

The chains slackened about her wrists, followed by a soft clink as they rested on top of her wrists instead of around them. She cracked open one eyelid, trying to gauge whether the guard had noticed. He seemed to have become aloof during the drive, staring out of the window. It worked...It worked, it worked!

She nudged the student next to her. He didn't budge. Across from her, the youngest student lay dormant, completely unconscious.

"You are freed from your chains now, little water wielder," that sweet voice whispered. *"Now break free from this trap. Your Goddess has blessed you, and you must survive this trial to repay the life-debt you now owe."*

Well, shit. Of course. "And how do I break free?" Sage quipped in her mind.

"Use your gifts, silly girl. You've hidden them long enough."

Sage felt a drop of water on her shoulder, and knew it was the Goddess parting ways. It seemed that breaking out of the chains was all the help she could expect.

Trying to move quietly, Sage managed to get her hands between her legs, away from the chains' touch. She reached deep into herself, reaching for whatever abilities lay deep inside her.

Shifting her head the slightest bit, she discovered there was a vehicle behind them, most likely tailing them just in case.

They were just reaching the bridge that spanned the river. Sage, nestled deep inside herself, and summoned the water with every ounce of energy she had left. She heard the water shift course, could feel its weight as it raced towards the bridge. Their van began crossing the bridge, the vehicle behind them slowing to match the speed limit. She could feel the second vehicle begin to lag behind slightly, and she tugged on that bond between her and the water. She pulled so mightily within herself, she thought she might faint.

"What's that?" the guard perked up, staring as a shadow began to envelope itself around the silhouette of the follow-up van. "Hey, up front, can you tell what that is?"

Another guard spoke into a radio, asking for updates. A rumble began shaking the bridge, and panic seemed to take over the guard in the back. "Hey!" he shouted. "Speed up, speed up!" Banging his fists against the wall that separated the prisoners from the drivers, the guard compelled his partners to "go, go, go!"

The van Sage traveled in sped up, shouts from the driver and the guards mingling with the roar of water. A mighty wave rocked over the bridge, slamming into the vehicle behind them. Screaming blasted from the guard's radio before going eerily silent, and Sage knew she'd hit her target, just as their van reached the other side of the bridge onto solid ground.

"What the fuck was that?" called an angry voice from the cockpit.

"Shit!" The guard looked out of the window at the back of the van, "something's kicking off. Get us back to base! Hurry!"

The thought that those people in the vehicle had been swept away to their deaths by her wave had her swallowing hard to push down the pizza she ate earlier.

There was no time for her to wallow in shame and guilt. She needed to act fast. The guard was on his feet, prodding at the students nearest to him with the butt of his rifle. He was armed with automatic weapons that would wipe them out in a snuff of light if he so chose. Firearms loaded with spells to stun, catch, or kill their targets.

Sage plummeted back into her magic, drawing on a thin cord of fire she could sense in the guard's rifle, just waiting to be unleashed. She focused her energy on that cord, and sent it barreling to the guard. The fire found the weapons, and they began to explode at his side. He screamed, blood splattering the sides of the van, and he collapsed to the floor.

He caught her eye, noticing them open, "You," he breathed, but before he could mutter anything else, Sage ripped the air from his chest. His mouth moved like a dying fish, as the guards in the front banged on the divider.

"What the hell's going on?"

"Pull the fuck over. We need to restrain the prisoners."

The driver began to pull over, but Sage sat up, bracing herself against the wheel well, and the corner of the van. She found her thread of earth power, and yanked on it as hard as she could. A wall of asphalt, stone, grass, and earth shot up directly in front of the van. The driver yanked the wheel, but it was too close; the van skittered sideways, and they slammed into the wall. Sage was catapulted to the other side of the van, and slammed against the side of it.

Her ears filled with ringing, and her head throbbed. Her shoulder ached, and her wrist was already swelling. She could hear one guard up front groaning as he tried to communicate into his radio.

She reached inward again, and robbed a second man of his breath. She didn't dare look around at the students on the floor around her, but a small lump caught her eye. The eleven year old boy lay on the floor, his arms and head at an awkward angle. A sob of rage escaped as she reached for more fire energy and blasted the doors off their hinges. The wall of earth still teetered over them and she walked to the side of it dazed.

The wall towered into the sky.

She'd done that. Never before had she reached so deep into herself and released the well of magic that lay inside. She had also killed tonight. If she wasn't a dead girl walking before, she was certainly one now.

She needed to hide, but she didn't think she could get very far with a broken wrist and collarbone, which throbbed in time with her racing heart. The river was at least five miles from them now. That would take her hours to get to. She couldn't do it without being caught. Not out in the open.

A sharp twang behind her ear reminded her of the chip implanted. She ran back to the overturned van, grappling with the lifeless guard tangled amongst the students and yanked free a knife clipped to his pocket. As quickly as she could manage, she felt for the lump lodged behind her ear. With a groan of pain, she dug the chip out from her skin until a bloody mass of flesh and metal sat in her hand. Summoning her fire magic once more, she burned the metal chip and then crushed it beneath her heel.

The distinctive sound of helicopters in the near distance caught her attention. It wouldn't be long before they were upon her, followed by large vehicles containing more guards with terrifying weapons. She reached down inside of herself again, and tunneled below the earth, bringing with her a pocket of air. She was encapsulated in a hollow tomb of soft, wet earth. She wondered if she would be able to move her little underground cave, so that she could just walk underground all the way to the river like a mole.

She waited, trying to listen to the sounds above her. Something loud and rumbling arrived at the spot. She could hear men shouting to each other, a helicopter circling above.

Her wrist and shoulder throbbed harder now, and she had to keep swallowing to keep from vomiting. She pressed her uninjured hand to the wound bleeding behind her ear. Holding her breath, trying to make as little sound as possible, she heard booted feet, the snarl of hound dogs, and machines stomp and crawl above her. She had chosen a spot of fresh dirt to tunnel, off the side of the wall she had raised, hoping it would look less suspicious.

How long would they look here? Could the dogs smell her underground? She redoubled her efforts not to breathe.

It felt like days before the sounds finally began to fade. The air was beginning to feel thin. As carefully as she could, Sage used her gifts to make a small channel from her pocket in the ground to above, so that fresh air could filter in.

A few more voices, far off to the left, remained, inspecting the scene, still making it too dangerous to leave her hiding spot.

She was cold, and so tired. She wanted to get out of here, to go home. She didn't remember falling asleep, but she awoke later, surprised to still be alive and uncaptured.

After sitting for a long time, she decided it was safe to try and tunnel towards the river. Reaching for the water as a guide, Sage stood, raising both palms and pushing against the soft, wet damp earth. It shifted, opening in front of her and closing behind her.

She began her descent to the river.

Sage surged up from the memory, sitting upright. Breath rasped out of her, and Raphael gripped her in a hug. Her skin felt hot to the touch, her hands shaking; she scanned the room, disoriented and afraid.

"I'm so sorry, Sage," he whispered in her hair, hugging her tightly. "I could see you, could see everything going on, but couldn't find a way back into it so I could get you out."

Sage nodded. Pulling away from her friend, she accepted and took a sip of water he offered, focusing on not spilling it from her shaking hands.

"Come, I will draw a bath for you, and you can tell me what you learned." He gently grabbed her hand, and they cast into her room.

He helped her up off the floor, her legs feeling like gelatin. Her heart was racing, and she felt trapped. She leaned into Raphael as he supported her around her waist. The tears burst from her eyes as she buried her face in his chest, "I killed them." The realization that she killed the guards, probably killed her fellow students, broke a piece of her.

Raphael wrapped her in his arms, and stroked her head. "It's ok, my dear. What's happened in the past will stay there."

"What if I'm broken, Raph? What if I'm bad? What if....what if everything I do leads to death?" She couldn't stop now, the tears streamed from her, and sobs tore through her chest.

"We will work this out together. And I think, you get to choose if you are bad, or good. And I think, whatever you decide, is how we will move forward." Raphael gave Sage a light squeeze, acknowledging that he knew what she was thinking, that she'd choose good, and then ushered her into the bathing room.

By the soft glow of candlelight, Sage sat in the warm bath and let the memory spill from her, surrendering every detail to Raphael. Talking about the memory was less painful than reliving it, and she found herself exhausted by the end, but feeling more whole than she had in weeks.

After a few hours, Sage allowed Raphael to help her dress, and she climbed into her bed where she slept, mercifully without the accompaniment of dreams or memories.

✧✦✧

Raphael took out his journal, hoping the King was awake. He held his pen above the journal, intent to inform His Majesty that he would be coming to the palace so he could tell Sage's story.

His pen hovered for long moments before he finally decided to wait, to hold on to the memory a bit longer. Hopefully, she would have a few more memories to fill in the gaps, answer more questions.

He closed the book, deciding to spend the early morning hours cataloging his supplies, and readying himself for a trip to the market. He reached out with his powers, sensed her sleeping soundly, and breathed a sigh of relief.

"You surely know how to catch someone's attention, my dear," he whispered to himself, and he turned his focus back to his task.

Chapter 11

In and around their dream walks, Sage and Raphael returned to Cerridos's temple every two or three days to continue her training in the physical world. With every visit, Sage's frustration grew as progress continued to linger outside her reach. Being accompanied by a sulking Gavin wasn't helping matters.

She still hadn't succeeded in getting the feather onto the insignia on the floor. In fact, if anything, she was farther from accomplishing her goal than the first time she'd tried. Sometimes she failed to summon the slightest hint of a breeze; other times, she would lose her temper and send a gush of wind so powerful, she would occasionally knock down trees. Once, she slammed her fists on the ground where she sat and ended up causing a small tremor in the earth, tearing down part of an already decomposing wall of the temple.

"I can't do this!" she finally huffed at Raphael, beginning to stand up. This was stupid, she thought to herself. A stupid, stupid, pointless task. If he wants that feather in there so bad, he should pick it up and put it there himself.

Raphael, ever the calm and patient teacher, just remained on his spot, smiling slightly as she began to pace. She had to move. She felt like a windup toy; like her crank had been twisted too many times and someone was holding the pin in place, refusing to let her spin.

"I feel....trapped. When I sit there, and breathe, and focus. I feel like I'm stuck," she stopped pacing, dropping her arms to her sides in defeat. "I can't do this, Raph," she whispered.

Raphael continued to look at Sage, took a deep breath, and began to walk toward her. "I notice, your power seems strongest when your emotions are high. That's a common problem for fae here, too. We have to train you to control your powers," Raphael had begun to circle the little clearing in front of the temple.

Sage stood her ground, "Or, maybe my power is just not something to control. Maybe it just does what it wants."

A chuckle rippled over the tension simmering below the surface. Snapping her head towards the rock Gavin perched atop, she glared at him. "Is there something you'd like to add?" she asked, saccharine dripping from her tone.

Gavin shrugged, not bothering to move from his rock. "You keep trying to control the wind. Like it's something you can grab hold of. It's kind of cute."

"Cute?! You think me sitting here every day and failing is...cute?"

"Sort of. I mean, usually, when something doesn't work for me-" Gavin approached from the rock, shoulders squared and gaze intent on Sage, "-I switch it up. Try something new. But, go ahead, keep trying to wield the wind like fire. What do I know?"

A slight tremor vibrated through the clearing, and Raphael's tsk snapped Sage back into control. With eyes closed, fists clenched, and her jaw locked, Sage asked Gavin, "Would you please explain? What should I do?"

"Try something different. Do whatever feels natural." Gavin grinned. He was close now. Close enough that she could feel his body heat through the warmth of the day. The sun sat behind him so that light seemed to radiate through his wavy hair. He'd be nearly angelic, thought Sage, if it weren't for the shit-eating grin.

A challenge, then; he was daring her to succeed. "Or, you could just give up now and never learn what makes you special." He waved a hand at her, walking back to his rock with an air of dismissal.

Sage took a sharp breath, holding back the smart remark she so desperately wanted to shoot back. But he was right. If she didn't learn how to use her powers, she might never discover why she was here; not to mention, better control of her powers meant better chances of fighting off those who wanted to hurt her.

"The wind isn't just energy. It's constant, it flows when and where it wants. You have to convince it to work with you, not for you." Gavin finished his remark, standing on his rock, then shifted into his hawk-eagle form and flew into the sky.

He said it like it was so easy. Like the answer was obvious.

She stood, rooted to the ground, and watched him soar into the sky. Watched as he rode wind currents as he circled the clearing. She might be imagining things, but it was almost like he was trying to prove his point. The wind was its own spirit. It needed to be cajoled.

She rolled her shoulders, trying to ease the tension she was holding there, and widened her stance. She began the breathing techniques Raphael had been so insistent she master. Slow-steady breaths, focusing on energy gathering throughout her body. She closed her eyes, envisioning the wind as something visible. She allowed it to become tangible in her mind, a flurry of blues, purples, and whites. She gathered one final breath and, as she exhaled, began to move. She freed her body from the spot and followed her instincts.

Sage stepped her feet together, windmilling her arms, one arm over her head and one out below her before they switched positions. She stepped back on one foot, extending the other leg so she was in a reverse lunge while simultaneously pulling her arms back to one side so that her body twisted. With her hands in fists, she extended her right hand out toward the feather and lifted her fingers.

A thread of wind grabbed the feather, and it fluttered upward. She extended the fingers of her other palm, and a second thread of wind began to guide the feather along. She danced: stepping, lifting, bending, twisting, extending, and pulling. The feather, as if tied to a marionette's string, floated into the temple and hovered over the insignia.

With a final flourish of both hands downward, and a bend of her knees, the feather sank to the center. Sage paused, not daring to move for several seconds, focusing on releasing the threads she had just pulled and prodded before she looked at Raphael.

His wide grin bounced back to her, and she jumped up and down on the spot, "I did it! I did it! Raph...I did it!" and she ran to the fae, where they hugged in celebration.

"I never had any doubts," Raphael replied in delight.

A bird's call broke through the clearing, and Gavin's hawk-eagle form swooped through in celebration before flying back into the sky. The bird circled twice more before disappearing from view.

Sage rolled her eyes, but her grin never faltered. "Thank you, Raph," she replied, "Now...can we go home? I'm starved."

Gavin landed on the balcony of the Obelisk. Meliza and Zeke stood on the balcony, scanning the bay that led to the city. Veritasailles, despite being Felysia's capital, held no port for trade or welcoming sea-faring visitors. The idea was to keep the city safe from sea-based attacks. Gavin shifted from his bird form when neither fae turned to welcome him, or even acknowledged his presence.

"What is it?" Gavin asked. He wasn't sure he wanted to learn what made the two so focused, so uneasy. At the same time, he'd be damned if he was caught unawares.

"There have been sightings of human ships, steering towards Maracadia," Zeke replied.

"Okay," said Gavin. "Meropoli and Maracadia have trade agreements that span centuries. That should seem normal."

"Yes-" Meliza interjected, turning to face Gavin for the first time. "But there were no humans, no sailors at all spotted on the ships. Maracadia has the vessels incapacitated, for now, their island's enchantments are working."

The implication of humanless, mortal ships settled onto Gavin. That's why the two commanders gazed into the sea. If there were bespelled ships heading towards Maracadia, how long would it take before ships aimed for Felysia? And what was held below deck?

"Tell Symon I won't need to accompany Sage and Raph anymore. She's begun controlling wind. I can do more air patrols across the sea."

Zeke snorted. "Oh, no you don't, youngin. Tomorrow, you'll take the girl for her robes fitting for the feast. And *you* get to pick up your robes as well."

Gavin groaned. He hated dress robes. He'd much rather wear his training or sentry uniform.

"And after that," continued Meliza, "You'll head to Mystaira. There's a handful of citizens who need reminding of who's in charge. We have two more weeks until the feast. You'll use that time to remind your citizens you are the Lord of the region, even if we haven't ordained you yet."

Meliza placed her hand on Gavin's shoulder when he dropped his head back, sighing with frustration. "Like it or not Gavin, you are a powerful fae. And that comes with responsibility. Mystaira is yours."

Without warning, the two commanders disappeared, casting back into the city they were so intent to protect. Gavin walked to the edge of the balcony, staring across the water before shifting back into bird form. A few hours of air patrol would likely not prevent anything, but it was better than sulking in his room, trying to avoid the girl he couldn't stop thinking about no matter how hard he tried.

Chapter 12

***

Walking down a crowded street with street lights buzzing overhead, she was dressed in a short black skirt, black fishnet stockings, thick black boots, a black shirt, and a black jacket. Black, just like her heart, she joked to herself. Her cinnamon hair was covered by a short blue wig, and fake piercings adorned her nose and lip. Her make-up, stolen from a drug store, was applied heavily tonight; eyeliner as thick as the rubber soles of her boots, and she wore dark, wine-colored lipstick.

It was the kind of outfit that was equal parts memorable while saying don't fucking talk to me—unless I grant permission. The kind of outfit that would have guys buying her drinks and backing off if she decided she preferred someone else's company. It was always a risk, going out like this; but sometimes she just had to...blow off some steam- feel the touch of someone else. It was worth it on those days when the reality of her life became more than she could bear. She'd find a loud place to blend in, get shitfaced, maybe find someone to go home with, and then move on with her life. Distraction. That was what she was after tonight.

Sage turned down an alley. She'd just gotten to Techeduin a few days ago. Having run out of cities to hide in, she'd decided the most unlikely place they'd go looking for her would be their own backyard, and she had already scoped out the area. Turning down an alley, she headed towards the underground dance hall. Taking the steps into the dark, she mentally noted any potential threats, anyone who seemed out of place. Then allowed the sound and vibration of the loud music to fill her bones, the tension beginning to leave her muscles.

The bar was dark, colder inside than it was outside to accommodate the writhing bodies on the dance floor. Strobing lights flared across the space at random, and a DJ meshed together tracks that were probably familiar to patrons who weren't normally trying to remain unseen in public. The music was mechanical; hard, driving beats supporting digital melodies.

She strutted to the bar like a lioness waking from her slumber, making eye contact with several men on the way. She had a stash of money back in the place she was squatting, but left it there so she wouldn't be tempted to use it on booze or drugs. A lean man in his thirties approached the bar, getting there at exactly the same time she did. Got him, she thought to herself. For some reason, the first guy always ended up being at least ten years older than her. She supposed she understood what would make a woman in her early twenties attractive to them, but if she thought about it too much it gave her the creeps.

"What are you drinking?" the man asked with a smirk. Ugh...she could tell he'd spent at least as long as she had getting ready to come here. His teeth glowed unnaturally under the blacklights, proof of his whitening routine. She couldn't decide if his cologne was pleasant or not, but assumed it might have been palatable had he used less. He was lean and muscled, of average height, and in daylight was probably artificially tanned. In other words, he was the type of guy good for buying drinks, but would be hopeless if she were looking for conversation.

Nevertheless, she grinned and said to the bartender, "Shot of tequila and an amber ale."

"Tequila...my kind of girl," the man said with a wink.

He fidgeted with his shirt collar, unbuttoning the top two buttons to show just a bit of his bare chest. Gods, he really was going to be insufferable. Sage just smiled, lifting the shot in a salute to the man. She threw the shot back and chased it with several large gulps of her beer.

"So what's your name?" the man asked.

"Lonnie," Sage lied.

He grimaced, "Isn't that a dude's name?"

She shrugged, taking another sip of her beer. The man motioned to the bartender, and two more shots of tequila appeared before them.

"Ok," said Sage, "but you're going to have to buy me another beer," she finished with a sweet smile.

He bought her a second beer, and Sage chugged the first, handing the empty bottle to the bartender. Sage and the strange man clinked their shot glasses, turned them up and she chased it down with her beer. He watched her drink and began prattling off something about her awesome outfit; his voice faded completely from her attention around the time when he began questioning whether all her hair was blue. Even not paying attention to what he was saying, she had to force herself to stop the eye-roll at his suggestive innuendo.

Sage scanned the dance floor, decided she'd had enough company for the time being, and chugged her beer before he could ask her any more questions. She slammed the bottle down onto the bar top, burped loudly, then said with all the iciness she could muster, "Thanks for the drinks," and stalked to the dancefloor.

Her dismissal of him obviously went over smashingly, as Sage could hear him over the thumping music curse her as she left him at the bar. She entered the dancefloor, blending in with the other dancing bodies. Women carrying trays of fluorescent-colored drinks walked around. If she played her cards right, she might be able to swipe one.

She wasn't sure how long she danced. She lost herself in the music and the feeling of other people brushing against her, consumed by the feeling of bodies next to her, not caring about who she was or why she was there. It was the feeling of belonging to a sea of others that had her so lost in sensation. So lost, she hadn't realized how much she'd pissed off the glowing-teeth man. She was dancing with another man, younger, likely close to her in age if she'd paid attention, when Glowing Teeth Guy yanked her by her elbow. "You owe me a dance, at least," he demanded.

Sage jerked her elbow away, "I don't fucking owe you anything."

"I bought you four drinks. I ought to make you suck my dick for that."

Sage grit her teeth, demanding the flames under her skin to stay put. "Like I said before, I don't owe you anything. I didn't see a contract placed in front of me before you asked me what I drink. Maybe next time, you should make sure you are actually talking to a whore before you try to close a deal," said Sage, with so much honey-sweetness it came out more like acid. Apparently, he also didn't like that.

Glowing Teeth Guy lunged for her, so quick she almost didn't recognize the threat, the alcohol dulling her reflexes. She evaded his grab but bumped into one of the women carrying drinks. Before she could gather her balance, the man grabbed her by her waist and pulled her up against him.

"No one turns me down, baby. Come on, we're dancing," he said between his teeth.

Sage twisted in his arms and elbowed him in the stomach. Deciding that he'd had enough, the man grabbed Sage by her neck and slammed her against a wall. Stars popped from behind her eyes, and she gasped as she tried to claw his hand from her neck. She was struggling to breathe, trying with all her might to keep her power in check and pry his fingers from her neck.

"Not so tough now, are you, slut?" he crooned in her ear, squeezing harder.

Shit. Shit-shit-shit-shit-shit... Where was security? Usually they made it to her way before things got this bad. He was leaning into her face, aiming to assault her mouth with his when something barreled into him. The younger guy from before seemed to have finally figured out what was going on and tackled the guy to the floor. With a short struggle and two quick hits to the face, Glowing Teeth Guy was knocked unconscious.

"You okay?" Younger Guy asked, a small trickle of blood smeared below his nose.

He was still straddling the unconscious man and had twisted just enough so he could see her. Sage nodded, still catching her breath. She offered him a hand to stand up. The place was so crowded, no one else seemed to have noticed what just happened. She rubbed at her neck, feeling the place where the man's hand had squeezed, and winced. It would probably start bruising within the next few minutes. Younger Guy noticed and pulled out a wand; quickly waving it over her, she felt immediate relief as his healing spell washed over her skin.

"Hey— I know another place...It's a bit different than this, but pricks like him don't usually end up there. Wanna go?" he grinned.

"Depends," Sage answered, rubbing her throat in admiration of his skill, "What's in it for me?"

He grinned, "How about I buy you a beer? In reparation for assholes like that? A token of apology from the stupider sex."

She laughed, "Oh, you're good. Does this place have a name?" She didn't think this guy was more of a threat, but he was stupid to think she'd go to his place...yet.

"The Engine Room. It's more of a live music venue. Like I said, much different than this. Better lighting," he said the last line with a smirk on his face.

She couldn't help her answering grin, and nodded, "Yeah, all right. But I'm not paying a cover."

He grabbed her hand and began leading her through the crowded bar, onto the streets beyond. After a thirty-minute walk, they made it to the bar. The fresh air and walk had managed to kill whatever buzz she had before, and she hoped he'd make true of his promise to buy her a beer. They stepped in the door, and her jaw dropped. He was right, this was different.

Whereas the bar before was cold, dark, and almost sterile in appearance, The Engine Room possessed a type of grimy, cozy ambiance that immediately had Sage smiling, despite herself. Nautical elements and mementos flooded the burgundy walls, and a long, shiny mahogany bar top spanned one side of the room. A small stage graced the neighboring wall, and a smattering of tables lined the third wall. Two levels of balconies rimmed the tall bar, and people mingled, drank their beers, or danced in front of the band onstage.

The punk band was in the middle of a song about a girl in fishnet stockings and combat boots when Younger Guy gestured, "Ehh? Perfect timing. They're singing your song."

He waggled his eyebrows a bit and she elbowed him playfully, "I thought you were trying to make your gender look good, not cheesy."

"Looks like I owe you two drinks then," he said.

Just then two guys yelled from the bar, "Oi! Ian! Fuck you doin?!"

"I'm looking for your ugly ass," Ian replied and gestured for Sage to follow him to the bar. Ian made it to the two men and grabbed hands with one, pulling him into a hug. The other guy landed a light punch to Ian's shoulder, and Ian ordered a pitcher of beer. They each grabbed a glass, Ian carrying the pitcher as well, and headed to the second level to find a table.

As they sat down, the taller of the men asked, "Who's this then?"

"I'll tell you mine, if you tell me yours," answered Sage.

The tall man answered, "My name's Brion. This," he said, pointing to the man with rich, dark skin, "is Duncan. And clearly, you met Ian already. I'll go ahead and tell you, he's the ugliest of the three of us, and he's horrible in bed."

Ian nearly spit his drink out when Sage purred, "Oh...please, tell me more. I'd love to know the story of how you learned that. I've always imagined what boy sleepovers are like."

Duncan nearly fell backwards out of his chair as he threw his head back in a laugh that bellowed through the second level. Ian continued to choke on his beer, and Brion's eyes went from wide to narrowed, "Why is it the pretty girls are always the cleverest?" he said playfully.

Sage shrugged, and Duncan replied, smacking Brion on the back, "The Gods made it so you'd have to wise up a little before you could actually go around and fuck all of Techeduin."

The four of them laughed over the idea of Brion's apparent bed-lust before Brion cheerfully asked again, "So, who are you?"

She was just about to answer when the band abruptly finished their song. The sudden silence emphasized the sound as her stomach rumbled loudly. She tried not to blush, realizing how obvious it was to the others that she was starving. Honestly, she was surprised she wasn't more drunk, considering how little food she had in her belly.

Before anyone could comment, Ian rose to his feet and said, "I was going to order some grub. Anyone want anything?" Brion and Duncan threw a couple of bills at him, prattling off their requests.

Sage, realizing now was opportune timing, decided she needed the ladies' room and headed off in that direction.

Ian was back at the table, with a second pitcher of beer, and promises that a server would be dropping off their food shortly. Duncan produced a deck of cards, and they proceeded to teach Sage the game of tails, a fast-paced card game that required little strategy, but quick reflexes. After some time, a server dropped off plates of sandwiches and fried potatoes, and a third pitcher of beer. They ate, drank, played cards, and had a wonderfully carefree time. By one in the morning, the band on the stage announced that a drinking competition would take place, the winning team receiving a year-long open bar tab for free, with some minor stipulations. Duncan shot to his feet, "Let's go, lets go lets go lets go!" and he ran to each of them, practically throwing each of them out of their chair.

"No. No way, I'm already drunk. I don't need a hangover tomorrow," Ian drawled. Brion put his hands up, "Nah, man. You get way too competitive in these things. I'd like to still be friends with your sorry ass when we finally leave."

"You guys are no fun, come on! You're in, right?" Duncan was staring at Sage; she had no idea why, but she couldn't say no to his wide-with-excitement eyes. "I'm in!" she shouted, raising her empty beer glass.

"Fine...I can't leave a girl to take my place as your best friend," Brion said, rolling his eyes, "I'm in."

Everyone looked at Ian. "No," he said. As a group, they all stuck their bottom lip out, "Gods, why do I introduce any-one to you two? You corrupt absolutely everyone. Fine..," he said, rubbing one hand down his face, "I'm in."

In the end, their team finished in fourth place. Fourth...out of five teams.

"Well, Duncan. Congrats on getting us drunker'n a sailor's tits," Brion drawled.

"What does that even mean?!" said Sage with a laugh. The four of them stumbled out of the bar, the guys split-ting the remaining tab. Brion and Duncan left Sage and Ian at the corner when Ian asked, "Where do you live? I'll walk you home."

Not wanting to show him the vacant building she'd been squatting in, she sighed, "Why don't you just walk me to your place instead."

Ian hesitated, and looked at Sage through narrowed eyes, "My place? And what do you think you'll find there?"

"Your place," repeated Sage, "And I don't know what I'll find. That's half the fun."

Ian hesitated a few moments more, and then seemed to make a decision. With a tilt of his head, he began walking in the opposite direction of Brion and Duncan.

It took almost an hour to walk to his house, and somehow Sage felt more drunk by the time they got there than when they'd left The Engine Room. Ian seemed to have suffered the same effects as they stumbled up a large wooden porch, Ian fumbling over some sort of locking spell to get his door to open. Sage stepped over the threshold, leaning into his side as he put his arm around her, and she admired the large, cozy sitting room that greeted them. Beyond an oversized lounge chair, she could see a comfortable kitchen and stairs to her left that must lead to bedrooms. He must do alright for himself, thought Sage, for being my age and living in such a nice place. "Nice place," she admitted out loud, walking toward the couch and leaning against its back.

"Uh- thanks. Couldn't afford it without a roommate, being so close to the University and all."

"How does a student afford a place like this, even with a roommate?" It might be rude, but she couldn't help her curiosity.

Ian, fumbling with his jacket and knocking over the coat rack, hesitated to respond. Finally, he shrugged, "I'm a researcher. I do some patent work and alchemical design work. Some of it is paid for through government contracts. Among other things."

"You work for the government?" She tried to hide the alarm in her voice but wasn't sure she succeeded.

Having righted the coat rack, Ian shrugged once more. "Sometimes. It's probably better if I don't get into it, honestly." That was good enough for Sage, and she walked further into the house, noting the homey furnishings.

Ian shut the door with his foot and muttered the locking spell under his breath. Sage heard the satisfactory sound of bolts clicking into place and she turned to face him as he walked to her. Leaning the full length of her body into his, she grinned up at him, and he wrapped his arms around her, grinning back at her.

"I...think I need some water," Sage giggled, just as a hiccup escaped her bosom. Ian snorted, shaking his index finger in the air as he led her into the kitchen, "A great idea." He filled glasses of water from the tap, and Sage leaned against a corner made of butcher block countertops. They smiled at each other as they sipped their water, Ian on one side of the sink, Sage on the other. Ian finished his glass, setting it on the counter, and stared at Sage as she slowly finished hers.

As she placed her glass carefully on the counter, he prowled over to her, "Your hair...it's um...crooked," he chuckled when he reached her. He leaned against her, pushing the front of his body against hers. She reached up, and pulled the blue wig off, tossing it on the counter next to her water. Her cinnamon hair fell to her jawline, and Ian brushed it out of her eyes. "What other secrets do you have?" Ian whispered, leaning his mouth against her neck, brushing his lips just behind her ear. A small, breathy gasp escaped Sage's throat, and she pushed him back, grinning like a sphinx. Without saying a word, she reached up to her face and removed the false piercings. Ian took the movement as an invitation, and leaned his face in, pushing his lips into hers. Sage opened for him and felt as he braced his arms on either side of her, pushing his body into hers. His lips were soft, and he caressed her mouth with gentle probes, a question of how far he should go. Sage cupped the back of his head, pressing him harder against her. That was all he needed, and Ian dragged his mouth from hers, running his lips along her jawline, nipping at the sensitive spot just between her ear and jaw. Sage pulled him harder still, demanding he go further. His hand slid to her, caressing her back, then dragging to her ribcage as he worked his way from one side of her neck to the other. A gasp escaped her, and she could feel his hardness answer as if she were beckoning him to go, keep going.

His hand worked up her front, cupping her breast and she moaned, hard. He was back at her mouth, this time demanding her to take. Her hands slid from his head, making their way down his back. As he slid his mouth away again, moving along the edges of her blouse, kissing and licking the parts of exposed breast that peaked from her shirt, she dug her nails into his back. He scooped her off the floor, setting her firmly on the counter. Her legs opened for him, and he pushed his body into her as he ripped her jacket off and began unbuttoning her blouse. He was halfway there when he stopped, eyes wide and muttered, "Shit...my roommate."

"Your room?" Sage questioned, and Ian scooped her off the counter. Sage wrapped her legs around him and he carried her to his room up the stairs, slamming the door with his foot. He was still holding her when she lifted her blouse over her head and he laid her on the bed. With thinly concealed restraint, Ian went back to her breasts, caressing them with his mouth as he removed her bra.

"Gods," Sage moaned as he took her breast into his mouth and she felt herself become liquid. Sage yanked at Ian's shirt and threw it on the ground. He laid against her, intent to work his way down her body again, and she moaned at the contact of his skin brushing against hers. With every kiss, and lick, and bite he gave, she felt her core become more slick in anticipation, his hardness a thundering echo of demand.

As he returned to her mouth once more, Sage ran her hand down the front of his body, and slid her palm home, under his pants. He shuddered, muttering, "Fuck," when she wrapped her fingers around him and squeezed lightly. She could feel the need throbbing along his shaft as she ran her hand upward once. That was all he could take, and Ian lifted away from her and quickly pulled her skirt and stockings off. He was tugging at his own pants as she removed her underwear when they heard the front door slam.

Quick, lively steps echoed through the house, and suddenly, Sage heard a woman's voice yell, "Ian?!" Sage sat bolt right, nearly knocking Ian in the nose. The question was written on her face as the woman again called, "Ian?!"

"Shit...it's my roommate."

"You live with a woman?" Sage demanded in a whisper. Ian was tugging his shirt back on, heading to the door as he sheepishly admitted, "Well...my mom. I live with my mom. Just...stay right there. Just like that. I'll be right back, I swear." Ian stumbled out of the door with one last look at Sage lying on his bed.

Sage snorted, trying to hold back her hysterics at his clumsiness, at the way he tried to conceal his circumstances. Honestly, for some reason, she found it utterly hilarious, charming even, that he called his mom his roommate. She wouldn't have cared; beyond the fact it was just one more person to consider seeing her away from her hiding place. Shit...a lot of people had seen her. Ian was taking longer explaining to his mom what was going on upstairs than she had expected. She grew cold and burrowed into his blankets. At some point, her eyes drifted closed. She thought she heard the door click shut, and tried to open her eyes, but decided against it as she felt lips press against her temple and footsteps move away again. In the distance, she could hear the sounds of a bathroom, running water, cabinets opening and closing; the last thing she recalled was a warm body pressing against her, a sigh followed by an easing of muscles.

She woke the next morning, disoriented, but grinning as she rolled over and found Ian laying against her, his arm draped around her waist. She stared at his sleeping face; even in sleep, she could tell he had kind, playful eyes. His fair hair, cut short to the scalp, complimented his fair coloring. He laid in bed shirtless, like her, and she admired his lean body. Not overly muscled, he had the kind of youthful physique that showed he led an active life but didn't seem to pay too much attention to his looks.

As quietly as she could, she lifted herself from the bed, taking care to place his hand gingerly onto the bed. She tiptoed around his room, slipping her skirt and boots on before grabbing one of his oversized flannel shirts draped over his desk chair. She spotted a canvas shopping bag and dumped her wig, which he must have brought up the night before, shirt and jacket into it. With every ounce of stealth she had acquired from her years on the run, Sage slipped from Ian's home and began the trek back to her headquarters. She kept her senses sharp as she wound her way through the streets of Techeduin, passing buses and cars busily making their way across the city. Shops were just opening, and she forced herself to ignore the tempting smells of bakeries and eateries getting ready for their morning rush.

Sage had made it back to her abandoned building, and taking the time to circle it twice, checking for anyone spying or following her, she wedged herself through a small opening in a boarded-up window. Sprinting up two floors brought her to the camp she'd set up. She tossed the canvas bag into the corner and began rummaging through her collection of snacks. She'd managed to swipe a full bag of apples the other day, a nice addition to her usual assortment of crackers, dried meats, and canned soups. Just as she bit into her apple, she heard a commotion on the first floor. Grabbing her kitchen knife and her wand, she ducked into the hallway and ran into the room she'd set up to hide from intruders. After several minutes of no following noises, no approaching footsteps, or any other signs of life, she crept down the stairs to investigate. Most likely the noise was from a feral animal in search of food or shelter. It wouldn't be the first time she'd learned to share space with the local animals.

A quick walk around the first floor declined to offer any answers, so she made her way back up to her living space upstairs. She stepped on the landing and quickly walked back to her room. She had her back to the entrance when she heard, "You know...it's like you forget we can do magic. You didn't even put up one defensive jinx."

Slowly, she turned; shit...she knew she'd forgotten something.

Ian was there, leaning against the doorway, arms folded.

"What are you doing here?" Sage demanded.

"Well, for one, you have my shirt. That happens to be my favorite shirt, and I'd kinda like it back." Sage made to unbutton the shirt, determined to fling it back to him when he held up his hand, "No, keep it for now. That's not what I'm here for. What I really came for...I got the sense you might be set up in something like this. Why are you living here?"

"That's really none of your business," Sage snapped, squaring her feet below her.

"I'm not trying to harass you. I just thought you could use some help," Ian replied calmly.

"I'm fine. I will be just fine. Don't worry."

"You never told me your name," Ian prodded.

"Lonnie," snapped Sage.

"Sure...and what's your real name?" Ian pressed. "I knew you wouldn't tell me honestly the first time, but something tells me you might want to."

Sage took a step back from him, contemplating how to proceed. "Why do you care?"

Ian shrugged, "Dunno. But I do."

She turned away from him; what was she doing? She rubbed both hands over her face, whipped back around, and said, "Sage. But if you tell anyone...I will..." she trailed off. What was she going to do? Kill him?

"Don't worry. I won't tell a soul. You can be Lonnie to everyone else."

Ian started walking around her room, noting the bedroll in the center, her little vanity set-up, complete with a stolen hand mirror and a full set of make-up swiped from various pharmacies. He nudged her go-bag with his toe before turning to her again. "I think you should stay with us."

Sage snorted, "Yeah..ok. Nothing creepy in that."

"We have an extra room. My mom thought about renting it, but I know if we told her your situation, whatever lie you want to make up about your situation is fine, I know she'll just let you stay there. She works at the university, I bet she could even find a place for you to work, make a little cash of your own. You don't ever have to sleep in my room again if you don't want. That's not what I'm here for."

Sage looked at Ian flatly, "And if I want to sleep in your room?" Without so much as cracking a smile, ignoring her attempt to bait him, Ian replied, "We can cross that road if we get there. What I'm saying, is you'd have a safe place to live, no strings attached. It's up to you."

Sage stared at him for a long time. She looked around her room, realizing just how pathetic her setup was, and suddenly feeling rather embarrassed that he was there in her slum.

"Just, give it a try. For a week. And if it doesn't work for you, you can leave and I won't follow you. No judgment." Sage gave the thought one more full minute of thought, glued to her spot, before she snapped, "Fine. One week. Just, give me a minute to get my things. You can wait downstairs."

She hadn't decided if she was going to go with him or just escape through one of her emergency exits as she tossed her make-up kit into the canvas bag she'd swiped from his house, when the thought of working at the university occurred to her. That was the point of hiding in Techeduin, after all. She knew Techeduin's university housed the biggest collection of elemental resources, books that might explain who she was and why Ranquer might be after her. That was the deciding factor, she told herself, as she stomped her way downstairs and met Ian. A look of relief broke over his face as he grabbed the canvas bag from her and they made their way back to his house.

Back at the house, Ian took her up to the spare room, showing her where everything was, promising to help her buy fresh clothes if she'd be interested.

Sage leaned against a chest of drawers with a mirror attached to it, realizing this would be the first time in five years she would be living with real furniture. The thought overwhelmed her, and Ian noticed her quiet disposition.

He made his way back to her, concern written on his face, "What's wrong?"

She shook her head, "Nothing." She looked into Ian's eyes, and pushed into him, tilting her face upward in invitation. He gently lowered his mouth to hers and caressed her mouth with his. Her hands drifted to the shirt that she wore and began unbuttoning it as his hands slid under the shirt. She gasped as his mouth found her neck and—

Sage rolled over in her bed, waking to sunlight flooding her room. "Just at the good part," she groaned to herself. She froze as she saw who sat in her room, grinning like a cat with a mouse he had cornered. "What are you doing here?" Sage growled at Raphael.

"Well, I was concerned when all our fireplaces lit at once, but it seems we were just recovering a memory? Obviously, it was a good one." he teased.

"Get out!" she shouted, tossing her pillow at him. He casted to the neighboring chair just before the pillow hit where he had been sitting.

"Tisk, tisk...so feisty!"

"OUT!" she commanded, and Raphael casted away from her room. She moaned in agony in her bed. Why? Why her? She asked herself. She rolled out of bed, still feeling the pressure of desire lingering from her dream, her memory, and decided a cold bath was in order before she could be seen in public.

She drew her bath and slipped into the frigid water, hoping the temperature would drive away the heat lingering and building in her core. After several minutes of agony, and relief still seeming eons away, Sage decided to take a different route. Using a combination of her water and fire magic, Sage heated the water to a comfortable temperature.

Tilting her head back against the tub, she closed her eyes and let herself relive those moments with Ian. She lifted her hands to her neck, allowing herself to caress her neck, her shoulders, and then finding their way to her breasts, heavy with want. She allowed one hand to continue descending, across the plane of her stomach, and lower. She kept her eyes closed, imagining Ian's touch as she found the center joining of her legs.

As she slid home, she gasped as a different face entered her imagination. Altering between a fair-haired man and the face of a dark-haired, tanned fae, Sage continued working her body until she finally found release. With a shudder, she allowed herself to relax into the water, willing her body to find calm.

Chapter 13

Gavin could smell her halfway up the stairs from the dining room to the balcony. The scent of honey, sage, and citrus were intensified in a way that suggested a certain...train of thought. She was standing at the railing that looked over the city, a plate of food balanced on the banister. Her cinnamon hair whipped away from her face and his breath caught as he stared at her.

She turned and he couldn't help but smile at the blush that immediately flooded her face, her neck. Her hand absentmindedly raised to her neck, and he heard her breath catch as he strode closer to her.

"Who are you thinking about?" Gavin teased.

"What?" Sage gasped. "What do you mean?"

"I mean, normally when someone blushes like that, they are having some pretty...pleasant thoughts." He waggled his eyebrows at her, hoping to push her a little further.

"Gods...you are all insufferable," Sage snapped. He couldn't help but notice the smell of want increase around her.

"Insufferable? I can agree with that. Fae are horrible at minding their own business."

She smirked, rolling her eyes as he walked to stand next to her. He hadn't noticed before, but her eyes were mesmerizing. He smiled in response as she stepped back, pushing herself against the pillar at her back. Her scent danced toward him on a breeze, more enticing than he had ever realized. He couldn't stop himself from stepping closer, unable to break his stare from hers. Her breathing increased, and damn if it didn't have the same effect on him. Her hand lingered on her throat, and he could hardly resist the urge to put his hand over it, to find out if her skin felt as soft as it looked.

His stare snagged on the soft swell of her breast, just visible over the edge of her dress. He was close enough now he could feel the soft thrum of power rolling off of her. The vibrato of power hummed around her, pulling him closer and closer to her. He realized he'd been lying to himself, that he didn't know why he was drawn to her. She was breathtaking. She was the embodiment of free will, untethered, drifting like the wind.

He brushed a strand of hair from her face as the wind pulled against it, and his control snapped when she gasped and closed her eyes. He leaned in, pressing his mouth into hers. Surprisingly, she opened for him, pulling him by his shirt closer to her.

In a moment he had her against the wall, kissing her. She kissed back in urgency. Her lips were soft. Her skin was soft. And she was warm, like sunshine. Her kiss felt like liberation. His hand wrapped around her neck, cradling her head, as his other arm wrapped around her waist. He pulled her closer, barely stopping a groan from escaping as her heat washed over him. He kissed her again, gripping tightly to the short leash of control he still commanded.

She pushed him away, "I need to get out of here." He could feel heat radiating from her palms, more intense now than moments before. "I need somewhere quiet. With water."

Pulling himself back into focus, he searched his mind for the perfect place to take her, "I know a place."

With all his years of training, Gavin willed his body to remain under his control as he lifted her into his arms, wings spreading behind him. He flew over the city, aiming toward the edge of the city boundaries.

Her hands were nearly scorching when they landed, and he had to grit his teeth to keep from imagining how they'd feel against his bare skin as he placed her on the ground.

They walked across an old bridge, the Philisian River running below it. Gavin kept his focus on the path but noticed Sage panting. Discomfort seemed to course through her, and that longing to shelter her, to make her smile resurfaced.

"This is an old trade route," Gavin explained, "Just a ways ahead of us we will find a creek. No one really uses this route into the city anymore. Actually, if you follow that path it'll lead to Mystaira." Gavin pointed down the larger road as they veered away from it, following a game trail into the woods. She nodded but didn't offer anything in return. He could see the focus to manage her power as she held her body tight, stiff, and began walking faster.

A few more minutes' walk brought them to a creek, babbling over rocks and boulders. Sage staggered to it, splashing into the water, allowing her dress to soak in the babbling brook. She fell to her hands and knees in the cool water, and he watched as she breathed deeply. After a few moments, she sat up on her knees, closing her eyes and beginning breathing patterns resembling what she'd practiced at the wind temple. Deciding to do his best to not disrupt her, Gavin found a flat, dry spot to sit down and watch.

Sage gracefully rose to her feet, and Gavin watched as she began moving. She stepped, lifted onto her toes, windmilled her arms, bent her knees, and floated into stances and poses. All the while shapes, ripples, and waves appeared and disappeared in the creek. At one point, she had gathered all the water on one side so that it formed a massive wall of water, damming the water behind it, before ultimately slamming the water down. In the process, she managed to soak him and about fifteen feet of the bank.

He was in awe. As far as he knew, she hadn't practiced water wielding at all with Raphael. After over an hour of her practice, she finally dropped back to her knees with a deep breath. Mist hung in the air and it almost looked like she was wrapped in rainbows. The sound of the creek seemed to applaud her performance. As she looked up at him, Gavin was struck by her beauty. Her hair was slicked back away from her face, drenched from the water. Her dress clung to her body, highlighting the dips and curves of her frame. The sun itself shone down on her like a celestial spotlight. In that moment, she was as radiant as the Goddess herself.

"Thank you," she whispered.

Gavin rose to his feet and offered her his hand. He could feel the tremble in her hand, her arms, a sign of the exhaustion she'd worked herself into. "Better?" Gavin asked.

Sage nodded, "And starving."

Gavin gathered her back into his arms, contemplating whether they should risk a visit into the city with both of them soaked as they were. Ultimately, he decided he didn't want anyone else seeing her with her dress plastered against her body the way it was, and brought her back to the tower.

He walked her to the kitchen, and with a wink said, "Thanks for the show," and strode back down the hall to catch up on his sentry duty. He could have sworn he heard her whisper, "Gods," as he made his way up the stairwell.

Sage was left dripping wet in the kitchen. The wood-burning oven was still alight from the morning breakfast rush, and Sage coaxed the air and flames to work together to dry her clothes. Sage called into the back bedroom, and a sleepy Hyacinth walked into the kitchen.

"Did I wake you?" Sage asked, palms still lifted to the fireplace.

"I was just taking a nap. Couldn't sleep last night."

"Dreams?" Sage asked knowingly.

Hyacinth nodded her answer as she walked towards the tea kettle and used her powers to fill it with water. Despite being sleepy, the female worked quickly to produce a pleasant spread of tea, small sandwiches, and cookies she'd stored away deep in the pantry. After stepping in one of the puddles from Sage's dripping dress, Hyacinth finally asked, "Why is my floor so wet?"

"Sorry about that. Turns out I'm really good at water magic," Sage answered.

"So that means I can have you work on tea and washing fruits and veggies instead of burning bread every morning?"

Hyacinth laughed when Sage gaped at her. "I don't burn the bread *every* morning!"

"If you say so," Hyacinth shrugged in response. "So...who took you to the water? Raph? Or Gavin?"

Sage cleared her throat a little before replying. She wasn't sure why she was hesitant to answer, or why she blushed when telling Hyacinth, "Gavin."

"Ohhh! I knew it! Tell me all about it. What happened?"

"What do you mean 'What happened?' Nothing happened. He just took me to the creek."

"Oh no. Something happened. Come on. You have to tell me; you woke me up from my nap after all."

Sage hesitated. This wasn't a big deal. They were both grown. There wasn't any reason for her to feel embarrassed. Except that the image of Ian kept replaying in her mind. Was she being dishonest? Should she have let it go so far with Gavin?

Quietly, she admitted, "He...kissed me."

Hyacinth's surprised face made Sage giggle nervously. She ran both hands down her face, a blush crept up her neck. "Why is this embarrassing? I shouldn't be embarrassed."

"Why would you be? Do you like him? He's good-looking."

"Good- looking?" Sage replied, laughing.

"I may not be able to talk to him, but I have eyes," Hyacinth explained. "Besides, so does he. I've seen how he looks at you."

Sage rolled her eyes, "Yeah, well. We'll see. Here, let me clean this up for you." Sage gathered up their dishes and began to tidy up the kitchen. The two pittered about the kitchen amiably, Hyacinth poking fun at Sage and both sharing stories from their past, as far as Sage could remember.

After cooking dinner, eating together, and cleaning up, Sage quickly ran to her room to change and then spent the night in Hyacinth's cozy room. It was the most normal feeling evening Sage could remember having. A bitter-sweet film of nostalgia coated the night as she thanked the gods for putting Hyacinth in her life, and prayed they watched over her own sister in Thuledain, worlds away.

The next morning, Gavin completed his air patrol quickly. His focus was on the task at hand for the day. He dreaded having to pick up his dress robes but was simultaneously curious to discover what the Queen had chosen for Sage.

He'd had dinner with the Queen the evening before. It was nice to finally have a moment with his old friend, and she couldn't hide her excitement when she explained she'd had a hand in designing Sage's robes. Not only that, Sage was to be the Queen's guest of honor. Symon had interjected when Gavin asked Aryael whether that was a smart decision given some of the citizens, his own people nevertheless, had begun raising concerns over leadership. News of disappearances and strange occurrences had started trickling throughout the continent. Not only was Felysia becoming wary, but other nations were beginning to reach out to allies in hopes of forestalling any major disasters. Symon's answering retort matched the weariness that seemed to cloak the King nowadays. Aryael, ever the optimist, had teased Symon until he eventually lightened up for the evening.

All of this was on his mind as he reached Sage's room. He knocked on her door but heard no response. He knocked again, pressing his ear to the door, straining to pick up any trace of her movement inside. After a third knock brought no response, he opened the door. The immediate lack of her scent in the room was enough to send him into high alert.

Could someone have broken through the wards on the Obelisk and taken her? Did she flee, somehow using wind power to glide to the ground?

As dread trickled through his veins, he heard a soft exhale of breath behind him at the door.

"If it isn't the Lord of Mystaira himself." Sage's voice was like a song as it danced across the room to him. Immediately, his shoulders relaxed, and he turned to find her leaning against the doorjamb, grinning like a cat.

"M'lady," Gavin replied, playfully bowing in her direction, quickly putting aside the anxiety he felt moments before. "I've come to escort you to your appointment."

"We are such dorks," Sage snorted.

Gavin grinned, "I don't understand the word, but if you are implying that I, the Great and Mighty Gavin, am anything less than mesmerizing, I take offense." He was grinning widely, obviously not offended at all, and enjoying the playful banter.

"Give me a few moments to finish getting ready?" She brushed past him as she headed towards the bathing room, and his heart thudded hard in his chest.

Swallowing thickly, he replied, "Sure. But be quick. I don't want to be late."

Sage's only answer was the click of the door.

Twenty minutes later, they were flying toward the city. He was still on edge as they entered the city, recalling their first trip to the market. His smile vanished as they landed, and his predatory instincts kicked in, allowing him to take in every detail of the commercial district they walked through.

The white stone buildings and red clay streets felt oppressive, and he had to suppress an urge to physically growl at any male fae who walked too closely by her. What was he doing? He'd never been the type of male to act possessively of another female. He'd been raised by his mother and sister to have irreverent respect for females and their autonomy.

They'd made it to the seamstress's business; a smallish building just a few scant blocks away from the palace. Gavin knew she was responsible for creating many of the royals' own garments and was slightly surprised Symon hadn't put up more of a fight over the choice of seamstress. Granted, Gavin knew that Symon stood little chance of convincing Aryael of changing her mind once it was made up.

They walked through the door, entering a dark, cool room, cluttered with full-length mirrors, spools and spools of fabric, and the sound of female chatter ringing through a back room. Gavin cleared his throat. An elderly fae female appeared in the doorway at the end of the room.

She was old, even by fae standards. Her face showed the signs of age with wrinkles, sun spots, and eyes that twinkled with the wisdom of a life long-lived. There was something more to her though. An expression of humor danced between the lines framing her eyes like she knew something no one else knew.

"You must be Sage, honored guest of Queen Aryael," said the old female. Sage nodded; "My name is Rahab. The Queen sent over some specific requests for your garments; we've nearly finished." The old seamstress smiled, ushering Sage to come to her. Rahab gestured to a small room, covered in tapestries, "Head in there, I will grab the dress, and we will begin the fitting."

Sage walked into the dressing room, closing the curtains behind her. Rahab bustled into the back, and entered with three other females, younger than Rahab, but none truly young. Rahab entered the dressing room, and Gavin could hear her instructing Sage as she stepped into the dress.

Miraculously, the dress seemed to fit Sage almost perfectly. His throat caught in his chest as she stepped through the curtains, heading to a raised stage designed to allow the seamstresses to pin and prod and fix.

The dress consisted of two layers; the bottom layer was a deep, vibrant emerald green that matched the eddies of her pale green eyes, while the top layer was a sheer material, iridescent and shining so that it looked like Rahab had caught a rainbow and wrapped Sage into it. Soft straps rested atop Sage's delicate shoulders, and two elegant swaths of fabric draped slightly down the tops of her arms. The empire waistline accentuated the slight dip of fabric at the center of her chest, accentuating her small but shapely breasts. The color, the shape, the texture of the dress elevated what was already beautiful. Then Rahab turned to another female, grabbing the sheer cape that would adorn her shoulders. Made of four panels, white, ruby red, cyan blue, and pale-sea green, the cape was embroidered in various shining threads of gold and silver, and adorned with small shining stones. The final touch was a headdress of delicate design; it looped over both sides of her head, along with a row of stones down the center, one large crystal marking the center and lying on her forehead. The females gasped.

"You look almost like the Goddess herself," Rahab beamed.

Sage looked at the cape. "These...the embroidery." She picked up the white panel, examining the delicate stitching. "These are the marks of Cerridos," she whispered.

Rahab nodded enthusiastically, "And Brighid, Allyra, and Therisyd. We know who you are, Realm Leaper. We've waited a long time to see another," said Rahab, bowing before stepping to Sage and embracing her, still grinning from ear to ear.

The statement hung in the air. Realm Leaper. Gavin had heard stories of Realm Leapers, of Cerridos and other gods visiting from other worlds. The thought of Sage being a Realm Leaper somehow hadn't occurred to Gavin. Even knowing so much of her backstory, dressed as she was, he couldn't help but wonder if she might actually be a goddess in disguise.

The seamstresses gathered themselves and began making small alterations to the robes. Sage remained standing on the pedestal and gaping at herself. After some convincing, Rahab agreed to close the dip of the dress just a little, which simultaneously relieved Gavin and filled him with regret. At least he'd had that one image of her; he doubted he'd ever forget it.

Once Rahab's alterations suited her expectations, the females set about fulfilling the other orders required. The first spectacular dress was for the formal reception and dinner which would follow. Sage would also be clothed in the traditional ceremonial clothes for the festival, an assortment of dresses and one-pieces of reds, golds, and ambers. She looked stunning in all of them, Gavin admitted to himself, but nothing compared to the green that she wore before. Rahab glanced toward him with a knowing smile, and he realized his thoughts had returned again to that dip in the dress, the one that revealed just enough of the swell of her breasts. He cleared his throat and began practicing the focus and determination he knew he would need to wield at the reception.

"And while I have you here, Young Lord," Rahab teased.

"Not Lord, yet," Gavin muttered.

Rahab waved him off impatiently, "I have your new uniform ready for the reception. It's been altered and set. Raquel will package it for you and bring it in," Rahab waved a hand, and one of the other females bustled to the back room.

"Oh, I see how it is. You get a preview, and I'm left to use my imagination?" Sage joked.

There was an insinuation in the comment Gavin wasn't sure she meant to make, and he cleared his throat as she seemed to realize what she said. He had to force himself back into focus, using immense willpower to compel himself not to imagine *her* imagining anything about him...especially not alone...in her room. Rahab laughed then, and he realized he'd failed.

Gavin swore under his breath, "I'll wait outside," he said as Raquel passed him a parcel containing his uniform.

They left the store shortly after. Rahab had ensured that all her robes would be sent directly to the palace, and would wait there for the reception. They walked down the busy street, stopping at a tavern for a simple dinner of roasted fish, grapes, hard cheese, and wine. They sat in a booth with an open window, the setting sun flooding Sage's skin as they ate. He found himself in awe then, seeing her in a way that hadn't ever quite occurred to him.

"Realm leaper," Gavin mused. "Is that what you are?"

Her eyes shifted, and he couldn't help but notice those dark lines of emerald, the smoky outline of dark grey-green.

"That's what I am," she replied. "'I don't know what it means, yet. But I recognized the term," Sage looked at Gavin, stared into his eyes, and he could tell she was contemplating how much more to tell him.

"That's fine," he whispered, "if you're not ready, you can tell me more later. When you're ready."

She nodded, taking a deep sip of her wine. "Let's go home," she said, her voice taking a huskier tone than he'd noticed. His heart thundered at those words.

The flight back to the Obelisk was torture; he tried not to notice the feel of her skin as she wrapped her hands around his neck, the feel of the front of her body as she pushed into him, clinging to him as he flew them up, up, up. He placed her gingerly back onto the balcony floor, and they stood there for a long moment holding each other.

"Thanks for the trip," she muttered, staring up at him. He nodded, distracted by the soft curves of her mouth.

He still had one arm around her, her arms wrapped around his neck. He dropped the parcel he was carrying to brush her hair from her face and whispered, "I have to leave, tonight. I'll be in Mystaira for the next two weeks on duty, but when I return we will move into the palace for the celebration."

Sage, still peering up at him, nodded. Her throat bobbed, and she looked like she might say something, but changed her mind. Slowly, he removed his hand from her back and stepped away. He felt her stiffen, then she said, "I guess I will see you when you get back then."

"Don't do anything silly like run off while I'm gone," he replied, and she rolled her eyes.

"You don't do anything silly, like get a big head and think I'll start following your orders." She smiled when he frowned down at her, then waved at him while heading towards the stairwell. "I'll be here when you get back."

Gavin stared at the empty stairwell after she left, feeling confused about their last conversation. He felt confused about how he felt. How had she gone from being a problem to solve, to whatever she was now? And why did he ache to touch her again?

Gavin didn't bother trying to figure it out. He shoved the parcel to the wall of the balcony and shifted into hawk form, launching himself into the sky towards the Tri-Goddess's temple. He would make an offering and send up a prayer; for what, he didn't know. He just needed some sort of sign that he was on the right path.

Chapter 14

Raphael was growing tired of being summoned to the King. Yes, Symon was the King, but Raphael was also the court's official healer. Not only was he in charge of maintaining the health and well-being of the Royal Family, but his duties extended to the city of Veritasailles. That included the sentries, who seemed determined to break as many of their bones in training as possible.

A sigh escaped from him as Symon continued on, explaining why Raphael must continue checking on Petra. "I've already told you, Symon, I cannot heal minds that are not ready to be healed."

Symon pinched the bridge of his nose, squeezing his eyes shut as he sank into the chair next to Raphael. "I know. But I can't help but worry for her."

Raphael leaned forward and squeezed his friend's hand. "No matter how much healing we achieve, it won't bring back the girl she was before."

Symon nodded. Quickly, he patted Raphael's hand and pushed out of his chair. "I didn't bring you here just about Petra. You've been summoned to the Rafalatriki. Shiphra has some new healers, and she thinks you are the best candidate for their orientation."

The Rafalatriki was an expansive commune in Mystaira where all of Felysia's healers went for training. Shiphra had trained Raphael herself and was known across fae lands as being the most skilled healer, possibly in fae history. A summons from her was not one a healer could refuse. Not even the King and Queen could deny such a call.

"I will leave this evening," Raphael nodded.

Symon tossed him a brown journal. "In the meantime, you will give this to the girl, so she can continue to record her memories as they return."

"You mean, so you can continue spying on her without her knowledge?" Raphael replied curtly. He recognized the same enchantments that adorned his own journal.

"Say what you like, Raph, but we still don't have the answers we need. We still need to know how and why she's he—"

They turned their heads towards the sound of stomping feet approaching the double door to Symon's study. Meliza, long blonde hair tied tightly in a low ponytail, wings shifting back into her, burst through them seconds later with such force, they banged into the walls on either side.

"Why is it that *my* spies can't give me the information I ask them for? I just received correspondence from Acantha and Epyllo informing me that they will tell *me* what they've learned after they speak with *you*."

She said the last word with a jab of her index finger in the air. She stood with her feet apart, her upper body leaning in towards her brother standing behind his desk. He was large, well-built even for a fae, but Meliza was the equal to him in female form. If it ever came down to a battle between them, excluding powers, it would be a fair fight, to say the least. Raphael doubted Meliza would let her brother forget that.

Symon placed a document he had just picked up back on his desk and exhaled deeply. Dropping his hand, he stared at Raphael with exasperation.

"Should I go?" Raphael asked. He could visit Aryael; he was on *her* council after all, despite Symon requiring his services so often of late.

"Stay," Symon ordered Raphael. Turning towards Meliza, Symon answered, "Because I've ordered Acantha and Epyllo not to tell anyone anything until they've corresponded with me first. Apparently, what they've discovered is not fit to be sent in writing."

Symon stared again at the document on the desk, leaning onto his palms. Raphael knew the contents. He and Symon had already discussed the cryptic response sent by the spies- *"We advise the city increase patrols and security. We will explain when we get there. -Epyllo"*

"Symon. What are you keeping from me? Tell me what you know. If it's about the girl...we can just put her in the dungeons for the time being, until Aryael's ceremonies are through. Tell me what you know," she repeated the last command through clenched teeth.

"The girl is not the problem. In fact, I think we may find that she is a boon from the Goddess herself," Raphael interjected. Symon glanced towards Raphael. Raph shrugged— they'd had this conversation multiple times over the last several weeks. Whether the King took his counsel, only time would tell.

Meliza exhaled sharply. "Respectfully, Raph, that doesn't answer any of the questions I've asked. Brother, how do you expect me to do my job, to protect you and Aryael, if I don't fully understand our threats?"

Meliza approached Symon, and he snapped his head upward to meet her glare, "Your job is not to protect your King and Queen. As you might remember, we can take care of ourselves. Your job is to protect the city, our people."

They stared at each other for a long moment, acknowledgment of the unspoken words hanging in the air. Understanding swept across her features; Symon and Aryael would die defending this city if need be. They would not allow their people to fall back into enslavement, to be tortured and slaughtered.

Meliza's face softened some, "So you're not going to tell me about the girl? About any of it?"

"I will tell you in due time; once I have all the pieces of the puzzle. Until then, I think having only parts of the story might...confuse the directive, cloud our judgment. I do have a request, however: that girl must be protected. Raphael is correct. Whatever threats are mounting, she is the key to surpassing them."

Meliza stood on the spot for a minute, then replied, "Fine. But you need to get yourself in order brother. We can't help you protect the city with only one eye open." Not waiting for a reply, she turned and left the study.

Well, at least Raphael had his answer. Sage was no longer the threat they had feared. What Symon thought she was? That answer would have to wait.

Raphael took his leave from the King. Maybe the Queen would divulge more.

Chapter 15

Gavin arrived at the formal estate that would one day become his, heading straight for the smaller home his family had claimed as their own. Once built as servants' quarters, the home was rustic, homey, and full of everything wonderful about his family. His mother's quilts hung over the backs of cozy chairs. Sturdy furniture and tables adorned every room, a testament of his father's craftsmanship. Books of all topics were scattered across the house, his brother's contribution as Levi continued his pursuit to answer every question that popped into his mind. And Delphia—well, she was the true master of the household. In many ways, he suspected she would have been a better candidate to lead Mystaira. He regretted not being able to spend more time visiting with his family and vowed to visit more often.

His formal tour of the province began the next morning, starting with the families along the borderlands. Mystaira, the agricultural capital of Felysia, had built walls around its borders as a failsafe against economic attacks. The wall was enchanted by healers and power wielders to stave off unwanted intruders and pestilence that an enemy may be tempted to slip through their defenses. So far, it appeared that the defenses were working. None of the families he met with reported suspicious behavior from outside Mystaira's walls.

The defenses did not, however, prevent people within the Mystaira borders from causing problems within the walls. The third family he'd visited shared disturbing reports of Felysian-born marauders. Some of the tradesmen had experienced raids on trails or roads. Their wagons and caravans sabotaged by packs of criminals intent on taking anything that could be moved. Food. Wares. Money. It all seemed fair game to the bandits.

He managed to meet with all five families that controlled the borderlands in two days, allowing himself one day with his family to recover before moving to the remaining families further in the interior. Flying was the swiftest way to travel but had exhausted him.

He was sitting by a creek that skirted around his estate, lost in his thoughts on how to lead.

"So what are you going to do about it?" His sister, Delphia, interrupted his thoughts. She had a knack for doing that.

"The raiders?"

"No, your shaggy hair," Delphia playfully tugged at a lock of his hair, then plopped down beside him. He tended to end up by the creek which ran along the back of their home. "Of course, I mean the raiders. It doesn't seem like an easy fix."

"It's not. First, I need to find out why we haven't heard about it sooner. Then, I've got to figure out how to manage the issue while not being here."

"Well, tell me what to do, and I'll do it. I've pretty much figured out the books for the province. Managing communication shouldn't be all that difficult."

Delphia had become Gavin's hand in his absence. In all honesty, she had been running the province since the Queen first announced Gavin would become Lord. Delphia had always been mature and steadfast. She was a natural fit to lead, and Gavin still struggled with the idea of taking responsibility from her someday.

"Ach- I know that face. Stop!" Delphia smacked Gavin on the back of his head. "I do not want to be Lord, or Lady, of this land or any land. I'm happy to help you out and make a difference on this side of things. You can keep your title. Let me keep track of the books and write pretty letters for you."

"Delphia, you would be so good at it, though. Don't you want recognition for your hard work?"

"Nope. Now, tell me what you really came out here to think about. It seems you've already got the other thing figured out."

Gavin sighed a little, dropping his attention to the ground. Despite his best efforts, he couldn't stop a smile from breaking across his face. His sister was the only person in the world that could disarm him so quickly. Even if she weren't a mind walker, he imagined she would still be the only person to know exactly what he was thinking just by looking at him.

"Oh! What's that smile about?" she exclaimed when he continued avoiding her gaze, and still smiling like an idiot.

"It's nothing," Gavin said. He tried, and failed, to stop his nervous laughter.

"It's not nothing. Gavin! Is there someone back in Veritasailles you came out here to think about?" Delphia had propped herself onto her knees and grabbed Gavin by his shoulders, forcing him to look at her. "There is!" she continued, taking in his goofy smile.

"Stop, Delphia. You're making a big deal out of nothing," Gavin said, shrugging off his sister and pushing off the ground. He made his way to the creek and began tossing pebbles into the water. Within seconds Delphia was standing right next to him, apparently not ready to drop the subject.

"You don't *have* to tell me. But you know you'd make me tell you. So it's only fair you tell me. Besides, I'm practically your formal advisor, so I'm really entitled to information of this manner. Plus–"

"Enough, alright? Goddess, Delphia." Gavin rolled his shoulders, he hoped he wouldn't regret sharing the information. "Her name is Sage."

"THE REALM LEAPER?!" Delphia's shock skittered around the clearing, and Gavin had to force himself not to grab his sister and slap his hand over her mouth.

"What? How do you know about that?"

"Because Seth, yes—that Seth, has been going around all of Mystaira spreading the news."

Lord Seth was the most prominent leader in Mystaira. One of the few original progeny of Mystaira, his family had held their estate since before steadfast records were kept. Not only was the family renowned for their orchards and wine, but they also provided a significant amount of livestock for export. Their family homestead's taxes could single-handedly pay Gavin's annual allowances.

"And what does Seth have to say about the Realm Leaper?" It wouldn't be good, Gavin was sure. Seth had always been outspoken about his concerns regarding an outsider becoming Queen, despite Symon's own mother being from Nysa as well. He also had plenty to say about Gavin's appointment as Lord of Mystaira. Seth obviously believed he would have been the better choice. And, usually, Gavin would have agreed.

"Seth claims that King Symon and Queen Aryael welcoming a stranger to the festival proves that they are unfit to rule. He claims it demonstrates their instability, especially with Speridisia openly organizing their forces."

"So he's willfully speaking against his King and Queen? What does he think that will accomplish?"

"I don't know brother, but you should be careful. He's been after your place since it was given to you, and—" she held up her hand when he attempted to interject, "—I know you would gladly give it up, but you and I both know that Seth is too hot-headed to be Lord. He would quickly unravel any good we've done."

"I know," Gavin rolled his shoulders once more. He looked at his sister, the look of wariness still on her face. "I have to go. I'll write to Symon, and let him know what you've told me."

Quickly, she hugged him, then turned back to look at the creek. "You've been given this opportunity for a reason Gavin. Don't sell yourself short."

He left his sister by the creek, aiming for his room in the small house. Luckily, everyone was still out for the day, tending to their daily chores. It wasn't often that the house was empty, but it meant that he could get from one point to another without being stopped to visit and catch up. He supposed that was his own fault for being so absent the last several years.

Once in his room, he sat down at the tiny writing desk his father made. Pulling out a stack of blank paper, Gavin prepared himself to record everything he'd learned in the last couple of days. The enchanted paper, given to him by the King, would disappear whenever he'd finished his letter and arrive wherever he told it to land. Despite the urgency of the matter, Gavin found himself crafting a note to Sage instead.

Checking in to make sure you haven't run off yet. I always forget the beauty of this place. Maybe one day I can show you this part of Felysia. -G

Before he could think too hard about it, he finished the note, folded it the way Symon had shown him, and thought of the side table in Sage's room, willing the note to land on top of whatever books she might have piled on it.

Once the note vanished, he rolled his shoulders once, recentered himself, and began recording everything he had learned over the last three days. Perhaps, if he played his cards right, he could finish in Mystaira early and be back in the Tower before having to move into the castle. Then he and Sage might have a few precious days to spend together before his world changed and he was pushed into his role as Lord for good.

Sage sat in her favorite chair, the one near the fireplace but angled just right so she could sit and stare out the expansive windows in her room. Three days had dragged on without Gavin or Raphael there to give her any distraction from her thoughts. Memories had been pouring back into her rapid-fire, but she hadn't actually sat to record them. Part of her was worried that putting them in writing would make them too real. She scrubbed her hands with her face.

"Right," she announced to herself, went to reach for the journal Raph had given her and stopped short when she noticed a note lying on top of it.

She couldn't stop smiling when she opened the paper and read the note Gavin had scrawled across it. Maybe he was as bored as she was. Quickly, not really knowing how the magic of the paper worked, she replied to his note. Scratching out something about still being in the tower, but actively plotting her escape, definitely wanting to see Mystaira one day, and admitting to maybe missing his presence at least a very little. She folded the note back how she found it and whispered, "Can you go back to him now? Go right back where you came from!"

To her delight, the note vanished. Hopefully, it would end up where she wanted it to. Hopefully, some poor fae wouldn't be eating supper and lean into their food only to find a folded-up piece of parchment nestled in their dinner.

"Okay. Time to write—for real!" she announced loudly to herself. She picked up her journal, opened to the first blank page, and began scribbling frantically as the memories poured out of her.

She was in Ian's house. Her memories flitted through scenes of meeting his mom, Stiofanie, a woman of fierce compassion who immediately latched on to "Lonnie," and flung herself into finding her work at the university. Stiofanie took Sage out to shops to find suitable clothes, helped her find out a way to get her school certifications so that she might one day be able to enroll as a university student, and welcomed Sage as a pseudo-member of her household, never questioning what she and Ian might get up to when they were left alone. Sage didn't have the heart to tell Stiofanie that no school records would ever appear for the false name she had given, and tried her hardest to work in the library in order to live up to the kindness Stiofanie had already given her.

Sage also didn't tell Stiofanie, or Ian, that the entire reason Sage was in Techeduin to begin with was to get into the library. On her lunch breaks, she would comb the stacks, looking for anything that might help her learn about her elemental abilities. She hid her magical ineptitude by being quick and quiet on her feet while the other assistants relied on spells to lift books to the highest stacks in the library. Sage, on the other hand, didn't dare to use her wind magic to lift books and wasn't skilled enough with her wand to even pretend to use the same magic. On the few times Stiofanie spied Sage taking the long way to put books away, she'd vowed to help Sage catch up on the lessons she'd missed since dropping out of school at fifteen. Stiof never asked Sage why she dropped out, where her parents were, or why she chose to live on the streets prior to moving in with them; but sometimes, she would approach Sage and hug her, seeming to need to give the girl some sort of comfort. A mother's intuition, Sage mused.

Sage, Ian, and Stiofanie developed a routine; Ian would go off in the morning, to his studies on campus as a promising alchemy student, studying ancient alchemical procedures and investigating how they might be integrated with modern techniques. Meanwhile, Stiofanie and Sage would walk together to the library. Sage often packed lunches for them all, a small repayment for the enormous kindness they'd given her. And in the evenings, Ian and Sage would work together to fix dinner, chatting about their day. At night, they would find their way to bed, sometimes in Ian's room, sometimes in Sage's room, and sometimes apart in their own rooms depending on what they each needed in terms of rest and solitude. Sometimes, they made love, deep into the night. Sometimes, they told stories about their past: Ian's often funny anecdotes that included himself, Brion, and Duncan making fools of themselves, while Sage's stories were memories of her family, and retelling everything she'd done to survive since her capture and escape. He informed her he'd heard of the earthquake caused by her escape, the official explanation by the government, the one that had killed the school group on their way to a sanctioned reception at the nation's capital. He had seemed shocked for days that she was actually the cause of it in her desperate attempt to flee. Ian vowed to help her find a way to elude Ranquer, and would occasionally pop into the library to help her search for certain materials. Other times, they would sleep soundly next to each other, just enjoying each other's company.

As much as she hated it, Sage continued to stash emergency items in her room. Hair dyes, colored eye contacts, a potion that would change her skin color for twenty-four hours, another potion that would allow her to swap genders for a brief period; all items that would help her make a run for it if she needed to, if she needed to leave to protect Ian and his mom. She'd do it, she knew; at the first sign of threats, she'd leave. She probably wouldn't even leave a note, just...poof, be gone.

It was Ian's discovery of her stash of emergency items that caused their first real fight. Hurt and betrayal flooded his face as she stepped into her room. "I was just trying to put away your clothes. They'd been in the washroom for like...three days, so I thought I'd just put them away for you. How long?" he demanded. "How long have you been planning to go?"

Sage stepped into the room, closing the door behind her; "Always," she replied flatly, "If anything happens...I couldn't let them hurt you, or your mom. I won't let them. That's here in case I need to go, Ian."

"You won't need to go. I can help; we can keep you safe," he pleaded, tears rimming his eyes.

"Ian," Sage whispered, cupping his hands in hers, not daring to look into his eyes, "You have to let me go. Ian...if they come, I need you to promise not to come after me, to let me go. They will hurt you, and your mom. Please...let me go."

He grabbed her face, crushing it to his, tears flowed freely now from both of their eyes. "I can't," he whispered.

"You have to," was the only reply she could give him.

That was probably when it happened; when the first part of her really broke. She had thought it was when she'd killed the guards, probably killed her fellow students, but it wasn't. That part of her had been holding on by a thread. Realizing just how much danger she put Ian and Stiofanie in cut that thread, and a piece of her heart plummeted into the darkest abyss. She hadn't allowed herself to dwell on losing her freedom, losing her family when she escaped, how she lost any promises of the life she could have had. But the prospect of Ian and Stiofanie becoming collateral in her journey to find some way out of the nightmare her life had become...a new urgency grew within her.

Over the course of a week, Sage worked to convince Ian that she was right. Eventually he gave in, but wouldn't let her refuse his help in tracking down the answers she needed. Sometimes, she worried her presence jeopardized his place in the alchemy department of the University. Ian shrugged off her questions, and insisted he was more attuned to government happenings than he'd let her believe before.

With Ian's help she had compiled a collection of resources describing elementals in the past, how their powers were developed and honed, and the manner in which their magic was different from other common forms of magic. She found descriptions of elemental practices, routines that allowed elementals to focus their power and command the energy forces that flowed around them. She found detailed figures and transcriptions of steps, forms, and poses an elemental would flow through in order to summon water, create fire, wield the wind, and shatter the earth. Ian helped make copies of the books. His knowledge of alchemy allowed him to create tools for her, so she could make duplicates of the materials on her own. He also used his skills to give her an edge should she ever need to make a run for it.

"Here. I call it an Egress Key," he said as he handed her a small bundled object.

Sage looked at Ian quizzically before unwrapping the bundle, "Egress? For what?" Under the wrappings lay a silver metal ring with a dark black stone attached to the center of it. The stone hovered, suspended in the center by a second silver piece, going directly through the stone so that it could spin in the ring.

"It's been enchanted. If you spin that stone in the center ten times it will transport you anywhere on the continent. I've actually been working on something similar in the lab and modified it to be something that'd help you, if you ever need to go. It's still a work in progress; this one should be good for two trips. I'm hoping, someday soon, to have an upgraded version that can work more times." His voice was clinical, a sign that he was working on keeping his emotions in check.

Tears spilled from her face, and she placed her hand on his cheek. She shook her head, setting the key onto the table they sat at in his kitchen. "Thank you," she whispered.

He grabbed her hand on his face, and tilted her chin so that her eyes met his, "If it comes down to it, you run," he said, "I've thought about it so many times. I know you will have to go." She kissed him, gently, and they sat in the kitchen, holding each other.

Sage continued her search for knowledge and practiced what she could glean from the manuals she had duplicated from the library. It was nearly a year when the first sign of threat occurred. She was far back in the stacks trying to find the home for a book on the ancient, elemental gods when she overheard two students talking. They spoke in whispers about a group of students who had been summoned to the capitol building for a private meeting with the President and his advisors. They were murmuring about the students, the unfairness of their professors choosing favorites who didn't deserve the honor, and how he was scheduled to visit the University at the end of the term. Sage dropped the books she was carrying and hurried to the front of the library. "Stiofanie," she whispered as she approached the front desk, "I'm not feeling very good."

Stiofanie looked over at Sage, "You look fine. What's wrong?"

"It's my stomach. I don't know; just, I feel really off. I think I need to go home, lie down for just a bit."

Stiofanie clucked her teeth, "Alright, go on then. Let me know if you feel much worse. I'll see if I can't get home a bit early. I'll pick up some ginger tea on the way home, ok?" Sage nodded and quickly made her way to the exit.

The entire way home, Sage felt as if there were eyes on her, as if she wore a target on her back. Everything on the outside seemed normal. Automobiles trundled down the city streets, buses pulling over as they made their way through their routes. Pedestrians hurriedly navigated the sidewalks. She saw a pair of vagrants get into some sort of fight by a liquor store, one of them procuring a wand and turning the other man's lower half into stone. She didn't notice the small flying drone that bounded from rooftop to rooftop above her, following her as she made her way home. She was nearly there when a van pulled up beside her, a man leaping out and grabbing her. A black canvas bag was forced over her head, and invisible ropes tied her hands and feet together. "Hello, Sage," drawled a familiar female voice.

Ms. Dullahan had found her. She had assumed the woman had drowned in the van following her all those years ago when she washed that bridge into the river. "The President has waited a very long time to see you again." No...no no no no! Sage's heart thundered in her chest, moisture slicked her hands. She couldn't get caught now. And so close to home. So close to Ian and Stiof.

An invisible gag materialized in her mouth when she began screaming for help, and Sage bit down on it as tears spilled from her eyes. They drove for what felt like hours, but was just as likely several minutes. The van stopped moving. She heard rustling and a door opening and slamming shut before the sack was ripped off her head. Ms. Dullahan was inches away from her, smiling wickedly. She wore the same smart, black and white suit as before, but something was different in the agent's appearance. Ms. Dullahan cuffed Sage with large, mechanical manacles that buzzed on her skin. "These will keep your powers at bay, so don't get any ideas," Ms. Dullahan said with a sing-songy voice.

Sage grit her teeth, willing the tears to stay put and not to spill over her cheeks. With a flourish from the agent, the invisible gag dissolved. "What do you want with me?" Sage growled out, keeping her teeth clenched.

"Well," purred Dullahan," before I deliver you to Mr. President, I've been tasked with the delightful job of finding out just how you evaded us for so long. Who helped you, where you were going...you get the picture."

"No one helped me. I've been on my own," Sage blurted.

Dullahan clucked behind her teeth, "Now, you don't actually expect me to believe that. I've seen you walking to work each day. My drones have been following you for some time now. Tell me who they are, and I promise to make their executions quick."

No...no no no no...this couldn't be happening, not now. "I haven't told the others yet; where you've been hiding. If you tell me, I will make sure that their punishment is over quickly." Dullahan had leaned in close, whispering the promise into Sage's face. There, in her eyes, was a flicker of light that was not human.

Sage recoiled, "What are you?"

"Oh," scoffed Dullahan, "you noticed. Thanks to your little prank five years ago, my mortal body was not of use to the President any longer. But, I had already started the process of uploading my consciousness, a new design our alchemical engineers have developed, and I was able to commandeer a new body. So, I guess a word of thanks is in order." She grinned at Sage, removing a glove to reveal mechanical fingers. Her hand lifted, and Dullahan slammed her fist in Sage's cheek. Bright stars burst into Sage's eyes, and she couldn't stop the sob that followed.

"They don't know...they don't know who I am," she sobbed.

"Liar," Dullahan purred again. "Tell the truth, little one, and all this can be over." Another blow, this time to her other cheek. She could feel her eye already begin to blossom, swelling below the point of impact.

"They don't know who I am!" Sage pleaded again. "Please...please, just leave them out of this. I'll go, I'll go with you." Wham! Another blow, to the center of Sage's nose. Blood bloomed across her face, coating her mouth, spurting out from a gash on the side of her nose caused by the mechanical knuckles.

"Just tell me," Dullahan crooned, "You know you are going to tell me. Eventually."

Sage sobbed, blood gurgling from her mouth. "No," she whispered.

"Say that again. Louder this time," Dullahan demanded.

"No. I won't tell you. You'll have to kill me." Dullahan grabbed Sage around her neck, squeezing tight; electricity pumped out of mechanical fingers, sparking through Sage's body. She writhed, gasping for air as she fought to remain conscious, stay alive. Ms. Dullahan squeezed tighter, and Sage's insides boiled; she wouldn't tell them, she thought. Dullahan leaned in close, "I already know who they are, you impertinent little bitch. I just want the pleasure of hearing you say their names. The satisfaction of seeing you condemn them will be payback for killing my old body," Dullahan said between her too-white teeth. Sage was slammed to the floor of the van, knocking her head as she landed. She rocked onto her side, curling up to protect her from any oncoming blows. Ms. Dullahan chuckled, "Not so tough without your stupid little powers, are you? Tell me their names."

"Allyra," whispered Sage.

"What?" demanded Dullahan.

"Allyra, Cerridos, Brighid, Therisyd," Sage whispered.

"Very clever girl. Those gods haven't been seen here in ages," spat Dullahan.

"Allyra, Cerridos, Brighid, Therisyd. Help me. Please," whispered Sage, again. Wham! Another blow, a kick this time to her center. "Allyra, Cerridos, Brighid, Therisyd. Help me," demanded Sage between her sharp gasps for air. Dullahan ripped Sage from the floor, pinning her to the side of the van with her fingers locked around her throat again. "Allyra, Cerridos, Brighid, Therisyd. Help me," Sage said, fighting against the strong mechanical fingers, trying to pry them from her windpipe so she could continue her chant. A wind began to buffet the side of the van, and Sage could hear water begin lapping around them.

Dullahan looked around, "Stop it, stop saying that," her eyes wide as she began to squeeze tighter.

"Allyra. Cerridos. Brighid. Therisyd. Help me!" Sage shouted as loud as she could while Dullahan continued to clamp down on Sage's throat. Black spots began to pop in the sides of her vision. No, she thought. She couldn't breathe, as Dullahan continued to squeeze her throat, cutting off her ability to suck in air. She could feel veins begin to bulge in her forehead as the wind continued to increase, and she began to feel heat build in the van. She thought she could see the walls begin to emit a red glow as she tried...tried...tried to pry those cold metal fingers away. But it was no use; she was no match for this machine, and she tried not to look into those cold dead eyes as she felt life slip away, as she slid into darkness. Her vision went black, and she thought she heard Ms. Dullahan scream, perhaps in triumph, as she released her body into the dark.

She was nowhere, and everywhere. It was made of stone, this place after death. There were little altars along the wall, altering between basins of water, large torches of flame, sparkling crystals or sculptures of clay, and finally, a display of small, ancient pinwheels which spun despite no obvious signs of a draft of any kind.

"Hello?" she called. Her voice echoed, bouncing off the walls. She walked, just a few steps, forward. Looking for any signs of life, any way out from this place she'd arrived. "Hello? Anyone here?" she spun around, looking for anything, anything that could help her determine where she was.

"You've come," a voice shot by her, around her, above her, inside her. Not one voice, but several voices. And yet it was the same voice all at once. "What-" she whispered, and immediately, she was standing on a dais, surrounded by four archways, no sign of where she stood moments before.

"You've come," said three voices. Sage circled, and through the archways, she saw three impressive figures step forward. A huge man, with white hair and a short trimmed beard carrying a spear; a woman wearing a flowing tunic of blue, carrying an ax of what looked like ice and a shield, her skin covered in blue tattoos along her arms and chest; and a woman clothed in leather armor, a helmet of blue and red flame upon her head, a bow and flaming arrows slung across her back. Sage circled on her spot again. "How?" she asked.

"You are Sage Brennan?" asked the white-haired man. Sage nodded. "You do not recognize us?" asked the blue woman. Sage shook her head again, opting to decline speech. "I thought you might at least recognize the one who helped you escape the last time," scoffed the blue woman.

Sage's eyes widened, "Allyra?" she whispered, and her knees buckled; she bowed her face, as tears began to stream down her face.

"Stand girl," said Brighid, goddess of flame. "Stand, and hear our command," said Cerridos.

Sage lifted her head, noting the empty fourth archway, "But where's Therisyd?"

"That is why we immortals have chosen to interfere. We have saved you twice, now, even though your people have declined to offer their gratitude to us, instead choosing to slaughter those we've blessed. You, girl, now get the honor to help bring us back into the light." The goddess of flame, Brighid, rippled with power as she spoke to Sage.

Sage shook her head, "What? Why? Why me?"

"Because you are one of our blessed, silly girl," Allyra crooned, "For too long, your people have squandered our gifts, slaughtered elementals, and eradicated our powers from the land. And now...one of our own is using our powers against us."

"Ranquer?"

Cerridos nodded, "He's been using elementals, such as you, in an attempt to gain enormous power and immortality. Not only that, but he's discovered a way to harness our own power for his benefit." Cerridos glanced at Therisyd's archway. "Ranquer has imprisoned Therisyd, and plans to use him alongside yourself in a final sacrifice to ensure his immortality."

Brighid lifted a palm, flame dancing in a ball at the center, "You, girl, have unbridled, untrained, and unchecked power at your disposal. You will wield these powers to abolish the evil in our land, to punish Ranquer, and to liberate my partner from bondage."

"How? How will I do this?" Sage pleaded.

"There is a book; we've placed it in the university library, disguised it as a children's book. Find that, and you will find your answers. Look for the Realm Leapers, and that will be your key," Allyra chimed. Sage nodded, and the three gods began to fade away in their archways. "We will be with you, Sage Brennan. Do not be afraid," called Cerridos. The gods faded into nothing, and Sage spun on the spot. She started to walk towards Allyra's archway, but before she could reach it, the temple around her began to fade as well. Slowly, the sounds of a river lapping softly and a gentle breeze swaying through the grass began to filter through her senses. She blinked...

Sage rolled over, ash and fire spurting around her. Everything had burned, except her. Small smudges of soot collected on her arms and hands, along her clothes, but she was unscathed. She gingerly touched her nose and noticed it felt unbroken. Blood still crusted the spot around her nose, and she started as she realized her swollen eye had been repaired as well. The scene around her became clearer. One-half of Ms. Dullahan's face was all that remained of her torturer, and Sage noted the sparks that continued to emit from the tiny wires still connected to the eyeball.

Sage ran to an outcropping of rock, recognizing it as the pillar of a bridge, before vomiting all over the rocks at the edge of the river. She heaved and heaved, finally gasping for air as her stomach realized it was fully empty. She waded into the water, letting the coolness along her ankles soothe the panic rising in her. She had to go, but she didn't have anything she needed. Sage turned slowly on the spot, and made her plan. She began jogging, heading to her old hideaway. She still had a few belongings there, a few stashes of getaway clothes, and materials. Her wand had been in the van, she realized and hoped her magic was good enough to get into the hiding place without it.

Her hand ached as she came to, realizing she'd filled page after page with a neat script she couldn't recall writing. So involved in her memories, reliving them as if they were real, she felt the pain in her body, her throat, of the ghostly hand that had gripped her there. Gingerly, she placed the pen on the table next to the journal, her hand going to her throat almost involuntarily. But the pain had gone, along with the memory.

Slowly, she peeled herself from the chair she sat in, heading for the large windows of her room. Part of her body still reacted to the memory, the urge to fly away, to run and hide a drumbeat. Questions of Ian and Stiofanie swarmed her.

Refusing to cry, sick of tears, Sage walked out of the room, grabbing the pen and folded paper that appeared on top of her journal. She wasn't in the mood for writing anymore. Perhaps a visit with Hyacinth would stop the phantom tremor in her hands.

Chapter 16

Sage finished scratching out a quick note to Gavin. She wasn't sure how the note paper worked, but she found herself passing the end table by her chair more often than she could remember doing before he left. Already they'd filled an entire sheet of paper, front and back, and had to start a new sheet. They had scribbled notes back and forth to each other until late in the night. According to Gavin, he was currently awaiting another meeting to begin. She hoped her latest note found him before he left.

In the back of her mind, she wrestled with feelings of unfaithfulness. Memories of Ian mingled with her desire to see Gavin again. She couldn't stop questioning herself about the morality of continuing on with Gavin, especially since she hadn't told him about Ian. At the same time, the urge to write to him, to see him again, continued hour after hour.

Groaning in self-deprecation, she forced herself not to look back at the table as she made her way down to the kitchens. Her only sources of occupation the last few days had been helping Hyacinth, reading in the library, and recording memories as they came in her journal.

220 ~ P.E. CRAVEN

Sage was just exiting the stairwell when Hyacinth's laughter twinkled from the kitchens. Sage smiled to herself before rounding into the kitchen, at the same time she recognized a second voice—too late. Petra was sitting with Hyacinth at the counter, a broad smile on her face that nearly made her unrecognizable. The atmosphere immediately turned frosty as Petra and Sage stared at each other.

"Oh- I'm sorry. I'll just come back."

Sage made to turn when Hyacinth called, "Oh, no you don't. Petra, I think it's time that we all have breakfast together."

"No, it's fine. Really, I can come back," Sage hesitated by the door. She really wasn't in the mood for Petra's bullshit this morning. In fact, if she never had to deal with it again, Sage would consider it a blessing from the gods themselves. She turned once more, intent on leaving when Petra's voice croaked.

"Sage...I would sincerely like to invite you to sit with us."

Sage inspected the scene before consenting. Petra's face, once again a stony mask, avoided Hyacinth's while Hyacinth looked at Petra like a mother scolding a child for stealing cookies.

Once Sage had settled at the table and Hyacinth fixed a plate of food for her, Hyacinth said, "See, isn't this nice."

One look at Petra, still avoiding anyone's eyes, and Sage couldn't stop a snort from escaping her body. Hyacinth cut her eyes at Sage, which only triggered a fit of laughter to bubble from her body. Petra, still not looking at Sage or Hyacinth, cracked a smile, which Hyacinth noticed causing her to start smiling. Seeing both fae smiling, but trying not to laugh then sent Sage deeper into her laughter, triggering

Hyacinth to start to laugh. The effect built until even Petra was laughing.

"See! She does laugh!" Hyacinth squealed in delight.

"I can't help it...This is just so damn awkward," Petra admitted.

"Oh my gods, I know," Sage sighed, finally getting ahold of herself. "Listen, Petra. I know this hasn't been easy for you. I get it—why you're so uncomfortable around me. It's fine."

Petra exhaled loudly, looking at Sage. Sage got the feeling it was the first time the female had truly looked at her as a person, and not a ghost or a ticking time bomb.

"You're right. It is really hard for me to see you, and that's not really your fault." She grinned, tight-lipped. "I'm sorry I've been...less than welcoming."

Just then, Hyacinth sniffed. Loudly. Petra and Sage looked quickly to Hyacinth, who was weeping and smiling broadly. "It's just, so...great. Having you two together."

"Hyacinth, don't cry!" Petra and Sage cried out simultaneously.

"See! You guys have so much in common," Hyacinth replied through happy tears. Sage wasn't sure about that, but she was thrilled to see Hyacinth happy. It took several minutes to calm her down, but once Hyacinth had dried her tears the three of them had an agreeable breakfast. Petra insisted on cleaning up, so Sage dismissed herself and headed to the library.

Sage had only begun perusing the library, scanning for a new book to read, when a cold voice cut through the quiet. "Don't think this means I've dropped my guard."

Sage dropped her head. It had been too good to be true. Slowly, she turned to find Petra standing in the doorway.

"You were right. You being here is hard for me. But that's not why I don't trust you."

"Right. It's because I'm the scary girl from the sky. I get it," Sage said.

"No. It's because wherever you go, everyone loses their minds. My brother hasn't been the same since you arrived, Gavin is distracted as ever. Even Raphael has gotten behind in his duties. And that—" Petra pointed a sharp finger at Sage— "is how you will bring us down. I don't care what the Goddess has planned, you will never convince me to trust you."

With a swish of skirts, Petra stalked away, leaving Sage in the library seething to prove Petra wrong.

Raphael was exhausted. The new healers seemed millennia behind where they should be. Sure, the Rafalatriki had only just been rebuilt enough to introduce new healers two years prior. Still, Raphael could not help but feel like he would need a whole year to acquaint the apprentices to their role, not a short two weeks. He sighed with relief as he arrived at the door to his temporary abode, a cozy room with a fire enchanted to light the room according to his preferred temperature, soft blankets, and a blessedly luxurious bed. The room was an obvious gratuity from Shiphrah, who was managing with the few on-site teachers she could muster.

Raphael pushed open his door, and nearly wept in anguish as Symon's voice rang out, "Oh, good, you're here."

"What could you possibly need from me tonight Symon? Are you trying to make me look my age?"

"Always," the King replied with a chuckle. "I came to update you on your girl's new memories. I just finished looking through the journal."

Raphael sighed as he sank into an armchair. "And?"

"You and Aryael were right. She's a Realm Leaper."

"Great. Now, on to the news I didn't know." Raphael usually tried to temper himself with Symon. But he was simply past pleasantries at this point.

"She met with them, her gods," Symon explained. His spectre sat in a chair that manifested in the room. The King leaned forward with zeal. "She met with Cerridos himself! And Brighid. And Allyra." Symon sat back in his chair. A mixture of excitement, bewilderment, and scheming rippled through his features. Slowly, his focus settled back on Raphael. "She also wrote about her President."

Symon paused, letting the implication settle over the room. Raphael sighed once again, leaning back into his chair and draping his hand across his face. "Yes, yes..." he waved off the king. "I already know all about that, which you know already." Raphael paused, compelling himself to focus his full attention on Symon. "Symon, you knew from the start how I felt about all of this. I was concerned that you would take the news of Rankor's duplicate badly. Can you look at me now and tell me you wouldn't have reacted swiftly to the news that she had been hunted by a replica of the man that killed your father? Your people?"

Symon's gaze burned toward Raphael. Even in his spectre form, a watery-airy version of the fae himself, his gaze could pierce a lesser fae's resolve. Luckily, Raphael was not like other fae and could will himself entirely to be unmoved by such a stare. Symon, grunting in frustration, slapped a hand on his thigh. "Fine. You win, Raph. But next time, let's try being honest with each other."

"That is a road traveled two ways, little cub."

Symon rolled his eyes, a begrudging grin breaking across his face at the nickname Raphael had pestered him with when they were young and careless. "I know. I'm not like my father, you know," Symon said.

"I know." Raphael and Symon smiled at each other for a moment. "Now, your majesty, if you don't mind. I am absolutely spent, and I have an appointment with a lovely bottle of wine and my bed. Please, see yourself out."

Raphael did not wait to see if the King had obeyed his request before heading for the shelf holding said bottle of wine, and tossing his shoes to the far corners of the room.

Chapter 17

✳✳✳

The first thing I remember after waking from the explosion is ash raining from the sky. At first, it was kind of pretty, like snow, except the temperature was so warm- way too warm for snow. Then I noticed the fire, all around me. And bits of metal were scattered around everywhere. I was singed in places, but I wasn't hurt. My nose wasn't even broken, so I guess the gods were nice enough to help with that.

Sage's pen hung in midair as she contemplated how to continue. Days had flown by, and she waited to learn what happened to her after being captured again. She hesitated at the open journal. The resolution hadn't been what she hoped for but knowing eased a small part of the wariness she felt. Her resolve solidifying itself within her, she sighed as she put the pen back to the paper.

I'd made it to the old building, reciting the enchantments to get inside. Fortunately, I was able to get inside without trouble. I had rigged an old shower in the building so that it would work and decided to stop and shower before changing clothes and trying to make a run for it. Who knew how long

I would be running again? Besides, being covered in soot and ash wouldn't help me blend into the city.

Thoughts raced through her mind as she showered. Shit. How the hell was she supposed to get that book? She'd finished showering, scrubbing fast and furiously at her skin, before jogging into her old room, flipping over her bedroll to reveal an outfit already laid out, waiting for her. She had just slipped her pants over her hips when she heard, "Were you even going to say goodbye?" Ian stood in the doorway.

Sage froze. Panic flooded her veins, icier than what she felt in Dullahan's van. "I. Ian...I can explain," Sage whispered.

"How about you start by explaining why the news is asking for help looking for a rogue elemental? What happened?"

"What do you mean?"

"I mean, you were missing for two days, Sage, and now the news is blaring about an escaped convict who used elemental magic against government agents. What. Happened." This time, he demanded an answer from her. Sage's mouth hung open, and she searched for words to explain. When her mind failed to comprehend how to tell him how close Ian and his mother had been to being caught, Sage sunk to her knees. The world was closing in on her; she sobbed, panted. She couldn't breathe.

Ian rushed to her and cupped her chin before pulling her into a tight embrace. "I thought you were lost. I thought they got you."

"They did," she whispered.

Ian pulled back in shock, alarm written all over his face. "So that woman you are accused of killing? She was one of them?" Sage balked, but nodded, then told Ian everything. How she was abducted, how Dullahan had known about Stiofanie and him, how she blacked out and ended up in the realm of the gods, about the book. Everything.

Ian sat silently for several minutes. "Come on, we've got to get home. My mom's worried sick."

"Ian, I can't go back there. They will find you guys, and kill you," Sage pulled her hand from his as they stood.

"Listen, you need us. We can help. We can help you get that book; help you figure out what the hell you've got to do." Sage stared at Ian for a long time and, remembering she'd stashed another wig in her old place, reached over to procure it.

"Ian, I need to know you and Stiofanie will go if it looks like you're in danger."

"We already are in danger, Sage," he whispered. With that solemn thought, Sage slipped her wig on her head, and they made their way home.

When they got to the house, Stiofanie was pacing the floor. Ian and Sage slipped inside, and Stiofanie's attention snagged on the wig on Sage's head. "Where have you been? You had us both worried sick!" she demanded, stopping on the spot.

"I'm sorry," whispered Sage, one tear rolling down her cheek.

Stiofanie huffed, clearly about to lay into her again, when Ian interjected, "Mom. We should talk." Taken aback, Stiofanie's words seemed to freeze in her mouth.

"Ian," Sage warned.

"She should know the truth," Ian growled and pushed Sage towards the kitchen table, his hand on her lower back. She stared at the floor as the three of them took their place at the table. Ian did most of the talking, telling the story exactly as Sage had told him, Sage interrupting only when absolutely necessary. Shock and understanding seemed to wash over Stiofanie as Ian finished the story.

"Oh, my poor girl," whispered Stiofanie, and she reached around the corner of the table and hugged Sage.

They all three cried silently, and Sage whispered, "I'm going to have to go soon. But I need that book first."

"Don't you worry, Lonnie-I'm sorry...Sage," Stiofanie declared, "We will get it."

"I can't go back to the library," Sage said quietly.

"You can't leave this house," demanded Ian. "If what Dullahan said was true, they don't know where you are. She did us a service by keeping that to herself, the greedy bitch. This is the only safe place for you right now." Sage nodded. She'd use the time to come up with a plan.

The next morning, Ian and Stiofanie got ready for work and school as usual, Stiofanie running the departure of Sage over with Ian one last time before heading to the university. Sage spent the day dying and cutting her hair, unpacking, repacking, unpacking again, and finally repacking her emergency bags, making sure everything was where she needed it. She re-read the texts on elementals as quickly and thoroughly as she could.

It took two days for Stiofanie to find the book. Titled *Realm Leapers and Other Myths for the Adventurous*, the book looked like a bygone era children's book about mysterious mythical creatures. Upon further investigation, Sage discovered it was a manual for traveling to other realms, other worlds beyond their own, disguised as a story.

She read the story of evil powers coming to the world, and how the elemental gods chased the dark lords through portals and into other worlds. She read how mortals such as herself were able to realm-leap, by gathering the four sacred insignias, hidden around the continent. She learned in her research that the place she had met the gods was actually the highest temple, high atop Mount Danu, a temple abandoned centuries ago due to the perilous climb. She would have to find the insignias, then bring them to the temple, and somehow wield them in order to escape into a new world. How and what she would do then, she hadn't discovered. But at least once she'd escaped, Ranquer couldn't find her.

Sage waited two more days, going over everything with Ian and Stiofanie. Finally, on the fifth morning after her truth had been revealed, Sage awoke in the early hours of the morning. Ian slept soundly; she allowed herself several moments to wonder at the beauty of him. His face looked boyish for its lack of tension, for all the ease that slumber offered. She implanted the memory of his face into her mind: his full lips, the playfully arching nose, his round eyes that lit up when he found something interesting or curious. She wanted to remember all the good things as she embarked on the next phase of her journey.

It was still fully dark outside as Sage crept from Ian's room to her own. With all the stealth she could muster, Sage gathered her things. She knew her destinations: Lyonesus for Brighid; Murias for Allyra; Goulain for Cerridos; and finally, Tiernan, her hometown, for Therisyd. The insignias would be hidden somewhere, in plain sight but unnoticed in those places where the gods were said to have originated. Lyonesus was the farthest away, requiring her to board a ship.

She took the skin color changing tonic, grabbed a boat ticket she had stolen off an old-lady years and years ago, and cast a spell Stiofanie had taught Sage to alter the credentials as Ian had instructed her. She would be able to call a car, ride to the docks, and board a recreational cruise ship without being noticed. If she kept to her room for the three-day voyage, she'd be able to make it to Lyonesus without causing a fuss.

She left a letter lying beside Ian's bedside table, not daring to risk waking him with a final, parting kiss. As she walked down the deserted streets toward the busier street corner where she could hail a car, she didn't allow herself to look back. She didn't let herself feel her sorrow. She only quietly thanked her temporary family for all they'd given her, for the joy she'd had, however temporary it had been.

Sage put down her pen. Her body warred between relief in knowing she'd left before Ian and Stiofanie were hurt and sadness. Every time she got close to someone, she left. It was the way her life had been since she was fifteen. She couldn't help but wonder how long she would be allowed to spend here. As much as she tried to ignore it, she had grown to love the people who kept her locked in a tower. Would she be able to leave without saying goodbye to Raph? Could she stand running away without Gavin knowing?

A note shimmered to life on her end table, and she smiled despite a small tear running down the side of her nose.

I'm at a new estate today. The lands here are so beautiful. I can't wait to show them to you one day. -G

Maybe she would have the chance to see them one day, after all.

✧✦✧

Symon sat at his desk. The sun had set hours ago, but he found himself glued to his chair instead of in bed with his wife. With the impending celebrations, the movement happening along the border of Nysa and Speridisia, and the arrival of a Realm Leaper, Symon had made his way to bed less often than he liked. And to make matters worse, the report of raiders in Mystaira added to the complex task of ruling a rebuilding nation.

Symon read over the correspondence from Gavin once more. He couldn't help but notice the paper was different from what was supplied before the trip, but he didn't spend long thinking over the oddity. The fact that Gavin sent such detailed reports, and suggestions on dealing with the raiders, proved that Aryael's intuition had been correct in naming the young fae Lord of the land. Quickly, Symon scratched out a reply: *I would like to know more about the raids. Gather more details. How many raiders are usually involved? Where and when do they strike? Perhaps your suggestion of sending more sentry from Veritasailles would work. -K.S.*

The note shimmered away, and Symon made to push away from his desk. Before he could stand from his chair, the journal containing Sage's latest memory caught his attention once more. The story of her and Ian interested him. Something of the male seemed...incomplete. Almost as if part of the story were missing. Especially as he so easily allowed Sage, whom he was supposedly in love with, to disappear on a dangerous journey. Symon couldn't imagine allowing Aryael to wade into peril on her own. In fact, it had been meeting Aryael that sparked his renewed desire to rebel and break free. He'd all but lost hope before she was transferred into his camp. Could a male who knew that depth of love actually let go when asked?

The other thing that bothered him was the matter of the insignias. No such item had fallen into their world with the girl. Could they be scattered across the continent? And if so, how likely was it they landed in Speridisia? The book, which was recovered in her pack, had proved a dead end. It contained some charming stories of the original Realm Leapers and the Gods. But in reality, not much of it seemed pertinent to their current situation.

Curiosity getting the best of him, Symon read through the journal entry one more time. Before he could reach the end, his eyes began drifting closed. A note shimmered onto his desk. Expecting a response from Gavin, despite the late hour, Symon unfolded the note.

Come to bed. I'll make it worth your while...

Knowing the Queen didn't appreciate repeating herself, Symon pushed himself from his chair and made his way to their rooms. He'd barely opened the door when her melodic voice purred, "It's about time." He smiled, the sound of her voice instantly putting him at ease.

Mystaira and Realm Leapers would have to wait until tomorrow.

Chapter 18

Raphael stood in the doorway of the Rafalatriki's great hall. Apprentices, Masters, and Scribes enjoyed the early morning bustle: grabbing plates of food and tea, discussing the latest research ventures, and gossiping about life on a sprawling campus closed off to the rest of the world. It felt like eons since Raphael had been an apprentice here before his sabbatical on the human continent, Meropoli.

Raphael took in the sight, basking in the strange combination of new and old, of tradition and innovation. While the stones and pillars were newly laid, the principle of the Rafalatriki remained as true as its founding day.

A whispered conversation in the corner pulled Raphael's attention away from the scene. Two apprentices, bright and fair-haired, talked in short, quiet spurts. As the lead Master for orientation, Raphael felt compelled to check on the younglings. It certainly wasn't his penchant for gossip.

"But what exactly did your letter say," said the girl with freckles scattered across her face.

"Is something the matter?" he asked sweetly, urging the girls to trust him as their proctor. Raphael struggled for a name, but luckily, the second girl interjected—

"Eva, he doesn't have time for the likes of this," her accent was thick, and their complexions made more sense as he took in their fair complexions anew. These were the recruits brought from the Maracadian Islands.

"Nonsense, ladies. I am here to assist as you get used to life as apprentices. Now, what seems to be the problem?"

"It's nothin', sir," girl two said....What was her name? Right! Tamara.

"Tamara– you insult me with your lack of confidence. Now, out with it. What is the issue?" Skeptical glances passed between the girls. Finally, Eva passed Raphael an over wrinkled letter. It was clear the letter had been unfolded, read over, and possibly wept over many times since receiving it. The penmanship looked rushed and scattered, as if someone had scratched the missive out in a hurry.

Details of a strange ship that had been reported earlier in the month dotted the notes, and woes over not being able to continue contact flowed across the page. According to the author, Maracadia was officially closing its borders to the outside world. Just as they had when Rankor had begun his campaign across the continent. It seemed that the enchanted island would continue its neutral stance. Cowards.

"I see," Raphael hummed as he reread the note. "It seems this might be the last we will hear from the islands for a while. Eva, dear, who wrote this?"

The girl's lip trembled slightly. "My older brother. He's all I've got back home. If I can't get back when my apprenticeship is done, I don't know what he'll do." Tamara reached out and patted her friend's back. Both girls looked downtrodden at losing contact with their homeland, and Raphael had to agree the island's actions could be a harbinger of troubles to come.

Shaking himself from his thoughts, he refocused on the problem at hand. "I assume Maracadia still honors the Realm Leapers? Does the original temple still stand?" It had been so long since he visited the islands, and he hadn't made the voyage since Felysia won its freedom.

Eva nodded in confirmation. "My brother is an acolyte for Brighid. He's a fire-wielder, so when our parents passed, he moved us both into the temple. They allowed me to stay for free in exchange for me using my healer gifts." She sniffed, daintily tapping the tears from her face with the edge of her robe. "I wasn't very good at first, but my brother always told me I had natural talent. That's why he took up a collection to send me here when the Rafalatriki reopened."

"And lucky for me, to meet you on the ship," Tamara replied. "I'd be awful homesick if it weren't for you."

"Speaking of–" Raphael interjected, "has anyone shown you two the temples to the Realm Leapers here? They surely pale in comparison to the original in your homeland, but I imagine it would be a place you might both enjoy."

Smiles lit both of the girls' faces, and they nodded enthusiastically. Tamara grabbed Eva's hand, and they followed Raphael, who set off towards the underground temple.

The Realm Leaper temples were buried below the Rafalatriki and remained one of the only original structures untouched by Rankor's terror. Sandstone stairs led a winding, but wide, path down, down, down, the temperature dropping steadily. Stairs broke into a wide, flat, open hallway darkly lit by torches.

"This was originally the site of Allyra's biggest temple. It's why the Rafalatriki was built here because she was also the Goddess of healing in her homeland. But the Goddess insisted before her final departure that the temple be converted to represent her fellows."

Raphael gestured above them to the expansive carvings. The most prominent being a depiction of Allyra, her hair flowing from her head into tiny creeks and streams, her hands outstretched in invitation. Water fauna seemed to dance along the carving before fading into separate depictions of the other gods.

Bypassing the first two rooms flanking the hallway, dedicated to Allyra and Cerridos, Raphael led the girls into the sacred temple room of Brighid. The chilly, damp air broke away into humid heat. Bowls of fire crackled in the room. A bronze statue of Brighid aiming a bow and arrow stood in the center of the room. The firelight danced along the grooves and curves of the statue so it looked as though she watched them from wary eyes.

"She's beautiful," Tamara marveled, approaching the statue. A small bowl of fire sat below the Goddess, and Tamara doubled back to collect Eva. Together, they kneeled at the feet of the Goddess and quickly wrote out their prayers on scraps of paper from the pockets of their robes. When each girl had completed the ritual of burning their prayers, they recited the story of Brighid defeating an army of demons that had invaded Nysa all by herself. Of all the Gods—Realm Leapers—she was possibly the fiercest fighter and definitely the least merciful.

Raphael smiled to himself as the girls finished their prayers and storytelling, content to listen and admire the carvings around the room. One particular carving showed Brighid with her palms outstretched toward the viewer. In her hands sat a coin with a design carved into it. The design was repeated in several places along the walls, and even in the four corners of the room. Five arrows studded the center of the coin, the group outlined in flame. Raphael pulled his own paper and charcoal pen from his pocket. Finding a smaller version of the carving, he placed his paper over the carving and rubbed the charcoal over it until he had a perfect replica of the image. He would redraw it later this evening when he wrote his reports to Symon.

Not only would he need to tell Symon about Maracadia, he wondered whether they should send out sentries to look for the missing insignias. If they were somewhere on the continent, leaving them unattended could have consequences later.

"Alright ladies, we should join the others. Don't want to be late. Although, I suppose they can't get started without their Proctor, now, can they?"

Quickly, the three of them ascended the stairs, a mood of contentment surrounding the girls. Raphael tried not to envy them, but his own mood remained plagued with anxious apprehension. Raphael squared his shoulders as they reached the top of the stairs, and pushed his worries to the back of his mind, forcing himself to turn his focus to the apprentices lining up in the great hall. His worries would have to rest until later that night.

Chapter 19

✳✳✳

It took me three days by boat to arrive at the port of Lyonesus. I'm sure the skin-color potion I took was the last for me on my journey; I'm not sure the hang-over I received after changing back was worth the safety it afforded me on my journey. Based on my most recent dream, I had to hole up in an abandoned house for two days to recover. I suppose that's why the pharmacies reserved the potions for extreme cases of dysmorphia.

Never mind all that. What's important is that I remember the fire temple for Brighid. It's strange. No one really visits the temples much anymore except on major holidays, one of which being a celebration to remember the last Great War- the one that targeted elementals. Ironic, really, that we go to elemental Gods' temples to celebrate a history of destroying their chosen blessed.

The temple was enormous. I'm not sure I can truly describe it, but I suppose I can give it a try...

The temple was vast, made of enormous square blocks of limestone. Cairn-like fire pits dotted the interior, all blazing with sacrifices made to Brighid on the last holy day.

A stone labyrinth lined with miniature fires along the top dominated the center of the holy building. At the labyrinth's end sat a gleaming copper basin of fire, The Heart of Brighid, or so it was called. The walls of the labyrinth were high enough that peeking over the edges to find the way was impossible, and the ditches of hot oil carved into the top of the walls prevented the temptation to try. Instead, faith and patience were required to find the center fire pit. It took Sage a day and a half to finish the maze. And when she found it, she'd also found the oracle.

Standing next to the copper basin of fire, Mugroi the Oracle's attention narrowed on Sage. Dark glasses clashed against the druid's filmy white robes, reflecting the bright firelight so much that Sage almost didn't notice the druid's sewn-shut mouth. Sage's stomach flip-flopped with unease, but she forced herself to approach the woman. Sage recognized the druid clothes and the tell-tale glasses announcing the druid's blindness. Before this moment, Sage believed all of Brighid's druids had been executed, but this druid had clearly managed to escape, or maybe there was a secret clan hidden somewhere on the continent.

Come closer and we will answer the questions you do not seek but must hear.

The words sifted through Sage like sand in a sieve. Several voices, and yet one echoed through her head, and Sage winced. Despite the sutures, the druid grinned, looking more like a grimace. Again, the croaking voice filtered through Sage.

Yes. That is us you hear. Come, and give us a fortune, and you shall receive the treasure you seek in repayment.

"A fortune?" Sage called out, still yards away from the fire and the druid. Sweat ran down the side of her face, and she resisted the temptation of wiping it away, afraid of making sudden movements and startling the creature ahead of her. "I'm afraid I'm broke."

It is not material wealth we seek. It is your future we yearn to tell. Seeing fate's designs is our sustenance. Come....let us get a peek.

The druid smiled again, an unsettling image, and extended her arms as if to offer a hug. Her ghastly pale skin glimmered slightly.

"Faith. This is about faith," Sage reminded herself.

Taking a deep breath, Sage gathered her courage and approached the basin. Before she could get too close, the druid gestured for her to stop. With a flourish, Mugroi the druid produced a blocky, old-fashioned instant camera.

"You....want to take my picture?" Sage asked apprehensively.

The druid held a finger to her sutures, signaling for Sage to be quiet. In a flash, the druid snapped a picture of Sage and held the developing square of picture paper to her eyes as if inspecting it with her sight. The whole scene would have been comical to Sage if she hadn't been terrified of the woman in white robes.

The druid began to glow. An eerie, star-bright blue light shimmered around the druid, and she began to rise off the floor. She dropped the picture, her head lifting to the ceiling, palms falling to her sides. A melodic harmony of voices rippled through the room, sweeping across Sage like the chiming of bells.

Realm Leaper.
Follow the one who walks on the wind.
Set to right what has been upended.
You will bring the one who is three back into power.
You will see all the worlds reunited in harmony.
There will be discord no more.

Just as quickly as the phenomenon began, the druid lightly dropped to the floor, her hands coming to clasp each other once more. Sage replayed the fortune in her head again. *The one who walks on the wind.* Who was that?!

"I don't know what any of that means. Can I just have the insignia now?" Sage moved towards the druid, pulling out her wand.

Brighid probably wouldn't love it if she knocked the oracle out, but the Goddess was kind of responsible for putting her there in the first place. So Sage considered it an even trade. Before she could act, the druid waved her arms in a flourish, and Sage found herself frozen to the spot. The croaking voice crackled through her again, buzzing in her head.

We know who you are now. You will get what you want, but first—a bargain.

"A bargain! I just gave you a bargain. You wanted to see my fortune, and I let you. Now hand over the insignia."

Give us a bargain, and you shall have it.

Fighting against the magic the druid wielded proved to be a losing battle for Sage. Begrudgingly, Sage acquiesced. "Fine. A bargain, but only one."

A twinkle of delight seemed to spark in the dark glasses covering the druid's eyes. Sage was whisked across the floor with another flourish from the druid's hands, so she stood nearly nose-to-nose with the woman. Dusty musk with an undertone of rot rolled off the druid's body, and Sage fought the urge to recoil.

A bargain...you will return to free my sisters so we can roam Lyonesus once more.

Return? That was the bargain? Somehow, it seemed too easy. "Okay. Deal?" Sage tried to keep the question from her reply. Shaking her head, she finalized the bargain, "Deal. It's a deal."

The flames in the basin grew to terrifying heights and pressure wrapped itself around Sage's heart so she thought it might burst. The druid's magic around her vanished and Sage fell to the floor.

Before she could master her breathing, heart still feeling squished like a grape, Sage looked up to see filmy white robes flutter to the floor, empty of the druid that once filled them. The pressure inside her dissipated and Sage scrambled forward, rummaging through the robes. In the center, Sage found a round medallion bearing Brighid's insignia. Five arrows and flame.

Her knuckles scraped the stone floor as she scooped the coin up and pushed herself to stand. She staggered to the entrance of the maze, grabbing the bag she dropped as she'd entered. Without waiting to see what happened next, Sage began the journey back through the maze to the sound of cackling echoing off the walls.

I'm not really sure how long it took me to exit the maze. I'm hoping it was a faster process than making it to the end. What I can't seem to get past is the bargain. Why would the druid make me bargain to come back? Wasn't that always the plan?

Chapter 20

Gavin finished writing his latest missive to Symon.

Already on this trip, Gavin had had to purchase two additional packs of enchanted paper in order to keep up his note-passing with Sage. He looked forward to her messages and found himself seeking small moments of solitude so he could send a message to her. Each time he saw her tight, looping script he felt pleasantly anxious. He pushed aside the questions that swarmed him about what that feeling was and instead focused on sending his notes.

In this case, his note was accompanied by a less-pleasant feeling of anxiety. Once again, he asked for guidance on handling the raiders. Was the movement on the Nysan borders more critical? Gavin supposed so, but losing massive quantities of export from Mystaira would have long-reaching consequences for all of Felysia. If they lost a season's worth of product, starvation might be their next battle.

Gavin knew Symon wouldn't let things get that dire. Most likely, Symon would cast directly into the raider camp and mind-control them into taking their own lives. But they were still a rebuilding nation. Compared to the humans in Meropoli, fae did not reproduce nearly as quickly or frequently. They were an aging population. Every life was precious. Gavin considered the likelihood that the raiders possessed legitimate grievances that went unanswered. Perhaps his next course of action should be trying to find the raiders' camps and trying to intervene on his own. To attempt to negotiate some kind of end to hostilities.

Gavin quickly shook that idea out of his head. Meliza would throttle him if he came back alive and found out about that plan. To go into a hostile camp without backup or reconnaissance, yeah— Meliza would probably skip straight to hanging him by his ankles to humiliate him. If he couldn't solve the problem on his own right now, he would have to continue reaching out to Symon. This was the third note he'd sent suggesting the King send additional sentries to guard exports from Mystaira to Veritasailles. The note shimmered into nothing just as he heard the crunching of approaching footsteps.

"Amos– good to see you!" Gavin called out to the hand of the latest estate he was visiting. He'd spent the morning with the minor Lord who owned the estate, but he was more interested in speaking with Amos. He was a male with his ears to the ground, so to speak. He hoped Amos could provide some answers on the raids.

"Lord Gavin, I could say the same." The farmhand's eyes crinkled in delight as he took Gavin's offered hand. His browned skin glistened with the barest hint of sweat having come straight from the fields.

"Just Gavin."

"For now," Amos's eyes crinkled even more. "How's Delphia? And Levi?"

"They are good, Amos. How about Lily?" Lily was Amos's daughter, his wife having died from an illness that had swept through the work camp. Lily was another rarity, born in the camps, and had been close friends with Delphia growing up.

"Oh, you know, still starting fights others don't believe she can finish. I'm afraid her mother and I did the world a disservice by giving her such a pretty name." Despite his words, Amos beamed as he talked about his daughter. "She's in charge of our livestock here. I've given her the task of breaking a mule that's as hard-headed as she is. Hopefully, that will keep her focused enough to keep her out of trouble."

As if on cue, a jarring bray rippled across the farm, startling a flock of crows that had been pecking along the path that led to a massive silo. A loud crash closely followed, and then a splash. A female's voice sputtered and cussed, fading into the distance as the braying signified a mule escaping whatever task Lily had been trying to accomplish. Amos and Gavin laughed riotously.

Gavin pulled himself together again and refocused on the task at hand. "I'm not here for a social call, Amos. Though I suppose I'm overdue for one."

"That you are, Lordling," Amos replied. "You're here about the raids?" Gavin nodded his response. "I was part of the last band of shipments that got hit. It was well-organized. Fast and brutal, but they didn't take any lives except one guard that was especially vigilant."

"What I don't understand is why we haven't heard about this before. At the very least, Delphia should have been sent word and she would have sent it to me."

"Well, that's probably because Seth's been going around and interfering. According to him, these raiders are the sons, daughters, nephews, and whatnot of Lords and Ladies who were executed or exiled when Symon took back the throne. He supposes he can handle it himself."

The details began to come together. Seth, who'd always thought it was his birthright to lead Mystaira, was actively campaigning to take over. Gavin felt a pang of empathy for the male because he was probably the better choice. The sentiment was short lived, however, as Gavin considered that Seth had neglected to seek outside help, the end result being a guard's life and continued economic terrorism.

"Right. Thanks, Amos. I'll get these details wrapped up, but I'll leave your name out of it. Don't want you on the hook with Seth. I'd bet he's got some sort of arrangement with your employers?"

Amos nodded, peering off into the distance as the sun began to set. "I'll be back again before the year is up. If you hear anything else, tell Lily to get the word to Delphia. They've got history so it won't seem suspicious if she goes to visit."

Gavin shook Amos's hand in farewell then shifted into his winged form. He flew towards the small town center that bordered the farm. He needed to pick up more enchanted paper before stopping in to visit the next estate. The next message to Symon would include a request to increase his allowance on this visit so he could continue his correspondence. The king didn't have to know where the rest of the paper was being sent.

Symon pondered Gavin's latest notes. A group of three sat in front of the King, two detailing the latest information gathered by the young Lord, and one requesting an allowance to buy yet more enchanted paper. The math didn't quite add up; Symon had sent Gavin with enough paper to allow for two reports per estate. The king had his suspicions about where the rest of the paper had gone.

Raphael appeared rather dramatically in the middle of Symon's study. "What are you grinning over?" he asked as he walked over to the king.

"Oh, just remembering what it was like to be young," Symon said.

"Ah– so that's from Gavin, I take it." Symon offered a knowing grin and a shrug in answer, and Raphael chuckled softly. "Right, I've not come this far to gossip about young love, although you know I love a good story to tell."

"Why are you this far from the Rafalatriki? Has Shiphrah kicked you out?"

"No. I came because...something strange happened last night. The apprentices have the day off, and even if they didn't...you need to hear—no— to see this."

"What is it?" Symon sat up in his chair, alarmed by Raphael's sudden change in demeanor.

"She's made a bargain," Raphael responded.

"You know about the druid?" Symon asked. Confusion swept across Raphael's face, and Symon didn't need to read minds to understand what was in Raphael's thoughts. "What happened?" Symon asked again.

"I don't quite understand," Raphael began, walking away from the desk and beginning to pace erratically—and somewhat annoyingly— around the room. Symon couldn't remember seeing the healer so out of sorts and self-conscious. "I suppose due to the difference in her biology, dream walking with Sage had different side effects than I anticipated. I'm not sure if it's an empathy link, that would explain the phenomena, but—"

"—What. Happened." Symon applied a dominance to his voice rarely used with Raphael.

Immediately, the healer stopped, turned toward the king, and replied, "I was in her dream. Almost as if I were...her. I felt everything she felt..." Raphael's face took on a haunted look. "But there was no...druid. A bargain was made, though." Raphael's eyes slid towards Symon, and he leaned onto his desk, almost as if to halt the tremor Symon detected in his hands. "If you know of another bargain, with a druid, then that makes two. And who knows how many more."

Symon sat back in his chair, rubbing his chin. This was worrisome indeed. The Fae didn't take bargains lightly. They were contracts that took dominion over a fae's fate, preventing the individual from moving forward in life until the terms had been met.

"We don't know that bargains hold the same power in her world." He looked back again at Raphael, the same doubt echoed in his eyes. "Yet something tells me we won't be so lucky. Sit down, Raph, and show me."

Raph nodded in agreement, making his way to a plush couch before lying down.

"Start from the beginning."

The journey to Cerridos had taken a month, most of it on foot. On the way there, in the back of unsuspecting trucks, or when she'd found a place to take shelter for a few days, she read the book. So when she reached Kailyoch, the tallest of the Ardernin Mountain Range, she was ready for the next task.

It took her a week to reach the summit of the mountain, the final day spent scaling the rugged, windswept face. Only her earth and wind magic prevented her from plummeting to her death on the jagged rocks below.

When she reached the top, she'd been amazed to find a druid circle. Great, square, stone pillars sat in perfect symmetry around a stone altar table in the center. The table featured a thin stone archway that held a stone pendant attached by a leather band. The pendant lay on the rim of a great copper basin; as the wind blew gently, the pendant circled the basin, causing a melodic ringing to fill the sacred space.

The stone pillars were covered with metal coins, tied through holes in their centers, and attached by leather throngs to the pillars. As the wind blew, the coins clinked against each other adding to the melodic quality of the altar. Sage sat in that stone circle for hours, or at least what felt like hours, marveling at the beauty.

Overlooking the Goulain terrain, picturesque between the stone pillars, Sage wept. She'd allowed herself those moments to weep for joy, that she hadn't fallen off the side of the mountain, and that she'd found Cerridos's sacred altar. She'd wept with grief, missing her mother, father, and sister. Missing the life she never got to have. The pain and loneliness she'd felt for Stiofanie and Ian. She'd wept in anger at the government who'd failed her, hunted her; the leaders, the powerful who'd slaughtered her kind and were hell-bent on slaughtering her too.

"Why do you weep little one?" a willowy voice brushed against Sage. A breeze sent the copper bowl ringing again as Sage peered up from her sodden eyelashes.

"Who said that?" she asked, only half caring.

"I am the one you cannot see until I've taken what you wish to be seen."

"That doesn't make any sense," Sage said flatly. "Look, I'm not in the mood right now for riddles. Just show yourself."

The willowy voice giggled cheerfully, "You can't see me. But here I am," and a forceful wind pushed against Sage, nearly knocking her over. No, it wasn't a wind. It was more solid than that.

"What are you then?" Sage asked warily, rising to her feet. She saw the sand before her move slightly, as if someone were dragging their feet through it.

"My name is Clionaugh," the mass before Sage shifted slightly, and giggled, "I'm a wraith."

"A wraith?" Sage questioned, "I thought those were made up."

"No, silly. You know, I used to be well known. I used to be the prettiest wraith of them all," the shape sighed, and Sage saw the imprint of a bottom and legs on the ground as Clionaugh sat on the ground.

"So, if you're not made up, then do you actually steal people's identities? Their bodies?"

"Now, wait just a second," the sand was brushed about as the wraith hurriedly rose to her feet. "We don't steal their identities. We trade them or borrow...or sometimes share. There's always a way to make all parties happy," the wraith let out a squeaky giggle.

"So, if you were the prettiest, does that mean you only made deals with the prettiest girls you met?"

"Uh-hmm...and boys, too, sometimes," Clionaugh replied, cheerily.

Sage finished wiping her face, her tears finally drying. "And I suppose you are here in some favor to Cerridos?"

"Ohh....do you know Cerridos? He's so handsome, eeee!" she squealed.

Gods, help her; Sage needed a faster way to get the wraith to focus. "Yes, I do. He sent me here to find something. Can you help me?"

"Oohh, what do you need to find?"

"Do you know where his insignia is? It should look like a medallion," Sage explained.

"I don't know if you noticed, but there are loads of medallions here. What's in it for me? If I help you?" the wraith harrumphed.

"I don't know; what do you want?" The sand in front of Sage twirled as if the wraith drew circles with a toe in the silt. "I want a form," the wraith declared.

"My form? You don't want my form," Sage tried to reason with the wraith.

"Oh, it won't hurt. All I need is just a little bit of you. A fingernail, a piece of skin, a lock of hair! That's all. It will be as painless as dreaming," the wraith cooed. Sage could just imagine her clasping her hands, the picture of innocence.

"Fine," huffed Sage, and she fished her pocket knife out of her pack. A moment later, Sage was holding a lock of her hair out in front of her. A swipe and Sage's hair spun around the wraith; the wind itself shimmered, sunlight refracting off the outline as the wraith's form began to take shape. Then Sage was staring at a duplicate copy of herself.

"Ohh...look how fun! I love this haircut. I've never had mine cut this short before, when I was in girl form, that is. I did once take the form of a soldier, he kept his hair buzzed. That's the last time I go for the butch look, let me tell you. It itched like the dickens when it grew back," Clionaugh prattled as she pranced around Sage, admiring her new form.

"Ok, you have your form. Which medallion is the right one?"

Clionaugh crossed her arms at Sage, "You're not very fun." Sage just peered back at Clionaugh. "Just...one more thing," Clio cooed.

"What now?" Sage groaned.

"You know, a bunch of us have heard about you. Gods-blessed children are the most delicious fodder for wraith-gossip circles. And you—" Sage watched as her own body pointed at her in delight, "have made quite the name for yourself."

Sage planted her feet. "Okay. What does that have to do with the insignia?"

"You made a bargain with that druid. I want one, too!" Clio announced, dancing away from Sage and towards the table.

"Nope. I did that once, and it hurt like hell. Not doing it again. We made a trade, now I want my half." Sage crossed her arms and rolled her eyes as Clio mimicked the movement.

"You've already done it once. So now you know what to expect. Come on....just a teensy little bargain." Clio waggled her eyebrows at Sage, and she cringed at how the movement looked on her own face. The idea of being indebted to another creature was alarming, but Sage considered the fact she'd basically entered a contract with the Gods themselves. How could things get any worse?

"Tell me the bargain first, and I'll consider it."

"Make a deal with me that when you come back, and you must come back, you will release the other wraiths. You see, that big, bad leader of yours did a good job of rounding us all up in the Great War. I'm one of the last to be free. He's keeping them locked up, guarding his tomb."

"My leader? You mean Ranquer? Clio—he wasn't even alive during the Great War."

"Oh, poo, never mind all that. We can discuss that later. Just make me a deal and I'll get that medallion for you!"

The bargain was practically the same she had made with Mugroi the Oracle. Despite not knowing how to find and save the druids or which tomb the wraiths were locked up in, Sage decided to take the bait. "Okay. You have a deal."

Clio shimmered, and faster than the blink of an eye she grabbed Sage's hand in a shake, confirming the deal. Rather than a vice-grip on her heart, the bargain wrapped itself around the organ like a bear hug: restrictive, but not painful.

"You're right, that wasn't that bad," Sage said, breaking her grip from Clio. A yawn broke from Sage so wide, tears welled in the corners of her eyes.

"Oh, deary," the wraith replied, waving at Sage. "How about this," she replied in her cheerful, sing-songy voice, "I look around, I know which medallion you're talking about, just don't know which pillar it got left on, and you take a rest. You look like a swamp hag that's been stranded in the desert." The wraith laughed merrily at her own joke as Sage scowled. Looking at the Clio, she decided she didn't look that bad if the wraith really was a copy of herself.

But the idea of lying down, of resting for a while was undeniably tempting. Sage rummaged through her pack, pulling out the thick blanket she'd managed to keep inside. She laid it out beneath the basin, pulled out the last of the dried meat from her pack, and finally rested once she'd eaten her meager meal.

Starlight flooded the sky when Clionaugh finally nudged Sage awake. "I found it. Here ya go," the wraith said with a smile wider than Sage reckoned she'd made in years and years. "You should probably get a move on. There's a bunch of people down at the bottom of the mount," Clionaugh said with a frown. "I don't think they're very nice." Sage sat up abruptly and began stuffing her pack with her blanket.

"Don't forget this," Clionaugh shoved the stone into Sage's hand. The smooth stone bore a hole through the center. Four spiraling cloud shapes surrounded the hole.

"Thank you," said Sage, even as she deposited the medallion into her pack, and made her way to the edge of the temple to peer down the mountain. Indeed, large trucks with lights were lined up at the bottom of the mountain. She could hear men and women shouting directions as they tried to figure out a way to bring their tools up the mountain. Large circular machines were warming up; drones, those were drones that would fly up here and find her, or capture her, or just destroy the temple. Shit. She had to get out of there.

"You need some help, don't ya?" the wraith asked Sage, peering over her shoulder.

"That'd be nice," Sage replied, not bothering to look at the wraith.

"Ok. Don't you worry. If you go down the back path, I can go make a bit of ruckus," Clionaugh said with a mischievous grin, wriggling her fingers towards the trucks.

"No, you can't do that. They will catch you and hurt you," Sage barked.

"Oh, don't be so dramatic. I've got your form now. That means I have your magic *and* my powers. Just watch," Clionaugh said the last sentence with a snap, and she was gone. Below, Sage could hear the yelling become more frantic. The sounds of boulders crashing, soldiers yelling–then screaming– filled the air. An explosion rocketed through the air as Sage stepped onto the path that led down the back of the mountain, and she swore she could hear musical cackling in the distance.

Sage reached the cliff edge where she'd have to descend the mountain face to reach the path leading to safety. Securing her pack to her back, she slipped over the edge, using her earth magic to create hand and footholds. She worked quickly, too quickly. Abruptly, she'd fallen through the air. But before she'd been able to make sense of what was happening, a gust of wind buffeted against her until she hovered atop the ground. The air popped around her, and she belly-flopped onto the ground.

The scene fizzled away in Symon's mind as Raphael's understanding of the dream and events at Cerridos's temple waned. "So she's made at least two bargains in her own world." Symon moved away from Raphael as the male adjusted to the light filtering through the curtains.

"It appears that way. What does that mean for us?" Raphael asked, sitting up on the couch.

"Nothing, yet. But it does mean she will need to figure out a way to get home. Let me discuss this with Aryael, she may have some suggestions."

"I would offer to come, but I'm afraid Shiphrah needs my assistance. A few more days and the apprentices should be ready to join in with the rest of the academy and begin their residencies."

"Take care, Raph. And thank you," Symon smiled at Raphael. "I know I've been a little...difficult to get along with lately, but—"

"Enough, Symon. I will see you when I return." Raphael gave Symon a nod that said he understood, and disappeared into the morning light.

Chapter 21

Gavin sat in an expansive sitting room overlooking fields of grape vines growing over rambling hills, rolling on and on into the distance. When he stared at the intricate patterns the trellises and vines made over the cresting hilltops his eyes went cross-eyed and made him dizzy. If he focused, he could pick out the sounds of livestock murmuring in a distant pasture. The whispering sounds of staff maintaining the massive household hummed around the quiet room. Despite the comfortable chairs and furnishings, Gavin grew weary of waiting to be received by the Lord of the house.

Seth, owner of the largest agricultural enterprise in Mystaira—and therefore Felysia— seemed content to allow Gavin to wither away in his garish salon. He grew restless as the hours dragged on. Writing notes to Sage had occupied a significant portion of his time, but he was once again down to the last few pages of enchanted paper. He'd already spent a good portion of his own coin replenishing the paper, plus the allowance sent by Symon. It was a good thing he would be going home tomorrow because Gavin doubted he could afford to continue the note-passing with Sage for much longer. Besides, he had to spare enough paper to send

Symon a final report before finally returning to the Obelisk. And then they would be heading to the castle for Aryael's celebration.

Gavin allowed his thoughts to wander. Before he knew it, his thoughts brought him back to that day on the balcony. The way Sage had looked with the wind tugging playfully at her hair. The way she had blushed when he stepped onto the balcony, and how that blush crept down her neck and towards her—

"I see you've made yourself quite comfortable in my house."

Gavin swallowed a sigh before standing, turning to meet the Lady of the house. "Megara—a pleasure as always." Gavin gave a sharp bow of the head, an indication of his status over her. In return, Megara should have dipped her head in a similar bow, only lower, but the Lady seemed incapable of such decency as she walked towards him.

Regal. Elegant. And haughty as hell. Her black chiton, encrusted in jewels along the bodice as if she were some sort of Goddess herself, swished across the stone floor as she advanced on Gavin. Her red hair, piled atop her head, was encircled in a headband that might as well have been a tiara for all the gold that adorned it. He couldn't help but get the feeling she had dressed for battle before finally making her way to greet him.

"I wish I could say I find it pleasurable to see you, Gavin, but I do not." Megara stopped several feet from Gavin. "Lord Seth, I am afraid, will not be able to make your meeting today. I am to meet with you in his stead."

Without offering a glass to Gavin, Megara turned to a decanter sitting on a table near them and poured herself a glass of wine. Sipping slowly from the glass, she glared at Gavin over the rim.

Summoning his willpower, Gavin asked as politely as he could manage, "May I ask what has detained Seth?"

"Lord. It is Lord Seth," Megara said curtly. "And no you may not."

"Then let me rephrase what I said. I demand you tell me what has detained *Lord* Seth. Because while he is Lord of this estate, I still outrank you both."

"Do you? I don't recall being invited to any ceremonies where you officially took the title. A title that rightfully belongs to my husband."

"Megara—you walk a very fine line between defiance and treason. Let me remind you that the title of Lord of Mystaira was granted to me by the Queen herself."

"A queen who was coronated before she understood her new people. A queen who did not know the land. Perhaps what you should be reminded of is that Symon's own father took a queen from Nysa as well, and look where that got us. Even now, there are mutterings of movement along the Speridisia and Nysa borders, ships going missing in the sea." Megara's skin flushed along her cheeks, anger apparent in her gaze and stature. Setting her glass on the table, she squared herself to Gavin. "What you should remember is that many of us were blindly loyal to a king once before, and paid for that loyalty."

Gavin let the last statement settle in the room. He could understand her frustration, and he couldn't even fully disagree with her. He did believe that Seth was more qualified to lead Mystaira. Seth understood the agriculture, understood the economics, and understood the history of the land and its people. He had remained loyal to Felysia and fought savagely, more than once, against their enemies. Gavin often wondered if Queen Aryael made a mistake overlooking Seth for leadership, favoring Gavin because of their friendship forged in battle.

"Lady Megara, I do not fault you for your questions. In fact, part of the purpose of my visit here was to discuss a partnership with your family. Lord Seth and yourself contain a wealth of knowledge that I would be unwise to ignore. It is my aim to reconcile our differences so that we may both serve the people of Mystaira." Gavin straightened, standing tall as he explained himself so that Megara could see what he said was true. "You are right that there are alarming things going on right now, but that's all the more reason for us to work together, in unity. To present an allied force to quash our shared enemies. Now is not the time to allow our differences to become our weakness."

"Alarming things? You mean like your Queen's special guest?" Megara smiled as she looked into Gavin's eyes. The statement had surprised him so quickly he was unable to conceal his reaction. "That's right. We've all heard about her falling from the sky. And how our little Lordling has been trotting around Veritasailles with her while we deal with raiders and real problems, here."

Megara's tone had taken a taunting tone, full of bitterness as her eyebrows drew together. Gavin took a plaintive step towards her, reaching with his hand extended, palm up, in an effort to try and persuade her to see things his way.

"I'm not sure what you are insinuating, but I will remind you once more of the line you are towing. Be careful how you speak about our Queen and those in her favor." Gavin locked eyes with the Lady standing across from him. A battle of dominance was not how he had expected his day to go, but working alongside Meliza and Zeke had prepared him for this.

"Or what, welp? What will you do?" Megara paused, waiting for his reply. "You've never seemed all that concerned with your duty to the crown before. You've left us here to fend for ourselves, running all our communications through your sister while you kept busy entertaining yourself in the capitol."

The truth of her words stung a little, but Gavin had always been humble enough to admit his shortcomings. "And I'm here now. Lady Megara, I ask that you give me the chance to fulfill my duty. With you and Lord Seth on our side, I don't think we can fail."

"So you expect a handout, just because now you decide to show up and act the part?" Megara scoffed, rolling her eyes before gazing out of the window. "You don't even truly understand the breadth of what we lost in the occupation. You didn't have to suffer the shock of being ripped from your home, your children being torn out of their beds in the middle of the night and thrown into wagons. If you had, I doubt you would be so naive as to believe that Symon and Aryael have the answers to the problems heading our way."

"But that's where you're wrong. King Symon and Queen Aryael have learned from the past. You're right, I didn't experience the destruction of our people. But I lost the only chance I had at a childhood. I lost the chance to know what it's like to have a home. And I would like Mystaira to be my home. All I am asking for is your help."

Gavin rolled his shoulders. Sharing that part of himself made him uncomfortable, but the fact that Megara had shared her fears with him made him want to reciprocate. If he could just get her on his side.

Megara's eyes fluttered slightly, and she turned her back on him. He thought that maybe he had made a break-through with her. Was it possible his words had hit their mark, and she would finally come around to reason?

Turning sharply, Gavin could taste the fire singing in-side her, dancing in her eyes. "You might have everyone else fooled, Lordling, but I for one cannot forget how you've abandoned your duties here. And I would advise you to stay out of our way when we make our sentiments known about the Queen harboring that dangerous little fiend you seem so fond of." With a swish of her skirts Megara turned towards the door.

True anger—rage—gripped Gavin then. Without warning, he sent a powerful gust of wind through the room, slam-ming the double doors that lead the way to the rest of the house and holding Megara in place. His aim was true, so true that hardly a paper skittered from its resting place. Wind spiraled around Megara, holding her tight as Gavin approached slowly.

"I've let your disrespect of our Queen slide once, but you've disrespected her again, and that was your mistake, *Lady* Megara." Gavin tucked his arms behind him in an effort to keep himself as restrained as possible. "Further-more, you speak of things you do not understand, despite your age. The Queen's special guests are her business, and her business alone."

"Not if it affects the safety of the rest of us." Megara spoke calmly, but her cheeks reddened with indignation. "So it's true, then? Our little Lordling *is* infatuated with the stranger."

"I can assure you that Sage does not affect you, or your estate, in the slightest. Now, tell me where *Lord* Seth is."

Gavin gripped his hands behind his back tighter, demanding himself to keep a hold of his anger.

Megara smiled wide, sweetly even. "He had important business to take care of. According to one of our close contacts, another raid occurred and he went to take the reports."

Gavin released his hold on Megara. "And you two both decided the best way to deal with it was to not tell me and deal with it yourselves?"

"The location is too far for air travel. Seth could only make it there in time by casting. He was worried you would take offense by his suggestion since you apparently couldn't travel with him. Better luck next time, welp." Megara spared Gavin one last scathing smile before she swept out of the room.

Gavin stood rooted to the spot, enraged by her dismissal. She had fired a fatal blow with her final statement. Fae were unlikely to submit to a Lord who couldn't cast, one of the most widely accepted attributes of power. Megara had beaten him this time, and they both knew it. He had to get back to Veritasailles and talk this over with Aryael.

Taking the time to gather his notes, Gavin shoved them into his pocket and shifted into hawk form. Circling the room twice, he speared into the foyer and shot out of the open front doors. Climbing high into the sky, he let out a shrill call into the wind, releasing his anger into the darkening night sky. Despite flying as fast and high as possible, his heart hammered with rage at Megara's threat.

He'd be damned if they came for his Queen...or Sage.

Chapter 22

Sage sat in the bright kitchen watching as Hyacinth merrily tidied up after their breakfast. The tower had been blissfully peaceful the last two days as Petra left the tower early in preparations for the Queen's birthday celebrations. Sage soaked in the moment of joy, listening to Hyacinth sing songs from her childhood about brave sailors making their way back to long-lost loves. Sunlight filtered in through the window she sat next to, and the feeling of it on her skin created a pleasant tingling along the back of her arm.

"Why are you grinning like that?" Hyacinth asked, looking at Sage with a side-eye.

"Like what? I was enjoying your singing, that's all. And these tarts!" Sage reached forward and grabbed one of the bite-sized tarts Hyacinth had whipped up and popped it in her mouth.

"Stop that!" Hyacinth snapped Sage's hand with her dish towel. "If you don't cut it out, there won't be any left for when Raph and Gavin get back tonight." Sage couldn't stop a grin from creeping across her face, and the tingling on her arms spread to other places along her body. "Ohhh....that's why you're grinning." Hyacinth wiggled her eyebrows at Sage.

"I don't know what you mean," Sage replied, turning to stare out the window.

And yet, she couldn't stop smiling. The anticipation of Gavin coming back had started a series of flutters in her stomach to come and go without warning. She also missed Raphael desperately and couldn't wait to hear about the Rafalatriki and everything he saw while he was there.

Based on her last note from Gavin, it would still be a few hours before he would manage to get back. "Ok. I think I'm going to wait in the library for a bit, so I don't ruin your surprise and eat every last one of those tarts. You sure you don't need my help on anything else?"

"Och— get out of here. If I have you try to bake anything else, you're liable to catch it on fire. Then I'll have double the work."

"Har, har...very funny," Sage quipped. Quickly, Sage skipped over to Hyacinth and laid her head on her friend's shoulder. "Thanks for breakfast. I'll come back down in a bit." Hyacinth patted Sage on the head, and then Sage made her way up the stairs to the library.

Two weeks. It had been two weeks of pacing the library, pacing the balcony, pacing her room, and writing, writing, writing. Raphael had warned her that once her memories started coming back they could start a floodgate. And that's exactly how it felt. Memories poured into her at all times of the day and night. Writing them down had been strangely therapeutic. She would have to thank Raphael for the suggestion.

And when she wasn't remembering her old life, she found herself remembering moments from her new life. She kept up with her elemental practices, going to the training room to practice fire wielding, and summoning water into fun shapes with Hyacinth, who was surprisingly good at the skill. Wind wielding proved to be tricky for her when she was calm, but on nights she felt restless she loved to go on the balcony and send ripples of air galloping out from her perch. Working with earth was the only element she couldn't freely practice in the tower. She was too afraid of making a mistake and sending the whole building crumbling to the ground. But she felt earth energy around her and knew if she called on it, she could make it bend to her will.

Some nights, after expending her extra energy on wind wielding, she found herself still restless. Thoughts of Gavin, and the balcony. And that kiss. Those thoughts were like her memories. They popped up when she least expected them, and always at night. Those thoughts were resurfacing now, and she wondered if he thought about that kiss as often as she did.

"I hope you missed me," a smoky voice said from behind her. Caught off guard, Sage whirled, finding Gavin leaning against the door frame, a mischievous smile on his face.

"Gavin!" Sage walked to him quickly, throwing her arms around his neck before she could second-guess herself. He hugged her back, his warm arms wrapping around her waist. And was that—did he just nuzzle her? Clearing her throat, she pushed out of his arms, though her skin protested at the sudden lack of his warmth. "I'm glad to see you. I thought you wouldn't get here until much later."

His cheeks were faintly pink, and his eyes seemed more intense than usual as he looked at her. He reached for her hand and held it as he replied, "I got in late last night, actually. There were some things I had to tell Aryael that couldn't wait. 'Slept in the barracks for a few hours then decided to just head over here."

He smelled good, like he'd freshly bathed. He smelled like rosemary and spice. Like sandalwood, and there was another scent that lingered that was distinctly him. Stepping back, she tried to stop focusing on his scent and act like a normal person, despite the fact that her stomach was fluttering like a wild bird, her heart beating fast in her chest. "Well, I'm glad you're back."

"So you did miss me." His playful grin did that thing to her stomach again.

"What do you think? I don't go around sending notes to all fae boys, you know."

"I hope not."

Just then, a soft clatter chimed from the table in the center of the library. A smattering of food, including those tasty tarts, appeared on the table alongside copious amounts of wine. Cheese, bread, and other snacks that Sage had witnessed Hyacinth arranging earlier covered the table. "I guess Hyacinth was excited about us returning as well?" Gavin asked tentatively.

"I think only cooking for me was getting boring for her."

"Oh– Thank the Goddess, you will not believe the time I've had." Raphael breezed past Sage and Gavin, heading straight for the table and pouring himself a glass of wine.

"I missed you, too, Raph," Sage sang to his back.

The healer took three large gulps from his wine, pointer finger extended. Finally, he lowered the glass with an exhale. "I missed you, too, dear. How did you get along?"

"Eh, fine. I thought me and Petra had come to an understanding, but that was short-lived," Sage said, pouring herself a glass of wine, and forcing herself not to eat another tart.

"What'd she do?" Gavin asked, joining Sage and Raphael as they sat at the table.

"Oh, nothing. I just think it's for the best if we avoid each other."

"If you want, I can have a talk with her," Gavin pushed.

Sage waved him off. "You guys tell me about your trip! I've been cooped up for so long, I want to hear everything!"

The hours flew by, and the Obelisk supplied more wine. Bottle after bottle disappeared as they all three caught up. By the time the sun set, Raphael was hiccupping through a story of an apprentice healer confusing the different fluids in a patient and somehow sending the poor male's blood pulsing in the opposite direction. Raphael had been forced to pry the fear-stricken student off the patient and save him. "You would think that would have been enough to toss the dearie out of the program, but Shiphrah is more patient than I. I tell you, I don't think teaching is for me."

Sage leaned towards Gavin, who was twirling a piece of her hair around his finger. "Well," she said to Raphael, definitely *not* slurring her words, "you taught me how to work with wind."

Gavin sat up a little, "Hey, I thought I did that."

"Yes, and either way, you were absolutely one of the quicker pupils I've had recently," said Raphael, his eyes closed and head tilted back against the plush chair he sat in.

Looking at Gavin, Sage asked, "Did he just say I was smart?"

Raphael smiled, eyes still closed. "Don't get used to it."

Sage grinned. "It's good to have you back, Raph." A slight lift of his pointer finger was all the response she received. She and Gavin stifled their laughter as deep breathing began flowing from Raphael.

At some point, Sage and Gavin nestled down on the floor in front of the crackling fire, lulled by the flicker of the flames, their backs resting against the chaise. Gavin wrapped his arm around her, draping it around her waist and pulling her closer. Sage rested her head on his shoulder.

"I missed having my friend here with me," she said softly.

"Yeah. Surprisingly, I found myself missing Raph, too."

"I meant you, you goof," Sage said, swatting at him before settling her head back on his shoulder.

"Is that what we are?" he asked, his voice lower and much deeper than before. That sound definitely made her stomach flutter.

She lifted her head to look into his eyes. "What else would we be?"

He stared at her for a long while, and she thought for a moment that he might kiss her again. He brushed the hair from her face, tucking it behind her ear, then said, "Friends is good." Pulling her back down to his shoulder, he pulled her close.

Sage wasn't sure if she was disappointed or not. Resting her head on his shoulder, she felt a strange combination of restless desire and contentment. "I'm glad you're home."

"I'm not home, though," said Gavin. "My home is Mystaira. I'm going to have to go there for good, soon."

She might have imagined it, but she thought he squeezed her tighter then.

They sat in silence for long moments; the fire crackled, and Raphael snored softly in the oversized armchair. Gavin's heart beat softly beneath her ear, and she didn't think she'd ever felt more warm and safe. She didn't even notice as she drifted off to sleep.

❊ ❊ ❊

Sage stood on the edge of Loch Leighis.

The silvery lake rippled on a soft breeze. The reeds lining the lake danced cheerfully in the morning mist. Clouds shrouded the rising sun, and fog clung to the ground like the softest fleece blanket, stubbornly resisting the rising sun's beckoning. The spring air chilled Sage as she stood, peering across the lake the book had led her to as if it would answer her questions. Hopefully, the sky would lighten soon and the lake would warm quickly.

She'd circled half of the border of the lake twice, stopping on both sides where the Meeran forest began. She referenced the book once more, pulling it from her pack to investigate how to proceed.

The book told the story of Allyra. How she'd built a city that once hovered over the lake. The city had been created to submerge itself below the surface in the face of danger. Allyra herself had blessed the waters with the powers to cure common ailments such as boils, rashes, and superficial wounds. Bathing in the sacred waters required payment and special permission, but was rarely withheld, and made Allyra one of the most treasured of the four gods.

Sage had never read anything about the city of Meera in school and wasn't completely sure the book was leading her in the right direction but resolved to look into it either way.

She paced the edge of the shore once more, looking for some sort of entryway into the water. She made her way back to the place where she'd laid her pack, and eyed the water again. Kicking off her socks and shoes, and packing them snugly into her bag, Sage took several deep breaths trying to ready herself for the frigid water she would soon wade into.

She glared at the sunlight rippling off the softly rolling water; the sun had fully risen, but the clouds kept the fog from burning off the ground and kept the temperature less than warm. She'd just psyched herself into wading into the water when a soft splash caught her attention; Sage peered again across the lake but didn't see anything beyond a faint ripple a hundred yards or so into the lake.

She'd taken several steps toward the water, just so it began lapping at her toes, when the sound echoed across the shore once more. Sage halted and stared across the expanse of the lake, scanning the surface for whatever creature was disturbing the sleepy lake.

In the distance, but closer than the initial ripples she'd seen, she spied a small fin peak over the glossy surface. The triangular dorsal was spined, the scales nearly translucent. Sage froze on the spot; the book hadn't warned about any malicious creatures, making it sound as though the lake were docile, abandoned by men and creatures alike. She kept her eyes glued to the fin as it rippled across the lake, swimming closer toward Sage.

When the fin was about twenty yards from the shore, it ceased its advance, circling on the spot twice. Sage bit down on a startled scream when a green and blue head popped above the surface of the lake. Not a fish's head, nor an amphibian's head, or reptile; but not wholly human either. It was scaled, hairless, and crowned with fins ribbing the back and sides.

Whereas every human she'd ever met possessed a vertically oblong shaped head, this creature's head was horizontally so, and possessed overly large eyes devoid of any white sclera. The creature tread water, its head bobbing along the surface, assessing her. It looked at her with what seemed to pass for amusement, as far as Sage could tell on the strange creature. Sage could see the outlines of finned arms as the creature hovered in place, suspended in the water. Sage frantically glanced around, using her peripheral vision as much as she could so as not to lose sight of the strange being staring at her in the lake.

Abruptly, the scaley head popped back below the surface. Sage took several steps back from the water, frantically scanning the lake, the shore, for any signs of disturbance—that she was about to be set upon.

The scaley head popped up again in the same spot as before and grinned. A blue-green, webbed hand reached in the air and waved a beckoning motion for Sage to come into the water. The creature plopped back below the surface, but Sage remained where she was. The head popped up again; the distinct frown on the creature's face might have been comical—cute even—had fear not begun settling over Sage's body. Sage walked along the shore a bit, pacing as she tried to make up her mind. The creature dived below again, popping its head back up to gesture at Sage over and over.

Finally, once the creature crossed its arms and gave an audible "Humpf," Sage decided to go for it. What did she have to lose, anyway? With as little trepidation as she could muster, Sage eased herself into the frigid water. The mud squished between her bare feet, and the cold water twisted beneath her clothing; reeds danced between her toes and skittered across her legs as she launched herself into the water. Her parents had seen to it that she could swim at an early age, claiming that drowning was the most likely danger to befall young children, and Sage leaned into the techniques she'd learned all those summers at swim camp.

The frigid water squeezed the breath out of her, and Sage had to fight the urge to use her fire powers against it. She reached the creature, who she now realized possessed rather sharp-looking teeth. And, she realized, she was the idiot who left her wand in her bag...on shore. The creature smiled, showing off their pointy-looking teeth, and tilted its head.

"Do you have a name?" Sage asked.

"Heh?" squeaked the creature.

"What do I call you?" Sage asked again, barely whispering over her chattering teeth.

The creature raised one clawed, webbed hand and pointed down. "You want me to swim down there?" The creature nodded and grinned with delight.

Shit; Sage had been prepared to do just that, but this felt more like a trap with every passing second. She took several deep breaths and nodded to the water nymph, or whatever it might be. On her third breath, Sage ducked her head under and began to swim through the clear water. They descended down, down, down, and Sage realized that though the water darkened as they descended, the nymph's scales glowed with bioluminescence so she could see the shapes and outlines of plants along the lake's bottom.

As they continued down, she realized she'd be out of air very soon. With a grunt, Sage was able to get the nymph's attention, and pointed back to the surface. With a burst of her water magic, Sage was able to propel herself skyward.

She was gasping by the time she reached the top. Several deep breaths later, Sage was looking again at the nymph who swam circles around her with a confused look on its face.

"Just a moment; I think I can make this work," Sage said.

As she tread water, Sage focused on the air around her. She willed the air to wrap itself around her body, encapsulating her. The nymph gasped, and Sage looked down to her feet to find the water carved away from her, creating a bowl of air that displaced the lake's water around her. With a flex and push of her fingers, Sage began to descend once more; she fought her instinct to hold her breath and focused on willing the air to seal the bubble she'd wrapped around herself.

She resembled an egg, or a capsule as the air bubble held its oblong shape around her and she dropped toward the bottom of the lake. The glowing nymph hovered next to Sage, awed by her ability to command the air at her will. They reached the bottom, and Sage willed the bubble to remain just above the ground, to avoid getting stuck in the squishy mud. The nymph swam a bit ahead of Sage, and circled back, signaling to her to keep following as they continued on along the lake. Sage walked inside her bubble, like a hamster inside a wheel, and they made their way towards whatever destination, or trap, the nymph was determined to drag Sage to.

The lake remained docile, disturbed only by the occasional curious fish swimming past Sage and the nymph, on business of their own. The latter paid little to no attention to any other creature, and Sage became more and more curious about this mysterious being and where it came from. Were there others of its kind here, or did it live a lonely life stranded in this lake somehow...or possibly by design?

As they progressed across the bottom of the lake, Sage made out the shapes of a plethora of lost junk. A sunken rowboat, various lost treasures, and trinkets that were either dropped into the lake, or possibly washed into it through the numerous estuaries and creeks that fed into the body of water. A cracked porcelain doll gazing with glazed eyes caught Sage's attention, and a shiver crawled up her spine.

"What's your name?" Sage called out once more, hoping to receive an answer this time.

The nymph spun towards Sage, and put a finger to its mouth in a universal sign for "Quiet!"

Sage clamped her lips together, and peered through the darkened waters, hoping she hadn't just somehow jeopardized both their safety. But the two of them continued on in silence, the nymph swimming through the reeds and grass of the lake, Sage pushing her bubble through the entangled mess. And then, unexpectedly, Sage found herself walking on cobblestone, covered in algae and slippery mud. Squinting through the dark, Sage could make out looming shapes of varying sizes jutting out from the lake floor.

As they continued to move forwards, the reeds and grasses were left behind in a tangled jungle at their backs. The nymph gestured to Sage, extending its hand in invitation for Sage to go towards it. The cobblestone extended on for as far as Sage could make out through what seemed to be a vast archway. A soft, blue glow undulated in the distance ahead, and Sage felt pulled towards it. Sage whispered a prayer to Allyra, asking for courage as she walked, pushing her bubble forward. The nymph scampered off through the water, leaving Sage alone as she continued across the cobblestone.

Ancient statues greeted her in all directions; she could just make out their shapes, but not much detail. Their shadows leered at her, stretching out as if they would swallow her whole. Without the nymph floating by her side, seeing through the waters was impossible, so Sage continued on towards the glow, beyond the archway of stone. Anxiety pushed her towards the safety of light, away from the darkened lake floor.

Sage reached the archway and observed a large, glowing basin at the center of what appeared to be an amphitheater. Stone benches lined the expanse of the amphitheater, and forty steps down brought Sage within a few yards of the basin. Sage took several moments to look around, noting the large stone pillars, the scattered bits of statue, carvings, and pottery. There were remnants of baskets, decaying and dismembered. What appeared to be a canvas bag of some sort lay in tatters at the foot of a statue. It was an abandoned city. As if the people who had once walked these steps, and gathered together in this place had simply dropped their belongings and left.

Sage's head was beginning to ache, a sign that the air in her bubble was waning—or her power was. Either way, it was time to find the insignia and go before anything bad could happen. She began approaching the basin, her feet now making contact with the smooth cobblestone floor. She was six feet from the edge when she felt rather than saw something slither in the darkness. Sage whirled towards the movement but saw nothing. A quick pivot around herself provided no further clues. She took one more cautious step toward the glowing, copper basin, tarnished and green from being submerged for so long. A pause, and no further movement to alarm her, Sage stepped again, advancing towards the glowing bowl.

Four more steps and Sage screamed as a large, black horse's head, covered in rough scales, emerged from behind the basin. Scrambling to get away, she bumped into something cold and jagged, her air bubble threatening to burst with the impact.

The creature rose up from its hiding spot, domineering over Sage. Its scales were as black as midnight, its serpent-like eyes the palest, coldest blue. The front half of the beast was equine in shape, with two front legs, powerful hooves the size of tires, and a massive head with pointed ears and a flowing mane that drifted with the ebb of the water.

Jets of boiling water streamed from its nostrils as it whinnied in delight, or rage, Sage couldn't be sure. Her knees gave out, rattling as she hit the floor. The creature whipped out its scaled, serpentine tail, tapering from its thick trunk. Coiling behind her, it scooted her along the slippery cobblestone, closer to its steaming snout, filled with sharp, pointed teeth.

A cold, booming voice echoed through her mind, making her ears pop as if she were in the smallest cave and the voice was shouted through a megaphone.

"Who dares to wake the loch dragon of Leighis?"

Sage peered into the creature's eyes, bound to the spot by some invisible force field or power that throbbed painfully through her body and brain. She struggled to speak, to move her hands and summon fire or wind or earth to her command but was fixed to the spot like a stone statue. A terrifying thought occurred to her then; the statues, all humanoid in shape, how old were they? Were they stone? Or was that the price for venturing into this loch dragon's lair?

"I asked who you are," the booming voice rattled through her mind, "Give me the name of the one so bold as to disturb my realm."

Sage tried to think, tried to summon thought, her voice, anything to offer this creature to appease him. The loch dragon contracted his massive tail, and Sage's knees scraped against stone as she was pushed closer to the monster. She squinted her eyes, willing her body to respond to her thoughts. Her head pounded; her throat ached with her desire to scream. She was mere feet from the monster's face and could make out the place where fangs peeked from his muzzle.

"Who. Are. You?!" the monster's voice rumbled through her mind, through the stone floor, scattering whatever small fish might have still lingered around the wreckage of the amphitheater.

In her mind, she screamed, "Sage. Sage Brennan!"

The monster's tail stopped coiling, and he surged toward her, his hooves pulling him forward over the rim of the basin. His enormous face peered at her, and he seemed to smile as the voice purred, "And what, Sage Brennan, has made you so brave as to venture into my territory, to disturb me as I rest at my goddess's feet?"

Sage looked past the dragon. She hadn't noticed it before, but sure enough, a massive statue of Allyra towered just beyond the amphitheater and seemed to have begun glowing, although not as brightly as the basin before her.

The dragon recoiled slightly, and moved to one side, clopping on the stone floor with its hooves, dragging its serpent's tail behind it. "You've made a foolish mistake coming here Sage Brennan; you, just like all the others, think your magic is powerful enough to sneak here, into my realm, and take what is mine, what my goddess gave me to protect. You humans, so boastful of the magic the gods blessed you with; so proud of your abilities, you've forgotten about the likes of me, of my brothers and sisters."

Sage cringed; she had, in fact, not even bothered to look into the myths of this lake. She knew of Allyra's healing abilities, but hadn't thought to research more, hadn't even had the chance to research, if she was honest. Of course, there was a powerful loch dragon guarding the insignia.

"So, Sage Brennan, tell me why you've sentenced yourself to an early death? What made you think you could enter my lake and steal what is mine?" the cold voice purred, his face now inches from hers, his tail coiling tighter behind her.

"I'm here at the behest of Allyra," Sage said, out loud and through clenched teeth.

The dragon's head reared back as if he'd been slapped, and he glared at Sage. "Do not lie to me," he roared.

"I'm not lying," sobbed Sage; jets of hot water from his nostrils pelted Sage's air bubble. "I'm here on orders by Allyra herself; Allyra, Cerridos, and Brighid have tasked me with finding their insignias. I've found the others. And I'll go to find Therisyd's next." Her voice wobbled, and she didn't dare look at the dragon, instead stared directly at the basin ahead of her.

The dragon floated down towards her, shrinking in size, and he placed his hooves on the stone floor.

"Then you are one of the blessed? One with water, fire, air, and earth magic in your blood?" the dragon asked. Sage nodded, squeezing her eyes shut, willing her body to stop its trembling. "Show me," the dragon hissed.

Sage cracked open one eye to look at the dragon. He remained to the side of her, his tail still pushing on her air bubble.

"Well, you see my command of air," she commented, gesturing to her air bubble, "fire," she said, and a small flame lit atop her pointer finger. "Earth," Sage said with a whisper, and with her other hand, she beckoned a pebble to float up to her palm. "Water," commanded Sage, and dropping the flame and the pebble, she drew a bubble of water from outside her air bubble, drawing it towards herself. "I can do more when I'm not so focused on one element. This air bubble is commanding most of my magic."

The dragon stood stock still, considering her for a moment. Then she noticed his size begin to diminish until he was the size of a large horse, his tail reaching behind him to just the other side of the basin. His color faded, from midnight black to the fairest, most shimmering white. Where his eyes had been the iciest blue, now they were the green of sea glass. "Then you are truly the chosen. You were sent by Allyra?" he asked once more. His voice still echoed, but now bounced around the amphitheater instead of in her mind.

Sage nodded again, acutely aware now of how little air she had left. "I need that insignia, nothing else."

"Then you shall have it," commanded the dragon, "but first, a trade."

Sage balked. Fucking hell. She really didn't learn, did she? She'd forgotten everything with the appearance of the nymph. "I've got nothing to trade with," muttered Sage, looking from the basin to the dragon with trepidation.

"Do you know my name?" asked the loch dragon.

Sage shook her head, "No."

"I am Eponis, guardian of the loch dragons, emissary, and ward for Allyra herself. I have many brothers and sisters," the dragon clopped and slithered his way back behind the basin, peering into its depths. The glimmering blue glow reflected off his muzzle, and Sage could see every glittering scale that covered his face. "My family, our kind, have been forced into hiding for millennia, forced to remain hidden in the deepest caverns of lakes, rivers, and oceans because your people hunt us. Because our blood is sacrificed and used for dark magic. Your leaders have decimated my kind to increase their lives, power their machines, and torment those who dared to rise up against them."

Sage's blood cooled even further. In school, they'd learned a very specific version of the truth. Of rebellions that had been violent and vicious. Of noble government leaders who put the safety of many before the demands of a few. Of how elementals had grown too powerful for their own good.

The dragon seemed to track her thoughts, "Ah, yes...your books like to paint a picture of a righteous government, one that had its people's best interest at heart. Do you know what kind of people they put down in the last uprising?"

"We were told they were infiltrators; they defiled Mount Danu and the gods' temples. They were trying to overthrow the government and enslave us," Sage panted. Her air was really beginning to thin. She fought to keep her concentration on the shimmering dragon before her.

"*NO*," rumbled the dragon. "Those were your people, Sage Brennan. The people of Mount Danu were the last community of elementals in Thuledain, the last on the whole continent of Magell. And your government," the dragon spit the last word, "slaughtered them, using their blood and bones to power their machines. Your people grew tired of being treated like chattel." The dragon let the words sink into Sage's consciousness.

"How does this help me make a trade with you? I know elementals, my people, as you say, have been sacrificed before. I know what kind of danger I face. How does that help you?"

"Sage Brennan, I will make a bargain with you," the dragon paced back to the center of the basin. "You will retrieve the insignia of Allyra, and in exchange, you will do something for me," the dragon's eyes flashed blue again with his words.

"What?" panted Sage, forcing herself to remain alert. "What is with you creatures and bargains?"

"You will complete the task given to you by the gods, and then, when the time comes, you will come back here and free my kind. And others. All the secret creatures, the ones your leaders want you to believe are myths, and you will free us from our need to hide. You will end the blood sacrifices."

Sage's head swam, felt like it was beginning to float away from her body as her air began to dissipate.

Without really thinking about the dragon's words, Sage nodded her head. "Fine, I agree to your bargain." She would do anything at this point to get that insignia and get back to dry land.

"Do you truly? You must say the words, that you understand the terms of our bargain. If you break this agreement, your life will be forfeit."

"Fine. I understand the terms of your deal; I swear on my life I will come back and end those who sacrifice your kind, and all the other magical creatures who've been hunted for their blood."

Sage looked back to the basin, whose glow turned from blue to gold. "Sage Brennan, I accept your bargain."

With his words, something clenched inside Sage, as if an iron chain were wrapped around her heart and locked. She staggered onto her hands, gasping at the pain as the bargain manifested itself in her chest, squeezing inside her. The weight of three bargains hammered into her, and Sage forced herself to accept it.

She staggered to her feet, looking toward the basin. Pushing herself forward, a hand gripping her chest, she advanced on the basin. Peering over its edge, Sage found the basin full of gold coins. Sage reached towards the pile with her magic, feeling along the collection, searching for the medallion made of stone, like all the others.

Her magic skittered along and halted on a river stone. Sage ushered it up towards her, and found a stone with etchings along one side of it. The insignia of Allyra: two axes lined the sides of the round pebble, and in between the axes were waves of water. The edges of the pebble were chiseled, similar to an arrowhead. Sage pulled the stone medallion to her, allowing it to breach her air bubble. The stone dropped into her palm, and she placed it securely into her pocket which zipped at the top. Sage was just about to thank the dragon once more when rushing filled her ears.

She felt the sides of her air bubble begin to push in, the edges of her vision begin to blur. Sage tried to take a deep breath, but the air was so thin now she felt as if nothing entered her lungs. The bubble burst, flooding Sage's senses as the water pummeled her. She leaped from the stone floor, trying to push her way up to the surface of the lake. She could barely make out the pale silhouette of the sun. She wasn't going to make it.

Sage kicked, clawed, and thrashed, trying to push herself up to the surface. Her mouth opened involuntarily; her lungs desperate for air that was really water. She gagged, hands grasping her throat as her legs continued to kick below her. She felt herself begin to drift back to the bottom, that sun-shaped orb becoming more faint. Suddenly, a swift push on her bottom sent her rocketing toward the sky.

The dragon had surged upward, supporting her with his nose, and he pushed her to the surface of the lake. Just as her vision went black, her face broke the surface. With a great heave, the dragon pushed Sage into the air and she landed hard on the shallow banks of the lake, mere feet from her pack. Sage retched, forcing the water to vacate her lungs. She panted, gasping for air. When she stopped reeling, and finally felt like she wasn't dying, Sage turned to look at the lake.

No one was there. The surface of the lake was undisturbed, silent. Not even a breath of wind or the croak of a bird disturbed the quiet.

She sat back on her haunches, turning towards her pack. A pair of elegant boots encased two feet standing next to her.

Raphael towered above her.

"What have you done?" he asked in a whisper, before shimmering into nothing.

Chapter 23

Sage's eyes fluttered open, sleep still tugging heavily at her eyelids. A warm arm draped across her center, and while she recognized that she was laying on the floor, she was so comfortable that the idea of waking up seemed like the very last thing she wanted to do. Instead, she snuggled into the wall of warmth pressed against her back. The arm squeezed her lightly, and she suddenly recognized the soft breath that brushed the back of her neck.

Gavin slept soundly, pressed against her. The creeping feeling of guilt crawled over her. She'd still never told him about Ian. They'd never discussed what it meant that she would have to leave one day. Was she being dishonest with him by not telling him that there was someone probably waiting for her back home?

"I can feel your mind racing," Gavin's voice said, gravelly with sleep.

Sage shifted, rolling onto her back. "It's nothing," she said, turning her head slightly so she could look at Gavin. "I'm fine."

"Best piece of advice my mother ever gave me: never believe a female when she says 'I'm fine.'"

"Your mom sounds very intelligent."

"She is." Gavin reached his free arm up, stretching, then rolled his neck slightly. Sage's heart raced a little. How could he be *more* attractive after sleeping on the floor?

"It was just a memory," Sage answered, rolling over so that she could sit up. "Where's Raph?"

"Probably already headed down to the castle. Which means we should probably get a move on as well."

As if in answer, a rattle came from the side table that sat next to Raph's chair. A pitcher of water and two glasses had appeared. "This place is awesome," Sage exclaimed. Her mouth felt extra dry, a dull headache hovering around her eyes.

Gavin filled his own glass. He was shirtless. How had she not noticed he was shirtless earlier? Sage tried to focus on her glass of water, but her gaze kept sticking on the way his shoulders rippled into a sculpted chest. Those muscles were probably from flying. Or training. Or just Gods-blessed. She didn't really care as her traitorous gaze slipped even further. Sage spluttered, nearly choking on her water as she realized Gavin was watching her look at him.

"Feeling better?" Gavin smirked.

"I'm *fine*, thank you very much."

"Good. We should get ready. You should probably do something with that," Gavin reached up and flicked a wild piece of her hair that stuck out at an awkward angle.

"Oh, my gods," Sage said, running her fingers through her hair. "Fine. Give me an hour and I'll be ready to go."

"Thirty minutes," Gavin said, crossing his arms.

"Right...thirty minutes," Sage said. She absolutely would not be ready in thirty minutes.

"I mean it. We have to go in thirty minutes."

"Sure," Sage replied sweetly. "Or, you could just let me go get ready, and agree that we will go when I'm ready. And avoid any disagreements that come from being late."

"Thirty. Minutes."

"Don't say I didn't warn you," Sage sang as she left the library and headed to her rooms.

Did she take her time bathing? Maybe a little. Did she slow her pace and become more thoughtful of how she packed her bag after the first knock on her door, warning her that time was up? Definitely. And did she grin like a cat when he rolled his eyes after she refused to leave without saying goodbye to Hyacinth? Oh, yes...she did.

Then they reached the balcony, and Sage realized she would have to wear the pack as Gavin carried her down. "I'm not so sure about this."

"Too late for that," Gavin said, scooping her into his arms and launching himself off the side of the balcony into the air.

The flight was awkward, slightly off balance, as Sage wore her heavy pack on her back, clinging to Gavin's neck. He didn't seem to struggle much, but she had to fight the constant pull of the pack, as if gravity itself was intent on ripping her and the pack off Gavin and down to the ground. She was about to whisper, to beg, for a brief break when a phantom wind rushed upward. The wind pushed against her, taking some of the pressure of the pack off her shoulders, assisting her as they made their way down to the palace. She looked up at Gavin, and he smiled slightly and gave her a quick nod. She squeezed him just a bit, and he returned the quick gesture.

They landed at the front gates of the palace, amid other Lords, Ladies, and honored guests, most of whom were

expected to stay in the grand palace throughout the ceremonies of the week. Gavin and Sage took up a spot in what
had turned into a queue, and waited patiently as the guards
checked each person in. The process moved smoothly, and
as soon as Gavin and Sage passed the front gates, they
heard a familiar voice beckoning to Gavin.

"I wondered when you might finally get your sorry ass
over here," bellowed a commanding, yet cheerful, voice.
Zeke strode over to the pair, and the males grasped each
other's forearms in familiar greeting.

"It's only been two weeks since you've seen me. Missed
me that much?" Gavin teased as they all began to walk
toward the palace.

"If only to distract Meliza some. The lionesses are wound
tightly at the moment," responded Zeke, rubbing his hands
down his face.

"Lionesses?" questioned Sage, peering at Zeke with bewilderment.

"Ah, yes," answered Zeke, pointing a finger at Sage, "you
likely haven't been filled in with regards to the siblings fully
yet. You know of their powers, respectively?" he asked.

"Well, I know about Symon; and from what I guessed,
Meliza can read people's minds, to see if they're telling
the truth. And I haven't got the slightest idea about Petra,
unless it's torturing people with that sour look on her
face." Sage froze, having forgotten that Zeke and Petra were
bonded.

The male stopped walking and surprised Sage as he
barked a laugh that startled a neighboring group of ladies
admiring a flower bed.

Zeke slapped a hand on his thigh. "Oh...that's a good
one. If I didn't fear the amount of time it'd take me to calm

her down, I might actually tell her that one! It's about time someone grew some balls when it comes to my partner."

"What? To replace yours?" Gavin teased.

Zeke stopped laughing and glared at Gavin as they continued down the path. Sage couldn't stop her grin, clearing her throat to stop the chuckle that tried to escape.

"Anyway," Zeke muttered, waving off Gavin's jab, "the royal siblings all have shifted forms as well. Like Gavin, sort of. Their other forms are lions, with wings. So they are called the Lion Born, like their father. 'The Lionesses' is a bit of a nickname we use for the sisters." Zeke finished his explanation with a wave of his hand.

"I've heard that not all fae can shift. Can you?"

Zeke nodded. "Harpy."

Sage shrugged. She'd never seen or heard of the animal before.

"It's an eagle, with gaudy feathers that stick out across his head. Massive, though...like his head," Gavin answered, whispering the last line.

Zeke pushed Gavin playfully. "Keep it up and I might decide we need one more for night duty."

Gavin held up his hands. "All right, I'm done."

They parted ways with Zeke at the entrance, Zeke giving Gavin a few parting commands, instructions on where to be and when. Then Gavin and Sage were shown to their rooms. Luckily— and likely not by accident— they were housed in the same hallway.

Sage could not get over how massive the estate was. This wing of the building contained three floors of guest rooms. Gavin and Sage were located on the second floor, Gavin across the hall and one door down from hers.

The walls were pristine white stone, with little flecks of minerals sparkling in the rock. The hallways were domed with silver filigree worked into the carved masonry covering the ceilings, molding, and occasional stone pillar that lined the hallway.

Scenes of mythical creatures and memorials of revered fae who made a mark in history danced along the surfaces of the stone building. Sage marveled at the delicate, pure beauty of it all.

Her room, equally beautiful, was more subdued in décor. A large woven carpet covered the majority of the floor. A modest fireplace centered the room, and Sage plopped herself onto the softest bed she had probably ever laid on. The furnishings were the most tranquil shades of blue and blue-green, and her open windows welcomed in the botanical scents from one of the many gardens. Ok...this week wouldn't be so bad, then.

After allowing herself time to enjoy and appreciate her bed—Gods, it really was comfortable—Sage busied herself putting away her few items. Two closets flanked the entrance to a private bathroom, and she was pleased to find the robes Rahab had created for her were already hung in one of them.

Running the fabric between two fingers, her stomach clenched slightly as she remembered what tomorrow meant. Tomorrow was the day she would be presented to all of Veritasailles, likely all of Felysia. She felt like some circus oddity. Maybe they'd ask her to perform a few tricks.

She blew a strong breath between her lips. Well, there really wasn't much she could do about it. Besides, she hadn't met the Queen yet, and curiosity overwhelmed her sense of dread. What kind of female would she have to be, to put up with a male like Symon, thought Sage. Her one and only impression of the Lion-born King wasn't all that favorable.

Further investigation of her room proved the large windows with the fluttering curtains were actually doors that lead to a private balcony. Sage leaned lightly on the banister of the balcony to peer into the gardens which lay sprawled below her.

A soft knock echoed from her door, and as Sage turned, she found Gavin striding into her room, a tray in hand. "I realized, by rushing you this morning, I forced you to skip breakfast. There is a room of refreshments on the first floor; I assumed you might like to wait for dinner before having to face the crowd." Gavin set the tray on the small round table on the balcony, a question on his face.

Sage grinned at him. "I guess that means we are required to attend tonight's dinner?"

Gavin nodded as he began attending to the tray, uncovering and unwrapping certain items. It was a meal similar to the first meal he'd brought her: breads, pastries, cheeses, olives, and fruit. He held up a finger to her, a gesture for her to just wait for a second, and he rushed to the door, speaking softly to someone on the other side.

In a matter of moments, he was back with a jug of wine and two glasses. The wine was sweet, red, and chilled—refreshing after the bustle of the morning—and the food satisfied whatever cravings she might have had.

He'd brought cherries again and she beamed at him. "You remembered."

"It was a happy coincidence," he shrugged.

They sat companionably, eating their meal, Sage sitting nearest to the wall. She leaned her head back onto the wall, lifting her face to the sun, letting it warm her skin and dance in her hair.

When she opened her eyes again, Gavin was staring at her. His eyes looked dark, lidded as he gazed at her, and she didn't dare to break her own gaze as she lifted her glass and sipped her wine. He did the same, and as he removed the glass and a bead of liquid remained on his lips, her stare snagged on his mouth as he gently licked it away. He had been gods-blessed with full lips, to match his broad, strong shoulders, his square jaw. His facial hair varied, some days cleanly shaved, other times he let it grow into a short and tidy beard.

Today, there was a shadow of two days' stubble on his face, highlighting the strong curve of his jaw joining with his neck. She thought of how that stubble might feel if she were to run her mouth along that jawline, and something inside her turned liquid and molten.

Gavin stiffened as if he could sense the direction of her thoughts. She set her glass back onto the table, straightening her spine, and tilting her head in question.

"What are you thinking?" Sage asked softly.

In answer, Gavin set his glass down, and leaned forward until he was standing, but still leaning over her. She had to look up at him as he placed both hands on the arms of her chair. Slowly, he pressed his mouth to hers, not hard like the last time, but gently. Slowly, they kissed, opening for each other, learning each other. Sage had to lean upwards, chasing his mouth as he loomed over her.

Finally, she broke from him, gasping for air, and he ran his mouth to her ear, caressing her neck with his mouth. Another gasp escaped her, and she was faintly aware of other fae down in the gardens, enjoying the ambiance.

Gavin's attention seemed to track hers, and he pulled away, scooping her into his arms and carrying her to the bed. After laying her down, he doubled back and gently closed the doors to the balcony. Her body trembled as he lay down alongside her, half on the bed, half on top of her. He reached his arm across her, cupping her face in his hand, and kissed her again. Sage wrapped her arms around his neck, pulling him down, a plea to keep going. A plea for more.

He kissed her deeply, and she nipped at his lower lip. He ran his tongue across hers in response. His hand drifted down her neck, skimming her skin as it drifted down. That hand lingered on the lining of her dress, the swell of her breasts peeking just above the edge. A sound of appreciation rumbled from his chest as he took her breast into his hand, and a moan escaped her. Her body heated in response, tightening and loosening at the same time. His mouth followed that line of her dress, and she felt her skin swell in response, her core dissolving into molten lava as that hand continued downward. His hand dragged across her chest, across the plane of her abdomen, and down along one thigh, all while his mouth caressed, licked, and bit. He bunched her skirts upward until his hand met bare skin along her thigh. His hand ran up and down her leg until it dragged up along that long plane of the leg to meet her hip.

"Goddess...fuck me," he ground out as he realized she wasn't wearing any undergarments.

"I didn't have time for them this morning. You rushed me," panted Sage.

"Good," Gavin said, just before crushing his mouth back onto hers. She dug her fingers into his hair, and his hand continued playful circles around her hip bone. Her hips bucked in response, and she kissed him back harder.

"Gavin," Sage whispered, pleading, when she didn't feel like she could wait any longer. A large, flat hand spread itself over her pelvis, pushing her back on the bed. "Gavin, please," Sage begged again, and she felt her legs move, opening without her commanding them to.

That hand, flat against the plane of her abdomen, between her navel and the joining of her thighs, turned downwards. Sage flung her hands down onto the bed, gripping the sheets, as one finger slipped down to that joining, finding the center of her and dipping down, then slowly up. A cry slipped out from Sage, and she bit down on her lip to keep herself from crying out again. Gavin swore, pushing his mouth back onto her breast as he dipped that finger down again. She could feel her slick desire as he ran his finger down, then up, then down again. Her hips bucked, moving to follow the finger, desperate for more, for more pressure, more friction. But Gavin continued his small, prodding movement, up and down and up and down. Finally, he moved in slow circles, which had Sage's toes curling, and she bit down on his shoulder. Gavin pushed his hips towards her in response, and she felt his hardness clearly now. She gasped, reaching for it, but pulled back as he slipped one finger inside her, pushing deep into her.

She wanted to touch him, to feel the length of him, and struggled to reach for him as he slowly pulled that finger out of her. She was still reaching for him, fumbling with the seam of his pants as he pushed back into her. All thought left her, and she arched, giving herself over to him, willing him to take however he might. Gavin swore again as she felt her muscles tighten, as her core beckoned for him to keep going. She felt him harden further, his desire throbbing beside her. But she was lost to the world as he continued, slipping another finger inside her, pumping into her. She felt her heat building, felt the stars themselves exploding as he continued, sliding in and out of her faster and faster. He dragged his face down, into the center of her breasts, and she felt her body reach its edge as he dragged his tongue up her chest, just as he mimicked the movement up her center with his fingers, before plunging back into her. Faster and harder, her legs shook, and she cried out, groaning his name as she felt the release take over her body.

For many moments, they lay against each other, Sage reeling all the tiny, shattered parts of her back inward. She rolled to him and realized his considerable length continued to push against her. She ran her hand down his chest, down to his hardness. She'd just reached him, when Gavin pushed her back onto her back, kissed her, and whispered, "I hate myself for this, but we need to get ready for dinner. We both will need to bathe before we meet the court."

Sage's hand froze, lying flat against him, feeling his reaction to her palm. A wicked grin spread across her face, and she brushed her mouth up to his ear as she said, "Ok. But when I repay the favor, I prefer to use my mouth, not my hand." She swore he grew another two inches into her palm, threatening the integrity of his pants as he gritted his teeth and rolled away from her.

He didn't even look at her as he said, "We have to be at dinner in one hour." He looked back at her then, her dress still hiked up along her thighs, and he exhaled, "We will finish this later."

Sage grinned at the promise, her core becoming molten and liquid again at the deep, gravelly tone of his voice. His eyes scanned her body once more, and her toes curled as she let him take inventory of her, making plans on how he'd claim her later. After she'd had her fun, of course. Rigidly, Gavin stalked to the door, looking at her once more and saying, "One hour," before hurrying to his own room.

Sage ran a hand from her neck down the length of her body, down to her mid-thigh. Well, fuck. She hadn't planned on *that* happening. Not that she was complaining. The feeling of his mouth on her neck was like a brand on her skin that refused to cool. Her fingers drifted to the spot where he had licked her chest and felt pleasant heat pooling in her stomach.

Ian's face drifted across her memory, and the icy feeling of guilt trickled through her veins. That thought alone was enough to cool whatever fire had been rekindled inside her. She wrestled herself from the bed, groaning with frustration as she made her way into the bathroom. What kind of person did this make her?

She was surprised to find that the closet in the bathroom wasn't a closet at all. After pulling on the chain, she discovered that water poured in from the ceiling of the empty room, mimicking rain. A shower; it was a shower. She loved her bath at the Obelisk, but there was something clean and simple about a shower that she hadn't realized she missed from her home.

The water was warm, and with further investigation, she found a valve that she could open and close to make the water warmer or colder. She spent most of her time in that shower. Once she'd had her fill of the warm, relaxing water, Sage climbed out of the shower and found a few cosmetics, oils for her skin, and hairpins in the bathroom.

She lightly rimmed her eyes with coal, adding a small dab of a rose paste to her cheeks and lips, and finished her look by pinning her hair back in multiple layers, arranged over the tops of her ears to disguise her un-faeness. She adorned her hair with a golden ribbon, tying it like a headband. She opted for a simple dress; a soft peachy, almost white color. The dress was flattering on her, but also shouldn't attract too much attention. She just had to go, eat the meal, keep quiet, and then get on with the rest of the week. Shouldn't be too hard. She gave herself one last appreciative look, then steeled herself to meet Gavin and the others.

Chapter 24

Goddess...it had been so long, too long, since he'd let himself be intimate with a female. He'd had sexual encounters, but had decided early on he didn't particularly care for frivolous hookups. But this girl, this woman... He found himself struggling to control his impulses. How many times had he laid in his bed thinking about her, about the first time they'd kissed? How many times had he been forced to disguise his lingering gaze, his appreciation of her figure, of her mouth? He was grateful she wasn't blessed with the fae's ability to smell arousal, otherwise, she might have never let him fly her to the city. How he'd managed to keep his desire disguised was a mystery and a blessing.

He showered; a cold, brutal shower. Still, he could smell her on him as he stepped out of the shower, and his cock stiffened in response. Gavin grit his teeth, and set about getting ready for dinner. Shaving, and dressing in his semi-formal dress uniform. Honestly, it was ridiculous that he had to be prepared with *two* separate dress uniforms. He supposed, being born a commoner and raised in a work camp would always make some court customs foreign and strange to him.

He dressed, and chugged a couple glasses of wine, hoping it would take the edge off before facing her again. "...I prefer to use my mouth," she had said with a wicked grin. Goddess, fuck him. She'd given him the most wicked grin he'd ever seen, and he'd almost hit his knees, willing her to take whatever she might from him right then and there. He would have done her bidding, too; days and days, he wanted to have her. He wanted to spend nights exploring her body, keep her in bed, in the shower...on the balcony.

Fuck. He might need one more cold shower.

Gavin took several breaths, trying to use the techniques Raphael had taught him to overcome the trauma of his early life. He focused his energy on his breath, focused on the task at hand. Once he felt like he might have control over his body, Gavin straightened and headed into the hall.

She was already waiting; dressed in a creamy peach dress that set her skin on fire. No, not fire; it was like radiant light, like the sun itself had nestled itself under her skin and she glowed for it. Her hair was piled into neat but soft layers, cleverly hiding the tops of her rounded ears, and he smiled as he walked to her.

"You look very pretty," he whispered.

She grinned. "So do you."

"Thank you, but I already know I'm the prettiest girl in the guard," he joked back. Laughing, she hooked her arm through his elbow, and playfully smacked his arm. They walked in silence, arm in arm, as they descended to one of the two ballrooms.

They entered the smaller ballroom where fae were already finding their seats along two long rows of tables. At the front of the room, facing the rest of the fae, Zeke and Meliza were seated in their dress uniforms, Petra in a silver dress of soft silk. There were no other seats open at the table, and Sage looked at Gavin questioningly.

"The King and Queen won't present themselves until tomorrow, during the formal reception. Petra and Meliza will hold court tonight."

Gavin led Sage to one of the tables nearest the head table. On their way, Gavin sensed the approach of another male, and his body tensed as he pulled Sage closer to him.

Raphael appeared on the other side of Sage, grinning at Gavin as they walked. "Gavin, we could smell her on you when you entered the room. No need to clutch her so tightly."

"I'm sorry, what?" Sage demanded. Color stained her cheeks, and he could feel the color rising in his own.

"It's a quirk of the fae," continued Raphael. "The male of our species have a territorial quality to them. They have a tendency to take on the scent of the ones they pursue...especially after an...encounter." Raphael was still grinning at Sage's apparent mortification.

"So, everyone here can tell we...we...?" Sage pressed. Raphael nodded.

Gavin squeezed her arm with the hand that rested there. "Relax; it's normal here." Just then, Gavin caught a male standing against the wall staring earnestly at Sage as they passed by.

"And I suppose male posturing is normal, too?" Sage questioned Gavin as he caught himself sending a death glare at the male. "Listen to me," whispered Sage, "I will accept the whole...scent thing. But I will not stand by and watch you glare at every male who looks at me. *If* I feel like someone is being disrespectful, *I* will take care of that."

Gavin exhaled sharply, gritting his teeth to avoid saying something he might regret.

"I will not suffer some...territorial, male posturing. Just because we...you know...doesn't mean I belong to you."

He ground his teeth again. She was right; he had no formal claim on her, and even if he did, he wasn't the type of male to expect his partner to obey his every command.

And yet, the urge to stand between her and every other male, besides Raphael, grew with every step. They made it to the top of the long table, Gavin taking the end chair, with Sage between him and Raphael. At least Raph would be a buffer between her and anyone else who sat at the table. Gavin nodded to Meliza, taking his seat after pulling the chair out for Sage.

The male from earlier swaggered behind Gavin, patting him on the shoulder as he made his way to his seat across from him. "Gavin, I see you brought entertainment to court," the honeyed voice purred as he took his seat.

"Suda. A pleasure to see you, as always."

The male fae grinned at Gavin with the kind of swaggering confidence that normally irked him; however, he had to admit that Suda usually brought a level of excitement on his visits that seldom disappointed. The male was blessed with the rich brown skin of Nysa. His brown eyes complimented their slightly elongated shape, and his black, cropped hair. He was dressed in the traditional robes of Nysa, which meant he was shirtless beneath the woven over-robe he wore, showcasing the sculpted body beneath. That alone usually had females hanging on his every last word.

Gavin worked to lighten his glare as Suda said, "Aren't you going to introduce us?"

"Gavin's *entertainment* can introduce herself. The name's Sage Brennan, honored guest of Queen Aryael," cut in Sage.

Suda's eyebrows shot to his forehead. "The girl of mysteries. Goddess above, Gavin, you have exquisite taste," Suda replied.

Raphael interjected before Gavin could finish clearing his throat, "Sage, this handsome male is the honorable Suda of Nysa; Senator of Nysa and Emissary to Felysia. And Queen Aryael's brother."

Suda's dark skin seemed to sparkle in response to Sage's momentary lapse of speech, her eyebrows shooting up, glancing to Raphael first, then Gavin. She realized her mouth hung open, and snapped it closed. When neither of her companions offered a lead on how to proceed, she shook her head and continued on, "It's an honor to meet you Senator Suda. I apologize for my sharp introduction."

She didn't look apologetic, and Gavin knew that would only prod Suda to behave rakishly. "No apologies required. In Nysa, we admire females who can fend for themselves. Perhaps at some point during the festivities this week we can find some time to...spar."

Raphael nearly spit out his wine, and glared at Suda, the unspoken question being just what in the Goddess Suda was up to.

Sage arched an eyebrow, looking Suda directly in the eye. "You don't strike me as a male who struggles to find company, Senator Suda. But if you are truly finding it difficult to find *entertainment* of your own, I'm sure there is some place in this city that can provide."

It was Gavin's turn now to choke on his drink, but Suda interjected with a booming laugh. A grin broke across Sage's face. Gavin relaxed slightly, as it seemed that Sage and Suda had reached some agreement, part of which being that she wasn't interested in playing *those* sorts of games.

The meal carried on rather uneventfully after that. Sage and Raphael spoke between themselves for most of the meal, while Suda and Gavin caught up on the comings and goings of their cities, the seat directly next to Suda remained blessedly empty. Suda answered questions about the movement of Speridisia's armies, passing along whatever information wasn't considered classified and above Gavin's status.

"Why aren't you seated with the other royal siblings?" Sage asked him near the end of the meal.

"Because he's too embarrassed to admit he got his ass kicked by Meliza the last time he was here," Raphael replied, chuckling.

"I wouldn't call it an ass-kicking. She just...managed to knock me down on my ass," Suda explained, casting a quick glance at the General.

"Suda thought he could waltz in and speak to Meliza the same way he speaks to all the ladies. It turns out, she doesn't respond well to unsanctioned advances," Gavin continued.

Suda shrugged, "Yeah, well, if I won all the beautiful females, there'd be none left for the rest of you."

The meal finished, and the servants cleared away the plates. The court, escorted by Petra, moved to the hall and the room was converted into an oversized salon with sofas, round tables, and collections of formal but comfortable chairs. Evidently, they were expected to mingle and greet each other. Gavin strode over to a grouping of chairs with a stiff spine, pleading internally for he and Sage to be overlooked.

Luck was not on their side in that regard. Several groups of fae made a point of visiting Gavin, Sage, and Raphael, Suda having abandoned them to join a group of females on a couch near the windows. Some approached them seeking out the healer, others were acquaintances of Gavin, fellow newly appointed Lords or Ladies, and the occasional sergeant or lieutenant. And then, others found their group in order to be introduced to Sage. Somehow her reputation had trickled through the land, and fae came over to be introduced to Queen Aryael's mysterious honored guest. Regardless, every fae who made it to their group eventually looked to her, then slid their eyes over to Gavin, understanding washing over them. The males made sure to leave a respectable berth between them and Sage, and the females grinned appreciatively at Gavin. This was why, partly, he had never made it a habit to sleep with a lot of females. The speculation of every single fae that would pass by was cloying enough.

After a while, Sage leaned in and whispered, "Any chance we can make a break for it?"

Gavin looked at her; she looked tired, and uncomfortable. "Should I cause a distraction? And we can run for the doors?" he teased.

"I was kind of just hoping we could scoot around the walls, try to blend in," she replied.

She'd drank her fair share of wine at dinner, and had a pleasant blush to her face, a relaxed demeanor to her posture despite her obvious discomfort of being introduced to so many new faces. She tilted her head, an invitation to take her back to her room, to finish what they started.

"Let's go," Gavin said, abruptly, and grabbed her hand. He didn't particularly care if it looked rude, he was getting her out of there.

A bit of a thrill went through Sage as Gavin dragged her through the crowded collection of fae. A few cast scandalized glares their way, but neither Sage nor Gavin seemed the least bit bothered by the attention. They were down the hallway in a matter of seconds when she first heard the sound.

That voice.

She stopped in her place, pulling her hand from Gavin's and listened. There it was again. It was *his* voice. Turning down a wing adjacent to the ballroom they'd been in, Sage followed the sound of the voice.

"Sage, we can't go that way. That's the King's study," Gavin whispered in her ear, trying to grab her hand again. She moved, fast enough to avoid his grasp, and hurried towards the sound. It was Ian's voice. Ian made it.

She didn't dare think of the consequences of Ian being here, of introducing him to Gavin. She turned a corner, and stopped, frozen.

It was him.

It was him; it was him!

"Ian!" Sage called.

He was standing next to a woman covered in tattoos and a shaved head and King Symon. They were talking to each other in greeting, casually catching up, it appeared. When she called out his name, all three turned to look at her. He looked just the same, his fair hair and skin, his smiling face.

"Ian!" Sage called out again, and launched into a run. Tears streamed down her face, and she leapt for him, wrapping her arms around his neck. She hardly noticed his arms fling out beside him, hesitant to hug her back.

"Epyllo....something you'd like to share with the group," the tattooed woman said between her teeth.

Sage pulled back from Ian, placing her hands on either side of his face. "Ian?" she whispered.

But no...it wasn't Ian.

"I'm sorry. I think you've got the wrong male," smiled the fae as he gently removed her hands. Because she noticed then, the pointed ears.

"No," she whispered. Her heart shattered, and she swallowed back the sob fighting to make its way out.

"Sage Brennan, meet Acantha and Epyllo. They are messengers of Felysia, just arrived from the borders of Nysa," King Symon explained, gesturing to each fae in introduction. Sage could feel her face contorting as she fought to retain her composure.

"I'm sorry," Sage whispered, and stepped back, bumping into Gavin.

"Take her back to her rooms," Symon whispered to Gavin, "Use the servants' stairs." She could feel him nod, but she couldn't stop staring at the fae who wasn't Ian.

Gavin steered her to a secret stairway, using gentle pressure against her back to help her move along, getting her safely to her room. She managed to choke back the tears, to keep her eyes somewhat clear until Gavin opened the door to her room. She made it three steps inside before her knees softened and she crumpled to the floor.

A sound somewhere between a wail and a death shudder tore from her, and she rested her face on the floor. Gavin was in front of her, gathering her upward into his arms. He let her weep into his chest, holding her as she sobbed and sobbed, both of them kneeling on the spot she fell. Eventually, her tears dried, and he continued to hold her.

"I'm sorry," she whispered.

She couldn't imagine how difficult it might have been for him to watch her fling her arms around another male. But he didn't mention it, just whispered in her ear, "Don't apologize. It's ok."

At some point, she let him help her to her feet. He helped her climb out of her dress, and into her nightgown. Her body trembled with the weight of sorrow, of grief. He helped her climb into her bed, then took off his shoes, his jacket, his shirt. He climbed into the bed, and lay next to her, draping his arm around her.

"Tell me about him," he said quietly.

"You don't have to do this Gavin. I'll be okay." Sage tried to push herself away from Gavin, but he gathered her closer to his side, tucking her head to his chest.

"It's okay, Sage. It will be okay." Gavin wrapped both arms around her and rested his chin on her head.

A shaky exhale rushed from her body. Her head ached from crying, and she felt like her eyes were wrapped in gauze. But being wrapped in Gavin's arms felt safe and solid. And the truth was, she wanted to remember her time with Ian and Stiofanie.

"Ian kind of...found me, while I was running. I had these reckless streaks sometimes, and he found me while I was going through one and offered me a place to stay. He was— or is, I suppose— a good, kind man. An inventor, and so bloody smart. And funny." Despite feeling so awful, she smiled as she remembered Ian's playful nature. "And Stiofanie, that's his mom. She was the first mom I had in almost ten years."

"Where is he now?"

"I don't know." The admission felt like a stone in her stomach. "The last thing I remember of him was me leaving to find the Gods' insignias. I didn't want to leave, but I guess that's just what I do: leave."

"What if I told you that you don't have to leave?"

The question surprised Sage. She shifted, moving so she could look at Gavin fully. "What do you mean? Eventually, I will have to leave this place, too. I have to go back home."

"What if...See—if it had been me...," Gavin paused, staring at the ceiling as if he were debating what to say next. "If I were Ian, I think I would have gone with you. Maybe I can come with you when it's time for you to go."

"I don't know if you can do that Gavin. That would mean leaving behind your family, your home."

Gavin shrugged. "I don't know Sage. I just know that, everything you just told me, it doesn't change anything for me. I'm still here, for as long as you are. And if I have the choice, I hope you'll let me come with you and see this thing through."

Sage tucked herself back into Gavin's side. What he said surprised her. She never anticipated finding someone willing to follow her into danger.

She wasn't even sure if she was capable of letting someone follow. Or if she deserved it.

After Sage's disruption, Symon gathered Epyllo and Acantha into his study. Closing the door, Epyllo used his powers to ensure that the study was soundproof; there were no servants' stairs in this room, so it was the most secure room to have conversations that needed to be kept secret.

"She's a realm leaper," Symon explained. Epyllo and Acantha both blinked at Symon. "It means she has the ability to travel between worlds. It appears, Epyllo, you have a duplicate where she is from." Neither Epyllo nor Acantha seemed more understanding with Symon's explanation, so Symon launched into the story of Cerridos and the other gods, explaining how they had voyaged here to defeat the first Dark Lords who threatened their continent in ancient times. "It appears that it's possible for some people, humans and fae alike, to have duplicate personas on various worlds. Already we've determined that Sage is a duplicate of Hyacinth's sister, Celia."

"Well, that explains our news then," said Acantha, plopping onto a sofa near a table piled high with books. Epyllo followed suit and sat next to her, draping his arm around her shoulder.

"How?" was all the King replied.

"Well, we camped along the tree line of the Nysan border. We wanted to observe the border for a bit before attempting any infiltration. For the most part, Abbadon seems to be keeping their troops to the edge of the border markings, just below the Spearsean Gap," Epyllo rattled off the details in his practiced manner.

"But then...we thought we'd both gone mad when we saw it...we were both shifted, and we had to leave our site, head into Nysa to shift and discuss what we saw to make sure we weren't crazy," Acantha rattled off, less organized in thought than Epyllo.

"What did you see?" questioned Symon. He knew the routine, Epyllo would be the one to give the details, but Acantha had the keenest observations. Her intuition was always reliable.

"It was him," Epyllo said coldly. Symon lifted his eyebrows.

"Rankor's back," stated Acantha, "Or, at first that's what we thought."

Symon stood from the chair he had sat in, and paced to a stack of books. He laid his hand on the pile, and tried to take deep steadying breaths.

"We both shifted, deciding we needed to get a better view. That's when we discovered who we thought was Rankor. Well he is Rankor, but different. They call him President Ranquer. And he's made an alliance with the brothers," the last sentence from Acantha's mouth carried icy steel.

"They are planning an attack, but we couldn't figure out when or where before deciding we needed to get back here to tell you. This...President, has made some arrangements to provide weapons, and supplies to Abbadon and Appylon's forces. In exchange, he wants the girl and our strongest elemental wielders. We couldn't find out why, though," Epyllo finished.

So, they were planning an attack. "I want you both to station your ears everywhere you can in the palace tomorrow," Symon ordered.

"I'll have the birds on watch outside," Epyllo offered.

"Are the flowers fresh?" asked Acantha.

The pair really made a perfect espionage team. Epyllo was charming, detail-oriented, Acantha colder, but cunning and creative. Epyllo could shift into numerous animal forms communicating with them with ease—control them even. Acantha's snake form was often very useful, and her ability to manipulate plants—use them as eyes and ears—had proven invaluable in the years following the war.

Symon nodded. "I'll expect you both at the ball tomorrow evening, but use the reception as a time to gather whatever intelligence you can." With that, Symon dismissed the spies, and continued to pace through his study.

Symon had known about Sage's pursuer, but the confirmation that the man had made an alliance with the Dark Born was a chilling premonition. It made him wish he had waited to send the extra guards to Mystaira. Never mind, Symon decided. The sentry would just have to double their rounds.

He just hoped it would be enough.

Chapter 25

❋❋❋

Three days later, having rested thoroughly, after four long months of fruitless searching, Sage was leaving the Meeran forests behind. The book had guided her to the forests, situated right in the center of three vast lakes, but with no indication of which lake held the Temple of Allyra.

In the time it had taken her to test all three lakes, she'd built a small earthen hut using her earth magic. That, combined with several spells Ian invented to distract or dissuade unwanted visitors, had kept her safe. She'd added an extra touch by constructing several rounded mounds, casting illusion spells so that anyone wandering through the area would believe they were burial mounds. Sage banked on the superstitions of wary folk leaving quickly, lest the restless spirits they contained became curious. The spells had worked so well they'd even kept a pair of government officials away.

Now, she stared longingly at the place she'd called home all this time. If she was honest, she was impressed with her ability to create such an intricate living space and cast such effective spells. The last four months had been lonely, but she'd felt more in control of herself than she had in years.

With a swipe of her hand through the air, her hut fell in on itself, destroying any trace of her ever having been there. A new resolve washed over her as a breeze rippled through the forest. As she squared her shoulders and turned toward the path that would lead her back into society, it felt as if the forest itself was wishing her a safe journey.

She might have made her way to Tiernan slower than she had voyaged to the other temples. She would be venturing into her hometown. The temptation to peek into her old life was overwhelming. It would be her first chance to catch any glimpses of her family since she first escaped Ranquer. Aimee, her sister, would be graduating from the academy this year. Would she venture on to university the following spring? The idea that she might pass her house to not find her family there had occurred, too. What would she do? If something had happened to them? Sage didn't have an answer.

So, she walked. Rather than hitching rides with farmers who hauled their livestock and produce across province lines, or sticking her thumb out in hopes of sweet talking some day-tripper into letting her bum a ride, Sage walked. And walked, and walked. She walked for two weeks, barely stopping to rest, but still not pushing herself to arrive quickly.

She crossed the border between Finias and Tiernan early one morning, walking past the loading docks of the commercial ships that provided Tiernan with most of its economic resources. A coastal province, Tiernan practically revolved around those docks; every road led back to them, and massive trucks rumbled through the streets. Sage's father worked there; had since before she was born. She walked quickly, hoping to avoid recognition from any of the workers. She'd have to pass the docks just once more on her way out of the province. Until then, best to avoid them completely.

Sage made her way to Tiernan Academy; she hoped the old buildings the school had occupied four decades ago were still left unused. The dilapidated buildings sat there mostly for nostalgia purposes. The old-timers loved to talk about how much better things had been back in their day.

Sage arrived by evening, purposefully timing her arrival after school hours, to make sneaking into the old building easier. Some of the kids from her time in school used to sneak into the buildings for whatever mischief they thought was fun; Sage had never been invited. At the time, she might have been on the bitter side of being excluded; now she was grateful not to have had too many attachments.

Thankfully, it appeared as though the school had cracked down on kids sneaking in and wreaking havoc. Sage paced through the first floor, noting the old bottles littering the ground. As she found the stairs leading to the upper floor, Sage knelt by a discarded school bag in a lurid hot pink. The name of one of the girls who'd been in that van with her all those years ago was written in black marker on it.

Memories of kids strewn about the van flashed through her mind. Bodies contorted in strange positions, blood pooling around the guards and kids alike, and the sound of helicopters flooded her senses. Sage rubbed the strap of the bag between her fingers and sent a prayer up to Allyra, Brighid, and Cerridos that the girl's soul had found a place to rest. Despite everything she knew, the guilt was difficult to shrug off.

Sage continued up the stairs, taking careful measures not to disturb anything, checking every room to make sure she was indeed alone. She settled herself on a couch in what surely must have been a teachers' lounge. She kicked off her filthy shoes, peeled off her worn socks, and rubbed at her tired feet.

When she finally felt relaxed, she pulled the old adventurer's book out of her pack, along with a satchel of berries and dried meats she collected during her journey to Tiernan. Sage opened the chapter dedicated to Therisyd. The story scrawled along the pages described secret catacombs lying deep underground, hidden beneath Tiernan. Sage had good reason to believe the school was built over them. The school had long boasted that it was built upon a powerful leyline, its intent to enhance the students' access to power, to better enable students to learn and experiment with magic, under supervision, of course.

She had little doubt the school's boasting was truthful. Back in her academy days, she'd always been more successful at spellcasting at school than anywhere else; now she understood that she required a little bit of her elemental magic combined with the traditional practices in order to make anything substantial happen.

Sage turned the page and found a map, outlining the path to the deepest part of the catacombs, ending in an underground temple dedicated to Therisyd.

She'd just begun the painstaking process of trying to memorize the map, deciphering any warnings of danger the book might allude to when a loud smash made her jump. The sound of smashing windows rang through the building. Shit…shit shit shit.

Sage had hoped that by avoiding any magic use, she would keep the government trackers at bay. Rushing to one of the windows, keeping plastered against a wall, she peered out at the scene below. Rather than finding black and white suited government agents or soldiers, Sage found a group of three students chucking old bricks at the decrepit building's windows.

A boy with dark brown curly hair picked up a brick and hurled it at a window, "That's how you do it!" he jeered as the window smashed apart.

A girl with stick-straight brown hair laughed, sitting on the top of the automobile's hood parked just behind the other two students. A girl with long, light-brown hair who sported an athletic looking tan walked over to the pile of bricks lying at the corner of the building. As she turned around, Sage's legs nearly gave out beneath her.

Her sister. She'd grown so tall; Sage could tell she'd continued playing sports. Her lean, muscular arms showed definition as she lifted two bricks, one in each arm, and threw them at an unshattered window. The crashing sound echoed through Sage's mind.

"Feel better, Aimee?" the dark brown-haired girl asked.

"Not really," Aimee muttered.

"Come here," the boy gestured to the girl. He hugged her; maybe they were dating? Sage wondered, her hand clasped to her mouth to keep herself from calling out to her sister.

The dark-brown haired girl patted the hood she sat upon, "Come on. Let's talk about it."

Aimee strutted to the car and plopped down on the hood. "I hate this time of year. It's fucking bullshit," Aimee said. A loud sniff told Sage that Aimee had been crying. She wanted so badly to run down the stairs, and hug her sister, to wipe away her tears.

"I know," her friend said, their voices carried up against the building. "I know it's hard, that Sage's birthday is always tough on you, on your family. But Sage wouldn't have wanted you to mope about. Would she?"

Aimee gazed at the building like she wasn't really seeing what was in front of her. "No," Aimee responded. "It's just...That whole story of her death. It's fucked up. You know, I still think it was a cover-up. There is NO way Sage was picked as one of those ambassadors; do you remember the rest of the kids that were picked? Fucking Derek was in that group, and he was the dumbest kid in our whole grade. Sage was smart, but she had to work freaking hard for every bit of skill she had," Aimee trailed off from her train of thought.

Her friend glared at Aimee, "Listen, I know you think that. But you need to be real careful who you say that shit to. The Inquisitor Squad only just left Tiernan yesterday. All those people they arrested for voicing their opinions...Aimee, you might be right, but you could get your whole family in trouble with talk like that."

Aimee nodded. "I know," she whispered. "I just wish Sage was still here. She'd know how to get through this."

"How's your mom and dad doing?" her friend asked.

"You know mom...she always plasters that big old smile on her face this time of year, plans a big supper in honor of Sage. But I know she cries, a lot. Her eyes are practically always red and puffy. Dad just gets really quiet. He'll snap out of it, but it's tough. I could be standing right in front of him and scream his name at the top of my lungs, and I don't think he'd hear me. And then, one day, he'll just...be kind of back to normal, ya'know?"

Hearing about her parents nearly made Sage sob in relief. They were alive; they were alive and healthy. Hearing about their sorrow, their grief, was nearly unbearable, but they were alive!

"Guys...Seamus just called," the curly-haired boy called out, walking back to the girls. "His parents went out of town for the weekend. He's throwing a party tonight; wanna go?"

The girls looked at each other, "Only to keep you out of trouble Aiden," the brown-haired girl chimed.

"Yeah, 'cause we all know you're going regardless, and you and Seamus without supervision is unacceptable," Aimee mused, hopping off the car.

The kids all climbed into the car, Aiden assuring the girls, "We aren't THAT bad." The car revved, and they were gone. Sage stood against the wall, staring at the place her sister had just been. For hours, she stood there. Eventually, she made her way back to the couch, and curled up, falling to sleep with memories of her family swimming through her mind.

The next morning, Sage made her plans to find the catacombs. Based on the map in the book, it was likely the entrance was actually inside the abandoned old building. A lucky coincidence, Sage mused. She supposed it was possible the school had originally been built with access to the catacombs eons ago. The building she was in now hadn't been the original building; the original had been destroyed in one of the uprisings in the past century. Sage studied the map again and decided her best option was to make her way to the cellar room, accessible through a pair of doors in the back exterior of the school. Sage packed her bag, making sure the book was easily accessible; she clipped her pocket knife to her pocket and fished out the miniature camp light she'd bought in Lyonesus months ago.

Sage crept out of the building through its back doors and spied the slanted, wooden doors which led into the cellar. A large chain and padlock were looped through the door handles, and Sage dared using the simplest unlocking spell she knew. The risk of some of her elemental magic being used, and the risk that the government agents tracking that kind of magic might be alerted was unavoidable.

Her first attempt was unsuccessful. The school had the forethought to ward the lock against the simplest spells. Her second try was more successful, opting for another one of Ian's invented spells, and Sage pocketed her wand quickly. She would have to find Ian when this was all over and kiss him just for his ingenuity. Hopefully, the spell was simple enough that she'd avoided detection.

Sage walked through the cellar, peering through the old metal shelves, still housing antique cans of food, cleaning supplies, chalk, potion ingredients, and even a display of embalmed magical creatures, most of which were extinct now due to being over-harvested for outdated spells and charms. Sage peeked through the shelves, around corners, and in the shadowy nooks of the cellar. Finally, she happened upon a small trapdoor, caddy corner to an empty shelf. Sage hoisted the door up, leaning it against the adjacent wall, and peered down the narrow staircase below it. Sage used her camp light to illuminate the passageway. Clear of any obvious dangers, Sage began her descent.

The cellar had been chilly; the tunnel in which Sage entered now was downright bitter with cold. Sage's fingers ached as she continued walking down, down, down the dark tunnels. The tunnel twisted, turning right, then left, then right again, as if it zigzagged downward. A second turn left, and the walls began featuring small, square cubbies, all filled with neat stacks of bones. The bones were arranged in an orderly, tidy manner as if someone had taken great care. Sage avoided staring too long at the piles of bones, the skulls peering at her through the shadows, and continued walking further into the tunnels.

A drip sounded through the hollow pathway, and Sage turned, peering behind her. Walking ahead a little further, Sage found a small, delicate stream of water running along the ceiling of the tunnel, a tiny bead of water dripping to the floor every few minutes. Sage continued. She had no way of keeping time without the sun as her guide, forgoing watches and phones long ago in fear the tech could make her easily traceable. After what could have been thirty minutes, the rows of bones petered out. The walls became as smooth as ice, almost polished looking. Touching them, Sage determined they were made of some sort of clay, but had been carefully smoothed and polished. More walking and Sage arrived at a wide, circular room. Again, a copper basin sat at the center of the room. Primitive-looking rock statues, carved in the likeness of ancient druid priests and priestesses lined the circular wall. Sage stood at the entrance of the room, taking her time to observe the room, looking for any hint of surprise. Time ticked by, and nothing appeared. Sage took one step into the room...nothing. Another step...still nothing. Two more steps...growling.

There it was.

Sage looked around, holding her camp light up in the air. The battery-powered lantern lit the room with an ethereal glow. Nothing. She couldn't see a damned thing past the couple feet her lantern shone. The growling faded. Sage took one more step, and the growling began anew. "I'm here on behalf of Therysid...does that mean anything to you?"

"Therysid is gone. I guard this temple now," growled the answering voice. Crystals growing from the wall began to glow, casting an eerie green glow to the room. The basin reflected the green color, throwing stark shadows against the wall.

"Who are you?" Sage asked, fighting the tremor in her voice as that ominous growl continued to fill the room. She stopped walking as an enormous black wolf stepped into the glowing chamber just beyond the basin.

"I'm the Wulver of Donn." Donn...the guardian and god of the otherworld, a reaper god whose sole purpose was ferrying people across the dimensions after death, and keeping those souls from re-entering where the living remained.

"You're...you're the Wulver? Nehalennia?" Sage stammered. "Why are you here?" The Wulver continued advancing toward Sage, lurking close to the circular walls.

"Donn now guards this temple; your people have desecrated the gods and their temples. Your people have abandoned the contracts made in the days before the first rebellion. Your people have doomed this world and all who live in it," Nehalennia spoke, her words rumbling through Sage's bones. "Donn works now to fulfill his end of the bargain made in the beginning of times. He will judge you and your fellows with the truth you deserve."

Sage searched within her own mind, looking for something of interest to give the enormous wolf. The Wulver, Nehalennia, was equal parts human, wolf, spirit, and living thing. She could shift into a humanoid, wolf-headed figure when she wished, and was rumored to carry a mace and shield into battle when enticed. It was also told that she would offer blessings to those in need and righteous in spirit.

Sage shook her head, trying to come up with the words to explain why she was there. "Nehalennia, Wulver of Donn, I am here in honor of the gods," she explained, opting to kneel on the floor, bowing her head. Sage set her lantern on the floor and bowed her head until it touched the floor as well.

"How do you honor the gods? You are trespassing on sacred land, and bring nothing to sacrifice or offer," growled the Wulver, now circling behind Sage. Sage could feel steamy breath along her spine as the Wulver spoke.

"I was visited by Allyra, Brighid, and Cerridos. I know what happened to Therysid; Allyra herself saved me and gave me her blessing. I've been tasked to find Therysid, and stop the sacrifices of my people, of the gods," Sage said, head still resting on the floor. The wulver's breath skated along her skin causing goosebumps to erupt across her entire body. Sage tried to stop the trembling that was taking over her body, but Nehalennia could kill her right then if she wanted.

"Sit up," growled the Wulver. Sage did and found herself nearly nose-to-nose with the lupine face. The Wulver's eyes glowed amber as they looked upon each other, the reflection of the crystals refracting off the glossy black fur. Sage held that gaze, felt the twinge as Nehalennia entered her mind, pilfering through her memories. She was run through her life at warp speed, as if it were a book someone opened and fanned through, pages blurring by. At last, Nehalennia released Sage, and she sagged, nearly dropping her head to the floor again.

"So you are to be the one to do the gods' bidding?" Nehalennia finally replied, sitting in front of Sage. Sage merely nodded in confirmation. "You understand there will be a price for retrieving the insignia?" the Wulver asked.

"Big surprise," Sage muttered, her head pounding from having her life rifled through so brutally.

The wolf's head snapped to the side, her ears perking as if she heard some distant noise. The room, already quiet, became stale, time pausing. Dust motes paused in mid-air, the flicker of Sage's dropped lantern froze as Nehalennia stared past the stone walls. Sage followed the lupine gaze, trying to discern what suddenly drew the massive wolf's attention away. "Your price has been already paid," Nehalennia whispered, dropping her face as she considered Sage.

"What do you mean? What price?" Sage questioned.

"The price to complete your task has been paid, by another. Do you know the currency in which Donn deals?" Nehalennia continued.

Sage froze, her trembling ceasing. Donn, god and guardian of the Otherworld; he would require a life. "Who?" Sage asked. "Who has he taken?" Sage demanded, panic rising into her throat.

"The price has not yet been paid, but you will not be in time to stop it," Nehalennia replied.

"Is it my family?" asked Sage, tears rimming her eyes. No...it couldn't be them; she'd only just discovered they were safe.

"It is not for me to tell you who it is, but it is not your family, no. It is a piece of your heart, however, Sage Brennan. You cannot stop what has been foretold."

The Wulver stalked to the basin, and sat next to it. Sage peeled herself from the floor and followed. "Why has Donn decided to do this? Why must someone else pay the price?" Sage asked in a whisper. "I already agreed to do it."

"Do you not fear death?" Nehalennia asked.

Sage shook her head. "It's not that I'm not afraid. I just...I've known I'm probably going to die sooner rather than later for so long. I don't understand why Donn is taking someone else. It should be me." Despite her best efforts, a lone tear rolled down her cheek.

"It was not Donn's doing; a contract between the living world and Otherworld was made long, long ago. If you must blame anyone, blame the living. They are the ones who have forfeited the protection of the gods." Sage knew the wolf guardian spoke true, but her fingers never stopped trembling as she reached into the basin to pull out the lone, stone medallion lying at the bottom of the great copper bowl.

"Stay the course, Sage Brennan. The fate of many worlds now rests on your shoulders. When you are ready to fulfill the contracts you have made, come and find me. I will see you on the battlefield." With the last of Nehalennia's soft-spoken words, the wulver vanished along with the glow of the crystals on the wall.

Standing in near darkness, her camp light glowing faintly behind her, Sage held the final insignia in her palm. Nehalennia's words weighed heavily on her heart. How could the Wulver meet her on the battlefield? Sage was no warrior.

She hated the gods; hated the government who'd started this path to destruction all those years ago; she hated this world, the otherworld. She hated all of it.

But she'd made a promise, many promises at this point. Sage pocketed the insignia, wiped away her tears, then walked to her camp light and scooped it up while simultaneously shouldering her pack. She walked with renewed determination through the catacombs. She didn't bother revisiting the room upstairs as she exited through the cellar. She left behind the blanket still laid out on the couch she'd slept on the night before. She walked straight to the dockyard, determined to sneak onto a boat that would take her to the Finian shores where Mount Danu was located.

She would have this stupid mission complete before the end of the week, she told herself.

Chapter 26

Sage woke to a breeze blowing across her body. She shuddered as the cool air rippled across her skin. Gavin was no longer lying next to her, and her balcony door was open. It was still dark outside, but she could just begin to make out the lightening of the sky, a rim of silver above the tree line as the sun began to peek over the ocean behind her. She wrapped herself in her blanket and went to sit on the balcony to watch as the sun gilded the garden below.

Slowly, birds, chipmunks, and a couple of cats began to move, sing, and call out as they woke from their slumber. The sun peeked over the palace and littered the garden with golden rays. The whole garden was flooded with sunbeams when a white hawk with black-tipped wings landed on her balcony floor. Gavin shifted, and Sage peered up at him with apologetic eyes.

"Good morning," she whispered sleepily to him. He stepped over to her, placing a soft kiss on her cheek.

"I didn't mean to wake you," Gavin replied.

Sage smiled up at him. "I'm sorry," she apologized again.

Gavin shrugged off her apology. "I told you, don't apologize. No one faults you for having a life before you got here.

And I know what it's like to lose someone you love; someone you care for."

"You lost people?" she asked. She already knew the answer; everyone had lost people in the war.

"I lost friends and relatives to sickness, injury, attacks in the work camps. I lost comrades in the war. If you need to grieve, I understand," he explained as he sat down.

A few moments went by, and Gavin rose to put on his shirt and step out of her room. He returned with a tray holding tea and breakfast pastries. They each fixed their cups of tea, Sage opting to let it cool on the table before sipping. "Can you tell me about them? The ones you lost?"

Gavin took a deep breath, leaning forward to set down his cup of tea. He looked away from Sage, staring into the gardens below. "My sister has this friend, Lily. I think you'd like her," Gavin grinned a little. "She's a hell-raiser."

"Hey! Why do you think that'd make me like her?"

"Because you are also a hell-raiser." Gavin grinned wider, then cleared his throat. "Her father, Amos, is still a good family friend of ours. He lost his first wife and two sons when Felysia was first invaded. His sons tried to fight off the soldiers and ended up dying in the process. Somehow, Amos found a new partner while we were in the work camps. Lily was born there, just a few months before my sister."

"I can't imagine being born into a place like that."

"It wasn't great," Gavin admitted. "And it was rare. The fact my parents had three children in the work camp makes them kind of legendary. It's still a bit of a mystery." Gavin waved his hand, attempting to move the story forward. "When we were really young, I think I was five, a plague swept through the camp. Lily caught it from us. It was this awful chest infection, and it killed so many of us. My little brother barely survived. Anyway, Lily caught it, and her mother did everything she could to nurse Lily back to health. Lily survived. But her mother ended up dying after she became sick. It happened so fast. I didn't think Amos, or Lily, would survive their grief. Somehow, they managed."

Sage nodded. "I feel guilty all the time for how my life has affected everyone around me." Her throat suddenly felt thick, and she had to work to keep the pastry she just finished from coming back up. "It's like, no matter how hard I tried, everyone else seems to pay a price just because I exist."

Gavin answered with a tight-lipped grimace. "I felt bad about Lily's mother for a long time. I was the first one in our house to get sick, and I thought it was my fault. Raphael is the one who helped me get past that."

"I can't believe how much you've gone through, and that you survived that at fifteen."

"It was the same age you escaped President Ranquer," replied Gavin.

She hadn't been able, all this time, to mutter the President's name. Hearing it brought painful flashbacks. How was it that his duplicate had managed to be so evil in this world, too? Eventually, Gavin leaned in, brushed a strand of hair from her face, and kissed her cheek again.

He held her hands as he said, "Whatever you need, let me know. For now," he continued, standing from his seat, "it's time we get ready for the reception. I imagine servants are already on their way here to help you dress."

"Help me dress? I can get dressed on my own," Sage exclaimed, the fog of grief quickly dissipating as she looked up at Gavin.

"Right, well...good luck with that," Gavin replied with a grin, leaving Sage with the sinking realization that the servants were going to help her dress regardless of her ability to do so on her own. She was scowling at him as he chuckled, waving at her as he closed her door.

Sage got up and hurried to her bathing chamber; as quickly as she could, while still marveling at the shower, she bathed and stepped out, wrapping herself in a towel.

She nearly fainted from the shock when a low voice sang, "Realm leaper." A petite female stood in the corner of her bathroom, bowing slightly to Sage.

"Who are you?" Sage demanded.

"We were sent by the Queen, to see that you are prepared for the ceremonies today. The others are readying your robes in the room. I will take care of your hair and cosmetics," the fae replied.

"How do you know who I am?" asked Sage, looking at the female through the sides of her eyes.

"The Queen warned—informed us...before we came."

Warned? So she still wasn't fully trusted by these people, then. Sage let loose a sigh, then beckoned the female to her. "So, what are we doing then?" Sage asked.

The female gestured to a chair pushed under the vanity counter of the bathroom, and Sage pulled it out and plopped onto it.

The female set to work combing out Sage's hair. Swiftly, the female had managed to dry Sage's hair, presumably with water powers, and began the process of sectioning off chunks of her hair. The female set her hair in delicate, but thick braids, allowing pieces to fall forward to frame Sage's face. The braids were pinned in place so that her hair looked like a rope coiled around her head. The design was elegant in a way that seemed to lengthen her neck and highlight her cheekbones.

Then, the female rummaged through the cosmetics provided in the bathroom and began to delicately line Sage's eyes in coal, pinken her cheeks with rose paste, and sweep something that looked like Sage's idea of stardust along the tops of her cheekbones. Soft shimmery powder subtly highlighted her eyelids, and the final touch was a comb of what Sage would have called mascara in her world.

The make-up was subtle, but impressive. The color of her eyes stood out, the slope of her forehead, the smooth plane across her cheeks all emphasized so she looked like a woman from a classical painting. Sage noticed that the female had not covered her ears, and turned to question her when Sage was beckoned into the main room.

Three other females occupied the room. They had laid out the necessary garments, including some special undergarments Sage had not seen before. Sage swatted away their hands as they tried to help her into the undergarments, and insisted she apply the "ceremonial oils," to her skin herself.

Apparently, a part of this ceremony required her to smell a certain way as well. The oils smelled of fresh honey, bergamot, and cardamom. She instantly felt like she was floating through a field of sunshine, and submitted to the relaxation that flooded her tense muscles.

The females proceeded to pull the dress onto Sage, securing the straps in place. They attached the glittering headdress to Sage's hair and pinned the cape behind the center of the headdress so that it looked more like a veil with a long train.

"I see Rahab made an adjustment to the cape," Sage noted, admiring the way in which the seamstress had made the material even more delicate, more fine in the few days since she'd had her fitting. Sage stared at her reflection in the mirror of her room, the iridescent overlay of her dress casting reflections onto her skin, the gems of the cape and headdress making prisms dance on the walls. She looked like an ancient priestess in this ensemble, something to be feared and awed at. Sage wondered whether that was the point of it all.

The females took their time, looking her over from top to bottom, and any tension that had been relieved from the oils before seeped out as Sage stood rigidly through their inspections. "Ugh...guys...what if I need to...you know...attend to business...privately?" Sage asked, embarrassed because she did indeed need to see to her own business.

The first fae smiled softly, "Come, I will show you now so you can do it alone later." Together, Sage carefully managed to balance her dress, the veil-cape, and keep her headdress intact while using the bathroom. As she reemerged into her room, Gavin stood alone, apparently waiting for her to reappear.

The look on his face made her blush.

"You...you look very nice," he said in an almost whisper. Sage smiled, nodding slightly, at a loss for words. She might look very nice, but he...oh, gods, he was a downright marvel to look at. His normal attire of loose white shirts and brown leather pants, along with the various training uniforms was not the sort of thing that hid his physique or charming smile. But this uniform: a dark blue jacket, nearly black, with shining silver buttons was left open to a white shirt underneath. His matching leather pants, customary of the military ranks in this city, tapered into formidable boots so that she could see the shape of his muscled thighs. Across his chest was a blazing red, gold, and white sash, meeting at the place where an impressive sword was buckled to his belt. She'd not seen him with a sword before, though he always wore his dagger, which was also buckled to the other side of his belt.

"I know...it's a bit over the top. I've always hated dress uniforms," Gavin began, placing his hands on his hips and looking out the window. She could see then, just how uncomfortable he looked.

"You look like Suda will have a run for his money," Sage said softly.

Gavin tried to hide his smile, didn't succeed, and replied, "Yeah, well, let's get on with it."

They walked into the hallway, crowded with fae making their way to the ceremony. Sage could feel the eyes roving across her body, assessing her as they strode to the throne room. Gavin squeezed her arm in reassurance, and Sage straightened her spine, determined to tamp down on any fear or apprehension in her body.

The hall, no, the building, was flooded with the scent of the oils she was given: honey, bergamot, and cardamom.

Sage couldn't stop herself from inhaling, and Gavin whispered, "It's the Queen's scent. Everyone is wearing the same oils in deference to her authority, a sign of fealty."

Sage hadn't noticed it before, but even Gavin smelled the same as everyone around her. She found herself equal parts reveling in the relaxing, invigorating smell surrounding her and missing the clean, sharp smell of rosemary, spice, and sandalwood that she now associated with Gavin.

They arrived in a gilded hallway, which led through massive double doors into a domed room. Rows and rows of fae lined the room, and Gavin led Sage toward the front. There were no seats or benches. Every fae, male and female, stood in their rows. Gavin and Sage took their spot along the front row on the left side of the room. As they settled, Sage felt the hordes of eyes dance on them, curious about the female in the colorful veil, no doubt. The male standing next to Gavin looked him over and nodded, seemingly in approval, and Gavin nodded back. Sage was reminded that this would be the first time Gavin took his place as the representative of Mystaira.

"So, after this...do you go back to your family?" Sage whispered to Gavin.

Gavin shook his head, "No. I've still got to prove my powers are capable. This is more just a formality."

Sage glanced at the stage before them, Petra stood on a stair further away from Sage and Gavin, Zeke on the stair above her. Meliza stood across from Zeke, just above Suda's position across from Petra. While Gavin's uniform was made for formal occasions, Meliza and Zeke's were equal parts formal and tactical. Made completely of leather, resembling armor more than clothing, Sage counted no less than four blades on each of the commanders. Petra, on the other hand, wore a gown of white silk. Rather than the fabric softening her appearance, she looked more like an ice sorceress than fae, and glared out at the crowd with indignance and challenge. Suda was dressed as handsome as the night before, with his open dress robe of red and yellow, smiling at the crowd, winking at a female or two while they waited.

Sage's gaze rose upward, to the two thrones which sat side by side. They were equal in size but different in composition. The throne furthest away was made of silver and bronze, the top of the throne sculpted into a lion's head, poised in mid-roar, whose mane flowed outward and wrapped itself all the way around the arms of the throne itself. The throne next to it was made like the sun it-self. Constructed of gold- not just one, but all types of gold: white gold, yellow gold, rose gold, burnished gold; the throne was crowned with flames of gold that radiated along the entirety of the throne.

The windows which encircled the towering domed roof cast rays of light down so that the throne of flame looked like it pulsated with the power of a hundred roaring fires. The longer Sage stared at it, the more the flames began to feel tangible. The feeling overwhelmed her as her mind raced with memories of wielding flames, her palms began to sweat, and she felt an intense pressure of heat begin to build inside her.

Raphael, who, unbeknownst to Sage, was behind them, whispered in her ear, "My dear, breath. It won't do for you to combust before the Queen even arrives." Sage snatched her stare away from the throne, choosing to stare at Petra instead.

Taking deep gulps of air, Sage let Petra's icy stare bore into her, the coldness in the female's eyes squelching the flame writhing within Sage's center. Well, the female had her uses then, Sage thought to herself.

Just then, a roar thundered through the room, rattling the mirrors and walls. As one, everyone in the hall kneeled gracefully, bowing their heads deep. Sage followed suit but tried to watch as Symon, the stately, formidable male, and his Queen shimmered into existence in front of the thrones, taking their place. Sage recognized Meliza's voice as she called, "You may rise." As one, the entire throne room stood to their feet, and Sage gaped at the scene before her. Symon sat on his lion throne; he wore an ornate crown on his head, and a suit made of dark charcoal fabric embroidered with the colors of Felysia scrawled along the entirety. Draped over one shoulder was a goldenrod cape. His dark blue eyes pierced the crowd. Sage recognized now the way in which the lion-born siblings favored each other; and yet, Symon's brown skin was darker than Meliza's, whose skin was darker than Petra's. It was almost as if they were shades of each other, shades of a similar power. And even as impressive as Symon might be, on his lion throne, assessing the room with ferocity and equanimity, it was Queen Aryael who stole Sage's breath.

The Queen, one hand resting in Symon's, contradicted and enhanced Symon in every manner. While his skin was darker than his siblings, Aryael's warm brown skin resembled her brother, Suda. Its darkness seemed to soak up the sun before reflecting all that heat, the energy of an eternally burning flame, onto the congregation before her. Her eyes glowed like topaz with smoldering yellow embers dancing in them; her long braids were the color of the clay bricks used to pave the streets of Veritasailles, and the sun entwined itself in her hair, adorned with golden beads. Her dress was made of panels of amber, coral, reds the color of the sweetest wine, and yellows that were almost white so that she resembled the multitude of colors in a living flame. Her shoulders were kept bare, and resting atop her head was a crown that peaked from her head in delicate strands of gold. The crown was adorned with small gems, all fine and elegant, which made Aryael appear to possess a halo of light encapsulating her. Symon finished with his assessment of their court, looked to Aryael, and gave her a small nod. A smile erupted from Aryael. If she hadn't looked like an angel before, the smile made her more radiant, more ethereal than anything Sage had witnessed before. It seemed to have similar effects on the rest of the court as Sage could feel a collective lean towards the radiant Queen, ready to do her every bidding.

"Lords, Ladies, loved people of Felysia and esteemed visitors from across Panchaia. Before we begin our formal ceremonies, I want to begin by expressing my gratitude to all of you. It has been ten years since we've overcome the darkness; it has been ten years since we have worked together to unite our continent and built a world for ourselves of peace and trust. I want to thank you all, for your continued dedication to our cause. So that we should never falter, never fall to darkness again. Our work together, our unity, makes this possible." The final notes of Queen Aryael's melodic voice danced through the room, her words carrying the timbre of hope and resilience in them.

As one, the room sank to one knee in salute to the King and Queen, Sage following the others. The bow was a quick movement, but represented the fervor in which the court agreed. They would not falter, would not succumb to an oppressor again, not any time soon.

Sage could sense the gratitude this land, this world, felt towards the Queen. She had not heard the full story of this woman, this savior, but understood that she was the apex on which success had balanced. Symon, clearly, was a powerful male, but it was this woman who had tipped the balance. Sage would ask Gavin more about that later.

The procession began, with Meliza calling out to the court, summoning Lords, Ladies, and visitors from other countries, up to the King and Queen. The Lords and Ladies vowed their fealty to the King and Queen, the visitors making vows of alliances, and partnerships. All of them brought gifts.

Sage looked at Gavin in a panic, "I didn't know we were supposed to provide a gift," whispered Sage.

Gavin looked at her, his lips pressing together. Apparently, neither had he.

She could see his eyes darting around the room, trying to problem-solve this new dilemma they found themselves in. They stood there, and stood there. Discomfort clawed itself up Sage's throat as they stood for hours on end, witnessing grand gestures and gifts laid at the royals' feet. Hour after hour ticked by, and still, it appeared Gavin and Sage would arrive at the front empty-handed. Raphael was called to the front; it was nearly time then. Finally, they were called forward, the last row of the court before those who stood on the stage's steps.

Sage and Gavin strode toward the bottommost stair, one below where Suda and Petra stood, and floated together to one knee, heads bowed.

Meliza called out, "Lord Gavin of Mystaira and Lady Sage, Honored Guest of Queen Aryael, please rise."

They did, though not before Sage felt the exhale of Gavin's breath when Meliza called out his title.

Gavin opened his mouth to speak, but Symon interjected, "Lord Gavin- we received your handsome gift earlier this month. Mystaira's renowned heritage of exceptional agriculture has blessed Veritasailles once again. The Queen and I are humbled by your supply of goods, which have been put to use for tonight's feasts."

Gavin opened his mouth once, closed it, then opened it again before shaking his head and gathering himself. "Of course," he replied with a fist to his chest and a bow of his head, "My Queen, it has been an honor and a joy to provide your city with goods. I thank the Goddess for her blessings, and that she brought you to us. I look forward to celebrating your birth and long reign this week."

Gavin finished his speech, and the Queen nodded with a broad smile to him.

"And you, Lady Sage?"

Sage straightened her spine, trying, and probably failing to hide her discomfort. Finally, she replied, "Majesty, I regret that I have arrived empty-handed."

The Queen cut in, "But it was such an arduous journey. Your apologies are unnecessary," she said with a wave of her hand.

"I offer you my services and company should you ever need it," Sage said quickly with a small curtsy. Had she not had an audience, Sage would have slapped her head with her palm. What was she doing? She couldn't be more awkward if her legs were tied together.

A slow, playful grin spread across the Queen's face. "Since you did come empty-handed, I suppose there is one thing you could bring to me. My council room has been in a tizzy with excitement as news of a Realm Leaper was brought in," the court burst into excited whispers. They'd obviously heard the rumors, and now they were getting the confirmation. "But little has been told of your powers, whether they are as great as the mighty Cerridos and Allyra. There have been rumors, of course, but no confirmation. In fact, the rumor is you are a goddess yourself."

Sage blurted out, cutting off the Queen, "No, Your Majesty, I'm no goddess."

Aryael pressed her lips together, apparently not fond of being interrupted. "I would like to see for myself. Please,

Lady Sage, demonstrate to me and my court your true powers."

Sage looked at Gavin, who looked back at her with wide eyes and stepped away from her, giving her the floor to begin. Sage slowly turned back, looking up at the Queen and King with narrowed eyes. Fine, they wanted a show, she'd give them a show. Thinking quickly, she didn't hesitate to execute her plan.

Sage took four quick strides back, not turning away from the royals. She flung the veil-cape back from her arms and lifted them in front of her. She began by summoning the wind: Sage lifted her arms, palms upturned, and let them float back to her. A gentle breeze flitted along the court, ruffling skirts and capes, making the few candles hanging from candelabras flicker but remain alight. Sage stepped to her left, gathering her arms to her side, and with a great circling motion of both arms collected the wind into a ball of energy.

That ball of wind circled into itself, creating a whirlwind, suspended in front of her; a gentle push and the whirlwind floated just ahead of her. The wind grabbed at the males and females nearest, and they all stepped back, pushing into the walls.

Sage bent her knees and pulled her arms and hands into herself. She extended both arms and hands, clutching something between them, and opened her clasped palms to reveal a small flicker of flame. Sage pressed her hands again, bending at her knees a second time, and as she opened her hands the flame grew into a burning orb. Mutterings and whispers, gasps and whistles echoed through the hall.

Holding her left hand stable, Sage used her right hand to drift behind the ball, and she pushed the flame into the wind. The whirlwind transformed into a burning cyclone, still small and controlled, hovering in place.

Sage stepped back onto her right foot, and hinged at her hips, her arms making a gathering motion. A stone tile from the floor floated upward, suspended in the air. Sage raised an arm, bending at her elbow, and clenched her hand into a fist. The tile crumpled into dust. Sage closed her eyes, envisioning the Queen's face, her crown, as she pushed her palms together, fingers flexed to the sky. The dust pushed into itself. Sage pushed harder. The dust took shape, and she sent the figure into the flame.

The figure in the center sparked, and darkened, then glowed from the inferno's intrepid heat. Sage bent at the knees once more, and wound her arms over her head, one at a time. She repeated the motion. Clouds, honest-to-goodness clouds gathered in the throne room. Sage repeated the movement with her arms, bigger now and with a sweeping movement upward of her hips.

Sage lifted her gaze to the ceiling, her arms outstretched. The flaming whirlwind grew in intensity, and Sage dropped her arms. A rainstorm erupted in the throne room, dousing the flames and drenching the congregation, save the royals on their stage. Floating, suspended in front of Sage was a tiny figurine, a bust of Queen Aryael's likeness. Sage sent it to the Queen on a rigid wind, whose face was a mix of awe and delight.

The Queen examined the bust, showing it to King Symon.

"That was quite the demonstration," said the Queen. "I see that I was right."

The King looked at his wife, eyebrows lifted. Aryael grinned, and he answered with a similar smile. Symon looked away, shaking his head slightly and laughing to himself.

Sage wondered if they had just used Symon's powers to have a private conversation.

Sage determined she would really like to have mind powers, so she could tell Gavin just where she thought those royals could put that bust she made. A riotous laugh boomed from Symon, followed by a peeling ring of laughter from Aryael. Symon gestured for Sage to come forward, and whispered when she was close enough to hear.

"I recommend keeping those types of thoughts away from those of us who can read minds."

The King winked, and Aryael grinned at her, apparently amused by Sage's insolence. "Please, rejoin the court. Thank you, Lady Sage for your most generous demonstration, and the lovely gift. I will cherish it always."

Sage stepped back into her place, sweat poured down her back, the veil clung to her neck, and she struggled to keep her knees from wobbling. That had been the most she had used her abilities together since arriving here.

A gentle hand reached up to her shoulder, and Raphael whispered, "Let me help."

Sage nodded, and could feel the healer's ripple of power dance around her body, offering her a bit of fortitude to make it through the final proceedings. From the looks of it, only Gavin and one more Lord remained to pay their respects. They were so close to the end. And it looked as if they would leave the ceremony mostly unscathed.

Despite her exhaustion, relief washed over her as she began anticipating making it back to her room to rest.

A cold voice slithered into her mind. *I have found you, my darling. You always knew you cannot outrun me.*

She looked to Gavin, forcing herself to remain upright. His features were a mixture of alarm and awe. Had he heard the voice as well? Sage shook her head, dislodging the thought and deciding the voice was a rogue memory working itself back to her. She would talk about it with Raphael later.

Chapter 27

Gavin felt the pull of the wind calling for his attention as Sage began her demonstration. The wind sang as it flitted through the room. A shiver made its way down his spine as voices seemed to mingle in the wind. Soft melodies called his name as the wind whipped tighter into itself.

Gavin's knees weakened as the sound of a woman's voice calling to him became clearer. Sage turned the whirlwind into a burning cyclone and the voice grew. No, not a voice...three voices.

"Gavin...." The voice, voices, called with a whispering tone like a billion grains of sand rushing through a timer. His vision narrowed, and the only thing he could focus on was the burning wind. Gravity itself tugged on his center like the cyclone would pull him in, but he found himself glued to the spot. His senses were siphoned into the flames, into the voices that called and called his name.

Gavin stared into the flames and was transported away from the throne room. Not away....the rest of the room fell away so that all that was left was Gavin and the flaming whirlwind.

In the center of the cyclone, a woman stood. Her figure changed, shifted so that Gavin couldn't discern her true appearance. At times she seemed to hold a bow and arrow, at other times she held a rod and scales or a basket of flowers and wheat.

"Gavin," the voices called out, stronger now. "Gavin, you know who I am," called the voice.

"Who are you?" Gavin called to the burning woman. Deep down he knew who the woman in the flame was, but fear kept him from admitting the truth.

"Gavin, you know who I am. I am the one who beckons you to the hunt," the woman held a bow, a golden helmet bracketing her face. Her appearance melted into something new, "I am the one who wakes you and calls you to pursue your truth." Scales replaced the bow and arrow, and a sound like ringing bells chorused through his body. Her helmet was replaced with a circlet of olive branches. "And I am the one who has grown you and loved you." The woman's features softened, almost looking as if she were carrying a child in her womb. Flowers spilled from a basket resting on the crook of her arm. Her loose hair of lovely curls blew in the wind. As Gavin looked upon the woman, her appearance began shifting again, this time faster. She changed over and over again, all of them wholly focused on him.

Gavin's legs gave way, and he knelt harshly on the stone floor. He had to look around to see who else was aware of what was happening.

"No one else can see this. We've come to *you*, and you alone," the voices called as one.

"Goddess?" Gavin asked.

The women in the flames nodded, smiling sweetly. "Gavin, I am here to call you to action. The realm leaper you have been sent will be tested; she has been sent by the gods of her home; gods made by myself in the days of beginning. She will need your help; our worlds will need the help of many, and you will be the one to call them into action when it is time."

Gavin shook his head, "No. I can't do this. You need Aryael. She's the one who can save us. If something is going to happen, you should tell her. Or Symon," Gavin pleaded.

"No, Gavin. You mustn't tell them; not until it is time. Everyone has their own part to play. For now, your charge is to stay with the realm leaper. Keep her safe. You are both part of the key that will unlock our worlds from the grips of shadow. Together, you will be able to usher in a new generation of illumination."

Gavin could see Sage now, her arms raised above her head. Clouds rippled overhead, and the chimes of fate reverberated through his chest.

"How? How will we do this?" Gavin asked the Goddess.

"Do you believe that I will not provide for those I charge to take action?" The Goddess flashed and took the form of the huntress, her bow and arrow glowing as she held them to her side. "I will provide you with the tools and knowledge you require when the time comes." Something like a cold breeze brushed across Gavin's neck, and he felt the weight of the Goddess's blessing.

Without warning, a rainstorm erupted and Gavin was back in the throne room. Sage sent something to the Queen on a swift current of air. The royals spoke softly to Sage, then she was returning to her place. A glance around proved that no one else had seen, no one had heard the Goddess. He was standing now without remembering rising to his feet. His heart beat like it would jump out of his chest, and he struggled to control his breathing. Remembering his training, he forced himself to breathe in as deeply as he could manage, hold for a count of two, then slowly release his breath. The exercise helped with the trembling in his hands, but his heart still beat wildly. Sweat dampened his upper lip and he felt the cool touch of the Goddess like a brand to the back of his neck.

"Lord Gavin," the Queen was saying, "if you will. Take your place before us."

The Queen gestured to the spot, squarely centered before the King and Queen.

Gavin hesitated. The revelation of the Tri-Goddess's interference made everything in the last ten years feel small. *He* felt small, almost like he wasn't real. Realizing that Aryael was beginning to look at him in a way he knew meant she was reading his emotions, he forced himself to approach the stairs. Symon peered down at him, and he knew that Symon was reading his mind. Perhaps the Goddess warded his thoughts to keep her visit secret.

"We are ready to hear your pledge, Lord Gavin. When you are ready," the Queen instructed.

Clearly, not when he was ready, thought Gavin. Otherwise, he would have a few more years before he was forced into this, or even a few extra moments to gather himself. Exhaling deeply, Gavin nodded at Aryael, and she nodded back. The faith his friend, his Queen, put in his actions steadied his heart and calmed his nerves. He didn't deserve the confidence she had in him, but he also knew he couldn't let her down. Furthermore, he knew she was up to something and had a sneaking suspicion it had to do with Lord Seth following him in pledging fealty.

Gavin kneeled, drawing the sword at his belt, balancing it on the tip of the blade, both hands clasping the hilt. The room stilled, any rustling that might have been happening ceased as the whole room waited to hear his first formal pledge to the King and Queen of Felysia.

He bowed his head and began, surprised to hear his voice full of authority, without a tremor despite feeling unbalanced. "I, Gavin, Lord of Mystaira and as a bearer of Felysia's arms, hereby pledge my fealty to Queen Aryael, Flame Wielder of Felysia, and King Symon the Destroyer and Lion-Born. I pledge my loyalty to my King, Queen, and country. I pledge the support of my lands and the faithfulness of my people. I pledge my life to the honor of my Queen and King, from hereon until the Goddess of Three claims me once again." The final line of the pledge seemed to boom through the room and he felt a collective exhale as it rushed through the congregation.

Gavin's pledge was different from the other pledges. He wondered why the line about the Goddess had been added to it, a thought that now plagued him as he waited for the King and Queen's recognition of his fealty. Time slowed as he waited for them to tell him to rise.

Queen Aryael rose from her seat, and approached Gavin, placing two delicate kisses upon his cheeks. Gavin gave her a nod in acknowledgment, secret meaning flitting through the Queen, King, and the fae flanking them on the stairs. There was more to this than Gavin understood, and he couldn't help but wonder if Aryael knew more about what the Goddess told him than he expected. Perhaps she had been visited as well.

Aryael's voice darted through his mind, pushed there by Symon's powers. "Be on your guard, Gavin." Once again,

Gavin nodded to the Queen as he took his place by Sage as Lord Seth made his way to the stairs. Lady Megara was nowhere to be seen in the congregation, something Gavin couldn't help but feel relieved for.

Expectation and wariness flooded Gavin's system. Energy seemed to hum along Gavin's body as he became hyperfocused on the Lord's posture. Sage must have picked up on the shift of energy because she looked sharply at him, but Gavin gestured for her to remain still.

"Queen Aryael, I am here to represent my estate and my family in wishing you many blessings on your birthday." Lord Seth spoke clearly, bowing stiffly at his waist in a way that was less formal than the others.

The Lord stood tall. His figure was long, lean, and distinguished. His salt-and-pepper hair was brushed away from his face, and a neat, trimmed beard added to the air of dignity. His dress uniform of dark purple and copper, contrasted the others in the room. Instead of wearing colors that reflected either King Symon, Queen Aryael, or even Felysia, Seth wore his own family's colors.

"It is good to see you, Lord Seth," Queen Aryael called. Her smile was less warm now, and a look of wariness dimmed the fire in her eyes.

"Thank you Queen Aryael," Seth called, his voice rising so that it echoed through the throne room. "I wish I were here with the same intent as the rest of my peers. While we wish you blessings on your birthday, our estate has concerns about your rule that must be addressed publicly."

Murmurs erupted throughout the throne room. Lords and Ladies whispered behind their hands, some gasped in shock, and Gavin couldn't help but notice that representatives from Nysa and Meropoli pulled away from the fray.

Gavin felt his blood pressure rise. He should have known from the smug nod Seth gave as he and Sage took their places at the beginning of the ceremony that something was afoot.

"I would be very careful how you proceed," Symon's voice rumbled over the crowd. Black fire seethed in Symon's eyes, and Gavin wasn't sure if he wanted to see how Symon would react to what else Seth had to say. But Aryael, ever the diplomat, placed a hand over Symon's.

"Lord Seth, I would be happy to hear your complaints. Should we proceed to a quieter location?"

"Your Highness, it is the right of your people to hear the complaints of one of their peers." Seth turned his back on the King and Queen, changing his focus to the crowd. Gavin felt power thrum through his blood, a rippling breeze winding itself between his fingers. He rolled his shoulders, willing the wind to calm.

Sage leaned close, and he could feel heat begin to radiate from her, a sign of her discomfort and confusion. "What's going on?" she whispered.

"Politics."

Seth began again, and Gavin noticed Symon clench his fists, Meliza's hand grip the hilt of her sword, and Zeke adjusting his stance into one that clearly signaled he was readying for a fight. "Lords and Ladies of Felysia: many of you are new to your positions, and the majority of you have earned the right to lead your provinces. Even so, it is not your place to blindly follow our King and Queen. Our history has taught us that our leaders are not infallible, that they do not always know what is best for our people. It is our *duty* to hold them accountable."

Aryael's head tilted with interest. "And what do you believe we should be held accountable for?" she asked Seth, his back still turned to the thrones.

Turning slowly so that his side faced the King and Queen, Seth answered, half addressing Aryael, and half speaking to the congregation. "You have brought a stranger into our midst. You have no knowledge of this Realm Leaper, or what her true intentions may be. And should we take it as mere coincidence that she arrived just as Speridisia began collecting alongside the borders of Nysa? Or that Speridisian ships have been spotted along our coastline?"

At the mention of her, Sage flinched. "That son of a..." Gavin cut her off with a squeeze of his hand. He hoped it reassured her; this arrogance would not go unchallenged.

The power coursing through Gavin's blood thrummed. The urge to assert his dominance over Seth vibrated so he couldn't stay still any longer. "Stay here," he whispered to Sage.

"Don't tell me what to do," she whispered back, causing Petra and Zeke to shoot glances at them both.

"Just—let me handle this please." Gavin didn't look at Sage as he stepped forward. With all the dominance he could muster, he addressed Seth. "Lord Seth, that is enough. If you have any further complaints, you can direct them to me and I will bring them to the court."

"Ah—and here," Seth gestured to Gavin, ignoring the order and continuing to speak to the crowd, "—here is your Queen's choice for Lord of Mystaira. A welp who fought in one battle, a fae who cannot even cast, who has failed to demonstrate the power necessary for leadership. This is the boy your Queen has chosen to lead the province tasked with maintaining our economy. He's failed to prove

himself worthy of the title, spent the last decade gallivant-
ing through the country, and avoiding the responsibility
he's been given. And we are supposed to just...accept her
choice?"

Aryael stood, holding her hand out to signal that Meliza
and Zeke should stand by. Striding towards Seth, she addressed both Gavin and Seth with an amused smile. "Seth,
it sounds to me like you would like the opportunity to prove
your worth. How do you suggest we solve this matter?"

Seth stared at the Queen, a look on his face that normally
would have caused Symon to attack. It appeared as though
Symon would allow Aryael to handle the matter on her
own, however. "Your Highness, it is my right to challenge
your leadership. Therefore, I challenge *Lord* Gavin to a duel.
Whoever wins will be the rightful Lord of Mystaira."

The congregation fell still, shock making its way through
the room as the reality of Seth's challenge settled. A challenge in power was a serious charge in Felysia, and could
not be denied, even by the King or Queen. A challenge for
power had to be fulfilled. Gavin smiled as Aryael looked at
him, giving him a nod of approval. Gavin approached Seth,
unable to hide his anticipation. "Name your terms," Gavin
said, shrugging out of his dress coat and unbuckling the
sash that held his sword. Excitement hammered through
his blood, coursing into his muscles. A predatory awareness
settled over his senses.

"Weapons," Seth replied, squaring his stance to Gavin.
"Do you plan to use anything besides your sword?" Gavin
nodded, pulling his sword from its sheath, and then gesturing to the dagger at his side. "I will offer to avoid the use
of my powers. It is only fair since I would clearly outmatch
you with my abilities." Seth waved a hand at Gavin, walking

down the aisle of the throne room, a self-satisfied smile diminishing the distinguished air he held earlier.

"Don't," Gavin called out. "Seth, don't hold back. The offer is generous, but you are about to find out, I don't need your generosity." Gavin widened his stance, sword lifted and ready. His body hummed, prickling with excitement. The adrenaline of meeting the Goddess melted into anticipation, and eagerness. A fight was just what he needed. Extending his palm out as if he were offering Seth a dance, Gavin smirked, "Ready when you are."

Without warning, Seth bolted forward with impressive speed. Gavin met the male, swords clashing. The blows of Seth's sword vibrated down his arm. The old male was surprisingly strong, and quick as lightning. But Gavin anticipated his every move, sensing his attacks before they came. Gavin blocked Seth's advances, playing defense against Seth. He knew the Lord thought little of his training, of his ability to hold his own. Gavin was enjoying proving him wrong.

Seth made a sweep with his sword across where he expected Gavin's center to be, and Gavin spun, the sword missing him altogether. Gavin, now behind Seth, kicked the old male in the back, sending him sprawling to the floor. Zeke laughed, and Gavin could sense anger radiating from Seth as he pushed himself up. Gavin wiped a sheen of sweat from his lip with his shirt, spinning the sword in his hand as Seth pushed himself up.

Seth stood, glaring at Gavin. Gavin smiled, waggling his eyebrows. He gestured with his hand, "Come on, then."

Seth ran forward, disappearing into thin air.

He was casting. But Gavin knew where he would end up, the wind whispering to him as Seth reappeared. Reaching back behind him, Gavin blocked Seth's sword, turning with his dagger in his other hand. Using both, dagger and sword, Gavin threw Seth's sword to the side. The sword remained in Seth's hand, and he retaliated, once again disappearing. Gavin turned, blocking the strike with his dagger, and kicked Seth in the center. The male flew back and disappeared once again. Wind whispered along Gavin's back, and he ducked. The sword rushed over Gavin's bent figure, and Gavin swept down and around, delivering another strike to the male's center with a quick-as-lightning punch.

As Seth was pushed back, he casted once more, appearing at the far end of the aisle which parted the congregation. Gavin relished the thrill of staring down the old fae, who glared at him through clenched teeth. Seth rose from a crouched position, and Gavin reveled in his rival's panting breaths. A force deep inside him seemed to stir, come to life as Seth clenched his sword. Gavin stood, sword dropped to the floor, sending a clear message that he was not intimidated.

A strong gust of wind began building behind Seth, and Gavin nearly laughed out loud. With a mighty push of his arms, Seth sent the wind rushing forward to Gavin, knocking over the nearest bystanders. The wind pummeled into Gavin, pushing him backwards, and he flexed as his wings stretched out to buffet the onrush. Gavin pulled in the wind, welcoming the air as it coursed around him. The cocky look on Seth's face faltered as Gavin absorbed more and more of the wind, drawing on the power as it rushed across and around him, his wings still stretched out, keeping him in place. The wind rushed into Gavin, pulsing through his body and he embraced the building pressure of power. He felt undiluted exhilaration as he held onto the wind for two heartbeats.

The last of the wind calmed, and Seth did not wait as he ran forward, his sword lifted like he would run Gavin through. Gavin held tight to the wind that he'd gathered, feeling the power surge through his veins as he waited for Seth to reach him. When the old fae was mere feet from him, Gavin unleashed.

Wind hit Seth dead-on like a solid wall, knocking the male flat on his back as if a bull had run him over. The wind erupted from Gavin with such force it looked to have a form. The shape of wings emerged within the wind, and the thunder of hooves echoed across the hall.

The old fae lay on the ground, gasping for air, gulping like a fish that had been yanked from a river. Slowly, so slowly, Gavin walked to Seth, his sword pointed to the ground. He knew he'd won. He wasn't even fatigued, and he knew Seth had run through his reserves.

Fae customs did not demand the death of whoever lost a challenge, but it was uncommon for a challenge to be declared finished unless one or both had been killed. Gavin always thought that was a stupid idea, especially when he could use this to his advantage.

Reaching Seth, who was pitifully attempting to rise up onto his elbows, Gavin knocked him back down onto his back with his foot, pushing his sword tip against the male's throat. "Do you forfeit?" Gavin's voice felt foreign, as if it were amplified. The question echoed throughout the throne room, and Gavin almost wished Seth would decline. A strange, predatory drive galloped through his body, something he hadn't felt since the last battle against Rankor.

Seth, finally getting his breathing under control, failed to look Gavin in the eyes, instead, opting to look off into the distance. "Lord Seth, you owe me an answer," Gavin said, pushing the sword tip against the male's flesh. A small bead of blood welled below the sword, and Gavin eased the pressure. "Do you forfeit?" With what looked to be all of Seth's willpower, Seth's eyes drifted up toward Gavin. He gave Gavin the faintest nod, indicating he knew he'd been beat. "You have to say it. So everyone can hear," Gavin said, speaking low so that only the closest bystanders could hear.

With a croaking voice, Seth answered, "I forfeit."

Surprise rippled through the crowd as Gavin sheathed his sword and extended a hand to Seth, pulling his former opponent up off the ground. Gripping the male by the elbow, Gavin shook the fae's arm as a sign of benevolence.

"Let it be known, that I, Gavin of Mystaira, hold no grudge against Lord Seth or his family." Seth squeezed Gavin's arm, his face betraying the alarm he clearly felt. "Furthermore, I would like to offer Lord Seth the position of Hand to the Lord of Mystaira. Until I am officially endowed with the title of Lord of Mystaira, Lord Seth will help lead the land in my stead. We will work in unison to make sure the province is maintained and secure." Gavin, his attention focused on the room around him, slid his eyes back to Seth. Grinning, he asked, "Do you accept?"

Gavin knew the male would accept. Not only that, but by first beating the male in combat without casting, he'd proven his worth. Even better, by offering his grace and his mercy, Seth had no political options than to accept and step in line. Why, who in their right mind would deny such a blessing, when the alternative could have been death, and an embarrassing one at that?

Seth knew he'd been bested. He knew Gavin had out-played him. The knowledge was written across Seth's entire body, and Gavin didn't need mind-reading powers to know that Seth was searching for some way out. But Seth had underestimated Gavin. Finally, Seth dropped to one knee, bowing his head in submission. "It would be an honor to serve my land and my people. I accept your generous offer, Lord Gavin."

Zeke broke the silence with a "Whoop!" Applause followed, and Aryael met Gavin and Seth on the floor. Symon stood at his throne, still glaring at Seth, but Aryael was all smiles. She looped one arm through the crook of Gavin's elbow and gestured for Seth to follow. "Lord Seth, if you would please remain behind the rest of the congregation, I will have the necessary paperwork drawn up immediately."

Gavin escorted Aryael back to her throne, and she whispered, "Very clever, *Lord* Gavin. Though, I lost a bet to Symon. I really thought we'd see you cast this time."

Gavin shrugged. "Maybe next time."

Once Aryael was seated at her throne once more, and Gavin had collected his jacket, Aryael thanked her guests. With a final bow from the congregation, everyone began their procession out of the throne room. Gavin couldn't help but smile as they left. Looking at Sage, he noticed she seemed paler than before, and her knuckles were white from being clenched. "Relax," he whispered as they exited the room.

"I'm trying," Sage said through clenched teeth.

"Maybe next time I'll let you join the fight."

That brought a small smile to her face. "*Let*? Maybe next time I'll just light them on fire." She nudged Gavin. "What's next? I'm starved."

"Me too." He grabbed her hand, interlacing their fingers, not caring who saw. The feeling of proving himself had left him with a heady sense of euphoria. The consequences of what just transpired hadn't quite caught up with him, and at the moment, he simply didn't care.

The Goddess, his title, his Queen...everyone else would have to wait.

Chapter 28

After the ceremony, Sage managed to close the door behind them as they walked into her room before demanding, "What in the gods' names was that about?" Sage stood with her thumb pointing behind her.

"You mean the challenge?"

"No, obviously Seth is a chauvinist who deserved what he got." Sage crossed her arms. "I mean the pledge. Why was your pledge different from the others?"

"Aryael is clever," Gavin said, avoiding the truth he suspected. He walked towards the balcony, hoping to distract her. "That was quite a spectacle you put on, by the way," Gavin replied.

"Stop," demanded Sage. "Stop that. Tell me what is going on, Gavin. Because from my point of view, she played you. She forced you into something you don't want. And if you expect me to keep my mouth closed...or keep certain thoughts quiet from Symon...tell me what that was about."

Gavin considered Sage's point for a moment. She was right; not giving Sage at least some of the truth would be as dangerous as telling her everything. Gavin sighed and rubbed his hands down his face as he sat on the edge of her bed. "Meliza came to me this morning and gave me that pledge. She told me that there were some in the court developing doubts about my ability to step into my lordship. She also informed me the Dark Born brothers are up to something. My pledge was to shut up those who question Aryael's ability to lead, to remind them that they are expected to pick up their swords when she calls them, and...I guess to mark me as a member of her council."

"So...you're going to be called away? To war?" Sage asked, walking closer to Gavin.

Gavin shrugged. "Possibly."

"And why would the Queen mark you so special, compared to the others who are so much older, more experienced?" Sage had reached Gavin and placed her hands on his shoulders.

The weight of old memories, the weight of loss and struggle bore down on him and he couldn't bring himself to meet her eyes. "Because in the midst of battle, she grabbed me and made me her second on the front lines. Because she saw me wield wind, and together, my wind and her fire incinerated a legion of enemy soldiers. Because she watched me cut down soldier after soldier; because even though I was untrained, unskilled really, I fought next to her without fear. Because I hadn't really expected to walk away from that battlefield."

Sage leaned forward and rested her head against his forehead. "Gavin," she whispered.

Gavin leaned back, shook his head free of the memories that clung to him, and patted the bed. "Sit. I'll tell you the full story." The adrenaline from fighting Seth began to wane, and a tiredness he wasn't sure belonged to memories or fighting wiggled its way into his body.

Sage sat next to him, grabbed his hand in hers, and listened as Gavin explained how he had hidden his powers as a child, but unleashed them when his people joined together to overthrow their guards. He walked, with forty other males and females, determined to join the main rebellion and fight for freedom against Speridisia's grip. His work camp had been the last to be liberated, a task taken on by Meliza herself, and he arrived just in time for the final battle. The battle had lasted four brutal days. He'd been kept in the base, given menial tasks, until a pivotal shift in momentum occurred and someone had run through the camp shoving weapons into every available hand.

Speridisia had advanced, pushing the rest of Panchaia's forces back. He fought first with a crossbow, allowing his wind wielding to make his aim more lethal. Then he fought with spear and shield. On the last day, he picked up a broadsword from a fallen fae and charged headlong into the fray. That's when Aryael spied him, hacking at his advancers. Gavin hadn't known the tide had begun to turn in their favor, or that Symon had infiltrated the enemy lines and broken them from inside their own minds. No, all he'd known was that he would die before being captured again, that he would die before allowing his siblings, his mother and father go back into that camp. So, he and Aryael rallied the legion and pushed forward. Him supplying the air to her infernal blasts, and then fighting by her side when long-range combat was not feasible.

Ultimately, it'd been Symon and Zeke who had reached the King and taken his head as a trophy. But it had been Aryael who had kept the forces united and fighting until the end. It'd been her skill, her enthusiasm to run headlong into battle with her soldiers that had truly made the difference.

Sage sat in silence, "I'm so sorry you had to go through that," she whispered.

Gavin smiled, "It's no worse than what you've been through."

She sighed in reply and looked away. "So, Aryael...she means for you to become her second again?"

"No, that honor goes to Meliza, in battle at least. Meliza is technically part of Symon's court and council, but in battle, it'd be Meliza behind Aryael. And Goddess help whoever stands opposite them." Sage looked inclined to agree. "There's something big happening, Sage. I can't help but think you might be a part of it."

"I know," whispered Sage, and she strode away from Gavin, aiming for the doors leading to the balcony. Gavin waited a second before following her onto the balcony, but remained behind her at the doors. "Sage, whatever happens, I won't leave you if you don't want me to. Whatever you need, just let me know."

Sage looked at Gavin and nodded, "I know. I've been thinking about the insignias lately, the medallions I collected." She looked at Gavin to see if he remembered that detail from the memories she'd shared with him. "Without those insignias or my book, I'm not sure how I can get back to my world. And I have to go back." She shrugged then reached her hands up, fiddling with the veil, trying to take it off. She struggled for a few moments before dropping both hands and blowing a long breath through her mouth, eyes glaring up at the sky in defeat.

"Here, let me," offered Gavin, and he stepped to her before beginning to remove the pins which anchored the veil to her hair. Her braids and headpiece remained intact, and he handed her the veil.

"Thank you." Relief colored her expression. "How much longer do we have to be dressed up?" Sage muttered. "I'm ready to put on my nightgown and go back to sleep."

Gavin raised his eyebrows at that, and he knew his ideas of what she might do in that nightgown other than sleep were written plainly across his face. A pleasant blush spread over Sage's cheeks, even as she tilted her head playfully and replied, "You beast."

"What? You brought it up," Gavin chuckled as Sage walked back into the room. "Who said we have to wait?" Gavin whispered as he caught up behind her.

He could sense her reaction to his words, even though she replied, "And let you ruin my hair? I don't think so."

Still, she paused, and let him step close to her, and he wrapped his arms around her from behind. Goddess, her scent drove him mad.

Gavin nuzzled her neck, "What if I promise not to mess up your hair?"

Goosebumps danced along her arms, and a slight flush bloomed across her cheek. She reached up to him, reaching up and back to run her fingers through his hair, "Liar," she whispered as one tendril of hair danced free of its braid.

Gavin continued nuzzling her, running his mouth along her neck. Quickly, she pivoted in his arms so that they faced each other. Gavin pulled his head away and felt himself shutter as his body responded to the softness of her pushing up against him. Not giving her a moment to respond, to tease him about her hair or dress, Gavin leaned in and pressed his mouth to hers. Mercifully, she responded by pushing into him, opening for him. He pulled her to him, tightening his hold around her. His hands found their way along her back, drifting up and then fully down until they rested on her backside.

She pulled away with a grin, "Really?"

He gave her a quick squeeze in response, "Really. Would it make it better if I told you how much I like this part of you?" Sage snorted, but didn't manage to wipe the smile from her face.

Gently, Gavin leaned in again, kissing her softly this time in question. Just then, a faint knock sounded on the door. They both moaned quietly before Sage pulled from Gavin and called, "Come in." A servant bearing refreshments entered, a note propped on the tray of fruit, cheese, and wine.

Her Majesty requests the attendance of Lord Gavin and Lady Sage at her private dinner reception this evening. Places at the High Table will be reserved.

Sage groaned, her eyes squeezing shut. "I'm assuming those servants will be back to help me get this back in order?" Sage asked, pointing at her hair, much more disheveled than Gavin had realized.

"Probably not, actually," Gavin replied. "That was a one-time thing as far as I'm aware. But stay here, I know someone who can help." Gavin left the room as Sage removed the headpiece.

When he returned, Gavin noticed she had helped herself to a few slices of cheese, and a copious amount of wine that had accompanied the note. The shock on her face with the help Gavin brought made him chuckle slightly as he announced, "Help has arrived."

✧✦✧

Ok- maybe Sage had finished off the whole decanter of wine. Should she have saved some for Gavin? Probably; but she'd needed something to unwind that thing in the center of her body that he had toyed with earlier. The thing that was coiled tight as a spring and grew tighter as she struggled to keep the memory of his mouth on her neck at bay. She drank deeply as that thought nipped at her again when he re-entered the room...with Raphael. In a dress.

Sage nearly spit out her drink when Raphael looked at her and bobbed his head to the side. "Raph...you...that dress...is stunning."

Indeed, it was. Raphael, who'd been wearing a more formal version of his usual healer's uniform at the ceremony, was now clad in a sleeveless, black jacket buttoned high at his neck, a ruffled white collar peeking from the top. Gold embroidery danced along the jacket, woven into botanical flora. And below the jacket, a stunning black skirt, full and sweeping, commanded the space around him. His hair was left unbound, loose, and flowing with curls; his eyes were rimmed with kohl, making his bright brown eyes stand out.

"Yes, well. Aryael knows how to throw a dinner party," drawled Raphael.

"I take it that not many males choose to dress this finely where you're from?" Gavin asked.

Sage shook her head, "No one that I knew," she admitted.

"It's less common in places like Meropoli," admitted Raphael, "The fae seemed to have abandoned stupid ideas such as what males and females are permitted or expected to do long ago. I suppose that's the benefit of living long lives." Raphael continued to speak as he looked at Sage's loose hair.

"So, I should expect to find Gavin in something as fine someday?" Sage said to the males in her room.

Gavin snorted, "I don't think you'll find me in anything finer than this...preferably ever again. I'm more at home in my sentry uniform, truth be told. Or a simple shirt and pants on my time off."

"Hmmph," replied Sage.

"Not all of us were born to be magnificent, Sage dear. Poor Gavin here will just have to do with our beauty for the time being," replied Raphael.

Raphael escorted Sage into her bathing room and had her sit on the chair in front of the vanity counter. He began untwining the braids and fussing with her short hair. She couldn't imagine what sort of magic he'd have to work to make her hair presentable again.

"Nearly done," Raphael sang, and Sage dared a peak in the mirror. Where her hair had been braided and coiled, Raphael had swept most of her hair back into a simple, but elegant bun. A swath of hair remained loose, framing her face, and Raphael said, "Sage, dear, warm this for me," as he handed her a metal rod.

With a confused look on her face, Sage summoned a flame and ran it over the length of the rod, careful to keep one end cool. Raphael carefully took the rod and used it to curl the hair that remained loose so that her hair gracefully arched away from her face. Then he pinned her headpiece back atop her head. "There. The portrait of Anthephone herself."

Sage admired herself in the mirror. Where the updo from earlier, paired with the veil-cape, made her look ethereal, Sage felt this hairstyle suited her better.

"Who is that? Anthephone?"

Raphael smiled coyly, "She's one of the forms our Goddess takes. She rules over love, marriage, and fertility."

Sage flinched a little. "Well, as long as Anthephone keeps her whims to herself." Sage smiled, though. "Thank you," she said, reaching back and squeezing Raph's hand. He gently squeezed her hand back.

"Anything for you, dear."

Gavin, Sage, and Raphael walked together to the ball-room where Aryael would receive her guests. The bottle of wine and Raphael's company had done wonders for Sage's nerves. It was nice to have a friend in this strange place; nice to have a good-looking male on her arm as well, she thought as she snuck a glance at Gavin. She caught him staring down at her, and they grinned at each other. Whatever was to come, Sage was glad she had Gavin and Raphael with her to suffer alongside.

The room was filled with fae males and females already mingling when they entered the ballroom; round tables filled the room, and attendants were ushering groups to their assigned tables. Sage and her partners were shown to a long table at the far end of the room. Miniature versions of the King and Queen's thrones were set in the middle of the table, and Gavin was sat directly beside Aryael's place. Meliza, Zeke, and Petra were seated alongside the other end of the table, making up Symon's court. As Sage went to sit next to Gavin, a smooth, musical voice echoed behind her, "Unfortunately, that would be my seat." Sage turned to find Suda grinning down at her.

"Oh. I'm sorry," Sage muttered, cutting a look at Gavin.

The attendant who had been speaking with Gavin turned and explained, "Lady Sage, Sir Raphael, your seats." He gestured to the seats just beside Suda. So, she would sit between Suda and Raphael, then. Sage sat in the seat indicated for her and peeked over at Gavin. He gave her an apologetic grin, and addressed Suda, asking about the news he'd pilfered from Acantha when they happened to meet in the gardens earlier.

"At least I have you," whispered Sage to Raphael.

Raphael smiled back at her, "I find myself grateful to be sitting next to you and not forced to hear Suda drone on about trade along Nysa's many river routes," Raphael said.

Suda barked a short laugh in reply.

"I guess there's no such thing as a private conversation among the fae, huh?" Sage asked Raphael.

"You don't know the start of it," Raphael mused.

Fae continued to be seated for several more minutes until at last, music began to play through the hall. Everyone rose to their feet, and Queen Aryael and King Symon arrived through the large doors of the ballroom. Candlelight danced off the couple, radiating from the crowns perched atop their heads, as they made their procession through the crowd. As they passed, each table bowed to one knee, remaining until the whole room waited, heads dipping low in supplication. The music ended, and Aryael's voice echoed through the room. "Thank you, all, for coming tonight." The room stood from their kneeling bow and took their seats once more.

While the room was not as full of fae as the throne room had been, there were still rows and rows of tables full of males and females, dressed in their finery. Aryael assessed the room, then gave a nod to one of the attendants. A flurry of motion began as servants started bringing out the first courses of the dinner. The room sat in silence until everyone was served, and the Queen took her first bite. With that, the room broke into merry chatter, forks and knives clattering as they ate.

Servants brought out additional courses as they finished their plates, lending the dinner into a more casual affair than Sage had expected. Sage also hadn't expected her wine glass to stay so full. Raphael and Sage chatted, making quiet jokes over what they thought of some of the more pompous lords and ladies attending the dinner, and of the gifts that had been given to Aryael. The plates were cleared, and the dinner party was dismissed to the salon while the room was converted for dancing.

Sage was standing alone in a corner, peering out of a window overlooking a different garden than the one from her balcony. She was admiring a row of pink flowering trees when a melodious voice chimed, "That bust was quite the work of art." Sage whirled to find Queen Aryael towering over her.

Feeling the effects of all the wine she'd had, Sage pressed her lips together to keep from blurting out the first thing that sprang to her mind. "I'm glad you like it, Your Majesty," was all she could muster.

"I know that request must have been a shock. But I hope you understand why I asked it of you," the Queen stated, still smiling softly.

"Truthfully?" Sage asked, and the Queen nodded her encouragement. "I don't honestly understand. Beyond entertaining your guests, I don't see what good that display did," Sage explained.

Aryael gave a patient sigh, "Well, if anyone thought to *test* your strength...they'll think twice about it now. And, I'm in need of an alliance to remind our people just how strong we are together. Now is not the time for our people to start quarreling amongst themselves. You, Sage, have been an unexpected boon to Gavin and myself." Sage stared at the Queen in disbelief. She shook her head as if trying to shake some sort of sense into the conversation. "I know," Aryael whispered, "I know what it's like, to be talked about like you're some sort of gift, some sort of tool to be wielded. I wish I could tell you it gets better. In reality, you just learn how to shoulder the burden." Aryael gave Sage a knowing and kind smile, then finished, "I'll be off to visit with more of my guests, but should you need anything, Sage Realm-Leaper, come find me. Us gods-gifted females need to hold each other up." With a wink and a final smile of alliance, the Queen waltzed away from Sage to greet her guests as they awaited entrance back into the ballroom.

Sage turned from the crowd, and stared out the window she stood next to. She wasn't sure how she'd gotten so tied up, so entangled in this new world. She still wasn't even sure what she was doing there, and now apparently these people expected her to be some sort of gods-gift. She wanted to crawl inside herself, to scream that they had it all wrong.

She was on the verge of letting the tears welling up inside her trickle down when a voice whispered, "I take it the conversation went well?" Sage hiccupped, tried unsuccessfully to hide it, and whirled around to find Gavin. The look on his face told her he knew what had just occurred.

"How much wine, exactly, have you had? Because I didn't expect you to be hiccupping already."

Sage hit his arm, "Oh, don't you tempt me you brute. I'm just getting started." They smiled quietly for a minute, then Sage asked, "How long is all this going to last? I wasn't kidding earlier when I said I was looking forward to crawling into bed." She'd spent enough hours standing and minding...well, trying to mind her manners today. She was ready to shed her undergarments and crawl into the loving embrace of her bed- that luxurious, soft bed. She nearly sighed at the thought of it.

"Oh, we haven't even got to the dancing," Gavin mused.

"Dancing?" Sage asked. It'd been an age since she'd danced. Not since Ian; they'd gone out, somewhere with dancing shortly before she left.

The memory of Ian pained her, but only shortly, as the thought of dancing raced through her mind. "What kind of dancing?" Sage asked.

"I'll leave the formal stuff to Suda and Raphael. But...well- you'll see," Gavin answered with a smirk. Just then, the attendants re-entered the salon. Sage had chosen to forgo the wine offered earlier, but gladly accepted a glass of water Gavin procured from somewhere. Petra stepped to the front of the room and beckoned everyone into the ball- room for the festivities. It was an amazing transformation. The torches that had lined the wall and the candelabras which had hung low with hundreds of candles flickering in them had been turned down somehow so the room had a more intimate feel. Couches lined the walls, along with high tables scattered periodically through the room. Glowing orbs of light skittered through the room, casting prismatic shades of pastel rays wherever they went. There was a band of string and percussion players set on a stage in the far corner of the room. Honestly, Sage thought it looked like the fae equivalent to some of the nightclubs she might have frequented in her home world. The thought brought a wide smile to her face, and she beamed at Gavin.

The band struck their first chord, and she and Gavin had no choice but to follow the crowd to the center of the room. "I hope you know what you're doing," Sage whispered between her teeth.

"Barely," admitted Gavin. The dance was simple enough, a circular pattern of four steps; Gavin, while definitely not being the most skilled dancer in the room, kept up with the crowd and managed to miss Sage's feet and keep them from bumping into any other couples they danced alongside. Still, Sage relished the feel of his arm along her back, the way that he steered her through the ballroom. She'd never danced like this with anyone before, and the movement felt freeing, made her feel light as air. Something in her chest loosened as they danced, around and around in circles, her skirts rushing over her ankles. She might have imagined it, but she swore she felt the wind entwining around her feet like a playful kitten as she and Gavin floated around the dancefloor.

She was breathless by the end of the music and had nearly pulled herself together when a silky, smooth voice crooned, "May I?" Sage turned to find a grinning Suda standing with his hand extended in offer.

"Yes, you may," she replied with a smile as wide as the sea. She felt Gavin stiffen behind her, and snapped, "Oh, you stop it. I've never been with a territorial male, and I won't start now."

Gavin hefted a sigh, and said, "Fine. But watch your hands, Suda." Suda winked at Gavin, and Sage added, "Yes...watch your hands, Suda. But I'd love a dance." Suda, graceful and elegant as a leopard on the prowl, led Sage through another version of the dance they'd just finished. This dance required the steps to meander more, through a figure-eight pattern. After a complete pass around the dancefloor, Sage felt confident enough to stop counting, and let herself lean into the music. The matching of steps to music seemed to release the ball of tension she'd been carrying in her chest.

At the end of the dance, Suda led Sage over to a couch where they were served water, and wine, and Sage peered around the room in search of Gavin. "He's over there," stated Suda, jutting his chin towards a crowd of older-looking fae. They were in deep conversation with Gavin, and Sage decided she would allow him to finish up rather than interrupt. She was still gazing at him when Suda drawled, "I couldn't help but overhear your conversation with my sister. It almost sounded as if you forgot she was a Queen." Sage couldn't stop her eye roll if she'd tried, and really...she didn't try.

"Well, where I come from, we don't have Queens. Or Kings."

"Really?" Suda questioned, "Neither does my homeland." Sage looked at Suda incredulously. "You think just because my sister is *Her Majesty* now that we came from some royal bloodline." Suda shook his head in disagreement, "No. In Nysa, we have elected officials; the Senate, broken into two parts: the High Senate, and the Low Senate, represent our people. It is very rare for multiple generations to be elected to the Senate. Our people have a general mistrust of power, or at least the corruption it can lead to."

"Where I'm from, we have a President. Though, he's practically made himself a King. From what I can remember, he was a wicked man; but...I don't think my people know that yet," Sage admitted, not really sure how much she should share with Suda.

"Power can do strange things to people. Our parents, Aryael and mine, were one of the few couples who managed to marry within the Senate and keep their seats. Normally, that form of inter-marrying would be viewed as power grabbing in Nysa; but our parents were genuine, loyal servants to their people. They did their best to protect them. I was a child when we were captured," Suda developed the faraway look that people tend to get when remembering important, painful memories.

Sage couldn't help herself as she patted his hand, "I'm sorry for what you, all of you had to go through."

He looked at her then, and waved his hand as he shook his head, "That's in the past now. Shall we dance again?" Sage was nodding, and just beginning to stand when Gavin interjected, "I think maybe it's my turn?" Gods...she couldn't stop that stupid smile on her face if Brighid herself had commanded her to. Sage beamed at Gavin and placed her hand in his. Just then, the music grew wilder, louder, and the ballroom filled with mostly younger-looking fae.

Meliza, Zeke, Petra, and Aryael ran onto the floor and began to dance. Where the dancing before was coordinated, something the court obviously knew, this was a free for all. Some fae jumped, some twirled in circles, and Zeke performed some sort of stomping side-to-side movement. It truly was the fae version of a nightclub Sage thought to herself.

Sage and Gavin danced, and danced, and drank for hours on end. Eventually, laughing and staggering, Sage and Gavin were gracefully dismissed with kisses on their cheeks by Aryael, who was clinging to Symon herself, as they made their way back to their rooms.

Gavin's arm was wrapped around Sage's side, caressing her ribs and her hips as they walked, and Sage wrapped an arm around Gavin. She gripped him with a fierceness, trying to signal to him what she hoped the evening would lead to as they approached their floor. His hand drifted below her waist, gripping her backside and she tried, and failed, to suppress the blush that crept across her face. They reached their floor, empty of anyone walking the hallway, and Sage stopped, pulling Gavin into her embrace. She kissed him, fully on the mouth. She wanted him and wanted him to know she wanted him. They walked, kissing, staggering, towards her door.

Gavin pushed her up against her door; she relished the feel of him against her. He caressed her mouth with his, and she pulled him into her. She ran her hands down his back, and grabbed his backside, pulling him closer to her. He was fumbling with the doorknob, dragging his mouth down her neck, lower when finally, the door released...and they heard a cough from down the hall. Both Sage and Gavin froze; a sideward glance revealed Suda, leaning on the banister of the stairway just a few yards from Sage's door. Sage still gripped Gavin's backside, and they both seemed to realize it at the same time as they straightened and tried to discreetly fix their disheveled clothing.

"Gavin, friend. I know that you might have had...plans," he winked at Sage, "But I'd hoped you'd join me for a few rounds before turning in for the night." Suda waggled his eyebrows, signaling mischief. Gavin peered down at Sage. She had been so ready to drag him into the room, but she hesitated. Could she expect Gavin to neglect his relationships when they didn't know how much longer she would be here? Sage shrugged, "Go have fun. I'll be in bed when you get back." Gavin looked at her, a question written on his face, but when Suda cleared his throat once again he leaned in and gave her a quick kiss, then whispered in her ear, "I look forward to finding you...in your bed when I get back."

Heat raced through her body, and not the magic-flame-wielding kind of heat. Gavin and Suda both stiffened, and she realized they could both sense the effect his words had on her. Gavin placed his hands on either side of the doorway, and Sage leaned up to his ear and whispered, "I'll be sure to be *un*—dressed and ready." Gavin practically growled as she slipped through her door and shut it demurely in front of him. She counted the beats before he began to walk towards Suda, and wasn't sure he was actually going to go before the shadow beneath the door finally crept away. Suda laughed, and she heard him say, "Oh, you got it bad."

Chapter 29

❋❋❋

Sage had just reached the docks and was peering around the corner of a building, trying to spy the best ship to board. Her dad—having worked there all her life—had talked often enough about work that Sage knew which dock Finian ships would be moored on. She was just about to make a run toward a pallet of goods covered with a tarp when a strong hand gripped her shoulder and spun her around.

Sage was reaching for her knife when the owner of the hand asked, "Lonnie?"

Sage gaped at Duncan, who looked at her incredulously. "Duncan? What are you doing here? I thought you were still at University?" Sage asked, pulling free from Duncan's grasp.

"I left, came here to find work and lie low. Where have you been? Some shit's gone down, Lonnie, and I have half a mind to knock you real good for leaving Ian and Stiofanie high and dry like you did."

"I know...I'm sorry, Duncan. I had some personal issues come up," Sage tried to vaguely explain her disappearance.

"Come off it, Lonnie. I know you were caught up in the same shit as Ian. I'm surprised you aren't back in

Techeduin, though. Today's the day they are going to put him down," Duncan explained, glaring at Sage with anger, sadness, and confusion, all of which warred for dominance as he assessed her.

"Put who down? What are you talking about? I haven't heard anything about Techeduin since I've been gone," Sage prodded.

"Right, right. You haven't heard of the mass arrests of anyone and everyone who's spoken their minds about the government, about all the missing people who keep disappearing. You haven't heard of your old boyfriend starting an underground periodical aimed at discrediting the government and inciting distrust. I'm sure that means you also haven't heard of his arrest, then, huh? You know...I never trusted you, Lonnie. Ian could have done so much better," Duncan jabbed Sage in the chest as he spoke, then turned to leave.

"Wait," Sage called, grabbing Duncan's elbow. "Wait," she repeated, "Stiofanie? What about her?"

Duncan glared at Sage. "We got her away," Duncan growled in a whisper, "We managed to sneak her onto a boat, and get her off the continent. She's hiding somewhere, even *I* don't know where. The agents got Ian before we could smuggle him out. The least you could have done, Lonnie, is been there. They're putting him down today; a public execution, to mock him and make an example out of him. And you haven't even bothered to care, to even know what's going on with him." Duncan shrugged off her hand, shaking his head in disgust.

"No," whispered Sage, as Duncan walked away down the alleyway.

Sage whipped her head, the pallet had already been moved. She needed to leave, had to get to Techeduin. Reality dawned as she realized no boat could get her to Techeduin in a day. A warning clanged through her mind as she began to understand the Wulver's words. *"The price has already been paid,"* Nehelannia had said.

The price; no....no no no.

Sage set down her pack; she still had the Egress Key Ian made all those months ago. Good for two uses. Maybe she could jump to his cell, and they could escape together. She had no idea if it worked for two people. She'd been saving it for a time of true emergency, and had almost opted to use it on the mountain in Goulain. Sage pulled out the Egress Key and moved the hand that kept the black stone in the center in place. She just had to spin it ten times, think of Ian, and she'd be there...she hoped. Sage spun the stone in the center...

A sharp popping of atmosphere...and Sage stood on a busy street corner in Techeduin. She looked around, panic pounding in her ears. A steady stream of people were headed in the same direction. Sage jostled her pack, freeing the hood of the jacket she wore from beneath it, and flipped it over her head. A poor disguise, but hopefully she'd be gone before anyone would notice her.

Sage followed the hordes of people, government agents blocking the alleyways. Apparently, the majority of people were required to attend the demonstration. Sage choked down a sob and continued following the throng of pedestrians. Everyone lined up, orderly and subdued, near the steps of the nation's capital building. The dark gray building seemed to devour the sparse sunlight that tried to peek through the heavy gray clouds. Sage had never noticed how gray the city was. The gray street blended in with the gray steps which fed into gray marble walls. And there, on the third to final step at the top, was Ian, chained to a chair. He sat, spine straight and stiff, looking straight ahead.

He was handsome, despite the dark purple shadows beneath his eyes, the scab of a cut running down his mouth. His stark white prisoner's jumpsuit seemed so sterile compared to the dark gray steps he sat upon. President Ranquer stood there, along with Ms. Dullahan and several other government agents.

"What the fuck?" Sage whispered, staring at Dullahan. The woman truly wouldn't—couldn't—die. Disbelief merged with terror and Sage felt like she would begin seizing from the dread invading her veins.

The President's advisors all sat in comfortable-looking chairs on a balcony high above the building's massive doors, looking down on the scene below them. Sage paced through the crowd, seeking any way to reach Ian, anyway she could get to him and get them both out of there.

The crowd stopped, everyone standing, waiting. No one dared to speak. Not a single whisper. The President stood, removed his wand from a pocket, and cast a charm that projected his voice across the entirety of the crowd.

"Citizens of Thuledain, residents of Techeduin. We are here today to enact the sentencing against Ian Dunbar. He sits here before you, found guilty of organizing and facilitating a terrorist group aimed at disrupting our peaceful nation."

The President paused, allowing the words to ripple through the crowd. Sage stood still, staring at Ian as the President spoke. She was short enough that she could hide among the crowd, barely reaching many of the men's shoulders. She stared and stared up at Ian, chained to the chair, hoping against hope that she could make eye contact with him, someway, somehow. She was running out of time, and if she could just get him to look at her.

She readied the Egress Key in her pocket. As soon as she had a plan, she would be ready to jump with Ian.

"We will not drag this out today," the President droned on. "We recognize the busy lives of our constituents in Techeduin. In order to proceed, we will give the guilty a final chance to confess to their crimes, before we honor our forefathers and serve justice at last." The President approached Ian, who continued to look forward; no, he wasn't looking forward. Very slightly his eyes roved across the assembly of people amassed in front of him, scanning—for what? Who? His gaze fell on Sage, but only for a second before he raised his eyes once more, looking above the crowd at the buildings which rose into the distance.

The President repeated the charm, allowing Ian's voice to be amplified once more. "Tell the people," the President demanded, "how sorry you are for leading your followers into despair; how you wronged your nation by acting against us, targeting us with your malicious intent." The President grinned widely at Ian as if daring him to say the wrong thing.

Ian spoke clearly and strongly, "I would like to apologize to those I love, and to the people of Thuledain...for not knowing the truth sooner. Do not come. Run...save yourself. Fight against the tyranny—" his voice cut off, the President ending the charm with a wave of his wand.

Ian was still speaking, trying to yell above the commands being given by President Ranquer. Four government agents approached Ian, wands out, and the mighty chains began to snake into the air, extending Ian's limbs so he floated in the air, sprawled into an X shape.

He was still yelling, "Go...Run!" as the agents held their wands.

Ms. Dullahan approached Ian smiling like a cat playing with a bird, along with two other agents. All three raised their wands in unison; electricity shot from their extended wands and wrapped around Ian. He thrashed, sparks flying from his mouth and eyes as the agents held their spells on the chains. It was over in a minute, Ms. Dullahan and the others lowered their wands, Ian slumping despite the chains continuing to hold him up.

He was gone. Ian was dead. Drums pounded in Sage's ears as reality set in. She'd been too late. He died because of her.

Sage bit down on her scream, her knees wobbled, and she stared at the scene ahead. Ian's eyes remained open, bulging from his face. Blood ran from his mouth, his nose, ears...a healer walked forward as the chains lowered his body, but Sage didn't need to see her nod her head in confirmation. She could feel it in her soul. Ian was gone. They'd killed him. She bit her tongue hard enough to draw blood, forcing her legs to hold her upright as the President began speaking once more.

The Egress Key was in her hand. He was speaking, she was turning the stone: one....two...three...four....tears streamed down her face......five...six...a sob finally to burst from her mouth....seven...eight...nine...the crowd lurched as if it were released from a spell....ten.

Her knees hit the soft, earthen ground of a forest. She screamed as she knelt in the dirt, laid her face on the ground as she screamed, hands clutching her head. Ian was gone. He was dead, and it was because of her. She'd done this. She left him there to fend for himself, hadn't dared to look back as she'd answered the gods' summons. How could she have done this?

Earth rattled around her, stones lurching up through the ground. Wind whipped in a frenzy, and she began hearing the crackling of fire. Smoke filled her lungs.

Sage screamed until her voice refused to work; she sobbed into the dirt until she was retching in the spot she sat. Tears refused to stop and she succumbed to the feeling of loss as raindrops poured around her. No clouds hung in the starry sky, but raindrops spontaneously appeared in the air and fell heavy and fat to the ground, squelching the pockets of fire that had sprouted around Sage. She pushed herself against the trunk of a massive tree and stayed there until she passed out against exhaustion.

"Get up, girl," a rough, female voice demanded.

Darkness wrapped itself around Sage, smothering her senses, smothering her will to live. She wasn't sure if her eyes drifted closed, or if this was what it felt like to finally give in to fate and quit fighting.

"Get up, now," it repeated. Light reappeared. As if she were blinking in slow motion, her awareness came back. The weight of truth threatened to bury her.

Darkness, like a heartbeat, wrapped around her once more. The breath was strangled from her, and she wished she could succumb to it once and for all.

Her eyes peeled open. Brighid stood before her; rough hands grabbed Sage and placed her on her feet. "Go. Now," Brighid pointed up the face of a large mountain. The goddess's hair whipped around her like flames. Her skin glowed with power.

Another heartbeat. Darkness again.

Sage was running now. She could see the lip of the cave she had to reach, the landing of it jutting away from the seemingly smooth mountain face. A silvery, round drone flew mere feet from her. Sage ran harder, feeling the heat of a flaming arrow shoot past her. The drone exploded, shards of metal whizzing past, slicing her cheek.

Darkness.

The drones were back. Hot breath sawed from Sage's chest, her fingers bled as she scraped herself across the rock face. She was scrambling over boulders and heard the hum of a drone as she crouched behind one of the massive stones, not daring to breathe. She reached into her power, searching for some sort of thread to pull, to squash the drone under a landslide.

She couldn't find it; she'd lost her magic. She was broken.

The ground shook, and before Sage could react, boiling jets of water burst from the earth's crust, engulfing the drone. Allyra stood next to Sage, and hoisted her to her feet, pushing her up the steep slope of Mount Danu. The Goddess's skin was slick, cold. Allyra turned sharply, releasing a wild battle cry as she let loose a wicked battle ax, smashing another drone. Sage's feet hit the ground hard as she ran. A wild laugh rang out as she heard more drones explode, and the ground rumbled as more jets burst from the rock face.

Darkness.

They were nearly there. Just ten more feet and they would be to the cave. The cave glowed red as if the heart of a volcano rested inside. Flaming arrows continued flying past Sage's face. Soldiers were down below now, gathering themselves and their weapons. Something exploded down below, and Sage felt part of the mountain slip away. A mighty wind barreled down the mountainside, knocking down the trucks and tanks lining up, preparing to climb up the mountain. A muscular arm grabbed her as she slipped.

Cerridos. He hauled her over the lip of the cliff. "Keep going," he urged. Spears appeared in each of his hands and he threw them down onto the soldiers below. Torrents of wind pummeled the trees, flattening the massive pillars, and squashing trucks like bugs. Sage ran.

Darkness.

She was inside. She stood on the portal. All four insignias were in place, she opened the book, and found what she was looking for. She would go to TupaGuara, a land full of rivers and forests. She was focusing on the land when she heard the voice. "My dear...you didn't think you would get away with it did you?"

Sage whipped her head around. He was here. The President had arrived. "Give me the insignias," he demanded. The archways were glowing. The insignia she stood on glowed. She was going, she could make it.

"TupaGuara," she said. "TupaGuara, TupaGuara, Tupa-Guara," she repeated over and over, as the President continued walking forward, flanked by Ms. Dullahan and another unreal-looking agent. "Give me the insignia," yelled the President.

Ms. Dullahan shot out, away from the President, running for Sage. Sage slapped the ground, steadying the final insignia.

She could feel the floor moving, falling away. But Ms. Dullahan was almost there. Without thinking, Sage reached forward and scooped up the four insignias. She couldn't let Dullahan get her hands on them.

Before Sage could react, the floor fell; Ms. Dullahan's outstretched hand was inside the glowing orb Sage was contained in, and then...

Darkness.

Chapter 30

Symon, Suda, and Gavin sat in Symon's study. Aryael had long gone to bed, having thoroughly enjoyed her feast. Symon looked forward to getting back to their room, something she had whispered in his ear was replaying in his mind.

But he was enjoying Gavin and Suda's company. The two had cleared part of Symon's study and had challenged each other to various wrestling and sparring challenges. Despite Suda's enhanced speed and strength powers, Gavin seemed to have a sixth sense, able to anticipate Suda's every move before the male made it. If Symon didn't know better, he would have guessed the young Lord possessed mind-reading abilities similar to himself.

Now the three of them sat on the comfortable, oversized chairs, laughing about stories from their youth—and Gavin's current youth. Suda found the stories of Meliza besting Symon in combat training especially entertaining.

Warning gripped Symon by the neck, and he shot to his feet. Something was wrong. Both Gavin and Suda stilled, looking to Symon in question.

The air across the entire city seemed to still. A sudden change in air pressure sent a pulse of pain through Symon's temples. The fire went out, strange because it was enchanted so it would burn continuously. Symon reached his power out across his city; he could feel the sea pull away from the shore. Then...

The wind howled against his palace, the fires roared back to life, candles lit, and the sea raged against the shore. Streets, buildings, and even the mountains in the distance rumbled like thunder.

It was over as quickly as it began, but he knew the source.

Symon cast into Sage's room. She was in her bed, her face stretched in a silent scream, back arching off the bed.

Her door burst open. Gavin barreling into the room.

"What's wrong," he demanded. Gavin stalked forward, going to reach for Sage, but Symon stopped him. Her skin glowed red hot and he could feel power pulsating from her.

Symon reached a hand down onto Sage's head just as Gavin reached her bed, "Wake," he whispered.

Sage bowed again, her eyes flying open. Her hands clenched her bedding. A moan escaped her lips and she shuddered as she inhaled.

The fire in her room banked, leaving only glowing embers in the hearth.

She gasped, looking up into Symon's eyes. Her body relaxed slightly, and she squeezed her eyes closed, rolling over into the fetal position.

"You remember, now, don't you?" Symon asked in a whisper.

Soft padding footsteps told Symon that Aryael was making her way to the room. Gavin looked from Sage to Symon and back again as Sage nodded in confirmation. Gavin placed his arm around her waist, shifting so he could make eye contact with her.

She inhaled, letting loose a soft sob, then whispered, "King Symon. I think you should gather the others. There's a lot to explain."

Aryael had just entered the room. Symon and his Queen looked at each other. *She remembers.* Aryael's hand went to her mouth. Empathetic grief creased his wife's eyes. "I'll get the others."

"It's nearly sunrise," the King said to Sage and Gavin. "We will meet in my private study in an hour. It will give us enough time to gather everyone and enough time for you to make yourself ready." Symon softly removed his hand from Sage's head before, looking at Gavin, whose eyes brimmed with worry. "One hour," Symon whispered.

Then he and Aryael left the pair behind, aiming for Raphael's private quarters.

Gavin sat with Sage for several minutes, letting her cry, and piece herself back together.

"It's ok, I'm here for you," Gavin said, stroking her hair as she curled tighter and tighter into a ball. He wanted so badly to scoop her up and cradle her.

She sobbed harder.

Shit. What had she seen? What happened to her? His chest felt like it would be split in two at the sight of her so frail.

Sage's eyes cracked open, and she looked into his eyes. "Gavin, what I'm going to tell you all...What I've done. Gavin, I can't bear it," and she sobbed again.

He couldn't stop himself then, he wrapped her into his arms, laying his forehead on the side of her face. "Sage, whatever you did, you did it and survived. I won't hold that against you."

"You will," she said, recoiling. "Gavin," she shook her head, "Gavin, it's so awful."

"I promise," he said, cupping her face with both hands, forcing her to look into his eyes, "I promise nothing you tell me will make me balk. You forget, everyone here has had to do questionable things to survive."

She stared into his eyes, he stared right back. Finally, she softly closed her eyes, blinking free the tears clinging to her eyelashes, and nodded. "Ok...ok," she sighed.

He wrapped her into a soft hug, and they began the process of getting ready for the meeting with the King, Queen, and their courts.

Forty-five minutes later, Sage and Gavin were striding toward the open doors of Symon's study. The cream, burgundy, and charcoal room seemed to have been tidied from the night's fun. It was a stark indication of how the mood had changed.

Symon was waiting for them outside the room.

Sage dared to grab Symon's elbow before the King could walk through the doors. "Symon...I know you have certain abilities...to...show things, see things...mental power," Sage stammered.

Symon placed a hand on hers, still holding his elbow. Gavin was surprised by the tenderness in that touch. He often forgot how aware Symon was of his peoples' trauma, he supposed it'd be no different with Sage.

"What I'm trying to ask," she continued, not daring to look at Symon in the face, "is whether it'd be possible for you to *see* my memories, and simultaneously show them?"

Sage looked then at Symon as if realizing how ludicrous her idea—her request— really was.

Symon considered her for a moment, then nodded. "Yes, I think that would work. I have many questions myself that I think would be best answered if I could see your story as well as hear it."

With that, Symon grabbed Sage's hand and ushered her into the study like a long-lost best friend.

Scattered about the room, in various postures of tense anticipation, were Meliza, Zeke, Petra, Aryael, Suda, Acantha, Epyllo, and Raphael. Aryael locked the door, giving them complete privacy.

Gavin was surprised to find not a single of the older fae leaders, even more surprised to find the spies included in the event, but strode to a vacant divan, Sage sitting next to him.

"Thank you all for being here. I think it's important for us all to witness Sage's story. We've come up with a unique plan, so we might all have the pertinent information together," Symon explained. Aryael arrived by his side. "Are you ready, Sage?" the King asked. She nodded her agreement.

Sage sat upright, the King placing his hands on both of her temples. Flashes of light filled the room. Symon closed his eyes, and the room was transformed.

The room was filled with the illusion of a field, two girls running through it. It was Sage, and the other girl was her sister. Then they were watching as Sage used her powers on a young boy, most likely while at school. The image flashed again, and they watched and listened as Sage's mother explained the danger she would face as an elemental.

The pictures, places, and sounds flashed as Sage and Symon showed the synopsis of her life, up until she was trapped in that van. Aryael gasped as the wall of asphalt surged to the sky, forcing the van to collide into it. Gavin forced himself not to grit his teeth as he watched Sage run for years and years, then find love with Ian. By the time Ms. Dullahan had captured Sage again, he felt like he might throw up.

How had she endured this?

"Cerridos," whispered Raphael as they witnessed Sage being blessed—chosen by the gods. They watched as Sage trekked her way across Thuledain, hunting down the insignias. When she'd faced the Wulver, the soft panting coming from Sage nearly brought Gavin to his knees.

A sob escaped her as they witnessed Ian—the one she had loved—brutally executed. Acantha let out a startled cry at the scene, and goosebumps erupted across Gavin's flesh.

He watched, mouth agape, as she ran from the machines the government had sent to track her, watched as the gods themselves defended her so she could escape.

"TupaGuara," she had said over and over.

Finally, with the last image of her grabbing the insignias and vanishing from the President's clutches, Sage slumped over her knees, wrenching herself free of Symon.

The room seemed too bright, too cheerful after what they'd witnessed. Gavin's throat was dry. He blinked to clear his vision of what he'd seen, now painful in the harsh light of day. Symon and Raphael shared a look of trepidation, and Gavin wondered how much of the story they had already learned, and how. Aryael gazed at Sage, and Gavin's questions of what and who knew about Sage's journey grew.

Discomfort and anger warred within him, and a feeling of foreboding pulsed through the room.

Sage wept softly as everyone else reacclimated to reality.

Gavin's throat was raw as Aryael said, soft as death, "That was Rankor."

Symon nodded, looking at Acantha and Epyllo.

"He's been here," Epyllo confirmed. "That was the version of Rankor we saw when we went to investigate the Speridisian movements at the border of Nysa."

"And you didn't think to warn the Nysan Senate?" asked Suda with a glare, rising to his feet.

A look from Aryael, and he sat back down.

"I wanted to have the full story," Symon explained. "I was hoping to avoid undue panic, but it appears that, yes, the Rankor of Sage's world has found his way here."

Sage fought to push the sobs back into herself. People in the room had begun looking at each other, speaking. She couldn't stop trembling as the image of Ian's head falling onto his chest, his arms and legs splayed in the air, played itself on repeat in her mind.

She didn't dare glance at Gavin; didn't dare look to see what she was sure was disgust at discovering how she'd betrayed Ian, her family. She'd inadvertently traded his life to pursue this task of hers, traded his life for hers. Buzzing filled her ears, and she shook her head trying to clear her mind enough to pay attention to what was happening in the present. She squeezed her eyes shut, willing her mind to stop showing her that last image of Ian, dead.

What was that they'd just said? Ranquer was here?

"What is he doing here? How did he get here? I grabbed the insignias to keep him from following." Her voice carried above the murmurs in the room. She was shocked by the lack of trembling in her voice, but it sounded distant. Empty.

Raphael chimed in, "TupaGuara...Symon, do you know what that is?" His tone was curious, but Sage couldn't help but feel its weighted implications.

"I believe that Sage's realm leaping went badly. As most of us know, from the legends of Cerridos, if she had done it correctly, she would have landed in the temple in Mystaira, where the Rafalatriki now stands. Or she could have landed in Maracadia. But by removing the insignias, she disrupted the process. That's why she fell from the sky," Symon explained.

He was walking around the room, heading towards his desk covered in books. "If she had jumped without the disruption, she and the insignias would have arrived together."

"TupaGuara is where I was trying to go," Sage cut in. Her voice was hollow, an echo of itself. Gavin was staring at her, his face full of worry and grief. She couldn't bear that look, so she looked away, settling on Petra.

Petra looked back, disgust and trepidation warring with each other. That was better. Sage didn't deserve sympathy. She'd left everyone behind, she'd abandoned her world. She'd *let* Ian die. Petra's glare mirrored the truth Sage knew about herself.

She was only half listening as Symon continued to explain: "It appears the Rankor from Sage's world has figured out some way to follow her here without the insignias, and he is intent on using *our* kind in his experiments. We still don't understand exactly what it is he is trying to do, but we do know that he has aligned himself with the Dark Born brothers."

The King had walked back to the group, a book in his hand. "I looked through this book, hoping to get an idea as to how the President had managed the feat, but I came up empty-handed. Sage's story corroborates much of what I found, however."

Book.

It was the book.

Sage looked slowly from the book the king placed on a coffee table near the divan she now sat, and met the eyes of the king.

"You have the book?" she asked.

"Yes," the king said. "I held onto it while we determined how to proceed—-"

"You had the book this whole time, and kept it from me?" she asked quietly.

Symon stopped his meandering through the room, meeting Sage's eyes with a look that dared her to lose her control. "At the time, we were unsure what sort of threat we might be dealing with. We decided, my court and I, that is, that you should regain your memories on your own. So that we might compare them with the information we found in the book," Symon explained carefully.

"Symon," whispered Aryael. Hurt was written on the Queen's face, and it seemed as though Symon hadn't included her in the deception.

"I used the time to research what information we had here as your memories resurfaced. We had to know what kind of threat you posed."

"What do you mean by research as my memories resurfaced? How did you learn about my memories?" Sage looked at Gavin, then to Raphael. "Were you both reporting everything to them? Spying on me?" The expression on Raphael's face was confirmation enough. "But you were gone," she whispered, looking at Raphael.

Then, it dawned on her. The magic paper. The journal. Could it have been a coincidence that Raphael gave her a journal to record her memories just as he was leaving her?

A cold finger seemed to skate across her mind, and her focus snapped to Symon. He was reading her thoughts. "Get out of my head."

"You have to understand, Sage. We had to be sure you were not a threat." Symon's voice was commanding, steely. But Sage didn't care. She knew now, none of the friendships, the comfort she'd allowed herself to slip into—none of it was real.

They'd all watched her, all spied on her. Sage rose to her feet, backing toward the door.

"You!?" she pointed at Gavin, "I suppose getting close to me was just orders? Just your job? To figure out what kind of messed up crazy I was."

Roaring filled her ears as the words tumbled out of her.

A couple of the others had started up from their seats. Before they could get nearer, Sage threw out both arms. The wind that surged through the room pinned everyone but Gavin to the walls, the seats, the floor. Papers and books flew about the room.

"You knew, and you kept it from me!" Sage raged, tears flowing down her face

She used the wind to throw open the doors behind her, leaping into the air to allow the gust to carry her away. Then she ran, leaving the wind to contain the fae in the study. She ran as fast as she could.

Sage ran through the gates of the palace, plummeting into the markets that lined the streets. A push downward with her arms sent the air buffeting around her so that when she leapt into the air, she was carried onto a rooftop. Running and leaping, she allowed the air to carry her from rooftop to rooftop; she didn't stop as she heard carts and wagons overturn from her wind, just kept on running and leaping until she'd reached the Obelisk. She didn't stop as she felt the ground rumble below her, or feel the call of the ocean as she stopped at the base of the tower.

She hadn't planned on running there but didn't know where else to go. She ran around the outside of the building. Gods be damned. She couldn't find the fucking stairs.

"Sage," said a soft voice behind her.

She whipped around, stunned to see Gavin.

"What?!" she demanded.

"Sage, I'm sorry. We were just trying to protect ourselves."

"I don't want to talk to you, to any of you," she cut in.

"Can I at least take you up? I won't bother you, just let me take you up there." Sage glared at Gavin, then looked up the tower. She *could* use her earth power to move the stones, then scale the tower. But that might ebb her anger, and she wanted to feel angry right now.

How could they have done this to her? How could *he* have done this?

Finally, she jabbed a finger into Gavin's chest, bared below his unbuttoned shirt; "Fine, but I don't forgive you. You lied by omission Gavin, and I trusted you."

Hurt washed over his face, but he nodded, shifting into his winged form. She turned around, crossing her arms. He wrapped strong arms around her waist, bent his knees, and launched into the sky. In less than a minute, she was on the balcony landing, striding away from him.

She ignored the pang in her heart as she heard him fly away again.

Sage didn't know why, but the only person she wanted to see was Hyacinth. Maybe it was remembering her sister, how tall she had become, how fierce. Hyacinth was so much like Aimee, despite the fae choosing to stay in the tower after losing her sister. Tears threatened to fall from her eyes as Sage made her way through the Obelisk. She was still in the stairwell when she could hear Hyacinth's bright voice as she sang in her kitchen. Sage once again wondered at the voice, and whether her own sister sang as sweetly.

Sage had just stepped through the kitchen entranceway when Hyacinth whirled to face Sage, worry flooding her features. Jars of fruit scattered the wooden work table, and something sweet smelling simmered on the wood-burning stove. The tears broke free as Hyacinth rushed to Sage and asked, "What's wrong?" Sage shook her head and allowed herself to be folded into Hyacinth's arms. Hyacinth was tall enough that her head perched on top of Sage's as she held her tightly, letting Sage work through her tears.

Hyacinth sat Sage at the table, sliding a chocolate pastry in front of her and commanding her to eat. Hyacinth quickly finished her task of making fruit preserves and left the tools scattered around the kitchen. Sage recounted the story, starting with the dream which had held all the secrets of her memories. Hyacinth wept alongside Sage as she told her about Aimee, and they both sobbed when Sage told her how Ian had died, and how Ian's duplicate was Epyllo. Sage talked about finding Epyllo the first night they were in the palace, and how her heart broke seeing Ian's likeness here. Once Sage had cried all the tears she could muster,

Hyacinth urged Sage to tell her all about her time in the palace, meeting Suda, whom Hyacinth blushed over, having apparently met him once in passing. Sage told Hyacinth about the ceremony in the throne room, the gift she'd given the Queen, and the food at the ball. Hyacinth even managed to pry a few details over those more secret moments between Sage and Gavin.

"He's a good male," Hyacinth whispered.

"He lied to me," Sage snapped. "Even if he didn't lie, how can I trust him now that I know the whole court has been working against me, keeping me trapped here?"

Sage winced when she noticed a brief flash of hurt on Hyacinth's face, but she just replied, "What else would you expect? How would you have responded to some stranger crashing down into your land? Especially after what our world has seen."

Sage looked at Hyacinth, considering her point. "The President, my world's duplicate of King Rankor, has come here. He's working with someone they called the Dark Born brothers."

Sage hadn't mentioned that information before, and she wished she hadn't mentioned it now. The color drained from Hyacinth's face before she brushed the skirt of her dress, "Well, I'm sure Symon and Aryael have some sort of plan for it. They won't let those two hurt us."

Sage looked at Hyacinth fully, acknowledging the equal parts of fear and bravery on her face. Sage searched for something encouraging to say.

Hyacinth rose from her stool, where they both sat, and announced, "I think, tonight, you and I will eat our way through all this fear and pain, and tomorrow we will both face the world feeling much better. Who knows, maybe I will let you take me down to the market, just for a bit."

Sage smiled at Hyacinth, "You don't have to do that."

"No, it's time. I've known it for a while now, and it's time I stop remaining cooped up in here. Celia wouldn't have wanted that." A quick nod from Hyacinth, and she strode over to the massive pantry. She came back to the island with armfuls of sweets, cheeses, breads, and pastries, then rushed back to the pantry for even more. They ate their way through piles and piles of food, shared wine, and shared happy stories of their families. Hyacinth told funny stories of the fae Sage had met, and Sage teased Hyacinth lightly over her obvious crush on the handsome Suda.

Exhausted, but feeling better, they curled onto Hyacinth's bed late that night. And though Sage was still angry at the world—worlds—over all she'd been through, a sense of peace had finally settled itself into her chest. She slept soundly and fully for the first time in what felt like years.

Gavin stormed back into the palace, intent on interrogating Symon over withholding Sage's belongings. Aryael intercepted him, "I know you're angry, but you'll be mindful of your place, Gavin," she said, placing a gentle hand on his chest. Gavin looked at the hand and fought the urge to rip it from the place she had set it. Aryael read the look on his face, and he found unwavering challenge in the look she returned. He knew how that fight would end; likely, with him sprawled out on the palace floor, at least one bone broken.

He made himself take a calming breath, then stared his Queen fully in the face. "Symon had no right," he bit out.

"He did. He has every right to do anything and everything in order to protect our Kingdom," Aryael countered.

"If he was so concerned whether Sage was a threat, why keep her in the Obelisk? Why not keep her here in the palace, with the guards?" Gavin questioned.

Aryael hooked Gavin's arm in her own, steering him to her own study. "First off, Gavin, is that really what you would have wanted? Suda has told me about you two, and I can't say I blame you for falling for the girl. Of course, you'd fall for the girl who hasn't got the slightest clue who you are, what you've been through," Gavin rolled his eyes, but allowed himself to be steered away from Symon. "Second, *we* agreed there would be no safer place to observe the girl than under the watchful eye of not only you, but Meliza, Petra, Zeke, *and* Raphael."

Gavin shouldn't have been surprised to learn Aryael had had something to do in the planning of how to treat Sage; she was Symon's equal in every way. She commanded an army of her own and even had spies of her own. And yet they ruled together and alongside each other's guidance. Full trust was the only way they were able to rule in such a way.

"We wanted to give the girl a chance to show her true colors." Aryael continued. "You know as well as the rest of us, being locked up in a cell is hardly the best way to learn who a person truly is." The Queen unhooked her arm with the last words, and walked over to her large, round table, covered in a map of Panchaia.

Small metal figures dotted the map, stacks of notes and reports were placed in various piles along the border of the table. Aryael stalked to the table and peered down at it.

"That's the Dark Born legion?" Gavin asked, pointing to a row of dark amethyst-colored figurines.

Aryael nodded her confirmation, "From what I've gathered from Acantha and Epyllo, they've been lining up here, and then leaving. They weren't able to get close enough to see what they would do while the legion lined up here. They've put up enchantments, barring Acantha from reaching out through the root systems in the area. Epyllo seems to believe the animals of the area have fled."

"Not a good sign," Gavin muttered.

"No," Aryael replied, "it is not." She looked at Gavin, "I want you to go to the Rafalatriki. Ask Shiphrah about blood magic and let's see if we can piece it together. You'll go once the celebrations have passed."

"And Sage?" Gavin asked.

"*I* will ask the girl where she'd like to go next. I think it's possible she might have some insight as to what Rankor...the duplicate, that is, might be up to. She might be able to tell us why he'd want our people, and what he might do with them."

Gavin knew he shouldn't ask, but he couldn't stop himself, "Should we ask the Goddess for guidance?"

Aryael gazed at Gavin, her face full of questioning, worry, and then finally acceptance. "I think, if you asked the Goddess, she would tell you that you already have the answer. So...what do you think the answer is?"

Gavin stood silent for a moment, considering. He stared at the map, the outline of Mystaira, where his family was right now. "I think, she'd tell me to take Sage to Shiphrah."

Aryael nodded her agreement, then clapped Gavin on the back. "Now that we've decided that, we will ask her opinion, and proceed from there. Now, let's go find that brother of mine and have a drink. This morning has been far too dramatic for my birthday celebration."

Gavin laughed, glad to be in the company of his friend and Queen. He was still angry with Symon, and even Raphael. But he understood their actions.

He would go to Sage tomorrow, make his apologies, and see how he could help her through everything she'd been through. A pang ran through him as he remembered the pain on her face, her thrashing in her sleep as she relived those painful days before she came here. But he vowed to allow his friend and Queen enjoy her day. Tomorrow, the final day of the festivities, he would bring Sage down here, and they would smooth it all over.

Tomorrow, he'd make things right.

Chapter 31

Sage woke the next morning, groggy, but rested. She laughed to herself at the sight of Hyacinth sprawled across the bed, so much like Aimee. The female lay in a starfish position, legs and arms sprawled equidistant from each other. A crick had formed in the side of Sage's neck from sleeping on the edge of Hyacinth's bed, but she was happy. Happy to have someone she could care for; someone she was sure would be safe. Petra, Gavin, Zeke...they would never let anything happen to Hyacinth, Sage knew.

Sage rolled out of the bed and headed into the kitchen. She rekindled the small fire and set about making tea. She decided she'd make breakfast, and clean the remaining mess in the kitchen. It was the least she could do.

Sage completed her task with an unfamiliar sense of peacefulness. Having been on the run so much of her life, she'd never really had much of a chance to develop much in the way of domestic skills beyond what Hyacinth had taught her, but scrambled eggs, toast, and sliced fruit was something she could manage with confidence. That, and a nice strong pot of tea.

Sage finished making breakfast and had nearly cleaned the entirety of the kitchen when Hyacinth stumbled sleepily into the kitchen.

"Oh my word..." Hyacinth yawned as she walked into the kitchen, "I'm afraid I've gotten used to sleeping in with you lot gone to the palace. I don't know if I'll be able to stand waking up so early once the celebrations have finished."

"Maybe I can start helping more?" Sage offered.

Hyacinth sat at the work table, and Sage set a plate of food and a cup of tea in front of her friend. Hyacinth beamed up at Sage.

"What?" Sage asked at Hyacinth's wide smile.

"Oh, nothing. Just, every once in a while, you bring me a happy memory of Celia. She was always offering to help people."

"I wish I could have met her," Sage whispered.

"Me, too," Hyacinth replied before biting into her toast.

The pair ate their breakfast and made plans for the afternoon. They both hoped one of the more powerful fae would be by to check on them. Then they could ask whether or not they could both go down to the festival. Sage wasn't sure she would be welcomed after her fit yesterday, but Hyacinth seemed to believe all would be forgiven.

Hyacinth told Sage about the parades, the live entertainment, and the dancing and fire shows that would take place at night. Sage decided, despite everything that had happened the day before, she would allow herself this chance to have a good time, to make sure that Hyacinth's first trip out of the Obelisk would be joyous and carefree.

Sage made her way up to her room and was surprised to find a package waiting for her. Inside were the clothes that had been made for her to celebrate the final day of Queen

Aryael's birthday festival. Sage placed the outfit onto her bed, a rust-colored jumpsuit made of a gauzy muslin material and a pair of leather sandals, and rummaged through the rest of the package's contents. Sage was surprised to find the book King Symon had kept from her, her wand which had been missing since she arrived, and a letter addressed to her. Astonishment washed over her. She hadn't expected to get her things back so suddenly. She took it as a sign that their opinion of her was changing. Still, she couldn't help but feel wary about her place among the fae.

She opened the letter to find Gavin's handwriting.

Sage- I'm sorry. I know we've betrayed your trust, and I'm not sure how to make it right. Let me make it right. I brought your clothes and convinced Symon to let you have the rest of your things. I'll be back to pick you up at lunchtime. -Your friend, Gavin.

Despite herself, Sage found the smallest hint of a smile tug at her lips. She *wanted* to still be upset with Gavin, with all of them. But if she was honest, she could understand where Symon came from. And, she realized, Gavin hadn't been told the whole truth either. It was as much Gavin's fault as it was her own. She'd let him make his apologies in person, she decided, and would figure out the rest afterward.

Sage bathed, got dressed, and felt more confident with herself than she had in ages. Yes, she would make this work. And after the festival had finished, she would talk with Symon and start the search for the missing insignias, assuming the King hadn't hidden those as well.

Sage left her room and was just closing the door behind her when a strange and sudden feeling of apprehension permeated the air around her. She checked the door, checked her person, and looked up and down the hallway. She had her wand safely tucked in her pocket, and nothing seemed out of place. Still, an overwhelming shadow of dread seemed to fall around her. She paused at the stairwell, listening for any signs of the others.

Nothing.

Sage continued down the stairwell towards Hyacinth. She passed windows in the stairwell and peered out of them.

Nothing.

Everything was normal. The sun shone, the sky was blue and nearly cloudless, a soft breeze tickled the tall grass lining the beachy shore. A picture-perfect day outside, full of the noises of an impending celebration from the city below.

Sage continued on down the stairwell, winding her way down to the kitchen. She'd just reached the landing when she heard a crash come from the kitchen. Sage rushed to the sound, breaking into a run. She'd been so focused on the sound, on checking on Hyacinth, Sage had forgotten the prickle of warning she had moments before. "Hyacinth?" Sage called as she turned the corner.

A strong, dark-haired arm wrapped around her chest, a knife tip pressing against her head before she could take in the scene before her. A tall, black-winged fae male stood behind Hyacinth. His eyes were rimmed with red, glowing red circles around his irises. He held Hyacinth by her neck, a mirror of the hold the male behind Sage held her in. Fear flooded Sage, and she could see the feeling reflected in Hyacinth's face.

"Make a noise, and we kill you both," the male behind Hyacinth hissed. "You will both come with us, and we won't destroy your city."

Sage tried thinking of any way she could get out of this and spare Hyacinth. Fire this close to Hyacinth would just as likely injure her, even if Hyacinth could reach her water powers.

"What do you want with me?" Sage asked.

"I said, be quiet," the male behind her commanded, and he jabbed her in the ribs with the butt end of the knife. Air whooshed out of her, and Sage fought to keep upright. Air...maybe she could suck the air from them? But how would she, if she was bound, couldn't move? Sage was reaching full panic now, her mind reeling, looking for any way she could at least get Hyacinth out.

"Just take me, leave her," Sage whispered from between clenched teeth.

"You don't make demands," the male said, making to hit her again.

"Don't," Hyacinth said, her voice full of cold fury. Her face had shifted. She no longer looked afraid. Fury encompassed her, her body had gone rigid with a rage that was palpable.

"Hyacinth...don't. Just let them take me," Sage pleaded. But before either male could respond, Hyacinth had clenched her fists.

Water began to seep through Sage's clothing. The male that clutched her was sweating—suddenly and profusely. Trying to ignore her disgust, Sage looked around. The other male, the one holding onto Hyacinth was perspiring heavily, as well. A look at Hyacinth, and Sage knew the source. The male behind her began to gasp. She felt him shudder against his back, dry rasps pulled from his chest.

He released her the same moment Hyacinth was released. Hyacinth stared at the male across from her, and Sage watched as water began to pool around the two intruders. Hyacinth was draining the males of all the water in their bodies. The skin on their faces began to change hue, pink, then red, then blue, then gray. Their skin shrunk and shriveled, clinging to their bodies. Their lips dried, and their skin became flakey and ashen. With a final rasp, the males both hit their knees and crashed forward onto their faces with a sickening thud.

Hyacinth released her clenched fists, then looked from the males to Sage. Her skin paled, her body drained from the sudden surge of power. Sage rushed forward to catch Hyacinth as she fell forward. Sage caught her just before she smacked her head on the island. Her skin was clammy and hot. Her eyes fluttered, then focused on Sage.

Gasping, they looked around. "Let's go," Sage said, breaking the silence. She shook Hyacinth lightly. "Come on, let's go. We've got to get out of here." Sage pulled Hyacinth to her feet.

They began walking to the stairwell, water splashing around their feet, and stopped as they heard footsteps coming toward them. Sage held out a hand, signaling to Hyacinth to stop, and they listened in apprehension for a sign of who approached. The steps were even paced, regimented, and Sage listened hard for any clue that the approaching steps were friendly.

Hyacinth's hand trembled in Sage's, and she looked back at her friend. Hyacinth's face was still pale, and her lips trembled with fear. "We are going to get out of here; look at me," Sage demanded in a whisper, "We are going to get out of here, together."

Hyacinth nodded. The footsteps drew nearer and Sage peered around the winding stairwell.

Three large males with black, leathery wings stalked down towards them. Before Sage could react, a black-tipped arrow whizzed by her. She dropped Hyacinth's hand and threw out her arms toward the males. Their red-rimmed eyes widened as a surge of wind threw them against the stone wall of the stairs. Sage used it to pin them there, immobilized. With a flexing splay of her fingers, stone spikes jutted from the wall, piercing the males where they stood. Thick, red blood oozed to the floor as their legs twitched below them.

One of the males was reaching for his crossbow as he continued to struggle, despite the recognition of his own death. He seemed determined to shoot Sage and Hyacinth. With a clap of her hands, Sage stole the air from his lungs and watched as he succumbed to his fate.

Hyacinth gasped behind Sage, but Sage didn't hesitate to grab her friend's hand, feeling Hyacinth squeeze back in confirmation. Together, they ran for the balcony. The open air would make it easier to anticipate further attacks, making it harder for the enemy to ambush them. As they ran up the stairs, taking care to check the corners as they made their way, sounds of distress began trickling into them.

The city was under siege.

Shouts and booms and rumbling filled the halls of the Obelisk as they got closer and closer to the balcony. With every flight they ascended, Sage pulled harder on Hyacinth's hand, urging them to go faster, faster, faster. They paused on one of the hallway landings, peering out of the window. Sage gasped as she watched Gavin and Zeke streak through the air, swords in hand. Gavin dove and banked, slicing through enemy soldiers.

They were coming to save them. They just had to make it to the balcony. They were nearly there—sunlight flooded the stairwell landing and Sage pulled harder. They bounded up the final two steps, and Sage screamed as she tried to stop their momentum.

A red-eyed male sat perched on the balcony railing, crossbow raised. Sage ducked as the arrow shot past her head. Hyacinth's hand squeezed hard in Sage's, and she turned to look just as the arrow plunged into Hyacinth's chest.

Time slowed as Hyacinth gasped, her hand slipping from Sage's. A sickening thud echoed through Sage. Hyacinth fell backward, and Sage couldn't hear anything even as she knew a scream erupted from her own mouth. Sage fumbled, trying to reach Hyacinth as she tripped up onto the balcony landing. Reaching for the floor, trying to break her fall, Sage saw as the male's head was ripped from his body as Zeke landed on the balcony floor. Petra ran to Hyacinth, fury written across her face. Sage stood on shaky feet and tried to make her way to Hyacinth as more enemies began to land on the balcony, surrounding them.

"Leave!" Petra ordered, a darkening mist beginning to encase her hands.

"Hyacinth?" Sage whispered.

"Get out of here," Petra ground out with a coldness that stopped Sage in her tracks.

Sage bumped into something solid when she moved again, and felt Gavin wrap his arms around her waist. She hadn't even noticed his arrival, and just kept staring as Petra stalked toward the males gathering on the opposite side of the balcony. "The little princess wants to play," said one of the males with red-rimmed eyes.

"Petra," warned Zeke, trepidation warring with fear in his features, but Sage could see that fury had carried Petra away.

Petra advanced on the males. Gavin backed up, pulling Sage toward the opposite balcony. Sage could just make out the outlines of shapes forming within Petra's dark mist. The males across from her grumbled, one of them smirking, and with a roar from Petra, the mist was set upon the males forcing itself through their nostrils, their opened mouths. Sage saw the first male begin to claw at himself, tearing at his own skin as Petra walked toward them. The mist devoured the soldiers, and crazed sounds escaped from their mouths. The one who had smirked at the sight of Petra advancing upon them now had a face twisted into an unnatural grimace of pain.

Zeke stood still as a statue, watching Petra's fury take its vengeance. Sage too, stood still, watching the scene unfold until Gavin hit the balcony railing and allowed them to fall before letting his wings keep them aloft.

He flew hard and fast, avoiding the arrows whizzing past them. Sage struggled to breathe, the image of Hyacinth's face grimacing as she fell, the arrow shaft protruding from her chest playing on repeat in her head. Enemy males flew above them, and Sage's heart thundered.

Rage boiled in her blood. Hyacinth. Ian. Her family.

Ripped from her.

Everything good and pure. Everything beautiful.

They had stolen Hyacinth.

And they would pay.

Sage barked, "There," pointing at a street as enemy soldiers advanced on the market square. "Get me down there," she demanded. She could feel the outline of Gavin's crossbow, slung across his shoulder. "Go there," she demanded again. There were innocent people there, running scared, and trying to find shelter and safety as danger approached.

"We're going to the palace," Gavin said, groaning as he made another sharp turn, an arrow narrowly missing his head.

"No," Sage said, smacking Gavin's hand around her chest. No, she would not allow herself to sit by again as innocent people were attacked because she didn't act.

She would not be the cause of anyone else being murdered.

"Put me down," Sage said through clenched teeth. He squeezed tighter, pulling up into the air and aiming for the castle. Her rage became a tangible object. Heat coursed through her hands and she slapped Gavin again. The heat, startling him, caused him to loosen his grip, and she plummeted to the ground, aiming for the legion of soldiers marching.

She released both arms beside her, commanding the wind to slow her fall just enough. She hit the ground, a little harder than she expected, and rolled out of the impact. Gavin landed heavily next to her, breaking into a run. Sage whipped out her wand and cast the protection spells she had once known so well over herself and Gavin.

With a smooth motion, Gavin whirled, taking aim with his crossbow. Two soldiers crashed to the ground, arrows sticking through their skulls. Sage ignored the feeling of satisfaction as they twitched and died. With predatory grace, Gavin swung the sword from his back and rushed into the crowd of soldiers.

Sage didn't wait to see as he took on four soldiers at once. She pivoted and ran toward the advancing regiment. She ran fast and hard, punching out a fist toward them. They fell as a strong wind pummeled them; she whipped her wand as they made to stand, and cast an immobilizing spell over them. A blast of fire erupted from beside her. Ducking, the flames missed her and she waved them away with her magic.

A lone soldier with glowing eyes advanced on her. With a strong step and a whip of her arm, Sage ripped a thin slab of stone from the building beside the enemy. The blade-like shape of stone sliced across the street, severing the male where he stood frozen, his body falling to the ground with a sickening, wet slap. Blood rained against the walls, and Sage pushed both hands out with flexed fingers, incinerating the bodies of those soldiers still getting to their feet.

She could hear Gavin swear behind her as six soldiers rushed him. A battle cry erupted and Meliza landed next to him. She unleashed. Whipping through soldiers with a spear and short sword. She fought with Gavin back to back. Sage had just enough time to witness their prowess as Meliza ripped through enemy soldiers. A yell, and she'd raised a pillar of stone from the ground, Gavin sending a burst of wind to her back as she leapt from the stone and impaled three soldiers at once.

Suddenly, a strong rope of wind wrapped around Sage's waist, and she was pulled back with a yank. Exactly where she had been standing a moment before, an enormous winged soldier landed, driving an iron-tipped stake into the stone street.

"Snap out of it," yelled Gavin as he blasted several males back into the street they had been advancing from.

Sage did snap out of it; her fury wailed as she stomped her foot and sliced downward with her arm. A hole opened below the male with the stake as he advanced on Sage. With a following swipe of her arm, the hole filled, sealing the male alive inside.

Above, Zeke flashed through the sky. Disappearing and reappearing rapidly as he cut through soldier after soldier. Body parts and blood rained to the ground. Zeke yelled as one soldier tried grabbing hold of Zeke from behind. His mistake. Zeke casted, appearing behind the soldier and punching his fist straight through the male.

It looked like the fight was on their side, but Felysian sentries were going down all around them. Falling to fire, stone, water, wind, speed, and arrows that rained from above. All the while, innocent fae ran through the streets, trying to avoid the onslaught.

With a mighty yell, Sage lashed out with her fire on another group of soldiers that marched toward her, this regiment marching without wings. A second gust of wind hurtled toward them, and Sage's flames grew. The soldiers didn't have a chance to so much as scream as they went down. More soldiers flew overhead, dive-bombing toward Sage. Sage reached out, and pulled the air from their lungs; their eyes bulging from their heads as they landed on the cobblestone streets, their bodies shattering with the impact.

Quiet filled the streets, Gavin breathed heavily behind her. He was bloodied, and a cut ran down his blade arm. A glance up showed them that more soldiers flew toward them.

"Those wings. They aren't natural," Sage said, noting the contraption strapped on the backs of the soldiers who lay dead in the streets.

"No," Gavin agreed.

"Up there," Sage signaled, pointing to a roof free from soldiers. She pushed down, wind gathering below her and she lifted into the air. A second push of air lifted her into the sky, then Gavin rose next to her. They landed, and he looked at her.

"We'll burn them down," she said coldly.

She hardly needed to summon the energy before glowing balls of flame encircled her fists, and she felt the hum of Gavin's power as air began to bolster the flames. Sage steadied her arms, reaching out as if she held a longbow. Pulling back with her right hand, she released her fists and watched as two bursts of flame went flying into the air. Gavin helped push the fire toward the flying enemy soldiers. Sage followed the flame with her eyes and splayed her fingers. The flames grew and separated into ten separate balls of flame. They crackled as they met their targets. Again, no screams followed as the burning soldiers fell to the ground.

Sage was just beginning to gather more flame when a roar erupted behind her. A great winged lion strode along the rooftop, roaring so mightily the sound engulfed the entire city. The lion roared again, and Aryael landed next to Sage. Aryael's leather armor and sword were bloodied, and her topaz eyes shined bright like the sun's energy coursed through them. The lion's maw was covered in blood and gore, but Sage recognized the piercing blue eyes of Symon as he padded next to his warrior Queen.

Winged enemy soldiers stopped attacking civilians and rose to the sky; those bound to the ground ran forward, lining up below the King and Queen. Symon roared once more, and they all turned to face Symon and Aryael. Aryael lifted one hand in front of her, and the enemies began to glow. Radiant, golden light filled the soldiers, streaming from their eyes and their mouths. Within seconds, the entirety of the invading army began to disintegrate, flaking away as they were incinerated from the inside out. Ashes rained throughout the city, and Gavin reached out with his wind, blowing the ash back across the sea.

Panic still flooded the streets as fires were put out, people called for healers, and loved ones searched for those misplaced in the initial chaos of seeking shelter.

Symon shifted with a flash of light. "Abbadon! Apyllon! Show yourselves," he commanded. Moments rolled by, all of them on the rooftop looking out against the sky. Suddenly, a shimmering outline made an appearance, and slowly, a great winged male began to form above them.

"Symon, Symon, Symon," the male called with a cold, elegant voice, as harsh and grating as a blade against bone. His wings were vast, and rather than feathers, were covered with scales, booming with each stroke that kept him aloft. The male was pale, with long, jet-black hair. Unlike the other soldiers, these wings were real. "You always ruin the fun."

"Apyllon," Aryael hissed.

"Yes, yes. My brother couldn't be bothered with this escapade. We've had a rather interesting guest lately. No doubt your little spies have told you." Apyllon smiled broadly, assessing the group gathered on the roof.

"What is the meaning of this?" Symon demanded. "Do you really wish to start this war again? To see the rest of Panchaia rise up to slaughter you and your people—again?" Symon grinned as his words found his mark, and Apyllon grimaced.

"Your people will regret the day my father died; we will have our vengeance. One day. But for now, all we want is the girl," Apyllon finished his explanation with a grin and gestured at Sage. "Give us the girl, and you will be able to rest easy, for now," Apyllon's hissing voice slithered across the city, echoing through the streets.

Sounds of panic continued to echo up through the roof-tops. No one made a move, then suddenly, Apyllon dove toward them. Gavin lurched forward at the same time as Aryael, and a blast of flame rocketed toward the Dark Born male. A shield of dark purple rippled in front of Apyllon as he reeled back, pushed by the impact of the fireball.

He hissed, and Symon growled upward, "Leave now Apyllon, or I will unleash the full force of my powers on you. You are alone, without your precious brother to protect you."

Apyllon grimaced, then began his ascent. "You will regret this King Symon." Apyllon somehow made the title, King, sound like an insult. "We will be back, and you will not like what we have in store for you," his hissing voice called out. Moments later, he was gone, vanishing with a ripple of dark purple power.

A rumble echoed across the city, and stones trembled along the streets. Screams filled the city as people prepared for a second wave of terror. The tremor stopped, and Sage knew that Apyllon had left at last. "I want you in my war room in five minutes or less," Aryael commanded, turning to look at Gavin. "All of you. Symon, call the others." A shimmer outlined the King and Queen, and they were gone, having cast to the palace.

Sage breathed deeply. Hyacinth was gone. She breathed and breathed, but the air didn't seem to reach her lungs. The screams of the people on the ground echoed the sorrow that quaked through her.

Her knees trembled, and she sank to the flat rooftop patio they stood on. She hadn't recognized it earlier, but they stood on the top of the tavern Gavin had brought her to all those weeks before. They were on that rooftop, in the part of the city Gavin loved so much. And the city burned and was reeling from the death that Apyllon had brought.

Death that Sage had brought just by being here.

Death that Sage had brought to Hyacinth, who was just beginning to find her joy again. She would never see her smile, never spend the night gossiping with her, or cook beside her. She was gone.

Gavin grabbed Sage's shoulders and hauled her back to her feet. "Let's go," he said with the coldness of a hundred winters.

Dread pooled in her stomach as he wrapped his arms around her waist once more. He'd dropped the crossbow somewhere, but the sword was sheathed again across his back. She let him gather her into his arms, barely feeling the drop in her stomach as he launched into the sky once more. They flew in silence; Gavin barely breathed as they landed in front of the palace.

"Are you okay?" he whispered as he set her down gently.

Crunching footsteps sounded behind them as Zeke and Petra landed. Petra ran forward, cold fury exploding from her face.

"You!" she screamed at Sage. Petra reached her and struck her across the face. Gavin reached out and pushed Petra away as Sage stumbled back. "You!" Petra screamed once more, "You did this. You did this, and she's dead now because of you."

Gavin had pushed Petra back into Zeke's arms who restrained Petra, even as she tried to advance on Sage once more.

The breath caught in Sage's throat, "I know," she whispered. "I know..."

"I hope you fucking rot in the pits of hell for this," Petra roared as Zeke ushered her through the front doors of the palace.

Meliza ran through the doors, seeking the disturbance. "Get her out of here," she commanded as she took in the scene below her.

"You think?" Zeke replied sarcastically, pushing Petra through the doors with a final and mighty heave. Sage could hear Petra wailing, Zeke's soft soothing as they made their way through the entranceway.

Meliza stared at Gavin and Sage. A deep sigh escaped her. Blood coated her armor, her hair was wild, escaping from an untidy braid. The commander looked exhausted as she said, "Sage, Gavin...take a few moments, but we need to gather soon. Aryael and Symon are already drawing up plans." Then she turned and strode back into the palace.

You did this. You did this...the words rang through Sage's head. Cold iron filled her stomach as she accepted the truth. It was her fault; her fault Hyacinth was dead, her fault Ian was dead, her fault Veritasailles had been assaulted.

It was her fault.

Gavin turned to Sage, "Don't listen to Petra." He said coldly. "Look at me. Look, at me," he demanded Sage. Sage took a shaky breath and forced herself to meet his stare. His eyes were cold, almost vacant looking, but he grabbed her shoulders and brought his face close to hers. "This is not your fault," he lied; Sage knew it was a lie. How could it not be her fault? "This is not your fault," he repeated. "We will protect you, Sage. You don't have to fight this alone. We will do it together, okay?" She nodded.

But no.

They couldn't do it together. She couldn't risk it. She had to go, had to get out. She couldn't bear the burden of knowing that more people, more innocents would die because she brought danger to their city. "You go on," she whispered, tears rimming her eyes. Gavin looked at her, concern washing over his face. "It's fine...I just...need a moment." She felt her gaze sliding to the side.

"You sure?" Gavin asked.

Sage nodded, "Yeah. You go. I just...I need to pull myself together." Gavin pulled her forward, placing a sweet kiss to her forehead. She grimaced. She didn't deserve that.

Gavin turned, then paused, "I'll send Acantha back for you, so you can find the war room." Then he left.

Sage waited until she could see him pass the windows next to the entrance, then slowly began backing away. She made it to the gates, then broke into a run. She ran, and ran, and ran. Past buildings still smoldering. Past healers leaning over injured soldiers, groans filling the air. Past mothers calling out for their young.

She made it all the way to the bridge crossing the Philias River. She would run to Mystaira, board a ship, and sail to Maracadia. She would make her way to Meropoli and figure out what to do then. She crossed the bridge, remembering the old road Gavin had told her would lead her to Mystaira. Sage paused, tears flooding her eyes. With a deep breath, Sage whipped her arms, gathering the water to her. As she stepped, spun, and circled her arms, a great fog rolled across the city, moving inland from the sea and the mighty river she stood over. She needed cover, she needed distraction. She needed something to hide the fact that she was leaving. The last thing she needed was one of them following her.

She glared upward, at the now shadowed sun. With a final breath, she turned to run...

And ran smack into a hard body.

Strong arms wrapped around her, and with a snap, she vanished from Veritasailles.

Gavin replayed that look on Sage's face, as Symon and Aryael cast from the rooftop. The look of panic, fear, dread, rage, and horror that overtook soldiers after a battle. The look of someone who'd lost everything; the look of a soul shattered. He'd seen Hyacinth lying on the steps. He'd seen the nightmares unleashed by Petra as she destroyed the soldiers responsible for that death. He'd be lying if he said it wasn't satisfying seeing the males rip themselves apart.

Fuck. Sage was teetering on a mental breakdown, he knew it.

Petra would be no fucking use to them like this, and the last thing they needed was Sage losing it now. He needed to get her inside, needed to get her to Mystaira, and needed to figure out what the fuck was going on. He would send Acantha out to get her as soon as he reached the war room. He understood her need for a few quiet moments. The power she'd unleashed out in the city had been impressive. And she barely seemed strained from it, but the aftershock of battle always claimed its prize. He knew she would need someone there when it came.

As Gavin walked through the palace, white-hot rage flowed through his body. He could pummel Petra for that. How could she blame Sage for this? The girl had been running for her life since she was fifteen. She had been evading powerful forces for nearly ten years; what else did Petra expect of her?

He must have been stomping as he made his way to Aryael's war room because the Queen intercepted him, once again. "Where's the girl?" she demanded. There was no friendliness in the tone; the killing calm of a warrior rang from the Queen.

"She's gathering herself, taking a moment. She's pretty shaken up," Gavin reported. "I'm sending Acantha to go get her."

The Queen nodded.

"How the fuck did this happen?" Gavin asked. The Queen cocked her head to the door, and they both walked inside, the Queen going straight to Acantha. The spy, daggers still in hand, strode out the door to check on Sage and bring her to the war room.

"Those soldiers were captives from Nysa," shouted Suda across the round table. He pointed a finger at Symon, then whirled to glare at Aryael. "You. You incinerated your own people," he bit out.

"Suda. Calm down," commanded Symon. A predator's growl laced the words, and Suda closed his mouth as if forcing words back down.

"Suda. You know as well as I what happens to the people possessed by the Dark Born. We've been witness to the madness that follows; there was nothing left to do," Aryael replied, approaching her map-strewn table.

"Killing them was a favor," Meliza finished.

The females looked at each other, agreement passing between them.

"Apyllon brought that legion to our shores for one purpose. He's sending a message. The Dark Born are going to try and finish what their father started," Symon declared.

"I suggest pulling our forces in now, taking the offensive, and heading off Speridisia's forces before they get a chance to strike," Zeke interjected.

Petra stood beside him, a vacant look on her face. Gavin forced himself to tear his gaze from the female, and looked back to Suda. "Did you know so many of your people had been captured?" Gavin asked.

"We'd had another regiment go missing. There had been rumors of great beasts roaming the bordering forests and had sent them in to deal with it. I hadn't been informed of the incident prior to coming here; word reached me just yesterday. I was hoping to discuss it with you today," he gestured to Aryael.

"They want the girl. Just give her to them, and we can be done with this," Petra bit out.

"Fuck you," Gavin replied.

Aryael slapped a hand across Gavin's chest as he leaned forward. "Petra, you and I both know that if we hand over the girl, we ensure our own doom. That girl is the key to beating the Dark Born *and* the Rankor duplicate." Aryael peered around the table, making eye contact with each person in the room as she spoke.

"We need to send the Lords and Ladies from the city immediately, check in on all of the territories. We can have them rally their forces while they're gone," Gavin replied.

A crash echoed through the room as the doors slammed open. Acantha reappeared at the doorway behind him.

"She's gone."

Ice ran down Gavin's spine at Acantha's words.

"What?!"Aryael snapped.

"A guard said he saw a female running through the gates. He said she looked like the Realm Leaper."

Gavin, Aryael, Meliza, Zeke, and Symon all cast to the gravel-lined pathway that led to the palace. Gavin spun on his spot, looking for her.

"Find her," Symon commanded. Meliza and Zeke launched into the air, Zeke in his harpy form which could fly impossibly fast.

A second later, Gavin had cast into Sage's room; he used his wind power to summon the pack Sage had carried around so protectively, making sure the book made it in. He cast into his room to grab a bag he had packed weeks ago on a whim. Without really knowing why he had obtained a set of female sentry clothing that would likely fit Sage. He cast out into the open sky over the city. A flash and he'd shifted into winged form, soaring over the city.

He scanned the roads, looking for her with his hawk-sharp sight, but couldn't see her among the smoke and panic that still flooded the streets. A mist was rolling in from the sea, and Gavin careened to watch. Surely Apyllon couldn't be back already. The chaos of the scene flooded Gavin with dread when Symon's voice boomed through his head. "The Phylias river," he said, "Meliza says the mist started there." A glance told Gavin she was flying back to the palace, away from the river. Gavin flew to the bridge, casting into the woods beyond it before whoever may be on the bridge could hear his approach.

Sage stood on the bridge, looking across the river, staring out at the mist she'd called in. Gavin stood in the shadows, watching her for a few moments before stealthily walking up behind her. A heartbreaking sigh wrenched free from Sage just before she turned to run. Gavin tightly grabbed hold of her as she ran into him and cast into the woods beyond.

✦✦✦

Symon had just received word from Zeke that the mist was receding. No word from Gavin had been received, but intuition said the young Lord had intercepted the girl. He was just finishing his brief with Meliza when Raphael appeared in front of both of them, stopping Meliza in her tracks.

"I thought you'd be out healing the injured," Meliza said, stepping back in surprise.

"I was. I thought you'd like to know that the sentry regiments are already finishing up their search and rescue assignments," Raphael replied with a tone of urgency.

"That's good news. They've worked fast," Meliza continued looking at Symon with a question.

"Symon. Meliza," Raphael barked, forcing them both to focus on him, "there are sixteen unaccounted citizens. Witnesses say they saw some of the soldiers grabbing a few of the missing and then...disappearing."

"Who were they?" Symon asked.

"Equal numbers of power wielders: wind walkers, water summoners, earth shifters, and flame wielders. I'm afraid Apyllon was not only here for Sage." Raphael's face was full of warning.

"We need to inform Aryael." Symon turned, rushing up the steps of the palace. He could hear the clipped steps of Raph and Meliza behind him.

A decade of peace, gone in a heartbeat.

The Dark Born brothers had finally come to call, Symon thought as he prepared himself to bring the news to his wife.

Chapter 32

Sage's feet hit dirt. Her knees shook with the impact, and she whirled within the grasp that held her tight. She shoved hard at the chest pushing against her, and gasped to find Gavin's cold stare peering down at her. Behind him, the massive rolling foothills that bordered Veritasailles loomed in the distance. They'd left the city, and she had no idea where she'd ended up.

His face was a mask of coldness. She thought she detected a feeling of loathing rippling off him. Horror gripped her tight. She had to get away from him, from all of them so no one else got hurt because of her.

"Gavin— let me go. You have to let me go!" His hands gripped her arms, preventing her from escaping, from saving him from the pain that would ultimately come from being close to her.

"Where! Where would you go, Sage? You think after all that has happened you can run? Again?" He squeezed her arms like he might shake her, then, without warning he released her. She stumbled back, still reeling from the surprise of his grasp. "You think running, again, is going to fix this?" Gavin asked. He held his hands, clenched by his sides. His body vibrated with tension. "You think by leaving us to clean up the mess in Veritasailles that the Dark Born are just going to leave us alone? Wake up, Sage! You aren't the only one who has faced death. You aren't the only one that has to fight to keep what you love safe."

The air felt too thin, her skin felt too tight. She just had to make him understand. "Gavin. If I hadn't been there, Hyacinth would still be alive. Your city wouldn't have been touched. Just let me get to Mystaira, leave me here, and I can board a ship and go to Meropoli. I'll figure out what's next when I get there. Just...leave me so I don't get you hurt," she begged. She looked him full in the face, every bit of pleading she could muster out in the open.

"And then what?" Gavin said, his voice dropping to a tone so low it made the air feel chilled. "You go to Meropoli, to the human lands, and you think Ranquer can't find you there? The humans have explosives, sure, but the kind of power that Ranquer and the Dark Born could unleash in Meropoli...you would bring that to *them*?" Sage hadn't thought about it like that. "It's time to stop running, Sage. Let us help you."

"I can't." Her voice was barely a whisper, but it landed on Gavin like a slap to the face. He flinched, and she didn't think she would ever get over the look of hurt that crossed his face.

"You won't," Gavin said.

His words reverberated around her. Despite her fear, despite her guilt, despite everything, a new feeling emerged. Anger. Bitterness.

Didn't he realize she would love nothing more than to stop running? That she would love to go back to her family, to find Stiofanie. The ground trembled below her as she stepped towards him, hands clenched so tightly her nails bit into her palms.

"Stop running?" she asked. "That's rich, coming from the male who's been running from his own responsibility for ten years." She knew it was a low blow, but she wasn't wrong, either.

The words hung in the air. Gavin barely reacted, instead, reached down to grab the bag he'd dropped when they landed. "Yeah, well, running won't be an option for me anymore, either."

Gavin turned and began walking down the path. Sage noticed her own pack on the ground and scooped it up. Staying in her spot, she called out to his back, "What do you mean it's not an option?"

"I casted. I used my powers. So, no more hiding for me," Gavin answered, still not looking back at her, still walking. "If I can't run, neither should you," he muttered, quiet enough that Sage barely heard him.

For reasons she couldn't understand, she found herself following behind him. They walked in silence, her trying desperately to catch up to his long strides. Fear still clung to her, but the bitterness she'd felt moments before had melted away. Her body trembled as she walked, and try as she might, she couldn't seem to catch her breath.

"Just...stop!" Sage doubled over, a cramp digging into her side.

She braced her hands on her knees, panting and staring at her sandals. Her stupid, blood-covered sandals. The sandals she had loved this morning. Whose blood splattered her shoes now? Was it Hyacinth's? The question sent a new wave of terror across her, and she shuddered. As she stood, she pushed the feelings down. Pushed away the memories of arrows hitting flesh, of bodies hitting the ground, of screams filling the streets.

Finally, when she didn't feel like she would immediately shatter, she straightened. Gavin had stopped a few feet from her and stared into the distance. "Where are we going?" Her voice was low, soft, sounding like it came from someone else.

"Mystaira. It will probably take us three days to walk there."

"Walk? Why not just fly? Or cast?"

"One, I can't cast that far. I'm a bit out of practice, and I pushed myself further than what most would have considered safe. Second, it will give them time to see us coming, to get prepared."

Sage pondered the answer, then asked, "Who needs to get ready?" wariness filled her question.

"My family," answered Gavin.

His answer was quiet. He still wouldn't look at her, and his distance grated along her senses. "Well, at least let me take off these shoes. They're already giving me blisters."

Gavin dropped his bag, and with a blank face, handed a set of clothes to her. "I've got an extra pair of boots here, too. I think they will fit."

He tossed the clothes and boots to her, and she scooped them up quickly, wandering off to a private area behind a tree to change. Gavin remained on the path.

She deserved this. She deserved his anger, his disgust. *You did this.*

She was the reason everything was crashing down around her, around them. Petra had been right all along. They never should have saved her from that crater. They never should have kept her in the tower. They should have let her die.

As she re-entered the path, Gavin began walking as soon as she picked up her bag. Despite the pain in her heart and the hollowness that was being carved inside of her, she couldn't help but notice the beauty of the forest. Tall, straight pines shot up to the sky from the forest floor. Lush ferns, creeping moss, and vines blanketed either side of the road. The birds sang merrily, rodents scampered through the brush, and soft-winged bugs fluttered across her path.

It was too much. Didn't the forest know who walked through it? Didn't the birds know the horror of what happened in the city? How could the sun shine so brightly now that Hyacinth was gone? Now that Ranquer had found her again? How could she possibly keep going?

You did this.

Gavin walked on. Sage followed, staring at his back. On and on they walked, and the hollowness continued to carve her from the inside out.

Eventually, she felt nothing. She no longer felt the stings of her blisters. She didn't feel the ache in her shoulders from fighting. She didn't feel the air begin to cool as the sun began to set.

Gavin veered off the path, following a game trail to an outcropping of boulders. He set down his bag and gestured for Sage to find a place to tend to her own business. When she'd come back, he had a small stack of logs and kindling arranged.

"Do you mind?" he asked. His voice sounded gravelly, thick with emotion. Nodding in confirmation, Sage approached the stack of wood. It took her a few tries, but she managed a small ball of flame which quickly ignited the stack.

Sage found a small boulder, and sat atop it, watching the firelight as the forest around them settled into night. She listened as the symphony of nocturnal bugs and animals began their calling, only the occasional pop of the fire disturbing the song. Everything seemed too stark, too real. The sound of bugs chirping slid sharply across her skin and she began to miss the numbness she felt earlier.

Gavin walked around the campsite once, then finally settled on his own rock a distance from Sage.

He rummaged through his bag and pulled out a satchel of hard bread and dried fruits and nuts. "We will make camp earlier tomorrow, probably along the river. We can hunt and fish before settling in. We'll have to make do with this tonight," he said, handing over a portion to Sage.

She took the food from him, forcing herself to eat. The food felt like ash on her tongue, like knives slipping down her throat. A canteen of water was placed by her feet. The cool fluid felt like it got stuck in her chest. Without waiting for Gavin to indicate it was time, she found a blanket in her bag and laid down on the forest floor. Her head throbbed, and she just wished she could melt into the ground and disappear. Hoping it would provide some sort of sanctuary, Sage willed herself to drift off to sleep.

Gavin strode back to the campsite. He had waited until he was sure Sage had fallen asleep to check their campsite once more. He built the fire back up, hoping it would continue burning through the night. The forest wasn't necessarily dangerous, at least, not any more dangerous than any other forest. There were a few large predators, mountain lions and the occasional bear, that roamed the woods. The most likely danger, Gavin knew, was potentially being tracked by Apyllon or Abbadon. He would have to remain alert. The fire was a risk, he knew, but the forest would become cold overnight. Plus, he really had taxed himself with so much use of his powers and casting. He wasn't sure he'd be able to summon enough wind to fend off a mountain lion should it wander into their camp.

He finished building the fire and looked at Sage again.

He understood her fear if he was honest with himself. He knew that pain, the weight of knowing that others sacrificed, and were sacrificed, on your behalf. His family was proof of it. But he also knew that a fight like the one they now faced couldn't be won alone, nor would it ever end if she kept running.

The weight of Hyacinth's death settled over him. He knew the burden of it would leave a lasting scar on those he cared about. Petra, Meliza, Raphael...how would they deal with the death? He was sure the funeral pyres had already started in the city. Would Hyacinth go with the others in the city? Or would Petra insist on something more private for her friend?

Gavin shook out his bedroll and settled himself down to rest. He wouldn't be likely to sleep, too alert for disturbances. Instead, he lay there for countless moments, looking up at the sky, listening for anything out of the ordinary. Despite his best efforts, his gaze kept returning to Sage.

Her running felt like a betrayal, and as foolish as it sounded, he was struggling to let it go. She lay there, wrapped in her bedroll, and he could see her arms folded against her chest. She looked small, and frail, like the girl he'd scooped off the floor of a steaming crater. She had grown into something different over the past months. He hated that she was letting herself be defeated once again.

He hated that she was being forced to go through the loss of someone she cared for. And he hated that they'd all been allowed to be caught off guard.

If he was honest with himself, he was angry with everyone. Symon. Aryael. Meliza, Zeke, Suda. They all should have known something was coming. They should have suspected that someone was coming after her. He should have been there to protect her.

He listened to the sounds of Sage's breathing. He'd be damned if he allowed that to happen again. Looking over at her, he vowed not to be caught off guard again.

Sage pushed herself off the ground. She'd been awake for gods only knew how long, listening as Gavin walked around their campsite once more, packed up his belongings, and put out the fire. She stood, straightening her spine.

Everything hurt. Her head still throbbed. Her shoulders ached. Her stomach felt like it was a swollen mass of knots. Her throat was dry and scratchy. But she relished the feeling.

She deserved it.

You did this.

As Gavin shrugged on his bag, he looked at her for what felt like the first time in ages. "We will continue on today, but stop a little earlier when we reach the river again. I can hunt or fish once we get there and we can actually have some warm food."

Sage nodded. She couldn't seem to form words.

They began walking, every step jarring Sage's joints. Eventually, the familiar numbness found her once again. A fog of nothing wrapped itself around her. She stopped hearing the birds. Stopped feeling the breeze as it skated across her arms.

All she wanted to do was to lie down and never get back up.

But Gavin kept walking, and somehow she kept following. Step after step, after step. On and on.

The sun was directly overhead when the road they were walking along began to run parallel to the river they had crossed the day before. The current moved quickly, and Gavin instructed Sage to drink and refresh herself for a few moments before they had to move on again.

A thought crossed her mind, flitting through her like a bird from one tree to the next. This walking through the woods in silence, sleeping in makeshift campsites, was more normal for her than living indoors. She had spent a significant portion of her life alone and unsheltered. A hysterical feeling bubbled inside her and she nearly laughed. She wanted to share the thought with Gavin, but couldn't find the energy to speak. She let the moment drift over her, a wave passing over the shore.

Gavin took them off the main road as the river bended away from the road. He set up a hasty camp and then shifted into his hawk form to hunt. On any other day, Sage might have been impressed when he finished hunting, bringing back a rabbit and several fish. He made quick work of cleaning the bounty, and she busied herself building a fire. The fish went down easily, but didn't fill the void that had tunneled itself into her abdomen. The sun was just setting when she lay down, rolling onto her side so her back faced Gavin.

Unlike the night before, sleep would not come. She didn't toss or turn. Her body remained glued to its spot, curled tight on itself. The fire warmed her back, but did nothing to chase away the dreams that kept her from falling fully asleep. Every time she managed to begin drifting away...

Visions of Ian's head dropping to his chest played over and over in her mind. The sound of Hyacinth's gasp of surprise was like a loop in her ears.

You did this.

You did this.

You did this.

Finally exasperated, Sage threw off the blanket she clung to. She couldn't lie still any longer and figured she might take a moment of privacy to relieve herself. She walked through the dark woods, seeking out a large fallen tree she'd used shortly after Gavin had taken flight earlier that evening. She clenched her fist, and a tiny ball of flame appeared as she opened her fingers. Stacking several small sticks on top of a large rock, Sage created a makeshift torch to see as she went about her business. She turned around herself, a twinge of unease wriggling beneath her skin, but nothing out of the ordinary could be seen. Sage quickly unfastened her pants and answered the demands of her aching bladder.

Finished, Sage refastened her pants. The cold air had wrapped itself around her bare skin, and she shivered painfully. She extinguished her tiny torch and began walking back towards the campfire, just visible over the shrubbery. Sage stepped out of the way of a crooked tree, taking care not to trip over the knobby roots jutting from the earth when a crack echoed out from the forest. She stopped; she swore the sound came from her side, but it easily could have been the popping of their campfire.

Gavin hadn't been bothered much by the idea of predators, so she really hadn't given much thought to the idea either. When no other noises followed, Sage continued on with a cautious step. A movement in the shrubbery to her side stopped her again. She stared into the darkness, her heart beating wildly.

Seconds ticked by, and nothing happened. The numbness she once felt was quickly being replaced with fear. Her heart pounded loudly in her chest, and she noticed how quiet the forest had become. Sage stepped again, readying herself to run should anything leap out. She nearly called out to Gavin before deciding she couldn't bear looking foolish if it turned out to just be one of the small nocturnal rodents that scavenged through the woods. Two more steps and Sage was just about to part through the shrubs that bordered their makeshift campsite.

Air was punched out of Sage's lungs by an enormous black shape bursting through the brush, tackling her to the ground. A bloodcurdling scream wrenched free from Sage. She collided hard with the ground, stars popping in front of her eyes as her head bounced off the root of a tree.

Instinctively, she pushed at the beast that pinned her to the floor, some kind of enormous wolf, black as a shadow. She covered her face as paws gripped her shoulders. Warm wetness trickled from the beast's maw as it growled over her. She pushed the great, black wolf's mouth away from her face, struggling to keep its sharp teeth from reaching her. With a mighty shove, she was able to create some space, and she blasted the beast back with a burst of flame. The wolf's head snapped back as a veil of purple light erupted in front of its face. But it was just enough.

Like quicksilver, she leaped to her feet and broke into a frantic run, away from the campfire, her only thought to get as far away from the beast as she could. One of the troublesome roots tripped her, crashing her hard onto the ground. She rolled, but still, pain radiated up her legs and into her hips. A whimper escaped her as she stood, her knee twinging beneath her when she stood up and turned to find the wolf stalking towards her with hackles raised, growling.

Its eyes glowed red, and Sage realized he was likely a possessed shifter sent to track her down. Several popping sounds followed and another realization clanged through her. Sage's heart raced. The wolf wasn't alone. A quick glance to her right and left showed other shadows with red glowing eyes creeping toward her. She tried pushing the wolves back using wind magic, and veils of purple covered the wolves' bodies. It was the same shield that covered Appylon in the city. She realized then, she couldn't fight them with her elemental power. Her breathing accelerated. She reached for the wand tucked into her pocket, but any idea of how to stop the wolves evaded her.

The wolf she faced rocked back on its haunches, preparing to leap towards her, and as if in slow motion, Sage watched as it launched into the air. Her hands raised up to shield her face, but then another figure burst through the shrubbery and intercepted the mighty wolf.

A leather-wrapped hilt protruded from the beast's throat, and Sage gaped. Gavin straddled the beast, a deep gash running down his arm.

Gavin yelled, "Run!" as he jumped to his feet.

It didn't take more than that for Sage to break free from her stupor. She turned and hauled ass through the opposite side of the clearing. Branches whipped at her face, and she could feel Gavin's presence behind her. She heard the whine of steel as he unsheathed his short sword. Growling surrounded them on either side, and Sage sent blasts of wind in opposite directions to push back their pursuers.

No use. Purple light glowed, and wolves continued running after them.

"Shift!" Sage yelled as she ran.

Gavin, not slowing, replied through gritted teeth, "Can't. Poison."

Sage saw it then. Black liquid mingled with the rust-colored blood already running down his arm where the wolf had clawed.

Her thinking cleared, memories suddenly coming back to her. She could hide them. She knew the spells, and she had her wand. "Get us somewhere secluded," Sage panted, soft enough so that only Gavin could hear her. "I can set up some distractions to hide us," she explained.

Gavin broke free, running ahead of her. He leaped over fallen trees, only slowing slightly to make sure Sage made it as well. Sage ran as fast and hard as she could, the chilled night air like blades in her throat as she breathed. Twice, Gavin cut down leaping wolves that had broken from their positions, intending to take one of them down.

They made it to another clearing, and wolves broke through the shrubbery on both sides. Sage and Gavin stopped abruptly. The wolves began creating a formation, trying to surround them. Their glowing red eyes were trained on Sage and Gavin, and she could feel malicious energy pulsating from the pack. Sage, not sure whether it would work, stomped her foot and pushed down with her arms. A canyon erupted beneath the wolves. Their purple veils shielded their bodies, but they still plummeted to the bottom. Yelps rang out from the canyon as the wolves hit the bottom. Gavin grabbed Sage's hand, pulling her after him, and they ran—not willing to stick around and see if the wolves were able to climb out of the pit.

They made it to another outcropping of stone, one of the random clusters of boulders that resembled playthings dropped and abandoned by giants. Sage pulled Gavin into a crevice of stone, then stepped out. She whipped her wand from her pocket to cast several protection and disguise spells around them. From the outside, it would appear that the crevice they huddled in was solid stone. They crouched together in silence, despite the sound barrier spell Sage had cast. She hoped her spell-casting was strong enough, and she huddled into Gavin as they strained their ears, listening for intruders.

Wolves howled in the distance. Snarls ripped through the woods, but never came close to their hiding spot. Sage sat still, her muscles coiled tightly. She shivered against Gavin, and she wasn't sure it was from the cold. Eventually, the howls dissipated through the woods, growing more and more distant.

Sage whispered, "No one should be able to find us or hear us. Do you think they will move on once they realize they can't find us?" Gavin nodded, and she exhaled sharply in relief. He rested his head back against the stone, closing his eyes.

She sat, crouched on her bottom, knees pulled tight to her chest. She willed her heart to slow, for her breathing to calm. The shuddering of her body slowed slightly as the forest finally fell silent.

"Why didn't you call for me?" Gavin asked, catching her off guard. His head was still tilted, eyes closed, but worry came off him in waves.

"I don't know," Sage admitted. The thought had occurred to her, but she wasn't ready to admit that she had been more concerned with looking foolish to him. In hindsight, that was what really made her a fool.

"You shouldn't have come for me," Sage said a long while later. Gavin looked at her in disbelief, then shook his head. "What?" Sage demanded.

"I just can't understand why you would say something like that." His head had fallen back again, eyes closed. Sage worried the poison was affecting him.

"Do you need me to heal that for you?" Sage pointed at the gash running along the edge of his bicep. The black poison was thick, like tar. She wondered if the wolves' mouths had been coated in the substance, but figured it didn't matter much now.

"If you can." Gavin's voice was rough, tight.

Quickly, she tore off bits of the long tunic she wore, using the strands to wipe off the blood and poison. She took a moment to remember some of the healing incantations Ian had taught her and did her best to draw out the poison in Gavin's arm. After several minutes, the wound was at least sealed, and the tenseness in Gavin's jaw had eased. Hopefully, that meant she'd removed enough poison for him to heal the rest of the way.

"Gavin," Sage whispered, not daring to speak fully. "You should have left me. Next time, promise me you'll leave me."

"I can't do that."

"You *have* to. If you keep saving me, people will keep getting hurt. I keep getting people hurt." Sage had turned now, angling her body to Gavin. "You deserve to be free of me, of any threat that I bring. The people of Felysia deserve to be free of any threat I bring."

"And you deserve that, too."

His reply was sharp. It hit her hard in her chest like he'd struck her with the sword laying at his feet. "No. I don't."

"Sage, no one deserves what you've been through. You deserve to be happy, and safe. Whatever has happened, it is *not* your fault, and I swear to the Goddess that the next person that makes you feel that way will be ripped to shreds."

The trembling returned to her body. How could he possibly think that? How could he not see that she was the common denominator, *she* was the thing that caused all these problems.

"You are not responsible for the evil things Ranquer, or Apyllon, or Abbadon have done. Sage—" Gavin exhaled sharply, and he looked at her in a way she didn't think he ever would again. It took her breath away. "I meant it when I said you have to stop running. It's time. Not because it's the only way to stop Ranquer, but because you deserve to stop running. You deserve the chance to live, and live freely. You can't do that by running."

"I don't know if I know how to." The truth felt strange to admit, sounded stranger as it came out of her mouth. Gavin sighed, resting his head back on the stone once more.

"You want to know why I was upset with you for leaving?" Gavin asked. Again, Sage was caught off guard. She wasn't sure how to answer, and Gavin continued, not waiting for a response. "When Acantha told us you were gone, the only thing I felt was fear. When we heard the city was under attack, and I saw those soldiers circling the Obelisk, I was afraid. I've fought soldiers hundreds of years older than me. I've seen people I cared about tortured. Yet somehow, the idea of you being hurt or gone made me more afraid than any of that."

Sage gaped. She opened her mouth to reply and closed it again. Realization drifted under the fog that had wrapped her so tightly over the last few days. A well of grief surged up in her. He was afraid of her leaving, but he had to realize that was exactly what had to happen, even if she stopped running. "Gavin...I'm going to have to leave, eventually. Even if I decide to stay and fight, eventually I will have to go back to Techeduin to take down Ranquer. You have to let me go," the familiar words echoed through her body. A painful shudder worked through her body as her heart squeezed. "You saw what I did in my world. The bargains."

"No, I don't," Gavin replied. He swiveled, pushing himself onto his knees. "I don't have to let you go alone. When you leave, let me come with you."

"What? No! No way. I can't let you do that. Your people need you here, you have a family that needs you here."

Gavin shook his head, "Let me come with you," he put his hands on her shoulders, forcing her to look into his eyes. "I was told not to tell anyone this, but fuck it. The Goddess came to me with a message. I think...I think she might have something to do with why you're here, why I was there the day you fell. She told me to stay with you and help you. But even if she hadn't, I'd say the same thing, Sage. I want to come with you, because..." He sat back on his heels, shaking his head. He squeezed her shoulders, and then finally whispered, "Sage, I've waited for someone like you my whole life.

I didn't know it, but it's *you* I've been waiting for. I couldn't accept the Lordship title because I knew, somehow, I knew there was something else I was meant to do. And you are a part of that." His voice was barely a whisper, and he wasn't looking at her anymore.

He towered over her in this position, she sitting on her bottom and he on his knees. She grabbed one of his arms and pulled herself up to her knees. "Gavin...if you go with me, it could mean you don't see your family again. Honestly, I have no idea what it could mean, or if you even could go with me."

He looked at her fully then, "I know."

She saw it; he did know, and he'd already accepted those terms. He'd accepted the terms a long time ago. She thought back to all the days they'd spent together, she thought about the secret moments they'd stolen on the Obelisk balcony, by the river, on the beach, and in her room. Something warm blossomed inside her. There was something solid in him, a connection between them that was stronger than she'd experienced before.

Sage reached her hands up to his face, and cupped it with her palms. He leaned into her touch; "I'm sorry," she whispered.

"I know," he said, eyes closed. "Promise me you won't run away from me. Let me do this."

He leaned forward then, his hands dropping down along her arms. He wrapped her in his arms and kissed her softly. She leaned into his embrace and melted into him as he held her. One hand slipped up her back and cradled her head, his fingers gently intertwined in her hair. The kiss was thorough, but so soft. It was a kiss symbolizing the terms of their arrangement: he would not abandon her, and she would not run away. Not anymore. They would fight this fight together, face down the obstacles together, and be victorious together, or die together.

She'd loved Ian, but she'd known they couldn't do this together. Somehow, she'd known deep in her bones that it wouldn't be him that was next to her in the end. That's why, as painful as it was, leaving Ian had been easy. But his life, his death, would not be for nothing. His actions had spurred a revolution, a revolution that was just beginning to take shape back home. And she and Gavin were going to be the ones to lead it, or die trying.

The next morning was rushed as they stealthily made their way through the forest, trying to avoid being tracked by any wolves that might remain.

The hours felt like they'd dragged on when Gavin finally pulled Sage to the side of the trail. He brought her to an overgrown thicket of berry vines. "Can you manage to hide here? I can shift now and make it to the nearest overlook tower in just over an hour. I can be back here with an escort before the sun sets."

Sage looked at the thicket and sighed. "It wouldn't be the worst place I've ever had to lie low."

"Okay. I will be back as soon as I can. If anything happens, you do what you need to in order to get to Mystaira. I don't care if you burn the whole forest down, just get to the border. You'll see it if you just keep going down this road." She looked at him and nodded.

"Why are you doing this?" she asked before he could step back and shift.

"What?" he asked.

"Leaving me here?" she asked, "I thought you were scared of leaving me."

"That's not what I said. I said I was scared of you being gone. You've been taking care of yourself for this long; don't think I'm stupid enough to think you couldn't make it to Mystaira alone. I trust you will do what you need to if it comes down to it." Gavin gave her a nod, shifted into his hawk form, and was gone.

As those words echoed through her, a strange feeling of floating settled over her. She had no idea why those words of confidence struck her so, but his words, *I trust you...* they were everything at that moment. She replayed that conversation over and over as she sat in the little earthen burrow she'd created in the midst of the thicket. Making her way to the center had been difficult, and she spent the first hour picking out tiny thorns. But the idea of any pursuer having to make their way through those thorns was worth it.

Hours later, she heard Gavin's voice calling her name.

"Here I come," she called as she picked her way through the brambles. She was covered in scratches, and Gavin carefully helped her extricate herself from a final tangle of vines as she emerged into the sunlight. She sighed with relief, even as a trickle of blood ran down her arm. Then she started; standing behind Gavin was a large mountain cat. The tawny-colored animal stared at her with interest, and Sage felt her eyes grow wide.

Gavin noticed her shock, then turned, "Sage, meet our escort: Levi." The cat stretched out before her, resembling a deep bow. Then, he sat up and pranced down the road.

"Levi seems...jaunty," Sage replied, before allowing Gavin to lead her down the familiar road.

"He is," Gavin replied. "He's also my younger brother. I expect there will be a lot of questions for you once we reach the Mystaira walls."

"Questions? About what?" Sage asked.

Gavin sighed his reply, "Everything."

Sage laughed; she imagined introducing Gavin to Aimee and realized she would likely be in the same position one day if everything worked out. The idea that, someday, she might actually be introducing Gavin to her family sent a small thrill through her body. Then, a yawning pit opened in her stomach as she realized she was about to meet *his* family. She wasn't sure if she was nervous, scared, or excited.

After the long journey, a wall came into focus at the end of the road. The forest thinned and they approached gates made of towering pine pillars. A wagon attached to a mule sat on the other side of the gates, and Sage sensed relief wash over Gavin. A female with curly black hair ran forward to greet them. Gavin brushed Sage's hand with his, and for the first time in as long as she could remember, she felt sure of where she was going next.

They'd made it to Mystaira.

Chapter 33

Aryael stood in her council chambers, staring at the expansive map which made up the large, circular table in the room. Little pieces representing troops and resources dotted the surface. Aryael's gaze swept across the table, eyeing each and every piece.

Symon entered the room, quietly closing the door behind him. His graceful gait betrayed no hint of his approach, but Aryael could always sense his presence.

"What are we planning now?" Symon whispered, his head perched just above her shoulder as he wrapped his arms around her waist from behind.

"Nothing. Yet," Aryael said. "Has there been any word from your spies?" She'd been staring at the map for hours. Days. If Symon hadn't dragged her from the room, she probably wouldn't have eaten, bathed, or slept. The destruction of the city weighed on her, and she knew their people would begin asking for answers. Answers she didn't have.

"Acantha and Epyllo have returned to the border. All seems normal in Nysa so far."

"All except they keep losing troops," Aryael snapped. "You heard what Suda reported. Four companies have gone missing so far this year. One of them is accounted for, ash on the wind after the attack this week."

Symon moved to stand next to her. She could feel dark heat rippling from him as his power begged to be released. "We could invade now. Avoid the developing conflict. Stop it before it begins." Symon spoke with his usual authority, but Aryael could sense the skepticism that floated beneath the surface.

"I don't think we can," Aryael sighed. "The Goddess came to me, months ago. I knew about Sage before she came." Aryael's voice dipped to a whisper as she finally confided in her mate. Her eyes slid to meet his. "She warned me not to tell anyone, but I think that's behind us now."

Symon met her stare, sorrow filling his eyes. They had both withheld information from each other lately, not something they made a habit of. He nodded, indicating he understood. To go against the Goddess's orders was not something he could ask of his partner. "So where does that leave us now?" he asked.

"Well, she was supposed to end up in Mystaira anyway. She needs to go to Shiphra. Meanwhile, you, me, and Suda will figure out what is to be done here.

Symon nodded, turning his attention back to the map. He reached out as if to move some of the figurines representing troops currently stationed in Mystaira when the chamber door opened with a slam. Acantha and Epyllo ran into the room panting.

Aryael scanned the spies. Epyllo's leathers were splattered with mud and blood. Acantha sported a bruise across her chest and up one side of her neck which seemed to blossom as they stood panting, leaning against the table.

"What's happened?" the Queen demanded. Symon strode around the circular table to attend to his spies.

Epyllo shrugged off the King and instead advanced toward the Queen. His eyes were clear, so he wasn't possessed. But there was a wildness to them. Dread tumbled in through his features as he approached her.

"Your Majesty," the spy said, "Aryael. I'm sorry. We arrived, and immediately heard the cries for help. We cast through the jungle, looking for the commotion. Their accents told us they were Nysian troops. It was an ambush, and we barely made it out ourselves."

Epyllo's eyes were haunted, full of horror and sadness.

"Are you hurt?" the Queen responded, trying to assess the spy for injury.

"What happened?" Symon growled, power lacing each word.

Acantha straightened, looking straight into the Queen's eyes, shrugging off Symon's hand on her shoulder. The look on the spy's face made Aryael's blood run cold. Time slowed as Acantha finally broke the news.

"The Dark Born have your brother."

Thank you for reading Book 1 of The Realm Leaper Series.

Follow me on Facebook and Instagram for updates on Book 2: Wind Walker.
@p.e.craven.writes

Visit my website to stay up to date on other projects including
The Realm Leaper Series and where to find other books.
www.pecravenauthor.com

Author Biography

P.E. Craven has spent her whole life engrossed in the fantasies of others. As a former dance teacher and choreographer, creative story-telling has always been a source of nourishment for her body and mind. Now, as a mother and teacher, telling stories in print is how she pours her creative soul into the world.

In her debut novel, she has answered the call to write stories about people facing down their destinies on their own terms. She continues this work with the next installment of *The Realm Leaper Series*, in addition to her next project: *The Tree Kings Series*.

In her spare time, P.E. Craven loves basking in the outdoors with her family, exploring her hometown Chattanooga, and jumping into perilous journeys written by other authors.

Milton Keynes UK
Ingram Content Group UK Ltd.
UKHW040730010823
426141UK00004B/313